D0503062

The

Ruby

in

Her Navel

ALSO BY BARRY UNSWORTH

The Partnership

The Greeks Have a Word for It

The Hide

Mooncranker's Gift

The Big Day

Pascali's Island
(published in the United States
under the title *The Idol Hunter*)

The Rage of the Vulture

Stone Virgin

Sugar and Rum

Sacred Hunger

Morality Play

After Hannibal

Losing Nelson

The Songs of the Kings

Nan A. Talese

DOUBLEDAY
New York London Toronto Sydney Auckland

The

Ruby

in

Her Navel

A Novel of Love and Intrigue
in the Twelfth Century

BARRY UNSWORTH

PUBLISHED BY NAN A. TALESE
AN IMPRINT OF DOUBLEDAY

Copyright © 2006 by Barry Unsworth

Published in the United States by Nan A. Talese, an imprint of The Doubleday
Broadway Publishing Group, a division of Random House, Inc., New York.
www.nanatalese.com

DOUBLEDAY is a registered trademark of Random House, Inc.

This book is a work of fiction. Names, characters, businesses, organizations,
places, events, and incidents either are the product of the author's imagination
or are used fictitiously. Any resemblance to actual persons, living or dead,
events, or locales is entirely coincidental.

BOOK DESIGN BY AMANDA DEWEY

Library of Congress Cataloging-in-Publication Data
Unsworth, Barry, 1930–
The ruby in her navel, a novel of love and intrigue in the twelfth century / Barry
Unsworth.— 1st ed.
p. cm.
1. Palermo (Italy)—Fiction. 2. Nobility—Fiction. I. Title.
PR6071.N8R83 2006
823'.94—dc22
2006040370

ISBN-13: 978-0-385-50963-3
ISBN-10: 0-385-50963-4

All Rights Reserved

PRINTED IN THE UNITED STATES OF AMERICA

1   3   5   7   9   10   8   6   4   2

First Edition

For Aira

The price of wisdom is above rubies.

THE BOOK OF JOB

The
Ruby
in
Her Navel

I

WHEN NESRIN THE DANCER became famous in the courts of Europe, many were the stories told about the ruby that glowed in her navel as she danced. Some said it had been stolen by a lover of hers—who had gone to the stake for it—from the crown of King Roger of Sicily, others that it had been a bribe from Conrad Hohenstaufen for her help in a plot to kill that same king. The plot had failed, they said, but she had kept the ruby and paid for it in a way that contented Conrad even more than the death of his enemy, vindictive as he was. As time passed the stories ranged further and grew wilder: the gem was a gift from the Caliph of Bagdad; it was sent her by secret courier from the Great Khan of the Mongols, with promises of more wealth if she would only come and dance for him and share his bed. And of course there were those who said that Nesrin was a shameless woman and the ruby was the reward of her pledge with the Devil. The troubadour who accompanied her made songs about the ruby, some happy, some sad, and this confused people even more. Neither of these two ever told the truth of it, no matter who asked, whether prince or peasant. I am the only one who knows the whole story: I, Thurstan.

Any human life lies in the future as well as in the past, of however short duration that future may prove to be; the two are hinged together like a door that swings, and that swinging is the present moment. To begin a story one must choose a time when the door swings wide, and this came for me on a day late in April of 1149 when Yusuf Ibn Mansur asked me to remain with him at the end of what we called the *majlis*, the gathering of officials that was held twice monthly in the royal palace of Palermo.

He asked me quite openly, rather carelessly, as if it was an afterthought, something that might have easily been overlooked. But it was rare indeed that Yusuf overlooked anything. What better way of disarming suspicion than to speak in the hearing of all? There was nothing strange about my remaining there, about our having things to say in private: he was the Lord of the Diwan of Control and I was his subordinate in the same chancery. But secrecy was ingrained in him; and he knew, as I knew—indeed, it was one of the things he had striven to teach me in the years I had served under him—that secrecy is best served by an appearance of openness.

The *majlis* itself has stayed in my memory because it was enlivened by a quarrel. I had only recently returned from Naples, where I had made an attempt to bribe the Count's jester, a dwarf named Leo, to return with me to Palermo as a gift to the King. Though much tempted, he had refused, being afraid of the Count's wrath, of being followed and strangled. This mission I had undertaken in my capacity as Purveyor of Pleasures and Shows, my official title in the Diwan of Control, a resounding one, but in fact there was only myself and my clerk and bookkeeper Stefanos and the doorman. I did not speak of this failure at the *majlis*; it was my practice in any case to say as little as possible at these meetings. I was distrusted as a man who belonged nowhere. I worked for a Moslem lord, I was not a Norman of France, being born in northern England of a Saxon mother and a landless Norman knight. My father brought us to Italy in the Year of Our Lord 1125, when I was still a child. He hoped to find advancement under the Norman rule, and he did so. My mother died some years later, struggling to give me a brother. My father . . . But more of my father later.

It was the eunuch Martin, a palace Saracen, that brought on the quarrel. He had words to say about a disrespectful incursion into the women's quarter of the palace on the part of certain drunken Norman knights. Spokesman for the Normans that morning was William of Vannes, who hotly denied the charge, clenching his huge fists and glaring at wizened Martin, in his green turban and saffron robe, as if he would like to pound him to pieces, which he would have been easily able to do. It is the Norman character to stress what they know causes adverse judgment. William knew the contempt of Greek and Arab alike for Norman uncouthness and barbarity, and he spoke the more loudly and roughly for it in the only language he knew, a dialect of northern France very difficult to follow. And Martin concealed whatever fear he may have felt and gave him look for look and repeated the charges in his querulous high-pitched voice. Only the presence of Yusuf, the host on this occasion and of a rank higher than either, restrained them from insult more personal and direct.

There were always tensions and hostility among us, moving just below the surface like a slow flame in damp grass. But open quarrels were rare, which is why this one has remained in my mind. Slight in itself, it was a mark of the deeper divisions that were opening among us, the rivalry for the King's favor between the Saracens in the palace service and the Norman nobility, a rivalry that was to grow fiercer in the time that followed.

Apart from this, what chiefly lives in my mind from that day, those hours, the beginning of my story, is a sort of amazement at the slightness and triviality of our words at such a time. Rarely had things looked worse for the Kingdom of Sicily than they did in this spring of 1149. A combined Venetian and Byzantine fleet was blockading Corfù and threatening Sicilian control of the Epirus coast and the Southern Adriatic. Conrad Hohenstaufen and Manuel Comnenus, rulers respectively of the Western and Eastern empires, the two most powerful men in the world, sworn enemies of our King, were now, after years of mutual distrust, dismayingly close in friendship and alliance, united in the purpose of invading Sicily and crushing our kingdom while still in its infancy: less than twenty years were gone by since our good Roger of Hauteville had been invested and anointed in the cathedral of Palermo, made King of Sicily, Calabria, and Apulia, the first Norman—the first of any race—to wear the crown. It was most of my years of life, but it was not long for a kingdom.

I cannot now remember what was said after this altercation, as if these few moments of heat had melted away what followed. I suppose my attention wandered. I had always liked this room, which was an antechamber to the two beyond, where the main work of our diwan was conducted. The ceiling was of wood, the work of Saracen carvers, very delicately fretted, with painted stars between the bosses. There was a thin band of Greek scrollwork in marble, running all round the walls, a frieze of tendrils and fronds. As sometimes before, I let my gaze follow the curves of the scroll and I was soon lost and mazed in them; each loop turned back on itself, doubled round to form the first curving line of a new loop; there was no break in it, no beginning and no end: wherever the eye fell, the mind was snared.

It happens to me when I dwell thus on the detail of form, when I look closely at things that are wrought for beauty and the upholding of power, my mind loosens and in some way dissolves and I feel the touch of heaven in the gross material of wood or stone. It has been with me from my early days, this sense of a crossing point between man and God that can lie in the work of hands. And on that April morning, still, the touch of heaven was the touch of my King, whose power was celebrated in that wood and that stone. My trance of mind was wonder at God's power and the King's; the voices around me still sounded, now loud, now soft, but the voice I heard was that unwavering one of majesty.

This drift of attention I would not have confessed to Yusuf, for fear it would damage me in his eyes—I wanted always to have his approval, though whether this was for increased pleasure in my own worth or to save him from disappointment I do not know. Can such things be truly known? In any case, suspicious as he was, I do not think he would have suspected such lapses on my part; they were too far from his own practice of unremitting alertness. Anything could be useful, could be vital, even the smallest thing, the very smallest—who could know? The sign of treason can lie in the flicker of an eyelid, he had once said to me. Without this acumen in seeing the signs, what can avail the rack and the wheel? So he tried to mold me and so I tried to fit the shape. As I say, I wanted to please him. But I was lacking, I was not an apt pupil—I knew it even then.

When we were alone I stood silently before him, awaiting his words. But he took my arm without speaking and walked with me to the smaller chamber that lay beyond, where his notary and scribes did their work, and through this to his own cabinet, closing the heavy door behind us and leading me to the narrow space within the embrasure of the window. It was no more than the habit of caution, bred by his many years in the palace service. I did not take it to mean that the matter was serious, nor did his first words give me any indications of this.

"Well, Thurstan Beauchamp," he said, "is that a new *sorcot* I see this morning?"

"Yes," I said, "so it is."

He made game of me sometimes about my extravagance in dress, using, with an accent of irony, the French terms that had become fashionable of recent months in Palermo. I like to be clean and neat and make a good figure, and I took much care with my appearance, shaving twice every week and spending a good part of my stipend on clothes and scent and oil for my hair, which is very light in color and reaches to my shoulders. That morning I was wearing a coat of dark blue silk, padded at the shoulders and pinched in the sleeves.

"And the *chainse*, that too? And the *chauces*?"

He smiled as he spoke and I returned the smile, knowing these questions were a way he had found of showing affection for me. No, I told him, the shirt was not new, but more of the embroidery showed because my new coat was cut low at the neck. I was rather relieved that he made no jokes on this occasion about my singing. He had discovered—but he discovered everything—that I had a good singing voice and a good stock of songs both sacred and profane. He threatened sometimes to set me singing through the corridors of the diwan, to enliven his work people.

"Yes, I see," he said. "Cut low at the neck, very striking." He himself dressed always with utmost simplicity, in white robe and high white turban and girdle of green silk, with for only ornament an emerald pin at his collar. Secretly I thought he made the better appearance, because he was also slender and graceful in movement, whereas I have more weight to me and more thickness in the shoulder.

His smile faded now and he looked at me more closely. "There is a mission for you," he said.

I should pause here to say something more about this *Diwan al-tahqiq al-ma' mur*, which some called the Diwan of Control and others the Diwan of Secrets. It is the central financial office of the palace administration, responsible for tax registers and for confirming grants of land and villeins out of the Royal Demesne. Much power lies in this chancery, since the royal grants and renewals of privilege can only be issued by its officers and not by the ordinary officers and scribes of the Royal Diwan. It is also concerned with the more secret operations of money, the management of blackmail and bribes, which both come under the heading of inducements, and the gathering of certain sorts of information, regularly reported by Yusuf in private audience with the King. Like all those who served in the palace chanceries, we took care to keep certain activities from public knowledge—and more particularly from the knowledge of other chanceries. Much of my work lay on this darker side. It was the King's policy to use bribes wherever possible; I was one of his purse bearers, and this consorted well with my official duties as purveyor, since my travels could always be explained as being in quest of new pleasures and shows.

"As you know," Yusuf said now, "we continue to have close relations with the Kingdom of Hungary." It was usual with him to begin with what was commonly known. Coloman, King of the Hungarians, was married to our King's cousin, Busilla, and all knew there was close friendship between the two thrones. "We are still receiving assurances that the Hungarians are ready to support an uprising in Serbia, if this could be brought about."

Yusuf's face was thin, and always seemed thinner by virtue of the tall, dome-shaped turban. His eyes were dark, set deep in his head, and very penetrating. They rested on me steadily, on a level with my own—he was tall for an Arab, as tall as I, though slighter, as I have said, and narrower-boned. "*Actively* support," he said after a moment, still looking closely at me.

My heart had been sinking ever lower since the mention of Serbia: I was already suspecting the nature of this mission. "My lord," I said, "how many times have we heard of this readiness of theirs?"

"True, but this time there is more ground for belief in it. We have it from sources close to the throne, and it is confirmed on the Serbian side. Hungarian cavalry units are massing on the border. The train is set. We are waiting only for a spark."

I nodded but made no immediate reply. This spark, so much awaited, was a Serbian uprising against Byzantine rule. This, aided by the Hungarians, who were eager to extend their eastern borders, would distract Manuel Comnenus, oblige him to send troops to Serbia to put down the rebellion, and so turn his attention from his plans to invade Sicily.

Privately I no longer believed either in Serbian uprising or Hungarian intervention; both had been promised so often before. Now I would have to travel somewhere to meet Lazar Pilic, the only Serbian rebel leader who spoke Greek. I did not trust Lazar, and I knew that wherever this meeting took place it would mean an uncomfortable and probably dangerous journey. To be sure, the danger to Lazar was greater. Byzantine rule in the Balkans was not secure. They felt the ground shifting, they feared for their footing, and so they became more watchful and more cruel. Blinding—the usual punishment for traitors and spies—was the least Lazar could expect if he came under suspicion.

The real difficulty lay in the fact that our diwan did not have full scope for action in the Balkans, being restricted to the payment of bribes. Elements in the Vice Chancellor's Office had formed a separate chancery that they called the Diwan of Command, a title confusing in its similarity to our own. They had gained the ear of the King and been granted the mission of diplomatic persuasion in Hungary. We had to rely on their reports, which came to us in garbled form with much that was significant omitted. Sometimes they did not come to us at all. So there were now two branches of the administration separately involved in fomenting rebellion in Serbia, each jealous of the other and neither sharing its information.

"We have already disbursed a good deal of the King's coin on these Serbs," I said. "So far without result. We do not know how they spend the gold—we have no means of knowing."

"This time there will be no gold. They have taken with both hands and made promises that were not kept. Now we in our turn will make promises, but we will keep our hands hidden."

He smiled a little, saying this; he had the Arab love for wordplay and reversed figures. I for my part felt some beginning of relief. He had spoken of a mission, but where was the mission in this?

"If we are to refuse them, there is no need for a meeting," I said.

"On the contrary, there is every need. If you are there in person to refuse, it will strike them the more. You are there, before their eyes. You are only the reach of a hand away. They reach out their hands, and lo, you give them nothing. The situation is serious for us; perhaps by these means we will make it more serious for them."

His tone had deepened slightly during these last words, a sign of feeling that he was perhaps not aware of. There was a gesture too that betrayed him. He wore as a talisman a scroll inscribed with the ninety-nine names of God in an embroidered leather case carried on a silk cord that passed over his left shoulder and across his body. In times of anxiety he would touch this case, brushing it slightly with his fingers. Unlike many of the Saracens in the Royal Diwan, who had converted to Christianity, Yusuf had kept the faith of his fathers.

That the matter was serious there could be no doubt. We were facing the most formidable military alliance anyone could conceive. Apart from the danger to our realm, we both had much to lose personally. Yusuf held great power in his hands, but the rise of the Vice Chancellor's Office was calling some of his prerogative into question. And now the King was to create a new post, that of Royal Chamberlain, with powers of supervision and control that extended over both offices in all matters of finance, renewal of privilege and grants of land. He who gained this post would be second in power and influence only to the King's First Minister, the Emir of Emirs, who at that time was George of Antioch. Yusuf wanted this post and on all hands he was spoken of as likely to obtain it. If he did, there was a good possibility that he would put my name forward to succeed him in his present position as Lord of the Diwan of Control. Then I would become rich like him, and have concubines, and white horses with gilded trappings, and Saracen attendants in uniform to make way for me in the streets, and a mansion of my own with gardens. I would inherit the marble frieze and the fretted ceiling and the breath that came through the molded casement of the window. I would send others on missions to meet people like Lazar. Yusuf had never made promises to me, but I was close to him, though different in most respects. He was not a man to demonstrate great warmth of feeling, but I knew he had some tenderness for me.

In a few words now he told me what he had in mind for me. We were then near the end of April, and the great pilgrimage to Bari in Apulia was already under way. From all over Europe, from Scandinavia and the Baltic, from Russia and the lands of the Slavs, bands of pilgrims were making slow convergence on the town of Bari for the Feast Day of Saint Nicholas, to visit the church where his holy relics were kept and wet their lips with the miraculous oil that was exuded from his uncorrupted body and had power to heal the sick and the lame. I would join this throng; I would travel to Bari in the guise of a pilgrim, and there I would meet Lazar and deny him the gold.

First, to lend natural color to my setting out, I would go in my own person, and openly, to Calabria, and there I would purchase the small white herons that are trapped at this time of the year in the marshes that lie between the town of Cosenza and the sea. I would have them shipped back to Palermo to restock the Royal Falconry—the King liked to use these swift-flighted birds for his goshawks. This accomplished, I would cross the peninsula on horseback. At a distance from Bari I judged suitable I would leave the horse and proceed on foot with hood and staff and satchel and mingle with the crowds of pilgrims.

"For the herons you must not exceed eight *folles* per bird," he said. "And that includes the price of the cage."

I could not help smiling at this. No detail was too small for him; he must have been to the falconers to get this figure. "Supplying birds for the King's sport has never been among my duties as purveyor," I said. "Why does the usual person not go?"

"I have inquired into it. The usual person was Filippo Maiella, and he decamped with the money last year and has not been seen since. A highly respected man in the Diwan of the Protonotary, he went to Calabria year after year to buy these birds. Twelve years at least. Then last year—only Allah the All Merciful knows why, who knows all things—he disappeared with the purchase money."

There was wonder in Yusuf's voice at a wildness so foreign to him, so much at odds with his own ordered life. "He walked away, he left everything," he said, and while the amazement still lingered in his voice I was assailed without warning by a demon, struck with sudden envy for this thievish Filippo. I knew it must be a demon who stabbed me thus: such a feeling could not dwell within me, who was always so careful, who counted every *follaris* of the King's money.

"He must have taken leave of his senses," I said, thinking of him there, with the money in his purse, setting his face toward the mountains and the sea.

"It was thought at first that his guards had murdered him and hidden the dinars," Yusuf said. "They were watched, but such people do not wait long if they have money to spend, and it was soon clear that these had not."

"Where will the meeting with Lazar take place?"

"In the basilica, beside the steps that lead down to the crypt."

"That will be his idea. The area around the steps will be crowded—the people will be jostling to get down to the crypt, to the tomb of the saint."

"No doubt that is his reason. In such a throng you will be the more likely to escape notice."

I looked at him in silence for some moments. His face wore its usual look of patient shrewdness. He was sending me. He did not

want me to come to harm; he may not have had much faith in the results, may even have felt, with me, that standing still in a moving
throng of people is not the best way to escape notice. But such missions formed part of the powers and prerogatives of his diwan; they
had to be exercised or they would be lost or expropriated, and that
would leave him the weaker.

"Lord," I said, "I am ready to do anything you ask of me, no matter what, but it is a long way to go just to show empty hands."

"We work by signs and gestures. Do you not know this yet? The
money has the same importance whether it is absent or present.
There is a verse in the Koran which speaks of this: 'But that
mankind would become one people we would have given those
who denied merciful God silver roofs for their houses and stairways
to mount to them.' "

I nodded as if I fully understood this, which was far from being
the case. In fact, I was often at a loss to understand quotations from
the Holy Book of the Moslems. I thought this one might mean that
God did not set store by gold or silver, but I did not see the rele-
vance of this, as we were talking about Lazar, who set great store by
both.

"The pains we take are part of the message," Yusuf said. "He will
have to take great care in making this clear to his own people, who
will be angry with him, not with us, and who may be inclined to
regard him as a spent force and seek to replace him. You see,
Thurstan Beauchamp?"

He used my name always, my full name, when he knew I was opposed and he wished to create an understanding between us, as if I
were a child, unwilling to see reason. And this annoyed me and
touched me in equal measure, which I think he knew. When he had
finished speaking he stood silent for a while. Tall and frail-seeming,

with his slight, scholarly stoop of the shoulders, he more resembled one of the Arab artists and men of letters with whom our King loved to surround himself than what he was, mission master, controller of the royal revenues, with a power that made him envied and feared, ruthless and devoted in serving this kingdom—a kingdom that his forebears had ruled for two centuries, ruled now by a Norman king, whose father and uncle had landed in Sicily as penniless adventurers and taken the island by conquest.

He started slightly now, as if he had forgotten something or allowed himself too much pause, too much silence. Then he inclined his head, said a brief word of farewell to me, and turned away. Thus dismissed, I left at once, this time not passing through the antechamber but stepping directly out into the passage, which followed the line of the wall facing toward the city. At the far end there were steps leading down in a spiral to the courtyard on this side. There was a narrow landing at the first curve of the staircase and in the recess of the wall an open casement with, at this hour of the day, sunlight slanting through it onto the steps and making a spill of light there. As I approached this I heard the wavering cries of the muezzins calling the faithful to prayer from the balconies of minarets throughout the city. I understood now why Yusuf had been so abrupt in his farewell: it was the noon call, he had heard the first notes.

I stopped and stood still there before the opening, as I had sometimes done before; it was scarcely two spans across at the broadest point, but I could see a section of sky through it. Yusuf would have needed time to summon his servant to bring water for the ritual ablution of his face and hands . . . I had been encouraged by him to use a faculty of picturing, of turning imagination like a directed light, a ray, onto the movements, thoughts, habits of others, to keep their continuing existence in my mind, see them in their times of vacancy or solitude, when they were unguarded. Where would such a person go, what might he do next? Even in the intimate details of his bodily life I would follow him. It was Yusuf, as I say, who had fostered this in me; now I turned the ray on him. He would shake his narrow feet loose from the slippers, he would clap his hands for his servant, a Berber boy slave he had named Matthew, who had a mat on the floor in the adjoining room. Matthew would know what to do without needing to be told. He would bring the ewer of water and the towel; he would pour the water very slowly into the basin that was always there; as the water flowed from the neck of the ewer, Yusuf would catch it in his hands and bring it to his face and wet his ears and nostrils and eyes and mouth, so that the organs of sense could be cleansed before he turned toward Mecca and intoned the intention to pray.

All this takes long to write, not long to see in the mind. The call was still continuing, rising from all directions, far and near, testifying to the greatness of God, calling upon the faithful to come to salvation, a clamorous, melodious hubbub that fell on the city five times a day, confused by varying distance and the overlapping of sound, since those chanting did not all begin at the same moment, one voice fell away as another was raised, like veils of sound laid one across the borders of another, veils that were then torn again by the movements of the muezzins themselves, since each had to address all quarters of the world and so pronounce his summons four times, each time facing in a different way. It was a ragged music, deeply familiar to all who had their lives in the city, and moving in its confusion, to me at least, though a Christian—like the loud plaints that lambs make, lost on the hillsides, one answering another near and far, which I remember from the dales of my childhood in England, a chorus that always seemed to me like sorrow and joy at the same time.

Now, as I still stood there in the thin shaft of sunlight, in response as it seemed to the human voices, but not in rivalry, there rose the brazen voices of bells from monasteries and churches all over the city, announcing the noon hour and the office of sext. And now again there was a confusion of sound, the clear silver bells that hang inside the cloisters, the deeper ones above convent gates, the clanging, deep-throated ones mounted in the towers of churches. For some moments more the throats of men and bells made that medley of loss and celebration, and as I glanced upward at the section of sky that was visible through the window I saw the swift-winged birds that live in the sky above the city and never alight on the ground, saw them flock together in the bright air, rising above the sound, not as in fear but as in joy.

With this I was swept by a familiar love for this city of Palermo, where I had spent most of my years, for the diversity these sounds expressed, the different faiths that lived together here, the different races that jostled in the markets and labored on the buildings that were rising everywhere, praying apart and having their cases tried in their own tongues, but all held together in unity by our great King. I thought of him now, the times on state occasions I had seen him, always at a distance. He rode with a canopy of pale-colored silk stretched above his head, and the light that fell through it seemed to obscure his face, a radiance that obscured. I had no picture in my mind of the King's face.

From here I could not see the Pisan Tower, where the royal apartments were, but I knew he spent his morning hours there, in the audience chamber on the second story. He would be there now, hearing ambassadors or studying documents that touched the lives of us all, or perhaps scanning details of the revenues from his estates—in that case, his eye might fall, just for the merest moment, on an entry I myself had made, some item of expenditure. He would see the marks I had traced! A sense of wonder descended on me with this thought, wonder at his nearness and farness. I tried to picture him, as I had just pictured Yusuf, but I could not, he was beyond my imagining, divinely appointed as he was, by God's grace invested with the scepter and the orb. I was eight years old that Christmas Day when he was crowned in the cathedral of Palermo. I saw him then for the first time, standing with my father in the ranks of the nobility. My father lifted me up and I saw him pass in sunlight and he was in a mantle of gold and the bridle of his horse was gold and its hooves made no sound because of the carpets they had laid over the pavement.

I had lived ever since in the protective shadow of his power. I felt ashamed now that I had been so grudging and reluctant in the way I had received the news of my mission to Bari, when it was in his service that I was sent. My life up till that time had contained disappointments. In fact, it had sometimes seemed to me that it was my fate never to arrive at a promised end. I had wanted with all my soul to fight in the King's cause as a knight and it had not been granted to me for reasons I will give more fully later. I had sought a command in his Household Guard, and this too had come to nothing because Yusuf had taken me from it. He had noticed me and greeted me in Arabic and I had answered him in the same language, which I knew, though at that time imperfectly, from the Arab nurse my parents had given me. With these few words I gave him in answer, my life was changed. I was to learn that he had wanted more Christians in the diwan, to broaden the base of his power. One like myself, of the Latin faith and of Norman descent, had been particularly suitable for this purpose of his. He had other reasons also, which I learned only later.

He had sent me to study Roman law at Bologna, so as to argue cases affecting the King's temporal power against ecclesiastical claims where property or revenue was involved. I studied but I felt no vocation for the law, and I was not among the most brilliant there. I had more success in the taverns, where I added to my stock of songs, both those in Latin that the students sang and the new ones in French that were coming from Poitou and Aquitaine. Somehow, returning to Palermo and the palace service, I had become Purveyor of Pleasures and purse bearer. Service in the sun, in the open, with no handling of coin, this is what I would have wanted. But I could still be of use to him in the shadows. And was I not going openly to Cosenza to buy for him the white marsh birds that he so loved to serve to his falcons?

Set aglow by these thoughts, I turned from the window to continue my way down. As I did so, by chance or by some instinct, I glanced behind me at the way I had come. There was a man at the head of the stairway, standing quite still, watching me. After a moment I knew him for Maurice Béroul, an ordained priest, employed now in the legal department of the Vice Chancery as an advisor in matters touching canon law. He had been present at the *majlis* but had not spoken. He did not speak now, though he seemed for a moment to hesitate as if he might come toward me. Then he turned, took some steps back along the passage, and disappeared from view.

II

THE STAIRS ENDED on the landward side of the palace, opening into a walled courtyard with a narrow portico and a fountain. Here I came upon Mark Glycas, who was taking the air in the shade of the arches, walking slowly, with his gait of an old man, unsteady and dragging. He had his back to me and did not hear my step. He did not see me until he came to the end of his paces and turned about, which he did by slow degrees—all his movements were slow except those of his head, which had an upward motion, rather frequent, as if he were following some faint sound in the air above. He was bareheaded, by which I knew he had come only for this brief respite from his writing table.

He gave me good-day and would have resumed his walk, but before he could do so I asked him the usual question, the same that he had been asked for twenty years: "And the studies, how are they proceeding?"

"We are building up a case," he said, his usual answer. "Yes, slowly and surely we are building up a case."

No one knew how old Glycas was. He had grown gray and his eyes had dimmed in the King's service, saddled always with the one task: to find convincing evidence, evidence that could be published, that Sicily had once, however long ago, been ruled by kings. If this could be done, it would make clear that our good Roger, in taking the crown, had not invented the monarchy or imposed it on the people but had merely resumed the royal line. Glycas was versed in the history of antiquity, conversant with legends and myths, adept at following up threads and finding links. He could read with equal ease the Greek of Hesiod and of Byzantium, the Latin of Ovid and of the Christian Fathers. He had brought all his enormous erudition to this task. No definite proof had so far been discovered; not many believed now that any would; some thought, and I was among this number, that Glycas was simply spinning out his time—he was comfortable there, the stipend was enough for his needs.

"Yes, yes," he said, cocking his head to catch that fugitive sound. "I am following a new line."

"What is that?"

I did not expect much response to this; he had already said more than was customary with him. But I had come upon him at a propitious moment, he was in garrulous vein. "Yes," he said, "I have long believed that the answer lies with the Siculi, and lately I have become more convinced of it than ever. No doubt you are familiar with the customs of this tribe?"

"Of course."

"I see that you are not," he said after a sly pause. "A very ancient tribe, they once occupied parts of this island. Their presence in

Sicily and the Italian peninsula is well attested. Thucydides speaks of them, as does also Polybius. We even have some words of their language, which in my opinion has an affinity with Latin."

"How does this touch upon the issue of kingship?"

"I am coming to that. You are too much in haste, like all the young. Haste is a very bad thing. The Siculi had gods, like all others—there has never been a people without gods. The most important were the Polici, protectors of farmers and sailors. These Polici had a father-god named Adranus. Now it is this Adranus who has been rousing my interest of late."

He might have meant lately or in the course of the last five years or so: it was impossible to tell with him. "Well," I said, "I hope your labors bear fruit."

I was beginning to move away, but he clutched at my sleeve to stop me. "Always this haste," he said. "I am coming round to the belief that Adranus was not a god at all, but a king. That is to say, he was a mortal, but because of his kingship he was revered as a god."

He smiled and raised his chin, as if that rustling had grown louder. There were more gaps than teeth in his mouth. "It fits together perfectly. Adranus was king, the Polici were his ministers, and the farmers and sailors formed the people. I am rereading the works of Polybius in search of a reference that will clinch the matter. But for this time is needed—the writings of Polybius run to many volumes."

He released his febrile clutch on my sleeve and I congratulated him on these discoveries and was finally able to move on. It did not seem to me at all likely that Glycas would live long enough to get through all the works of Polybius, that most long-winded of authors. But no doubt someone else would be appointed to continue. As I made my way across the courtyard I was filled yet again with wonder at the might of the King, how it infused all our lives. His title was not in dispute within the realm; it was recognized by all. True, he had potent enemies: the King of the Germans and the Emperor of the Byzantines both regarded him as usurper, and Pope Eugenius had not yet formally recognized his rule. But it was hard to believe that any of these would be brought to a new state of mind by learning that the ancient tribe of the Siculi had kings. Yet the labors of Glycas continued, and they would be continued by others when Glycas was no more. Perhaps King Roger himself was no longer aware of the scholar's existence. At some time in the past he had taken a mortal life between finger and thumb and set it down in a room among books and left it there, warm enough, ignored, like an insect in a sunny corner. How many there were in forgotten corners, kept alive by the warmth of his power! I too, I thought, as I saddled my horse in its stable near the gate and led it past the uniformed guards and so out into the street. When the heron took flight and the blindfold was removed from the hawk's eyes, how much space would Thurstan the Purveyor occupy in the King's mind?

That sun of April was hot when it was trapped between walls. It was the hour when people were closing their shutters for the afternoon rest. Those in the streets were making for home or for a place in the shade. The water sellers were calling with their high-pitched cries, their pails and dippers swinging from the yoke and scattering drops that flashed as they fell and dried before the marks could show. I passed a group of the King's Saracen footguards returning to their barracks after some display—they were in dress uniform of green caftan and white turban, with the short curved swords at their belts. Two Norman serjeants in chain mail rode by, and I saw the hostile looks they exchanged with the Saracens, who were the King's favorite troops.

I arrived at my house to find the shutters already closed against the sun. The gatekeeper, Pietro, was in his shed at the side, half asleep on his cot, and he was slow to open to me. It was his wife, Caterina, a woman from Amalfi, who took care of my two rooms and kept my water jug full and cooked for me, as she cooked for others in the house, wheezing slowly up the stairs with food she had prepared in the kitchen below—I call it a kitchen but it was no more than an angle in the wall with a fireplace. Today she came with wheat cakes made with a filling of chives and melted goat cheese. With this I drank a little of the good Sicilian wine from the royal vineyards in the Conca d'Oro, to which the first three degrees of palace officials are entitled by contract.

Afterward I slept a little and woke to feelings of unease, something like foreboding, remembering, as I still lay reclined on my couch, the marks of division so evident at the *majlis* that morning, the antagonisms that stirred among us. I wondered why Maurice Béroul had watched me so, what had been in his mind when he had seemed to hesitate. And I wondered who our King listened to, Norman or Lombard, Arab or Greek or Jew. Then I remembered I was to go all the way to Bari on a mission I did not believe in, simply for Yusuf to maintain the prerogatives of his diwan.

Mainly to expel these gloomy thoughts, but also because I would be away from Palermo for some time, I decided to go that evening to the Royal Chapel to see the progress of the mosaics. I felt the need for movement, I would go on foot, there had been no rain to muddy the streets. Also, I wanted to visit a goldsmith's shop near the Buscemi Gate, because I had it in mind, after seeing the mosaics, to spend some time with the women of the Tiraz, the silk workshop in the precincts of the palace, and in particular with a woman called Sara, who was my favorite among them.

These women were from Thebes, of Jewish race, experts in the cultivation of the silkworm and the manufacture of robes and vestments for court occasions, who had been carried off from their homes and brought as a gift to the city of Palermo by the Admiral of the Fleet, the Emir of Emirs, George of Antioch, on a raid he had made into Greece two years before. Usually I gave Sara coin—it was what she preferred. But I handled money so much in my work that I liked sometimes to make her a present, some small trinket. Along with my clothes and the rent for my lodgings and the care of my horse, my visits to the Tiraz were a main part of my monthly expenditure.

The light was fading as I set out, and the lamps at street corners were being lit. There was the smell of spilt water around the troughs of the pump near my house, a strangely strong odor, though made from nothing but slaked dust and hot stones; as always, it evoked some longing in me, though I did not know for what, or whether it was more than merely a feeling of loneliness.

This was the time of day when the street sweepers came into their own; sweepers they called themselves, but they were scavengers in fact. They were out now in force, sacks roped across their bodies. Of late months they had been coming to the attention of our diwan. They were unruly; they were too successful. It was a closed company now, impossible to enter without a permit from one of the clan chiefs who controlled the various districts of the city and had armed men at their bidding and skimmed off a portion of the sweepers' takings, as they did with beggars and whores. This was made more complicated by the fact that the dominant clans were of different races, Arabs in the Kalsa, Greeks on the south side, Sicilians in the area of the harbor. Disputes over territory arose from time to time and killings occurred. This was acceptable so long as a proper balance was maintained. Lately, however, the balance had begun to tilt. There had been pitched battles between bands of sweepers, the number of deaths had increased very noticeably. From being a simple matter of bribes and intimidation, it had been dignified with the title of fiscal malpractice, and so it had come to the attention of the Diwan of Control. So far no remedy had been found. It was obvious that the sweeping, or scavenging, or whatever one called it, mainly took the form of theft; the people were poor, there were not pickings enough in the streets of Palermo to main-tain more than a handful of lawful scavengers.

I fell to pondering the matter again as I walked along. The prob-lem was threefold: how to stop the thefts, enlarge the King's coffers, and have the streets swept clean. The sweepers could be made to wear a uniform of some kind, with a color that would mark them out, yellow perhaps. Then people would be able to watch them more narrowly, especially when they were gathered in groups. Bolder, more likely to come to the notice of the King and gain his approval, would be to change their constitution altogether, form them into a single company with a new name, The Noble Company of Street Cleaners, wearing the royal emblem and regularly paying a fixed sum, or perhaps a portion of their earnings, into the Royal Treasury. In that case it would no longer be a bribe but a tax, and so quite lawful. But the difficulty here, apart from the hostility it would arouse among the chiefs, was that they had no earnings, properly speaking, only the proceeds of their thefts. Could people be per-suaded to pay to have their streets cleaned? It seemed unlikely. Perhaps this too could be imposed as a tax. Meanwhile the scavengers might be required to carry broom and shovel; thus encumbered they would find it less easy to steal, but on the other hand a shovel in the wrong hands could be a formidable weapon . . .

These fruitless thoughts occupied my mind until I came to the little square close to the Buscemi Gate where the goldsmith had his furnace. I watched him work for a little while, hammering out softened gold to thin leaf on his anvil. When he saw me he gave the work to his son, who was as brawny as he and always there to assist him, and came toward me, the sweat gleaming on his arms and face. He had a glass counter with the things for sale in boxes below the glass, so that they could be seen but not touched until he took them out. After some hesitation I chose a garnet stone with a painted foil on the underside to make it glow. I thought Sara could wear it on a chain round her neck, or have it set in a ring if she so chose. He asked three silver ducats for it.

Making a purchase often lightens my spirits and it did so now. As I made my way through the darkening streets toward the chapel, my anticipation quickened. I had been following the progress of the mosaics for some years and was on close terms of friendship with the man whose charge it was to see them completed, the Byzantine master mosaicist Demetrius Karamides, who had come to oversee the work by personal invitation of our King Roger.

I entered by the west doorway and the wonder of the place struck me anew, a familiar awe but one that had never lost its power over me. The nave was in shadow as I moved forward, but there was lamplight at the far end, in the area of the sanctuary, where they were working. A gleaming light was cast upward on the saints and apostles in the arches of the crossing, holy ranks of those who intercede for us. Light fell on the raised right hand of Christ Pantocrator and on the open book with its message of salvation: *I am the light of the world.* I could not see the words but I knew them. Christ's face was in shadow, but a tremulous radiance lay on the hem of the Virgin's robe and on the gold of her halo and on the outstretched hand of the Angel of the Annunciation. The shadows shifted as I drew nearer, and I saw God's fingers and the bright wings of the Dove.

As I walked forward through the shadow I felt that the light beyond was casting for me as an angler might draw his net for a fish to bring it up from the deep. There is no accident in our lives: everything has been foreseen. I had entered at a certain time, in a certain light. There was the open book, the shining disc, the wings; there were the hands above all, hands blessing, hands sending. For a moment I felt the dazzle of a different light, but then it receded and was lost to me. I saw Demetrius move into the light. He came toward me and we clasped hands in the way the Byzantine Greeks are used to doing it, gripping high up above the wrist. He had been more than eight years on the island, first at Cefalù and then at Palermo, yet he had made no smallest effort to adopt the manners or style of dress of his hosts, keeping still the ceremonious ways of Constantinople and the high-necked, loosely belted dalmatic. I had wondered if this were due to pride or a feeling of patriotism, dangerous if so, now that his emperor was preparing for war with Sicily. Perhaps just an unyieldingness of nature. Or was my own too yielding, too loose? This also I had wondered about. Greek among Greeks, Frank among Franks—what was Thurstan?

I knew as I answered his greeting that something was amiss, not from his face, which was always somber, but from his tone, from the way he at once drew me aside and led me into the south side of the crossing, out of hearing of the two working in the sanctuary. There was a man slung high against the opposite wall, suspended by ropes on a platform of wood, with lamps attached to the ropes on either side. He was working on the decoration on the inside of the arch immediately above the Flight into Egypt. He was very fair; in the light his hair looked golden.

"What is it?" I asked, immediately responsive to this silent guiding of me. As a plant knows the source of light and turns its face there, so I knew the manners of secrecy.

But he said nothing for the moment, merely regarded me. He had eyes as black as jet, high-lidded and very lustrous, compelling in their gaze. When displeased he had a way of lowering the lids over them that gave his face an expression of suffering not patiently borne.

"Is the work not proceeding well?"

"We will not be permitted to finish the work. We will soon be leaving here."

"Leaving? But there is so much still to do. There is the west wall, and the arcades, and the apostolic sequence in . . ."

"Yes, as you say, there is much to do still, but it will not be my people to do it—new people will be coming. We will finish the mosaics in the sanctuary and the crossing because they do not want so evident a mixture of styles, but we will be leaving before the end of the year."

"New people?" I was bewildered. "Who are they that do not want mixed styles?"

Demetrius indicated with a movement of his head the man on the platform high on the north wall of the crossing. "He is one of the new ones. They are Latins from the north, Franks. We set this one to do the *fleurs délices* decoration on the arch because it is all we can trust him to do."

I glanced upward. There was an aureole of light around the

man's head; he was like a heedless angel, suspended there with his back to us. To the right of him, level with his shining head, were the emerald fronds of the Egyptian palm and the infant Christ sitting upright on Joseph's shoulder. When I looked back at Demetrius my sight was dimmed for some moments, as if I had been looking into the sun. "It cannot be," I said. "It cannot be to replace you that they are sent. To work with you, to learn, yes. You are known for a master, you made the mosaics at Cefalù for our King Roger, and all of us know how much they pleased him."

The King's gratitude had been lavish: five hundred gold dinars as a gift on the completion of the mosaics, this sum in addition to the wages and the maintenance written in the contract. I knew this for a fact, as the accounts had been drawn up in our diwan. "There must be some mistake," I said.

Demetrius made the strange, angular gesture of the Byzantine Greek, angry and resigned at the same time, shrugging his right shoulder and slightly raising his right arm, palm upward, as if throwing some object awkwardly up into the air. "There is no mistake. Unless it be the mistake of employing lesser craftsmen in our stead. We have the wrong liturgy. The Latin Christians will take our place."

"By whose order?"

"By order of the King."

I was dumbfounded at this; in fact, for some moments I could not believe the words had been said. A long course of persuasion and many promises had been needed to bring Demetrius Karamides to Sicily. In Cefalù first, and now here in the Royal Chapel, in the apse and sanctuary and crossing, he and those he had brought with him from Constantinople had made mosaics that were the wonder of the world. Whose the skill of tongue that had persuaded the King to order this dismissing of them? It could only be as Demetrius said, those of the Roman church, wanting mosaic workers of their own liturgy in this place where the Latin mass would be celebrated. But what filled my mind, once the shock of surprise was over, excluding all else, was that this decision had been taken and these orders carried out without the smallest trickle of information reaching the Diwan of Control—not even rumor had come to us. This it was that gave me the beginnings of fear as I looked beyond Demetrius into the shadows of the nave. Such secrecy was the mark of power. By what paths had they reached it?

"It cannot be," I said, but I was speaking now of this discord, this enmity of faiths, here where Saracens had carved the wood of the ceiling, Latins made the marble inlays, Greeks set the stones of the mosaics, all working together to make a church where our Norman King could hear the mass.

Perhaps hearing the trouble of my spirit in my voice, Demetrius moved toward me and again took my arm. "Come this way a little," he said. "You cannot see well in the lamplight. Not well enough to make a full judgment. But the medallions in the soffits of the arcade here, these were done by our people, working alongside Lombards from the mainland. Working together, you understand? The work is fine, just as it is in the apse and the sanctuary and the side chapels. They worked well, but it was always under our guidance. They have learned, but it is not yet enough. Now these newcomers, who know even less, will have charge of all the work in the nave. You will see how the mosaics will be coarsened, they will hold less light."

His eyes opened wide as he spoke. "Light," he said, "the art of mosaic is the art of light. It is in the setting of the pieces, not in the color. We see where one color ends and another begins, but light is splendor, and splendor has no bounds. Who does not know how to catch the light will never make truly fine mosaic. Their work will never be as ours here. You will see where our work ended and theirs began."

He had spoken with much feeling, and his eyes, as he opened them full upon me, gleamed in the lamplight as if they too had caught the light he was extolling. But it seemed to me that he was exaggerating because of his hurt at being supplanted—a feeling natural enough. I could not believe the King had allowed himself to be persuaded to entrust the mosaics of his own chapel to people of inferior skill, knowing them for such. Demetrius spoke as if there were no other makers of mosaic in the world.

"Yes," he said now, "in all the time to come, while this church stands, they will see where our work ended and their coarser work began. That is a consolation to me, that it will be seen and known through all the ages."

"Demetrius," I said, "please believe me when I say how unhappy this news has made me. I will try to discover more about it. There must be reasons, urgent reasons, that we know nothing of."

I had spoken these words with eyes cast down, as is the custom among us when we share the sadness of others or commiserate with them in loss or misfortune. When I looked again at Demetrius's face I saw that its expression had changed: a smile had come to it, but not a pleasant one. "The urgent reason we know nothing of is that your King wishes to please the Bishop of Rome by filling all offices with Latin Christians. He hopes that this, if continued long enough, will gain him the recognition of Rome, which so far he has failed to obtain."

There was almost a sneer in this, something unusual in him. I was offended by the slight on our good King Roger, especially as there was some small part of truth in it, not as regarded his motives—of

these what could either of us know, who were so far beneath him?—
but in the fact that Pope Eugenius still continued to address him as
Signore, unjustly withholding recognition of his royal title.

"I believe the King has been deceived," I said. "He has been advised wrongly."

"What does it matter how he was advised? He has set his seal on
it. You will have the decoration of the nave arcade, on both sides.
You will be obliged to keep to the book of Genesis—that was agreed
on all hands when we started our work here. But you will turn it
into stories."

His face was close to mine as he spoke and I saw his mouth twist
with contempt. "It is all that you of the west know how to do. You
go from left to right, from one scene to the next, in a line. You have
no understanding. God's grace is not different from his power, they
fall from above to below, one face of splendor, like the light. And this
grace and power, what do you do with it? You make stories. God
creating light, a little figure in the corner, making a gesture, then we
move on to the next scene. God lives in the light he creates, but you
do not know this—you make stories."

The contempt was in his voice and it was for me also. I had never
heard him speak in such a way and it made me think I did not really
know him, though for years I had counted him as a friend. His pride
had been hurt, yes, he had suffered a heavy blow. But the contempt
had been there already, some lesser blow would have brought it out.
When there is a flaw, any tremor will break the rock asunder. I think
it is Saint Paul who says this, in his Epistle to the Thessalonians, ex-
horting unity of faith and practice among his brethren in Christ.
But it was only later that the words of St. Paul—if indeed it was he—
came to my mind. What should have made me sad, had I been
wiser, only made me angry now. I said, "It is usual in those who lack

a thing to be jealous of those who possess it. God's revelation is made known to us by unfolding, like turning pages. We have the gift of narrative—you have not. So you make it a fault in us."

After this not much more was said between us. He accompanied me some way down the aisle but we parted coldly. I stood alone at the door for a little while, looking back down the nave toward the sanctuary and apse. Where the light fell I could see the colored marble inlays on the balustrades and lower walls, set like gems on the lid of a casket, work of Italian craftsmen. Beyond this was the radiance of the mosaics. In the dimness above me, hardly visible now but closely familiar from previous visits, was the Arab stalactite ceiling in carved wood, with its painted scenes and Kufic inscriptions. Latin, Byzantine and Saracen had worked together here to make a single harmony, to make this, though still unfinished, the most beautiful church ever before seen in Palermo. There had been times when the interior had sounded to their separate languages and the chipping and hammering and scraping of their work.

But it was not a question only of the edifice itself. This blending of all that was best in the separate traditions was to my mind a figure for the unity in diversity of our realm, a harmony that our King had known how to protect and preserve. It was my obscure service to aid him in this great task. It was why I struggled to curtail the abuses of the street sweepers. It was why I was going to meet Lazar Pilic.

III

I CANNOT SAY that I found much comfort in these thoughts after the news I had heard and the manner of my parting with Demetrius. I felt heavy-hearted and needful of solace, and as I made the sign of the cross in the shadows before leaving, I thought again about the women of the Tiraz and more particularly about Sara and the gift I had for her in my purse, which would make her welcome the warmer—or so I hoped, feeling the need for her arms about me and the yield of her body.

As I reached the foot of the steps and began to make my way across the courtyard, a man came toward me from the shadows close to the wall. He came on my left side, and he was silent and his step was light. The courtyard was deserted and I thought for a moment that he meant to attack me. I swung round to face him and my hand went to the dagger at my belt, that being quicker than a sword to draw and use in the short space there was between us.

"No," he said, "I am a friend, I am Béroul. I was crossing the square and saw you in the light from the doorway as you began to descend the steps."

"Light from the doorway?" I glanced back up the stairway. "You have good eyes."

I saw him smile, as if he knew my thoughts. "I have been wanting to speak with you for some time," he said. "I took the opportunity thus presented."

We were still standing in the shadow of the wall. He was wearing a hooded cloak and I could make out little of his face, except that the smile gave the set of his jaws a famished look.

"I am on my way to a visit of some importance," I said. "Can this not wait until another time?"

"It is something that concerns you closely. You would do well to hear me."

There was a coloring of threat in this, or so it seemed to me. I did not fear Béroul, but if he was prepared to use such a tone, he must deem the matter serious. "Very well," I said, infusing my voice with weariness. "I am listening."

"No, not here," he said. "What are you thinking of? A poor light will not make us less likely to be noticed, ill-wishers can more easily draw near."

"As you drew near to me."

"I am your friend and you will know it soon. If we talk here we will seem like conspirators. If we talk in a tavern I know of, not far away, we are Thurstan Beauchamp and Maurice Béroul, two servants of the Douana Regia, having a cup of wine together and not caring who sees us."

He had used the Latin title of the Royal Diwan with a certain deliberate emphasis, and this, when afterward I thought back on our talk, seemed the first pointer to his intent. He began to move across the courtyard as he finished speaking, and I fell into step beside him without more words.

The tavern was a poor enough place, no more than a cellar, ill lit and almost deserted—there was a man asleep or befuddled sitting at a table with his head hanging low, and three others playing dice in a corner and disputing among themselves at every throw. The man who served us wore an evil-smelling leather apron and the wine was sour. I was surprised that Béroul should choose such a place. There were taverns in Palermo frequented by the people of the Palace, but this was not one of them. We were conspicuous here, I with my plumed hat and loose-sleeved pelisse, he with his dark mantle and the fringe and dome of his tonsure—he had thrown the hood back now to reveal this.

He drank a little from his cup, then set it down carefully. After a moment he smiled his lean-jawed smile and said, "We have always taken a great interest in you, Thurstan."

"Indeed?" I said. "Is this the plural of majesty we are using?"

"We in the Vice Chancery, the Magistri Camerarii Palatii. We have been watching over you when little you knew of it."

This I could well believe. "We do our watching too," I said, "we in the *Diwan al-tahqiq al-ma' mur*." I had used the Arab title deliberately, and it seemed to me that his face hardened, but there was no change in his tone when he spoke again.

"We have seen your diligence and your devotion to the King's service. It is our opinion that your talents are being wasted."

He seemed to wait for a reply but I made none. After a moment he said, "In spite of your high abilities you will not go far in a douana conducted by Saracens, with a Saracen at its head."

"There are Christians in my diwan besides myself."

Now, for the second time that evening, I saw a face made ugly by contempt. "Christians? You put yourself on a level with them, you who are of Christian birth? You call them Christians, these filthy palace Saracens that claim to be converted to our faith and secretly continue to practice their own?"

"I have seen no evidence of this," I said, but he did not hear me or showed no sign of doing so.

"Once a Saracen, always a Saracen—it is in their blood," he said. His eyes had a staring look now, that famished smile gone, and with it all pretense of benevolent interest in me. He leaned forward across the table, bringing his face close to mine. "It is in their corrupted blood," he said, "and they will corrupt our blood with it if we allow them. The terrible warning is there for us in the words of Ezekiel: 'And when I passed by thee and saw thee polluted in thine own blood, I said unto thee: In thy blood live!' The Christian life as lived in Sicily can be summed up as a struggle against contamination, a struggle to keep our blood clean. It is a long struggle, one that has no ending. The threat is always there—no conquest can ever be more than provisional. Tell me, Thurstan, what does Christendom mean to you?"

"It is the term we use for those regions where our Roman faith is predominant."

"That is all it signifies to you? This great spread of our faith no more than a matter of geography? I will tell you what Christendom is. Christendom is the universal Christian church, the universal Christian society. Christendom is a mighty host that is destined to bring the world under its sway."

Rarely had I seen such exaltation on a human face. The constraint he was under to keep his voice low intensified the vehemence of his speech. It was quieter now inside the room. The dice game was over, one of the three had left; the head of the solitary sleeper had declined onto the table.

"This Christendom of ours is young," Béroul said, more calmly. "Bear with me, travel back with me in time a little. A hundred years ago almost to the day, you might have seen a company of men making their way from Worms to Rome. If you had been fortunate enough to be of that company, you would have known one of them for Bruno of Egisheim, newly elected Pope Leo IX, another for Hugh, Abbot of Cluny, and the third for Hildebrand, who would later become Pope Gregory VII. Think of it, Thurstan. When, before or since, have three such men traveled in a single company? Three future saints, three men of genius, each dedicated to extending the power and influence of the Holy Church. They saw more clearly than ever before that the danger lay in diverse practices, in their different ways they worked to transcend the local, to make our Church one single body. These were the founders of Christendom. Theirs was the spirit that inspired the First Crusade and took the Holy Land for Christ."

He said nothing of the Second Crusade, which had ended in disastrous failure only the year before, and I understood the reason for this and it brought me, if only for that moment, closer to Béroul than I was ever to come again: we were briefly united in the sorrow all Christians felt for our loss of Edessa, for our humiliation before the walls of Damascus, for the disorderly and ignominious retreat of the greatest army that the Franks had ever put into the field.

"We see further than they did," Béroul said after a moment of repose. "Not because we have sharper eyes but because of the foundation they laid for us. They were giants, we are dwarfs. We see further because we are sitting on their shoulders. This is a figure of my own invention that I sometimes use when I want to explain these matters."

"It bears a resemblance to some words of Bernard of Chartres, written at a time before I was born."

"Well done, Thurstan! I made a little test for you. They have not exaggerated who praise your accomplishments. But I was intending to say that while the danger still lies in local practices, we see now today, here in Sicily, that the great threat to our Church is the existence among us of a militant faith hostile to our own. These Moslems are allowed to live and breed among us, and their blood is corrupted—they will corrupt the blood of Holy Church, *our* blood." The calmer mood that had come to him when he spoke of those great men of the past was broken now, that fixed and staring look had returned to his face. "We will be condemned to live in our polluted blood, and the words of Ezekiel will come to pass."

"Is it to tell me this that you brought me here?" I said.

His eyes fell away from mine. He reached out a hand and moved his cup a little to one side, no more than a fraction, as if to find an ideal place for it. "You can help us in this sacred task. Your douana is a source of corruption. Will you say you have not noticed how year by year the language of the Saracens has supplanted all others in the documents produced by your douana? It was formerly Greek. Then Latin, the language of our religion, began to be used. But this was suppressed through their cunning. Now all is in their Saracen language. Will you say you have not noticed this?"

"It is not true that all is in Arabic. Greek also is used—my clerk is a Greek. Arabic is more usual now and the reason for that is not difficult to see. We use Saracen scribes because they have better instruction and write a better hand. We are occupied with land holdings and the grants and fees belonging to them. Clarity is essential. Those set to write in Latin could not make themselves clear in that or in any other language."

"Do you not see that this rise of their language is part of a conspiracy that goes far beyond the shores of this island? The Saracens ruled here once—not long ago. They are working to undermine the King's realm and to regain the power they had. They are assisted from abroad. Have you followed the rise of the Almohads in North Africa? One after another our colonies are falling to them: they are taking our ports and our trade, they are recovering the land for Islam. They send their spies across the water to stir up rebellion and acts of violence among their fellow Moslems here."

He spoke as if no one else knew of these Almohads, the Berbers of Morocco who were taking all by storm, whereas most of Palermo knew of them, and all those in the palace service. I myself knew more about it than he did, as I had carried the King's money over the water to stiffen the resistance of the Emir of Bougie, who was favorable to our trade interests there, but all to no avail. Every day our Arab friends were losing ground; these Almohads were already west of the Zurid Kingdom.

"They make use of the *alamat* to send secret signals among them," he said now.

"That cannot be true." The *alamat* were a form of signature in the Kufic script used by Arab scribes in documents that circulated through the chanceries. "They are extremely difficult to read," I said. "Almost impossible."

"That is the cunning of it. They make the writing intricate not for the sake of ornament but so as to deceive. We have used trained scribes to decipher them. They are quotations from the Koran. Let me give you an example. 'On the Day of Judgment to whom will the

Kingdom belong? To God, the One, the Victorious.' " He paused, staring across at me in a manner of one who has made a point impossible to refute. "It could hardly be clearer," he said. "That is an incitement to rebellion. Have you seen them pray? Hundreds of men moving together like a single beast."

I watched him in silence as he again paused to make a small adjustment to the position of his cup. His fingers were very white and the nails well cared for.

"The Beast that waits to devour us," he said. "Who is it that gives your Saracen scribes their employment and oversees their work? Is it not the lord of your douana?"

"You know it is."

"Yusuf Ibn Mansur. He is close to the throne and seeks to come even closer. But he will not leave his place to you, Thurstan, he will leave it to a creature of his own. We know already the successor he has in mind."

If he was hoping I would question him on this, he was disappointed. In any case, I did not believe it. By spying we can find the nest of the lark, the lair of the fox, the place where a man hides his treasure. But the spy was not born who could see into the purposes of a man like Yusuf. Nevertheless, though confident of this, I felt stricken by Béroul's words as if they took some shelter from me. "I do not seek his place," I said, and this I felt to be true in the sense of actively seeking.

"We know certain other things about him. We know that he and certain others, Saracens subordinate to him, are engaged in perverting our faith by offering bribes to any who will convert to Islam."

This was so insensate a thing that for some moments I could not find words to answer him. By a law newly introduced by the

Council of Justiciars—a council appointed by the King—such attempts at conversion, whether by bribes or coercion, were defined as crimes tantamount to treason. "But you are mad," I said at last.

"No, believe me, we have been watching him for a long time now. He has not made any such attempt on you?"

"No, of course not, never."

Béroul remained silent for some time, glancing away from me across the room. Then, still without looking at me, he said, "Think carefully, my fine young man. It is a capital offense. You would not want to be associated with him in guilt. It may be that you remember something, some form of words."

"What do you mean?"

"Something perhaps scarcely noticed at the time, but coming together afterward in memory to form a particular significance."

Slowly he turned his face toward me and I saw the smile return and the attempted look of benevolence, which would always be defeated by the needy set of his jaws. "From you it would have great force," he said. "Who came with evidence of this kind would earn the gratitude of some of the highest in the kingdom, those able to grant any wish, able to change a man's life with a word, with the stroke of a pen."

My understanding of his meaning had been delayed by disbelief. It came now, leaving no room for surprise but only for rage. This was the urgent matter he had wanted to discuss, this was where that talk of Christendom had been tending. I got to my feet and looked down at him, feeling the rush of blood to my face.

"You dare to ask me to give false evidence against my benefactor? You think my honor so slight a thing?"

"No, no," he said. "I ask you only to search your memory."

He had not moved, which was fortunate for us both: if he had stood to face me, I think I would have struck him, even in holy orders as he was. "They who set you on did well to choose a priest," I said. "Your cloth has been your protection tonight."

With this I left him sitting there. I threw a coin to the landlord as I went, not wanting to be beholden to Béroul, even to that small degree. Anger contended with shame in me, though the nature of this shame I could not determine. That I had listened so far? That I had been deemed a fit subject? More questions to plague myself with. Below anger and shame there stirred something of the fear I had felt in the chapel at the news of Demetrius's supplanting. There was a sickness in Béroul that was all his own. But Béroul was no more than a messenger, a lackey. Those behind him would be less concerned with the triumph of Christendom than with the gathering of power into their hands on this our island of Sicily.

Such was the disorder of my spirits that all desire for the women of the Tiraz left me. I went home by the shortest way, heavy-hearted after the rage, with Sara's ring stone still in my purse.

IV

I SAID NOTHING to Yusuf about this encounter, and this was the
first and perhaps the gravest of the mistakes I made with him.
Some of the shame I had felt at the time stayed with me. I was afraid
he would think, as I had not been able to help thinking even in the
midst of my anger, that I had been singled out as a likely traitor because so I was regarded. And if so I was regarded, perhaps so I was.
And truth compels me to admit that a thought had come to me, suppressed at once but piercing nonetheless, when Béroul had spoken
of those who have power to change a man's life; there had been a
moment when I thought of my disappointed hopes and my failure
to become a knight.

I did not think Yusuf could detect such flickerings of my mind,
but I feared he would place less trust in me, that I would lose his
regard—and his favor, on which depended my advancement.
Frankness then would have saved much sorrow later. But secrecy
and suspicion were in the air we breathed, both of us—I was his

pupil after all. And I thought it unlikely that the meeting with Béroul would come to his knowledge.

I spent the days before leaving in a way not different from usual. The mornings were passed at my desk in the small room I shared with my clerk Stefanos, and we did the work there that we were accustomed to do. There were accounts to look through that were not entered on the account books of the Royal Demesne, though they could be sent for at any time for the King's scrutiny: monies paid out for information, as rewards and inducements of various kinds, monies used to foment revolt in the Balkans and, more recently, in Germany, where we were hoping to unsettle Conrad Hohenstaufen, one of the King's bitterest enemies, by financing a league of German princes headed by Count Welf of Bavaria, who claimed a better title than Conrad's to the imperial throne. Our King Roger would use force of arms if necessary, but he was the first of his warlike line to prefer the undermining of his enemies by diplomatic means, and to me this was one of the marks of his greatness.

I visited Sara and gave her the garnet and benefited from her gratitude. I made some further inquiries about the birds I was to purchase in Calabria, though without learning a great deal more than Yusuf had told me. Every year they migrated to the marshes that lie between the sea and the town of Cosenza. They came in the spring, grew long crests for their courtship, and in this heedless time of mating were snared easily by the people of the marshes. All I knew beyond this was the price I was to pay—or at least not to exceed.

On the day following my visit to the Royal Chapel a man asked to see me and he was brought in, one of the palace attendants accompanying him. My room was no more than an adjunct of Yusuf's much more spacious quarters, but it was on the other side of the passage and had its own entrance. I insisted that anyone who came asking for me should be required to lay down his arms before entering and always be accompanied into the room. This was for the dignity of my office, it was not owing to fear; I was aware that I might have enemies whose names and faces I did not know, but I was strong and quick and I had been trained to arms before coming into the palace service.

The man was a trader in a small way, a Greek from the colony at Messina, who carried salt and our hard Sicilian grain to Salerno and Naples and cities farther north, traveling in all weathers by boat and mule train, a stocky, grizzled man, no longer young, used to hardship and danger in the pursuit of small profits. He had seen, he said, just west of Benevento, a troupe of dancers and musicians of a kind never seen before, the women half naked or more than half—he said this with a narrowing of the eye and a droop of the mouth.

If that was the great new thing about them, I told him, he was wasting my time. Did he think the King had not seen women in every stage of dress or undress, right down to nothing but a ring on the finger or a ribbon in the hair? Where was the need for a journey to Benevento when there were a dozen places here in Palermo where women danced and took off their clothes while dancing and did all manner of things besides—Saracens, Jews, Greeks, Italians, singly or in groups, according to taste and the preferences of race and religion?

Undeterred, he continued with his praises. Beautiful women. They could touch the earth at heels and head only, the body arched up like a bow, as if inviting the love of a god. They could make their bellies ripple without strain or effort . . .

"The dancing girls of Tunis can do as much," I said.

"No," he said, "the bellies one moment smooth, the next moment rolling, while the rest of the body remains still, the face composed, a very amazing thing." The dancers were the women, the men made the music. They were from the east, from Anatolia, and spoke a language no one could understand.

He himself spoke the language of cupidity. He was eager to interest me in these dancers, knowing me for the King's Purveyor, knowing that if they were brought to the court on his information he would be well paid. He even found occasion to describe the instruments played by the men, of a very unusual kind, he said, drums the shape of hourglasses with a skin across at both ends, a kind of dulcimer with a neck longer than a swan's, played with a bow that was the span of a man's arms . . .

He was eloquent, thoughts of coin had silvered his tongue, exalted his fancy too—I did not believe his words about the bow: the span of a man's arms is a very variable measure. However, I was interested in what he had said about the body remaining still and only the belly moving. The dancers of the Mahgreb could sway the hips to simulate the thrusts of love, but I had not seen any with this ability to concentrate all on the muscles of the stomach. On the other hand, if this man could exaggerate about one thing, he could exaggerate about another. I had in the past been deceived sometimes by accounts of dancers, jugglers, acrobats, and paid out good money for performers who proved to be mediocre at best and not fit for the King's attention. On occasion, he who spoke so well of them was discovered to be in their pay, or even to be one of their number. Certainly I did not suspect anything like this in the man before me, but there is a saying among Sicilians that while to give your trust is good, to withhold it is even better.

"Well," I said, "they may be all you say, and it is true that we have not had Anatolian dancers in Palermo before, but they are in the neighborhood of Benevento and I am not going there."

"They are traveling people," he said, sensing my interest. "They move here and there. Just at this time they will be following the pilgrims."

"I will keep it in mind." I did not tell him I was soon to leave for Calabria; even when we have nothing to hide, the less said the better—another of Yusuf's precepts. Perhaps he had got wind of it somehow, or perhaps his coming to me at this time was no more than coincidence. "Here is for your trouble," I said, and I gave him two *tari* from the stock of coins I keep in a box on my desk. "If we bring the dancers to Palermo, you will have more."

He seemed well enough pleased with this. Paying for information, something in which I was well versed, is always a matter of difficult judgment, no matter what the nature of it. If you are too ready you are taken for gullible, one who will believe anything; if you are too grudging no one comes forward—it is not worth the trouble, or the risk. Like so much else in our lives, it is a question of balance.

It was in the interest of balance that later the same day I went into the Kalsa, the Arab quarter that lies south of the harbor, riding as far as the Martorana and leaving my horse in the square behind the church at stables I had used before: it was better to go on foot and make sure of being unnoticed when visiting Mohammed ar-Rahman.

Here the streets were narrow and the walls high, and the houses had few windows and those closely barred. I walked with eyes cast down, watching my shoes as they scuffled the dust; to look upward was painful to the eyes in this late-afternoon sunlight that came in dazzling reflections from the whitewashed walls. In this district of

Palermo there is nothing to tell you where you are; the streets have no names. But I knew the way to Mohammed's house. I had been there before more than once. There was a small mosque in an open space, a simple *mesjid* with undecorated stone portals and a narrow portico. Close behind this ran a blind alley with a single door. A bell rope hung at the side. This was the entrance used by those who wanted to keep their visits private; there was another entrance, on a different street, one with wide gates and armed guards. I heard footfalls beyond the door, there was a brief pause while I was scanned through the eyehole; then the door was opened to me by the enormous Hafiz, who had lost an eye, in what circumstances I had never inquired, and who acted as cook, chamberlain, food taster, and body shield. He led me into the courtyard and there I found Mohammed in the shade of the colonnade, half reclining on a low couch padded with cushions. I heard some notes of a lute and a woman's voice singing low, but this ceased at my entrance.

I felt immediately grateful for the cool here, after the close heat of the streets. Now that the singing had ceased there was for these few moments, as I advanced at Hafiz's side, only the slappings and tinklings of the water from the fountain, as it fell from the tiled niche into the stone basin and down into the channel below.

Mohammed had begun the process of rising, which dignity and corpulence rendered slow. His skullcap and robe were of an impeccable, luminous whiteness. Perhaps my eyes had been affected by the dazzle of reflections outside, because this whiteness seemed stronger than any color could be, it seemed to draw to itself all the light in the courtyard and even the light from Mohammed's face, so that as he rose to his feet he looked, for all his bulk, strangely like a figure in some theater of effigies where only the dress and accoutrements indicate the nature of the personage. This lasted a few moments only. As I drew near, his features were restored to him, the short beard, the dark eyes slanting slightly downward like a melancholy dog's, the high-bridged prow of the nose.

"Welcome," he said. "Thurstan the Viking, welcome to my house."

He spoke to me in Arabic, though he knew also Greek, and I answered in the same language, with the conventional invoking of God's blessing on his house. It was his joke to call me Viking, because of my first name, which I think derives from the god Thor, and because I am tall and have blue eyes and fair hair that I wear long. It was also a kind of compliment, or at least I took it for such because he thought of Vikings, in their history of seafaring and raiding and settlement, as being a people similar to the Arabs. It was a joke, as I say, but there may have been truth in it; I was born in the township of Norton, close by the River Tees, and that is country where the Danes settled in great numbers in times past, so much so that all that eastern part of England is still known as the Danelaw.

Mohammed made a gesture toward a narrow alcove within the colonnade, where there were low benches against the wall in the angle of the corner. We sat here facing each other, he against one wall and I against the other.

"You have come on foot, the last part of the way, yes?" he said. "It is hot in the streets, this year the hot weather has come early." He leaned forward and clapped his hands together lightly. "You will take a *sarba*?"

Hafiz appeared as if by magic. I saw now that he had been waiting out of sight but very close, just inside the arch that led from the courtyard into the interior of the house; from here he could keep us both under his eyes.

I took care to show no haste in accepting this: the alacrity thought courteous by the Franks and the Greeks seems lack of dignity to an Arab. In fact, I was thirsty after my walk and I remembered Hafiz's sherbet as being particularly good, with just the right mixture of pomegranate and lemon. Nothing much was said as we waited; Mohammed was much too polite to inquire into the purpose of my visit, and I wanted to avoid the appearance of haste.

Hafiz served the sherbet in our full view, pouring from a stoneware jug into the metal cups, making it plain that we both drank from the same vessel, a notable piece of hospitable reassurance. When he had again retired, and after some compliments on the quality of the sherbet, I began.

"Yahuda Mari came to us with a complaint some days ago."

"Yes?"

"He came in person."

"I see, yes, a serious matter." Nothing had changed in Mohammed's face.

"There is a complaint that some Jewish cemeteries have been broken into during the hours of night and damage done to the graves."

Mohammed made a brief humming sound, perhaps to show interest or perhaps merely to encourage me in my narrative. He was leaning back comfortably against his cushions.

"Following upon this there is the further complaint that members of the Jewish community have had money extorted from them under the threat that their family tombs will be desecrated if they refuse to pay. According to Yahuda this has been going on for some time, but the people were too much afraid of injury to come forward."

Mohammed nodded, with a full appearance of understanding. "That is often the reason for silence."

After a moment's pause, in a tone I took care to keep dispassionate, I said, "It seems that these threats come from Arabs."

"Do they say that? Surely Yahuda himself has not been threatened?"

"Of course not." He was prevaricating now, and he knew that I knew this. The Mari were an ancient and powerful family with their main strength in Marseilles but with trade connections throughout Italy. Yahuda was the leader of the Palermo Jews, a man of great wealth. "Who threatens Yahuda?" I said. "We do not threaten the strong but the weak."

"My Viking, you speak with the simplicity of youth. When you have fullness of years you will know that the strongest are those that can be threatened most, because they have most to lose."

"He came to speak on behalf of his people. And it came to the attention of our diwan because no taxes or dues are paid on sums deriving from extortion, and so there is a possible loss of revenue to the crown. There is also the question of preserving harmony between races and religions. Yusuf Ibn Mansur, who sends his warmest greetings and God's blessing upon you, asked me to seek your advice because of the close friendship that is known to exist between us."

I was not sure how close it was, or whether it could truly be called friendship. The fact was that I had recently been able to do a favor for Mohammed. The porters that loaded the grain for North Africa on the docks of Palermo were all Saracens. The occupation was handed down from father to son, and it was profitable—a certain amount of the grain never reached the holds of the ships, never left Palermo in fact, but was sold by private contract. There was also a considerable trade in hashish from the ports of Tunis and Susa. All this being so, these porters were greatly envied by others working on the docks, and from time to time attempts were made to break in, especially by the Sicilians, who lived close by, but also sometimes by the Greeks. This resulted in bloodshed and feuds and all manner of evils. Some months previously, after protracted effort and with the support of Yusuf, I had succeeded in obtaining a charter from the Curia Regis granting exclusive right to the Saracens to engage in the loading of grain to North Africa, thus giving the force of law to what had previously been sanctified by custom only. Mohammed, whose people controlled the porters and extracted from each a monthly contribution, had been grateful.

"You did well to come to me," he said now. "However, it is not my people who have done this."

This might have been true or it might not; I had no means of knowing. If true, it meant that there was a band of Arabs in Palermo acting without his authority, a thing that could not have been pleasing to him. "I fully believe you," I said. "You are a man of honor. I know you would not, simply for the sake of a handful of dinars, so deeply wound the religious feelings of another race."

"Thank you, I am honored by your trust. This is a very serious matter."

"So it is."

"It is not just a handful. Think of the number of Jews living in this city and the number of the dead in their graveyards."

"True, the number is very great."

I paused on this, not quite sure of the best way to proceed. I was experiencing the usual difficulties in finding common ground with Mohammed. He was old enough to be my father, and his power and wealth and force of will and readiness to do wrong made an aura round him. He was devious but at the same time strangely simple. Unlike myself, he had no sense of service or dedication to a higher cause. I could not appeal to his better nature; he had not enough of this for my words to take lodgement. But this was not the reason: in my work I encountered many who were without a better nature, but I could still appeal to it because they made a pretense, whereas Mohammed made no pretense at all. He was a good family man, kind to his wives and his numerous children; he would defend his own interests and his own clan to the utmost sanguinary limit; he was faithful and recognizant when he felt himself indebted. These were his guiding principles and it was important to understand them, because Mohammed was of utmost importance to the ordering of life in Palermo. Adding to my difficulty was the fact that I liked him, despite myself, and felt that he liked me.

His lineage was ancient, going back to the tribal group of Yaman. He claimed descent from Hamza al-Basri, the famous philologist and reciter, who came to Sicily in the days before the Norman Conquest. However, Mohammed himself, though possessing a taste for poetry and music, had not followed in these illustrious footsteps. He was the chief of the strongest and most numerous criminal clan among the Arabs of the city, formed mainly from his own family members but reinforced—for the moment at least—by loose alliance with the Ahmad Francu family.

"We knew it could not be your people," I said. "That thought did not so much as enter our minds. I have not come to make accusations. It is in all our interests to keep a proper balance. The Jews have broken silence. If they do not find redress, their young men will start killing Moslems. There will be bloodshed. We have seen this before."

"So we have," he said, "so we have."

"Bloodshed within one community, that is normal, but between communities it is dangerous . . . it spreads quickly, it undermines the peace of the realm."

"It is bad for trade."

"Very bad indeed," I said, seeing in this the first sign he had given that he might be disposed to help. There was no doubt that he could do this if he would, and easily enough. If he did not know the culprits already, he could soon find out—it would be a small matter to him. He was on close terms with Al-Mawla al-Nasir, the hereditary Sayyid of the Sicilian Moslems, and so at the heart of a network of information extending from the Fatimids of Egypt to all Saracen communities in Sicily and the south of Italy. He enjoyed rhetoric and I sensed the time for this had come.

"Our great King inherited a land that was inhabited by Jew and Arab and Italian and Greek, races and faiths existing side by side. In his wisdom he understood that this harmony had to be preserved, that the well-being of all depended on it. He has devoted twenty years to this great task, with the loyal support of people like you and me, his servants. We have different ideas of paradise, which is quite natural. For us it is to join the ranks of the blessed. You perhaps lay more emphasis on physical ease and the gratification of—"

"We will have the supreme happiness of seeing God face-to-face."

I did not think it likely that he would attain to this joy but naturally did not let my doubts show. "However," I said, "there is one aspect of paradise we can all agree on and recognize, and that is the earthly paradise that comes from good governance. Our King is striving to create that paradise, and we are his agents."

I was sincere in saying this, though not believing that my words truly applied to Mohammed's activities. At Bologna, where I had studied law, they had set me to read the disputes of the churchmen, and I had seen from these, and absorbed the lesson well, that even for the godly there is always in argument the need for persuasion, and this need makes for suppression, or at least dilution, of the truth. My true feeling was that Mohammed, like all those who battled for power and wealth and preyed on one another below the surface, was necessary to the order and harmony of the kingdom, though not himself interested in achieving this settled state, but only in winning battles that in the end nobody won. I had formed in my mind a figure that I thought well expressed this feeling of mine. The King was rowed on a silver barge with silver banners; he was shining in silver and so were the oars that rowed him. This shining was reflected on the water so that it dazzled the eyes and made the figure of the King difficult to gaze upon. But the silver shone so brilliantly by virtue of the dark water; below the surface were creatures who stalked and feasted and fought and maintained themselves, some by force and some by cunning, and in doing so they maintained that shining world above them and kept the King's barge afloat.

As I waited now for Mohammed to reply, Hafiz must have changed his position, or perhaps there had been some shift in the sun's rays that had gone unnoticed, for I now could see the shadow of his head and turban lying across the pavement. I inferred his presence there only from this shadow and it seemed strange to me that this should be so. And it brought back my sensation as I entered the courtyard and could not see the face of Mohammed but only the whiteness of his form, like a white shadow, and with this a feeling of uncertainty came over me and I felt a momentary threat to my balance.

I was brought from this by the sound of Mohammed's voice. "A great responsibility indeed," he said. "The King's agents! But even the King's agents have to accept their limits."

He had been looking away as he spoke but now he turned his face toward me. His air of indolence had disappeared. His eyes were wider and he looked intently at me. "They must accept their limits, whether Christian or Moslem or Jew. We do but they do not."

This had to be answered quickly, before he was launched on the grievances of the Arabs. "You are right, you show the wisdom you are everywhere known for, the secret lies in limits. The extortion of money from the Jews, the threat of insult to their dead, these go beyond the limits, I think we are agreed on that. Let Arab quarrel with Arab and Jew with Jew. That is natural and belongs to the order of things. You are here in the Kalsa, the Greeks are in their district of the Martorana, the Lombards in the Albergheria, and so on. We do not pray together, but we can live together."

"Thurstan the Viking, tell me, is it worse for one Arab to kill another than for an Arab to kill a Jew?"

"It is worse in its results. It is worse in the degree of harm to our realm. I do not make a judgment about the wickedness of it."

"A wise reply. We cannot make such a judgment, do you not agree? No two killings could ever be exactly alike in all particulars, even to the temper of the blade or the knotting of the silk. And how can degrees of provocation be compared? As it has been truly said, though clouds in the sky are constantly changing, two might be the same for the briefest of moments. However, this moment can only be witnessed by God, the All-Seeing."

"True," I said, "true." I did not know whether this was a verse from the Koran, the words of an Arab sage, or merely an invention of Mohammed's own. But I did know that he was seeking to draw

me away into one of the discussions he so much enjoyed: interminable, abounding in metaphor, always inconclusive. "Our great
King has given us an example to follow," I said. "In his Assizes at
Ariano he made a code of laws and in this he laid it down that all the
subject people within his realm should live under the laws and customs of their fathers."

I heard Mohammed sigh, which was what he intended. "In
which court, and by whose custom and tradition, would it be tried
if those disputing were a Roman Christian—a Norman, let us say—
and a Moslem? Thurstan, I have a place for you in my heart, but we
must speak of things as they are, not as we would wish them to be.
This is a lesson you have yet to learn. The balance is changing—this
balance you speak of with such eloquence. Every day brings new
numbers of Franks and Lombards, people differing in degree but
all of the Latin Rite. The King gives grants of Arab land to Lombard
farmers, who turn our people into serfs. He founds monasteries for
the Latin clergy, and he gives fiefs to the Norman knights, as he did
to your father."

"How do you know this?" I had never spoken of my father to
him, and it was almost fourteen years now since our estates had
been made over to the Church.

"As it has been truly said, a man with many friends is like a fortunate fisherman. He casts his net wide and the catch is always good."

"Yes, I see." I did not want to talk of this with Mohammed; the
loss of the land had seen the end of my hopes of knighthood, and it
was still bitter to me. "It is true that many have come from the north
to make their homes with us," I said. "When the balance is threatened, there is the more need for care."

Mohammed sighed again. "We do not like the Jews," he said.
"They do not respect this balance. They lend money at exorbitant

rates to our people and send violent men to frighten them if payment is delayed."

"But you also have your moneylenders, is it not so? Their rates must be even higher, if your people go to the Jews."

"Palermo is getting richer," Mohammed said, looking at me very steadily. "And the sign of this is that everyone wants to borrow money. We do not like the Greeks any better. Greek cripples put on turbans and beg in our streets, using our own language, because they know that our religion enjoins charity on us. Where is the balance in that? It is deceitful and shows a low level of morality. Some of them are not even true cripples. The Sicilians of Palermo we do not like. They want to take everything into their own hands, they are not interested in sharing. They kill our people and try to take over our trade with our fellow Moslems. Tell me, Thurstan the Viking, where is the balance in that?"

He was talking now about the trade in drugs, the hashish that came from North Africa and the opium from Anatolia. This last was costly: the caravans from the poppy fields of Mersin passed through Byzantine lands on their journey westward and so were subject to high dues, which greatly increased the price on the streets of Palermo and Messina.

"You cannot answer," he said. "Answer there is none. There are also the Normans."

He paused for a long moment on this. Then he said, "We like the Normans, our King is a Norman, we live under his rule. We call him the Powerful Through God. You yourself have Norman blood. But this is Sicily, the Normans of Sicily have lived in the sun. Thurstan, I will say this to you because we are friends, we speak our minds to each other. They have lived in the sun, their brains are not damaged by ice. This freezing of the brains in cold climates was remarked first by Said al-Andalusi. In his writings on the subject of Europe he says that the cold winters stunt the brains of the Franks, and his words have been proved true before the walls of Damascus."

I knew what was coming now, knew it from the extreme gravity that had appeared like a mask on Mohammed's face. It was impossible during these months to talk to any Moslem about events in the world without becoming aware of the secret joy they felt at the disastrous failure of the Second Crusade, which had ended some months before in the ignominious defeat of the Christian army. It might be cloaked by an air of grave moral reflection, it might be concealed beneath an appearance of regret, but it was always there.

"They sat in counsel together and decided to attack Damascus," Mohammed said, shaking his head and pursing his lips. "Oh, what a catastrophe! Oh, what a terrible mistake! The Burids of Damascus were their natural allies against the power of Nur ad–Din. And where did they set up their camp? In the orchards below the walls? No, on the plain before the city, where there was no water, no shade. In this situation the only thing was to attack at once, but no, they sat there for four days, quarreling among themselves, dying like flies. On the fifth day they abandoned the siege. They set off back to Palestine without even making the assault! The greatest army the Franks have ever put in the field. Oh, what a calamity! Oh, what a humiliation! And just think—before that they were considered invincible."

As on similar occasions before, I found that the best response to this was silence. And in fact Mohammed, who understood the need for dignity, clearly did not expect a reply. After a moment, in changed tones, he said, "It is not my people who have desecrated the graves of the Jews and used threats to extort money from them.

But you have come to me and we are friends. We will find out who these people are, and we will speak sharply to them."

"These words of yours afford me great pleasure," I said. "Yusuf Ibn Mansur will also be delighted."

"God's blessings on his head. They will not be able to walk without sticks for a week or two. So we keep our paradise, eh?"

He looked at me with a humorous narrowing of his eyes. I sensed that our conversation was coming to a close and began to rise. I heard Hafiz shift his feet and after a moment saw him come into view. Mohammed rose also; his, as the person of greater consequence, would be the final words on parting.

"No, rest assured, Thurstan the Viking. We cannot repay the money—it will all be spent by now on harlots and evil courses. But we will talk to them. To offend against the natural human respect for the dead! What animals! The fault lies in their upbringing. They are not taught respect. Young men of good instruction, if such an intention had formed in their minds, what would they do? Would they not come to discuss the matter, ask our permission?"

V

THE DAY BEFORE LEAVING I rode out to the Monastery of Santo
Spirito, where my father was a monk. Always, before setting
out on a mission that might hold danger for me, I felt the need to see
him, though he showed little interest in me, or in my life or doings.
He had not lost all affection for me, but I belonged to the world outside his gates, the world he had turned his back on.

The monastery lay in the foothills to the west of Carini, over
toward the sea on that side, a morning's ride, starting early. The day
was beautiful, still fresh when I set out, with the sun rising over the
bay. The plain of the Conca d'Oro opened before me, with its park-
lands and gardens and its groves of orange trees, and the first rays
touched the crags of Monte Pellino and made them glow red as fire.
I cannot know now if it is merely to be wise after the event, looking
back to find signs that were not truly there, but it seems now to me
that I had a presentiment that morning as I rode out so early, some
foreknowledge that my life was soon to change.

I followed the plain westward as it widened in its shape of a shell, through orchards of almonds and figs, where the land on that side comes closer to the sea and the air is sharpened with salt. It was here that the Kelbite Arabs, in the days before the Normans came, founded the industries that made the island rich, sugar and cotton and silk. They mined for mercury and sulfur and silver also, but these mines have been long abandoned—my way led past some of the disused workings.

The sun was already high as I passed through Carini, a town full of stone houses, whose people have grown rich through the exporting of carob beans and dried figs, in their own ships, to every part of Italy. An hour more and I was entering the narrow track, loose-surfaced in places and difficult for the horse, that winds steeply up on the seaward side overlooking the gulf named after the town and ends at the gates of the monastery.

On the terraces of olives below the walls there were men working, lay brothers in their white habits and some who seemed common laborers. Arriving, I asked the monk on duty at the gate, who recognized me from other visits, if he would send word to my father. I waited in the cold room where we always talked together when I came to see him, a square, stone-flagged room with a raftered ceiling and a low stone bench running along one wall. I was heated from riding in the sun, urging my horse up the rough track, and I seemed to feel the chill of walls and floor on my face, a sensation familiar to me, waiting for my father in this room. To see him at all was a privilege: the Cistercian Order, to which he belonged, was founded on a strict return to the rule of Saint Benedict enjoining solitude and silence on the brothers. The privilege was for him, however, not for me; coming from the knightly class and bringing with him the revenues from his estate, which he had granted to the monastery *in perpetuum*, he was given a certain latitude. All the same, as far as I knew, I was the only one from the world beyond the monastery walls that he ever saw.

He came at last, walking slow and very upright, as always. He was tall—he had given his tallness to me; he had to incline his tonsured head a little as he passed below the stone arch of the doorway. He had laid aside cowl and scapular and wore only the white habit of his order. He apologized for the time I had spent waiting but gave no reason for it. He would have come from the oratory, from the singing of the midday office, I thought, in company with his fellow choir monks—the lay brethren did not take part in this. He would not have much time for me: soon there would be the afternoon liturgy that came between sext and none. I knew all the offices and the times they kept, all the observances of my father's life. To bring him closer to me in my imagination, I had made careful study of the Benedictine Rule and read the *Parvum Exordium* of Steven Harding, where he gives the history of this new foundation.

He did not approach very close to me or offer to take my hand, but he smiled as he motioned to the bench, and this I took as a sign of some pleasure at my visit—I chose to take it thus, to give myself heart. He was firm of step and sure in the carriage of his body, as I always remembered him. But abstinence, which I suspected went far beyond the requirements of the Rule—Saint Benedict had never asked his followers to go hungry—had wasted him; every time I saw him it seemed to me that his habit was looser on his frame and the bones of his face more prominent. It was a handsome face, though very fixed and unmoving, with blue eyes like my own, and a big chin and an obstinate molding of the mouth.

We sat together on the bench, and I asked after his health. He was well, he said, with the grave courtesy that belonged to him, but his eyes did not stay on mine. I began to say something about the journey I was soon to undertake, not that to Bari, I would not have burdened him with that, but the one I was making to Calabria in my capacity of purveyor. And I was aware as I spoke, by no means for the first time, of the paradox in this: my father's retiring from the lures and pleasures of this world had led to my career of providing them.

He listened to me and I saw a flicker of interest come into his eyes at my mention of the quarry birds I was to buy. He had had a passion for hawking in his other life; as a small boy I had sometimes gone with him, riding my pony at his side, watched him unhood the hawk and fly it loose in the hunting field, seen his pleasure when, through his own training and handling of it, a peregrine would swoop down on a gray heron, a bird accounted too big for it in the wild state, bind to it and bring it down, or else kill it with a stroke of the talons. This, and seeing him dressed for the lists, mounted on his black charger, plumed and burnished and splendid in his armor, with our colors on his shield and the pennant of his lance, were among my earliest memories of him, hardly quite believed in now, like scenes in a story I had been told and had begun to doubt now that the storyteller had gone away and there was no one to ask.

"What type of bird will you be looking for?" he asked. "Those marshes of Calabria close by the sea, I remember them for the cranes you found there, huge birds, you could hear the ruffle of their wings when they were still far." His voice had quickened, saying this, and he raised his head as if to follow those great birds in their flight.

"One would need an eagle to take birds of that size," I said. "One of the King's golden eagles."

"The King keeps eagles for the pride of it, and it is right he should do so, for it is a kingly bird. But an eagle is not biddable enough for good hawking, it does not give heed, no skill can train it beyond a certain point. No, you need a short-winged hawk for the cranes, one that can climb quickly. A goshawk is good."

"I am hoping to get the smaller birds, the white egrets. The Royal Falconer has asked for those, as he does every year. They fly faster and change direction more swiftly and suddenly, so they make better sport."

He nodded, but that life of interest had already left his face, subdued by the long habit of discipline. He cast his eyes down and listened soberly as I talked, and I looked at his face and sought there, again fruitlessly, something to account for the decision that had brought him here, the greatest single gesture of his life. Fourteen years ago he had walked barefoot up the stony track, beat at the gate of the monastery, and asked them to take him in, denying in that moment everything he had been brought up to think of as his duty and his destiny as a Norman knight.

No clue in the face—how could there be? All the struggle was over now. He had held his fief as a vassal of the Duke of Apulia, to whom he had vowed his service. In fulfilment of this vow he had left home to take part in the duke's wars against Robert of Capua, whose forces, aided by a contingent of German knights under Henry the Proud of Bavaria, were besieging Salerno. In a skirmish outside the walls he had been taken by the Capuans and kept six months in prison while they haggled over the ransom. During this time my mother, who had been pregnant when he left for the wars, died in childbirth, and he who would have been my brother died with her.

The ransom left us poorer, but it was not this that so changed the course of my life, nor was it the loss of my mother, much as I grieved for her. The land was tenanted; with thrift the loss could have been made good. It was my father who ruined us, making the estates over to the monastery, together with his own person and the rents that went with them. By a chance I could not help regarding as malign, the earlier devotion of the Cistercians to poverty, their refusal to accept manorial endowments, had for some time been relaxed. And so, at a stroke, I was disinherited.

Part of the pain of this was not to know why. I was sixteen years old, I loved my father, I would have put all my mind to understanding him. But he had never spoken of it to me, never tried to explain. He had never talked to me of the solace he had found here or the grace he had discovered; he had never, that I could remember, uttered God's name. And in the years that followed, the resentment that came to dress the wound had prevented me from asking. Had he witnessed some scene of cruelty or carnage that had charged his soul with horror for war? But he was no stranger to bloodshed. Perhaps in that prolonged captivity his heart had changed, he had discovered a love of solitude or a need for it, made greater by sorrow at the death of my mother, or even remorse, as if it might have been prevented had he been there by her side—theirs had been a love match, so I remember my mother telling me.

Whatever the cause, it had cost me dearly. Once again, as I looked at the face that was slightly turned from me, and spoke to him—I was talking now of recent events in Palermo—I was struck by the strange congruity of our lives. Those barefoot steps that had taken him from knight to monk had taken me by degrees from aspirant knight to the Office of Control and its workings, open and hidden. We had both, in our different ways, gone into hiding. On that December day when my father begged for admittance at the monastery gate I had been within eighteen months of my dubbing as knight; I had been trained to arms from the age of ten and I was gifted in it; all my heart was in achieving knighthood, it was all in the world that I wanted.

This disappointment, and the reproach I felt in my heart, lay always between us; it was between us now as we sat together there. When I might still have been freed from it he had kept himself away, behind these walls. It was too late to speak of it now. On this visit, as always before, I spoke of things that might interest him, among them what I had learned from Demetrius, that the Byzantine mosaicists were leaving with their work still unfinished, to be replaced by others of the Roman liturgy, Italians from the mainland and some Franks from beyond the Alps.

With this topic I succeeded in rousing some interest in him, but his feeling about the matter was the reverse of mine; he approved of it entirely. "They should all be expelled," he said. "Or kept belowground in dungeons. It is wrong that they should be allowed to walk the streets of our cities."

"Well," I said, "I do not see them as dangerous, but of course, speaking strictly, they are enemies to our realm, now that their emperor is preparing to invade us."

"Not dangerous? Not dangerous when they paint their faces and pad their bodies and go abroad in the clothing of women?"

"There are some who behave in this manner, so much is true. The population of Palermo is very great and many are the needs there that seek satisfaction."

"*Needs*," he said, and he looked at me as if I were a stranger.

"Franks and Saracens and Lombards could be found who do the same."

"No, it is a vice of the Byzantine Greeks. That is common knowledge. They darken their eyelids and hang rings from their ears."

Common knowledge where? Inside these walls? I felt the usual stirring of dislike for these communities of monks, a feeling I knew to be childish and unjust, as many worthy men, and scholars of note among them, have lived cloistered lives. But it was bred by my father's desertion, the ruining of my dreams of glory. He thought of the Byzantine Greeks as decadent and womanish and as poor soldiers, and this was not anything to do with his life in the monastery—what did he see of them? It came from his life of before, the common prejudice of the class to which he had belonged, to which he still belonged in some part of him. The Greek was womanish, the Lombard was treacherous, the Saracen was a worthy foe . . . The years of toil in the fields, of prayers and vigils, of mortifying the flesh, had made no smallest difference to these views of his.

As I say, anger with him made me childish. I wanted to say that I preferred the company of Greeks to that of Normans, which in fact was true; I wanted to ask him if darkening the eyelids was not better, since it might be thought by some to improve the appearance, than shaving the pate clean and leaving a fringe all round, which could not be thought by any to do so.

But of course I did not. My feelings for him were divided, but I could not have hurt or offended him. I had love for him, and something else that was not love but in some way bound up with it, something stronger than merely blaming: I felt he had betrayed me, that he betrayed me over again at every parting. Always, as the parting approached, I tried to bring him closer and to punish him by using those powers of speculation that Yusuf had fostered in me, figuring to myself the life to which he was returning. And always my imaginings leapt over the daylight hours and lingered on the night, and this, I think, because I so much hate the dark. I saw him lying in the common dormitory, still clothed in his habit; he would have been sleeping there since nightfall. Then, in the darkness, long before first light, the bells would ring for matins and he would rise, still full of sleep, and fumble to put on his night shoes. He would throw the covers over his bed, he would put on his cowl to go to the privy—to go bareheaded was forbidden, I knew this from my reading, but the wherefore of it was not said, and such a question I could never have asked him, but supposed these functions of the body, performed always in company with others, were too intimate for the face to be shown, each was protected by not knowing who squatted beside him. All this while the bell would still be sounding, and they would shuffle down the stairs into the cavern of the church, dark here too save for some scattered light of candles, and assemble in the choir to sing the night offices.

There was always some horror for me in this thought, that my father, once so splendid to view in face and form, should submit himself to this nighttime hooding and groping, that he should have become a creature of the dark to me when he had been like the sun. He had been a knight of modest estate and modest following, but he had been my model of all a knight should be. I was my own model now, and far from perfect I found it. Perhaps some of the sadness of this knowledge showed in my face as we said goodbye, because this time he clasped my arm for a moment and his eyes looked into mine and we saw each other and there was something that perhaps he would have said to me, but the moment passed and he drew back.

At first, as I rode away, though the sun was high now and the countryside flooded with light, thoughts of my father's night life continued to obscure my mind, like mist that was slow to disperse. I saw him still in the dimness of the church, groping to his place in the choir, with scarce light enough to give him guidance. Sometimes, perhaps, being old and drowsy, he would fall asleep during the singing. Would there be someone appointed to watch for this? If my father slept, would someone lay hands on him, shake him awake?

From this I fell to thinking yet again of all I had lost by the change in him, and neither the beauty of the day nor the exercise of riding could take my mind from this. Perhaps it is true that the frustrating of hope makes the desire seem in memory stronger, as Saint Augustine maintains in his *Confessions*—I think it is to be found there. I do not know, after these years that have passed, whether it was the idea of knighthood that drew me, to battle for the good under God and the King, or whether it was simply the wish to join an order that belonged to my rank in life, to do what was required of me, as my father had done, and his father before him. I know only that I wanted it with all my being.

I was seven years old when my father sent me from our home in Apulia to the court of Richard of Bernalda, where I spent seven years as a page. The loneliness and the longing for home were tempered—even then—by pride in the calling. There were ten other boys of my age there and eight girls, all the children of nobles. We boys shared the pride and did our best to conceal the sorrow, and with the girls it was something of the same—there was one girl there that I loved, and we talked together when we could contrive to meet.

This is what you were born for, my father said, on this our first parting—my father, who not many years later was to give my birthright away. You are the only son, the destiny of knighthood began with your birth, it is for this you must be sent away, to learn manners, wait on the ladies, serve at meals, help to take care of the armor and the horses. He did not expect tears from me, so there were none, but my mother wept.

The sense of destiny was there already, even in unhappiness; it grew greater as the unhappiness grew less, as I learned to ride and fight. By the age of fourteen I had abandoned miniature weapons and was already practiced at managing lance and sword on horseback; true, it was not a charger yet, but a stallion and restive enough. Now, riding home through the smiling countryside, bright spring flowers at my feet, larks singing overhead, on the eve of a mission for which I felt no eagerness, I remembered my ardor of those days; with a sort of arid pride I remembered that I had been the strongest of my companions, always first at the practice lists.

I was bareheaded and the sun was hot; I stopped to pull on my velvet cap that came fashionably low over the brow. Then I allowed the mare to go her own placid pace, remembering the dusty courtyard where we practiced, the heavy, snorting breaths of the horses, the gallop, the leveled lance, the straw-filled effigy twitching and swaying there as they jerked it on the ropes, the triumph when I pierced it and dashed it to the ground, the sacking agape as the belly of straw was spilled out.

A year later and I was shield bearer to Hubert of Venosa, went hunting with him and attended him at the lists and learned to manage his war horses and to fight on foot with sword and dagger so I could protect him in battle if he was unhorsed. Then, in a skirmish outside the walls of Salerno, my father advanced too far, was surrounded, tumbled from his horse, and taken captive. And with that recklessness of his my dream of knighthood was over, the splendor of the armor, the shine of the silver on the shield, the bright silk across the saddle, the enemy before your face.

On the day when my father beat at the monastery gates I still had more than a year to wait before my time came for the vigil and the blessing of the weapons and the flat of the sword against my neck. Hubert might have kept me for the time, he was always generous. But the armor I would wear when I knelt to be dubbed, who would pay for that? Who would buy for me the war horse, an animal bred for weight and very costly? How would I come by the weapons, and the trappings for the horse, more costly still?

What would have become of me I do not know. I might have returned to England, to my mother's people, and sought my fortune there. Then came delegates from the Seneschal's Office on a visit. Shows of various kinds were put on for them. We squires did our tilting at effigies and our mounting at the gallop and our sword exercises. I distinguished myself and was noticed, and my situation was explained to the visitors. A question or two, a quick reply, and I returned with them to Palermo, to the Palace, where I entered on a different kind of preparation. I was to be one of the King's Household Guard, a body whose duty it was to guard his person when he appeared in public, and whose numbers were kept small—there were never more than fifty at any one time, including officers, all of good family. There was no bar to enrollment on grounds of race or creed, and this by the King's own wish who put his trust more in diversity than sameness. Shared by all were loyalty, skill with weapons, and the obligation to speak Greek, the common language of the island.

I was set to study Greek, my knowledge of which was imperfect at that time since I had grown up in courts where the language was French. These lessons were a great boon to me, as it proved: they led me to a love of studying, and this is with me still. My teacher, finding me an apt pupil, perhaps unusually so, introduced me to

Latin, though in the main it was later, during my years in the diwan, that I made strides in this language. I was also taught wrestling and the ways of fighting when space is limited and the opponent close, which was mainly the use of the dagger and of a sword shorter and lighter than the one I had been used to. There were holds and blows that we learned, designed to disable a man or even to kill him, and we spent some time each day in lifting weights and doing exercises that make the body strong.

In all these matters I think I can say I did my best to excel. My disappointment at failing to become a knight was still keen, but I looked forward to the day when I would don the uniform of the Household Guard, a splendid uniform with a plumed cap and a tunic worked in silver thread on a scarlet background and a polished leather belt and embroidered leggings that had a line of silver at the sides. My role would still be one of service: I would be protecting the King's sacred person and helping to uphold his state, I would be near him, I would live in the light of his presence.

However, none of this came about. Another question, another answer, in Arabic this time, changed my life again. Now, as I made my way back through the Conca d'Oro, as it narrows toward the city and the harbor beyond, where I would take ship the next day, I felt my life narrowing too, and the knowledge of loss constricted my heart.

VI

It was still dark when I embarked next morning. The two who were to accompany me to Cosenza were waiting at the dock. One of them, Sigismond, I recognized; the other, who gave his name as Mario, was new. Both were brawny and impassive, as usual with those who are engaged in these duties. I would have been happier without an escort, but the rules of the diwan obliged me to have one: I was carrying money to pay for the birds and to meet my expenses for the second part of my journey; there were some who knew this and others who would guess it. In accordance with my usual custom, I kept some coin in the purse at my belt—an empty purse convinces no one. But the bulk of the money I wore strapped across my abdomen below the shirt.

The captain too was waiting at the dock. The ship was a small merchant vessel like a thousand others, with a crew of three, all Greeks from Cefalù, trading along the western shore of Calabria as far as Maratea. This time, as they knew, they would be going only as far as Paola, and taking no cargo there but the birds. It was on the King's orders—they knew that too and were happy at it, they were counting the coin already, but they would not touch any till they were back in Palermo, and this too formed part of the knowledge that lay between us. What did not was the fact that I would not be returning with the ship; neither captain nor crew would know this till the last moment.

The wind was favorable, the sea untroubled; we made good time, arriving at the harbor of Paola as dusk was falling. There was only one inn, very ill kept. I was given the best room in it, or so the innkeeper told me, but a foul and damp room it proved to be, the bed aswarm with creatures eager for my blood—I could see the lively stirrings of them as I stood there, talking of the price. He asked three times what the room was worth, naturally, since I was a stranger and he knew the errand I was on. We haggled, I brought the price down; this was the King's money, I would not be wasteful with it, I would not overspend by a single *folaris*; it was a point of honor with me, a mark of my devotion. The result of this haggling was that the innkeeper grew surly. However, the lentil soup they served us in the room below was welcome enough, as were the sardines, freshly caught and fried with black olives.

After supper, since it was still early, I walked for a while among the steep streets of the town, my two guards following close behind. Higher up it was pleasant: a light breeze was coming off the sea and the moon was near the full, giving light enough to see by. It was a question of passing some few hours. The people of the marshes would know of my arrival, word had been sent; next day the bird catchers would come down to the harbor, having walked through the night with their caged herons. We would agree on the price, I would make the payment and see the birds carried on board. I would send my escort back with the ship; their presence was oppressive to me, and once I had paid over the money there would be no more need of them. With the departure of the ship I would be free to continue my journey to Bari.

I descended again to the harbor and walked there for a while. I was restless, my nerves were tense, there seemed some edge of promise in the night. I was unwilling to return to my cramped and windowless room at the inn, the scrape of rats behind the walls, the verminous tribe in the bedclothes. This last was a particularly disagreeable thought to me. In Palermo I nagged at Caterina and paid her a monthly sum additional to the rent to keep my sleeping room aired and swept, to strip the bed and hang the sheets in the sun and scrub the bed frame with vinegar and water. Thinking of this made me wish I were home again. It came suddenly to my mind to sleep that night on the deck of the ship, where at least there was air and space enough. I told my guards of this decision and if they were displeased at the idea they knew better than to show it.

I returned to the inn to tell them that after all I would not be staying there. But they had made the room ready, after a fashion, and I had agreed on the price with the landlord; it seemed to me now that this would have to be paid; I was the King's purse bearer, I saw it as my equal duty to save him from cheats and to preserve his name for justice and fair dealing. But when I arrived I found only the wife, a slatternly woman with tangled black hair and a look of discontent. He had gone to Passo di Lupo, she said, to see the new dancers.

"What is new about them?" I asked her.

"Why," she said, "they are the ones that are traveling here and there in the country." And she looked at me as if there must be something sadly lacking in a person who did not know even this much.

"Woman," I said, as patiently as possible, "that they are traveling about is nothing to the point. It is what dancers very often do. I was inquiring into what is new about them."

"They come from far, it is dancing not seen before."

"Will they not come here?"

"No, it is why he is gone. People say they will go next to Melfi, but nobody can know, they go here and there wherever the fancy takes them. They sleep by the roadside."

She spoke sourly; perhaps in her heart she envied this freedom. "The women are whores," she said. "They have demons in the belly—and in what lies below. That is why he has gone there, the pig, along with all the others—the town is empty of men tonight, only the priest is left. They are whores and pagans, no one can understand their speech."

"Demons in the belly?" I said, but she made no answer. Suddenly it came to me that these might be the dancers that the Greek trader had spoken of and at once I formed the intention of going to see if this was indeed so. It was a diversion that made strong appeal to me in my restless mood; it would take up some of the slack time of waiting.

"Are there horses here?" I asked her.

"No, he has taken the horse. There are mules that can be hired in the town."

I sent Mario to conduct this business while I waited with the other in the inn yard. He returned after not much time, leading three mules in a train. The money I had given him, he said, had proved exactly enough for the hire. He affected to admire me for my judgment in giving him just the right amount, but I did not believe his words, feeling sure that he had kept back some of the coin. However, it would have been difficult to prove, and I did not want the delay. There was something displeasing to me about this Mario: he was too eager to ingratiate himself. He was a thick-shouldered, towheaded fellow with small eyes that did not rest long on anything, and there was a pale knife scar across his cheekbone on the left side. The other man, Sigismond, was taller, raw-boned and taciturn, with slow blue eyes.

The boy who served there came forward, offering to go with us and show us the way. The moon was high as we set off. Our guide went in front with a lantern, but the moonlight was enough to see by, glinting on the stones of the track. The memory of that moonlit journey often comes to me now, and I still find it strange that but for the coincidence of the dancers being close by when I had already heard mention of them, and the fact that I had felt some sort of promise in the night, I would have done the safer thing and waited in the town to finish the task I was saddled with, and so my life would have taken a different course and I would not be the same person as the one who is writing this. Certain things about myself I would not have discovered, and what is not discovered can never truly belong to us; it is only that knowledge of itself the soul knows how to summon that can truly be said to dwell within the soul. It is Boethius who says this in his *Consolation of Philosophy*—I believe it is to be found there.

Passo di Lupo was a cluster of low buildings hanging on a hillside, with the castle of the lord above it and the openness of the sea below. There was the light of a fire in an open space below the castle walls. We saw the movements of the flames and heard the swirl of the music before we caught any glimpse of the dancers—a dark mass of bodies blocked our view.

We tied the mules a little way below and left the boy in charge of them. Above us were a beat of drums and a play of shadows, movements that resembled those of a flail when corn is threshed, half obscured by the forms of the people watching. We pressed forward, the three of us forming a wedge to drive a way through to the front.

My sight was confused at first. The red of the flames contended with the white of the moon to make a light that belonged to neither. Something dipped in pitch had been put in the fire and it made the flames leap and caused a smoke that was black and acrid. There were three dancers, all women, moving in a slow circle, one younger than the other two and a little taller. They were barefoot and they wore bands of copper round their ankles and they were dressed in the same manner, in long skirts worn low on the hips and black girdles with tassels that swung as they moved, and bodices that left the arms bare and came well short of the waist, so that their midriffs would have been exposed had they not worn light-colored sashes wound about them.

They stepped in and out of the light and the flames leapt and fell as if the fire itself were dancing with them. The hands of the two men seated beyond them also entered the light and left it as they played, the one tapping with fluttering fingers at both ends of a pot waisted like an hourglass, the other playing on a kind of dulcimer with a round body and a long neck, such as the trader had described to me; he had exaggerated the length of the bow, but not greatly—it was longer by far than any I had seen. The music they made was wild and plaintive, with trailing notes and half tones and dying falls that then flared up again, like the fire, a strange mood of music, neither lightness nor despondency but somewhere in between.

It seemed to me that the music quickened, and the dancing with it, from the moment I appeared at the front of the crowd with my companions flanking me. It was as if some signal had passed among them, though the nature of this I did not perceive. In fact, it was only some time afterward that I understood the reason for the change, and this may seem strange, that I did not realize at once how apparent it must have been to them that I was a stranger and more prosperous than those I stood among, did not realize how my tallness and my clothes marked me out: I was dressed for traveling and so not richly, and I wore no jewellery or fine brocade, but my pelisse was of black velvet and my hat was one such as the Franks wear, of velvet too, and flat, worn low over the brow. Usually I am very conscious of the figure I make, too much so perhaps—yes, certainly too much so, it is vanity. But I had forgotten myself in the excitement of the music and the dancing. From what I know of her now I feel sure it was the younger woman who noticed me first, who gave the signal for this conspiracy to secure my pleasure and with it some contribution from my purse.

It was she, in any event, who marked the change, broke the circle, stepped toward me, raising bare brown arms that gleamed as if oiled in the now softer, steadier light of the fire. She had something fitted on the thumb and the long finger of both hands—small caps, I could not see them but thought they were of wood by the rattle they made when she snapped them together. She stood with feet planted, looking full at me, turning her shoulders slightly from side to side, raising her arms high, and there was something defiant in this that stirred me.

Still facing me with arms raised, she began to dance, setting her feet within a short compass, very rapidly but carefully too, as if there might be something jagged and dangerous there that would wound her if she made a false step, a prudence belied by the languorous sway of hips and abdomen inside the covering scarves.

The other two had fallen back and she spoke to them over her shoulder and laughed, and they replied, also laughing, and this was the first time I had ever seen such a thing, dancers laughing and talking among themselves in the midst of the dance, as if they cared little for those watching. Then, a moment after the laughter, her face grew somber and intent, a fine-boned face, very dark, something sorrowful in its repose, the lines of the mouth looked suffering almost, as if her drink had been bitter. She was beautiful in body, high-breasted and straight-shouldered, with long, slender thighs that showed against the stuff of her skirt as she stepped in the dance. Her hair was tied with a red ribbon, but now, with a quick, impatient movement, she tore the ribbon loose and shook her head and the black hair fell down below her shoulders and swung as she turned away from me.

The other women came forward, joined the dance, and at the same moment the drummer, without ceasing his finger-tapping, raised his voice in a high nasal chant, lugubrious in its rising and falling, like the song of the wind in some desolate place. The three women danced to this chanting, but they set their feet as they chose, each in her own way, they were possessed by the music but not obedient to it. This will be deemed a contradiction by the reader, but it was so. And it was this, or so I now believe, this way they had of dancing within the music but quite alone, different from anything I had seen, that gave me first the idea of hiring these people if I could and having them shipped back to Palermo along with the herons.

There was more to come, however. The music of drum and dulcimer ceased. The singing lost all melody and variety of pitch, it drew into a wild droning sound, loud, like the lamentation of some vast swarm of bees at the ruin of their hive. The women moved to a slower rhythm, the heavy tresses swinging round their heads. Then their step quickened, they began to revolve, the colored scarves round their waists unfurled and fell away like streamers, revealing nude abdomens decorated with thin strands of bead chains. In the dimple of the belly, set in the umbilicus itself, each wore a pebble of clear glass that caught the firelight and the moonlight and flashed now paler, now ruddier, as they moved.

The droning ceased, and in the silence that followed the bodies of the dancers shuddered once and were still again. Then, while the rest of the body remained motionless, the bellies of the women began to roll and gyrate with amazing smoothness. There was no sense of effort or strain; they moved as if at the bidding of a power not their own. I felt some awe at this, and the words of the women at the inn came back to me. *They have demons in the belly.*

Indeed it seemed so. More than ever I was determined now to have them dance at court, where people had seen many things, but not, I thought, dancing like this. I had heard the exclamations of the men around me, felt the pulse of excitement in the crowd; they were rutting with the women in imagination, they were thinking, *If they can do this with their bellies, what wonderful things might they do with the part lower down?* I too, in spite of my higher station, in spite of being there as the King's Purveyor, in the interest of truth I will admit to the same thoughts that prevailed in the common folk around me.

The movements of the dancers came to an end. The fire had died down and contended with the moon no more. The women went with canvas bags among the people there. I noted that, while there were those who turned away, most gave something. The younger woman came first to me. She smiled at me and her teeth were white and she had them all. She held the bag out to me boldly, as if she were offering, not asking. I put a quarter-ducat into the bag, the only silver they would get that night, from such a crowd. As she turned away, I spoke to her in Arabic, a compliment on her dancing, hoping she would understand, but she did not. She was smiling no longer and she moved away.

With my guards still keeping close I walked over to where the two men were squatting together, their instruments laid aside. I did not know how to talk to them, fearing there was no language we shared. They were somber in regard and wild-looking, with black shaggy hair that grew thick over the forehead. Their features were similar, especially in the setting of the eyes, and I wondered if they were brothers. I greeted them in Greek and asked them where they came from, taking care to speak slowly, and was delighted when they replied in the same tongue, though in a slurred and broken version of it. I was to learn later that they had brought their music to Lydia and Cilicia and spent time along the shores there, where the people speak Greek.

They returned the greeting but they had not understood my question. He who played the drum and sang, and who I took to be the leader, or the spokesman at least, made a swift gesture with his right hand as if throwing something behind him, over his shoulder. "We crossed the water," he said. "We came to Taranto."

The women approached now, having collected what money they could. They stood close but they did not speak. I could smell the long roads these people had traveled, a compound of sweat and resinous dust and wood smoke, with something scented in it from the women, like crushed leaves.

"The places, we do not know their names," the man said. "We make music always in the same way."

"No," I said, "I wanted to ask where you come from. Where is your home?"

There was a laugh at this from the youngest of the women, and the dulcimer player looked at her soberly, perhaps in reproof, I could not tell, but she met his eyes boldly—she was not one easily abashed, this I already sensed about her. "She laughs because our home is far," he said, as if to apologize for her, "and because it is many summers since we are there."

"We come from beyond the Toros," the first man said. He raised one arm to show the height of the mountains. "We are from a town they call Sivas. It is beside a great river." He nodded toward the girl who had laughed. "She comes from a different place, she comes from Niksar. She says she is born on top of the mountain called Ararat. She says that giants live on that mountain."

There was laughter at this, and I saw that it was an accustomed joke among them. "Giants carry her to Niksar," the other man said. However, the girl did not join in this laughter but compressed her lips and looked away, and this gave her face a look of obstinacy that I think made them laugh all the more. For my part I was more than ever eager to hire them: not only did the men sing in outlandish accents and play on instruments of a shape not seen before, not only did the women do things with their abdomens that seemed to defy our corporeal nature, but they came from lands that no one knew anything of, and one of them had been born on the peak where the ark had rested on the seventeenth day of the seventh month, when God saved the world from flood! I saw already how I would lay emphasis on these things when I made the announcements. If this did not gain me the King's favor, it was hard to see what would.

I spoke to the men still, believing—as it turned out, mistakenly—

that it was they who made the decisions; in fact, decisions were made by all five together, often speaking all at the same time. I think they understood quickly but affected not to, out of caution or cunning. Whatever the truth of this, much had to be repeated before they admitted to an understanding of the offer I was making, which was that they should come to Palermo to perform at the royal court, before the King himself and his guests; that they would be housed well all through their stay, given beautiful new clothes to wear, and paid in gold. The King's generosity was proverbial, I told them. If they pleased him they would receive presents of great value. In any case, whether they pleased or not, I would guarantee them a fee of eight gold dinars, far more than a year of wandering would bring them. Also, they would see the great city of Palermo.

They now fell to discussing the matter among themselves, but in a manner far different from the way in which the men had spoken to me, with raised voices and fierce gestures, not waiting for one to finish before another began. I could not tell what was dividing them, not knowing a word of the language they spoke, which had strange nasal inflections and sounds made far back in the mouth so that the lips drew back in making them. As I say, I could form no idea of why they argued so, whether from distrust of me or some other matter. But I knew already, watching them cluster together and shout with their faces close, that my troubles with these people were just beginning. Loud among them was the younger one, she who claimed Ararat for her birthplace, who had come forward and danced before me, and spoken some laughing words to the others. Suddenly now I wondered if that laughter of hers had concerned me.

They fell silent, and the man I had first addressed turned to me. "It is the mules," he said. "We have three mules. They are good mules, very valuable."

I was offering them a royal reception, with the chance of royal favor, I was promising them more gold than they could ever have had at any one time in all their lives. And they were holding out against it for the sake of three miserable mules that were not worth more than two ducats each, and a good deal less if in bad condition!

"So we are asking," he said. "Can we keep our mules?"

"Take them with you? You mean on the ship?"

I paused on this, daunted by the prospect of explaining, in terms that he would understand, the cargo of caged birds that we would be taking next day, and how much more difficult, and even chaotic, it would be if in addition to the five of them and my two guards and the crew we had mules trampling about on the deck. "We will return to the inn," I said, "and sell the mules to the innkeeper. He can keep them there until he finds a buyer."

This proposal led to further lively talk among them, but finally it was agreed, and we set off, the women riding, the two men walking, and we three making up the rear. The night was far advanced when we reached the inn, and both the innkeeper and his wife were abed, but I wanted the business done, so woke the serving lad, who was sleeping in the yard, and told him to rouse them. The man came down, though in an ill temper that he took little care to conceal. When I asked him to make an offer for the mules, he answered in surly fashion that he had no need of mules. Then, no doubt realizing his advantage—he could see I was in haste to conclude the sale—he made an offer of derisory smallness, eight *folles* for the three, and in spite of all my efforts he would not budge from this.

"I am here on the King's service," I said. "This contemptible behavior of yours will be included in my report, and the consequences to you will be serious." By this I sought to put him in fear, but it was an empty threat, and in his lowness and insignificance he knew it for such. Palermo was far; he knew he was a beetle not worth the crushing. Besides, what offense had he committed? He could hardly be punished for shrewdness in commerce; it was a virtue of our good King Roger himself, one widely admired as enriching the realm and therefore all who lived within it.

So I was in a quandary. It was long past midnight, the town was sleeping. If I wanted to keep the trust of these people and show my good intentions, they would have to be given a fair price for their mules. The only way I could see of achieving this was to buy the mules myself. But there was the purchase of the birds next day; I knew the price I was to pay per bird but could have no knowledge of how many birds there would be. Furthermore, there was the expense of my journey to Bari and the return. And there might be other claims on my purse that I could not foresee. On the other hand, I had to get these people on board ship as soon as possible, so as to make it the less likely they would change their minds about going.

"I will buy your mules," I said. "I will give you four silver ducats for them."

This offer set up a clamor among them, the nature of which I understood only when the drummer turned to me and said, in the quieter tone he used for commerce outside the group, "We want nine ducats for the mules." And he showed me the backs of his hands with the thumb of the left one folded inward to make his meaning plain.

Nine ducats! It was far more than they were worth. The innkeeper and these traveling people between them gave me a memorable example of human rapacity that night. It was true that I had offered less than a fair price, but this was because I was worried about my expenses. If I paid what they asked they would take me for a fool and all our future dealings would be colored by it.

I paused for a moment or two, wondering what line it would be best to take. The yard felt crowded with mules and people, the people full of noise and exclamation, the mules for the moment docile, tethered companionably together in the moonlight, their ears laid back as if they were quietly aware of being under discussion. There were six altogether, with the three we had hired. Sometimes, unexpectedly, a man is struck with wonder at where he finds himself and what he finds himself doing. Glancing now at these animals, I had such a feeling: I had come to this place on a quest for herons, only to find myself beset with mules.

I took six ducats from the purse at my belt, where I kept the stock needed from day to day, and displayed them on my open palm. The moon was high now, its light reached every corner of the yard, and the silver coins gleamed as I held them out. "Six ducats," I said. "Not a *kharruba* more."

They did not know the Arabic word but they understood my meaning well enough and this time the talk among them was of the briefest. As I had shrewdly thought might be the case, the sight of the coin was more than they could withstand. They were poor and ragged, they lived without knowing what the next day would bring. The price they had set on the mules had been in the nature of a dream: the night had brought them dreams of wealth already—why not one more?

There and then the sale was agreed and the ducats handed over. I was pleased for a while with my own sagacity, and the decisive gesture with which I had won them over. But then it came to me that I had after all paid somewhat more for the beasts than they were really worth; moreover, there was nothing in the world I could do with them but leave them with this miscreated innkeeper.

"I make you responsible for these animals, purchased in the King's name," I said sternly to him. "You will be held to account."

He gave me a ruinous grin but said nothing. I knew beyond question that he would sell the beasts then give them out as having died or strayed. I was heartily sick by now both of him and them, and it was a relief to get clear of his foul-smelling yard.

By the time we had reached the harbor and roused the captain and told him to treat his passengers kindly and got them on board with their instruments and their bundles, the moon was over the sky and there was a feeling of dawn soon coming. I was tired but my mind was active, I had no inclination for sleep, nor desire for any company but my own at this quiet time before daybreak. I told Mario and Sigismond that they could share the room I had paid for or sleep in the yard as they liked. If that pig of an innkeeper was asleep they could shout till they woke him. I would keep to myself a little, wait for the day.

VII

As I look back on it now, this choosing to walk abroad, alone and in unfamiliar surroundings, when I was carrying money belonging to the crown, was a sign in me of disaffection, of desire for change. It is true that not many were stirring at such an hour, true also that I had not full trust in my guards when we were in deserted places together. But the chanceries of the palace, no matter in which you served, schooled you to guard against mishap, however remote the chance of it, and this then became a rooted habit—one which I broke that night on no more than a whim. I knew that if anything went amiss with the purchase of the birds, I would be called to account. It might be that Yusuf would protect me and I would keep my place but it would count against me in future—in his mind too. I had been a success in the Diwan of Control, balking at nothing that was given me to do, even things that might be thought base or unworthy if it were not that they were done in the King's service. But one thing botched could outweigh all this and tip the scales against my succeeding to Yusuf's place when he became Royal Chamberlain. And I wanted this, as I have said, wanted the wealth and state of it, the release from bad roads and bad inns and purse carrying.

Nothing untoward occurred; I saw no one. With daylight I returned to the inn, where I was served by the innkeeper's wife with bread and cheese and thin ale. Then I slept for perhaps an hour, in my chair as I sat there. Waking, I found Mario and sent him back with our mules. Afterward, my two men once more at my shoulders, I mounted the steep streets until I was above the town, looking inland to where the marsh people would come from. They would come sometime in the morning, having set off the evening before on news of my arrival and traveled through the night. They would not arrive much before noon, I thought; they would be on foot, encumbered with the caged birds. I found a place where there was a ruined house, part of the stone terrace still remaining, and sat down here with my back against a broken wall. There was a view of the plain below, and the road they would come by.

I was content to wait quietly here. It was a cloudless morning, there were gulls wheeling above on the seaward side, from somewhere close by there came the sound of goat bells. The dancing of the night before came back to me as I sat there: the firelight and the moonlight, the strains of that wild music, sad and fierce at the same time, the languorous sway of the bodies, the quick-stepping feet, the strange moment of shuddering before the body was stilled again and that rippling of the belly began. I remembered the gleaming arms of the one I had watched—I had watched only her, it now seemed to me. That posture of the body savage in its pride, that suffering look about the mouth, dissolving in joy when she smiled. Straight shoulders and a deep curve from the waist to the hips.

Then at the inn, loud-voiced and bold-eyed, people used to contempt, careless of it. Outcast people. Ararat, where the ark came to rest for mankind to be saved, and where giants lived in old times. Was she beautiful of face or not? I could remember only the mouth and the smile . . .

I was still thinking of this girl in a rather sleepy fashion when the sun rose clear of the hills and I saw a flash of white in the distance, where the road descended, like a swift signal one might make with some bright surface of metal held up to the sun. It came again, then again, then there were many, and the first of the men came into view at the point where the road finished its descent and curved round into the open plain.

They had come earlier than I expected. They walked in single file, the caged birds hanging from yokes that went across their shoulders, two on either side, as far as I could make out, and swaying with the motion of their walking, so that the newly risen sun elicited flashes of light as rapid as blinking from their breasts and wings. I counted twelve men, and as they came into the sun they were robed in splendor by the birds.

The splendor was less, however, both in the men and in the birds, on closer view at the harbor where I went down to wait for them. The cages were made of thin cane and they were tall, to accommodate the long, slender legs, with their black shanks and yellow toes. But they were narrow; the herons could not turn, they were forced to stay in the one position, hunched and dejected. The men were like specters, pale and hollow-eyed, and I took this to be the result of the marsh sickness that people speak of, that comes from dwelling constantly in the flooded lands, among the mists that rise there.

At the harborside the scene was one of great confusion. There were mules tethered there also, for what purpose I knew not—my visit to this town was plagued by mules from beginning to end. Disturbed by the swinging cages and the people milling round, these beasts began to bray and shift about, and one or two of them kicked back in that spirit of indiscipline and revolt that descends on mules at certain accursed moments. The tortured sounds they made and the clatter of their hooves on the stone disturbed the birds and they tried to flap their wings but could not, and first one then another set up a desolate wailing sound, *wulla-wulla-wulla*, like the loud grief cries that Arab women make when they raise their heads and let the sounds come from far back in the throat. To add to this, the bird catchers were thronging round me with their feverish faces, clamoring for my attention, telling me how particularly fine these birds were, what pains it had cost to trap them. They had singing voices despite the fervor of their pleas, every phrase reaching a high note then sonorously descending, with the last word amazingly drawn out, as if indeed they had decided to end in song. As I strove to understand them—no easy matter, they sang all at the same time—I caught sight of the Anatolians standing at the stern of the ship, looking down at the spectacle and laughing among themselves.

Fortunately the theme before us was one of extreme simplicity, they asking more for the herons, I offering less. They knew quite well that the price for bird and cage was established beforehand, but there was still a hope in them, which I supposed perennial, quenched one year only to be renewed the next, that they could get more if only the right arguments could be found. They spoke of adverse weather, changed patterns of flight, fewer numbers. One man, more inventive than the others, tried to make me believe that the herons had grown in cunning.

These last had quieted now but looked far from cunning, their yellow eyes staring and fearful, as if knowing their fate, knowing the cruel talons that awaited them, though I thought that when the moment came, when they were struck down by the hawk like a bolt from the sky, their eyes would have a different look, their wings would be outspread, till that moment of death they would be in possession of freedom. Unluckier, as it seemed to me, were those already sickening, those who had spent too much time in the cage. But I knew no way to detect this and refuse payment, so saving my master from wasteful expenditure: drawing near to the town, the men would have cleaned the cages, washed the putrid excrement from the elegant dark legs . . .

There were forty-eight birds. Payment, when we finally agreed on it and struck hands together, came to sixteen silver ducats, money that would keep these people and their families in oatmeal and salt and oil through the winter to come.

The bargaining, though no more than a pretense, had been a lengthy process, and I was much relieved when all was settled and we had the birds on board and the catchers had set off on their journey homeward. Soon the ship would be casting off and I would be free to proceed with my mission. I was about to go aboard again to give final instruction to the master, who at that moment was nowhere to be seen—I thought perhaps he had gone somewhere below to take refuge from all that tumult. He had done this run before, more than once, with my predecessor, Filippo Maiella, a person who had become more real to me in the course of this transaction with the herons, so much so that I found it hard not to see things through his eyes. Eleven years of the wailing birds in their cages—the twelfth had been too much for him. There was the money in his purse, the beckoning distance . . .

I needed to find the master and talk to him. He had carried
herons to Palermo before, but he had not carried dancers and musicians, or so I supposed. He was the best person to trust with the
matter, as he had touched no coin yet—the reverse of the case with
Filippo. He would have to accompany them to the Diwan of
Control and deliver them to the care of my clerk, Stefanos, who
would arrange for their lodgings. Then, and only then, he would receive his payment and give the crew their part of it.

Thinking these thoughts and seeing the master nowhere on
land, I was mounting from the quayside to the deck when I heard a
sudden outcry, a female voice raised to a pitch like that of the
screech owls that live in the hills round Lake Poma. The sound startled the herons, who set up that desolate wailing again, *wulla-
wulla-wulla*, and tried to flap their wings inside the cages. When I
reached the top of the ladder I saw, across the ranks of lamenting
herons, the furious face of the younger dancer, who was standing in
the stern a little apart from the others. I say standing but she had
crouched a little, drawing her shoulders together as if about to
spring. Facing her at some two or three paces' distance, foolishly
leering in spite of the girl's rage, was one of my guards, the hulking
Sigismond. It came to my mind immediately that he had offered her
some insult, perhaps laid hands on her, even tried to pull her away;
he was a brutish fellow and must have been roused by her dancing
of the night before—in my sudden anger at his behavior I forgot that
I too had been roused by it.

She had moved away from the others, perhaps to see better what
was going on below, but now I saw the two men come forward, saw
how they widened the distance between them as they drew nearer
to Sigismond, saw that one had a hand inside his shirt. I moved
quickly toward them, overturning cages in my haste. Strangely, the

herons bore this in silence; they had all fallen silent now, as had the girl at my approach. Her hair was loose about her face and she had a long pin in one hand, copper, I thought—it shone with a dull light.

Drawing nearer to Sigismond I saw at once, even before I smelled the wine on his breath, that he had been drinking, saw it from the way he had planted his feet and the foolish bravado of his smiling. "What is this?" I said.

He was grinning still, as if seeking to indicate by this that it was some sort of a joke. Perhaps, in his primitive way, he had lost sight of the borders between public and private, thought that a woman who danced before men could be any man's.

I did not intend to make much of the matter. No harm was done, the fellow had been routed, and he would know better than to try again. But when I gestured to him with the back of my hand, indicating that he should back away and give ground, his grin faded and he did not lower his eyes but stared back at me with what seemed deliberate insolence. Nor did he give room, as ordered.

I felt my anger rise. To reach this state he must have started with the flagon on his own, before any money had been handed over, probably while the marsh people were thronging round me: in other words, while he should still have been fulfilling his duties as my guard. "You misbegotten wretch," I said. "How dare you brave me in this way? Step back."

It seemed to me that his hand moved a little, up toward his belt and the knife there. Or perhaps this was only the pretext I gave myself. I knew I would have to be quick. He was thickset and strong, and no doubt an accustomed brawler. Whether he would return a blow from one set in authority over him I could not know; it would earn him a flogging if he returned to Palermo and cost him his place, but he might think he had lost that already. It could not be left to chance in any case—the blow would have to be heavy. I could only do what I had been taught in my days of training for the King's Guard. I took a step forward and flicked at his eyes with the fingers of my left hand. He pulled back his head, which is always the first movement when the eyes are threatened. In so doing he lifted his chin a little and exposed his neck. My right-hand blow came hard upon this, while his hands were still lowered, a hooking blow with as much weight as I could put into it, driving my fist into the neck tendons on his left side. It was strange, but my anger left me as I struck him. I had never struck any man in this way before, only a bag of sand in the exercise yard. He did not fall but he leaned over, fighting for breath. Now indeed I could have struck him a blow, with his head hanging low in that fashion, but I did not, and two men of the crew came forward and took his arms to lead him away. Even then for some moments he set his feet against going, and this roused some respect in me after the grievous blow I had given him.

The girl had been silent all this time. When I looked back to her I saw that her face was composed, that eye-snapping fury quite departed. She was regarding me intently, not with the self-absorbed look of her dancing but openly, in a way that was neither friendly nor hostile, but as if dwelling on my face, as if considering. It seemed to me too that her look had something more gentle in it than I remembered from the night before. I understood then, and it took me by surprise, so enraged had I been by Sigismond's defiance, that she believed I had struck the man in anger at his insolence toward her, whereas in truth it had been his insolence toward me that had driven me to it. But looking at her face now more attentively than I had done before in our short acquaintance, and in this clearer light, at the thick black hair still in disorder, the dark eyes, not large but full of life, slanting upward a little toward the temples, the bones of her cheeks that lay so close below the skin, the mouth that had bitterness in it but something tender too, noting all this, I could discover in myself no smallest inclination to set her right in the mistake I thought she had made. I smiled at her and inclined my head a little and laid a hand on my breast. "Thurstan," I said. "I am Thurstan."

"Nesrin," she said, without returning the smile, and she touched herself at the base of the throat. Then she turned to her companions, who had gathered close behind, and she pointed and named them, one by one. He who played the drum and sang was Ozgur, the dulcimer player was Temel, the two women were Yildiz and Havva. Then Ozgur, smiling broadly, pointed at the drum and said, "Davul," and Temel named the dulcimer for me, "Kemanche." All five of them were smiling now, as people do when they are named. But there was an uncertainty in the pause that followed, as often happens when there is this naming, especially when there is some obstacle of language to overcome, and I think the girl felt this—she was quick in her sensing of things, as I was to learn—because she laughed suddenly and made a gesture to include the captive birds, whose cages occupied most of the deck, raising a hand and slackening the wrist and letting the fingers dangle loosely down. I saw after a moment that this was in imitation of the long crest plumes of the herons, which in the wretchedness of captivity drooped down along their backs.

After rage there comes some feeling of sorrow, at least so it is with me. I looked at the birds, at these limp crests of theirs, grown for their time of mating, useless now that their courtship had been cut short. God had made them this gift in the dawn of creation; he had endowed them with this plume to wear for their marriage. And now they were penned and could only shuffle their wings and wail, and they would never mount or be mounted.

I could not see cause for laughter in this, and I let none show on my face. Nesrin, as I have said, was quick in her sensing of things. She was equally quick in her defiance, and this too I was to learn. She showed it now, deliberately prolonging both gesture and laughter, looking directly at me all the while, as if to say, *You do not govern my laughter*, and I looked back steadily at her and my look said, *You are no more than a savage—why should I laugh at your bidding?* So something was exchanged between us without words, and when we looked away from each other it was like a truce, but not of the kind where pledges are made or weapons laid aside. I was glad I had not yielded, for immediate personal reasons and then because, as is well known, small things lead to great, and when I returned to Palermo I would be responsible for their appearance before the King. They would need to give heed to my words, from the very beginning they would have to understand that I was not one of them, to laugh at their jokes, but a person in authority, moving on a higher plane, the provider of rewards and the source of benefits: in short, the King's Purveyor.

In spite of this excellent reasoning, I was already beginning to feel some compunction. I know not why it is, but I can never stay self-contented for very long. I see a settled state of self-content on some faces, see how they can bask in the sunshine of it, but with me some shadow always intrudes. The girl had felt grateful for my defense of her. That she was mistaken in her gratitude was not the point at issue. She had tried to show her goodwill by jesting, and I had rebuffed her. I would have said something, even now, in an attempt to repair matters, but she turned away from me, raising her hands to her head and gathering her hair at the nape so as to tie it, and the loose sleeves fell back from her arms, which were beautiful—but indeed it is a beautiful movement in women, whether they be young or old.

I saw now that the master had come on deck and I remembered I had intended to speak to him before the altercation with Sigismond had put it out of my mind. Only then, as I gave him his instructions and informed him that I would not be returning with the ship, did it occur to me to wonder why Mario had made no appearance, why he had left it to the men of the crew to restrain his fellow and lead him away. Sigismond was standing at the prow, well away from the dancers, but there was no sign of Mario. He was not below either, so the master told me. He was nowhere to be seen on the ship or on the quay. I realized now that I had not seen him since the people had come down with the birds. But I would not have noticed him anyway, probably, distracted as I had been by those singing voices and that pretense of bargaining.

It was disagreeable to me to address Sigismond so soon after what had happened between us, but I had little choice. He answered me with his usual gruffness, but readily enough and without truculence. His hair was wet as if he had thrown water over it and he had tied a rag of cotton round his neck to cover the bruise. Mario had said he was going for a piss and he had not come back, this while I was purchasing the herons. He, Sigismond, had said nothing about this absence, supposing Mario would return before the ship sailed.

"Your first loyalty should have been to me, not to him," I said. "Two fine guards they gave me: one is away drinking when he should be at my shoulder, the other disappears at the time he is most needed."

Sigismond surprised me now: I had expected no more than a shrug, but he looked me doggedly in the face and said, "Lord, forgive this ignorant man that I am, no better than a beast. I thought the girl gave me a look. Then I felt a fool. I have a wife and children in Palermo. Have pity for them, let me keep my place."

This might have been the longest speech he had ever made in his life. Some grace had descended on him and I could not do less than share in it. Besides, whether by accident or design, he had given me my title, acknowledged my birth. "You can keep your place," I said. "I will not make mention of this in my report, but you must take better care in the future." At this he ducked his head and made a shuffling bow, and I again noticed the poor scrap of cloth round his neck and felt sorry for what had happened. I smiled at him and said, "The girl belongs to the King now, no matter which way she glances. It is easy to make mistakes about the look in a girl's eyes. And then, it is always our fault, no?"

He returned my smile with one of his own, as broad as any I have seen on a human face, and the first I had ever seen on his. He turned away without more words, but I felt I had healed the hurt to his pride if not that to his neck, and perhaps gained his goodwill, something I think I had not had before.

Mario was still nowhere to be seen, but we could not delay longer. I waited at the quayside while the ship put off. As she pulled away from the wharf and passed beyond the harbor wall, the sun caught the birds in their cages and for some moments the deck of the ship flashed along all its length.

VIII

I HAD NOW TO MAKE my preparations for the continuing journey. I would have to secure a horse in good enough condition.
But first I retraced my steps to the inn. I had changed my mind
in the matter of the mules: I had been too tame with that foul innkeeper. Why should I leave three mules as the King's gift to him?
I was more at my ease now, not harassed by conflicting claims as
I had been the night before.

The innkeeper showed no pleasure at seeing me. "I have decided to sell these mules to you," I said to him in the manner of one
conferring favors.

He was inclined to sneer at first, having set me down as a soft fellow. But when I threatened to lead the beasts away there and then
and sell them to the first who made me a fair offer, he saw his advantage slipping away. In the end I recovered four ducats and sixty
kharruba from the six ducats I had given. "Life is not always kind,"
I said to him in parting. "Otherwise a man of noble birth would not

be haggling about mules with a scoundrel. But I hope at least I will be spared the sight of your ugly face again." I had prepared this insult in advance, but even as I spoke the disagreeable suspicion came to my mind that I was destined to be Filippo's successor, that this annual purchasing of herons for the Royal Falconry would henceforth be one of my settled duties.

Within the hour I had found a horse, a brown mare. Her teeth were good, her back was straight enough, she was well shod; she had no disability that I could see and the price was fair—for horse and trappings, twenty ducats. My better clothes, and the pilgrim's hooded robe, went into a saddlebag, together with a loaf of bread and a flask of water. I was dressed now for the second stage of my journey, in the rough style of the country, in clothes I had brought with me, the surcoat and leggings and wooden-soled shoes that are common among the people. I had not cut my hair, of which I am proud, but I had tied it back and it was concealed under a snood cap, which fitted closely round my head. My purse was inside my shirt, strapped against the skin. My knife I wore openly at my belt, and I had another weapon, a thin-bladed dagger with a weighted handle for throwing, in a sheath in my saddlebag. I also had a heavy cudgel tied to the saddle. Bands of robbers were not common in these parts, they worked more usually in pairs. The horse alone made me worth robbing, but I hoped that I would be taken for a peasant and so have the advantage of surprise if it came to fighting. This was my hope, as I say, but I was not altogether confident in it.

I reached Cosenza in two days, traveling from sunrise to dusk, but never in the dark, making my way through the valley of the River Crati. The first night I found no lodging but slept by the river, and soon after dawn I was lucky to meet a man on his way to market with baskets of the small white fish that live in the river shallows and are netted in great numbers by the local people. He was ready enough to sell me some, and I made a low fire and cooked the fish on a cane spit and very good they were.

After Cosenza I continued northward, always following the line of the valley, taking what lodging I could find, all of it mean and dirty. I let the hair grow on my face, and when I could I used the river water for washing. I was fortunate in the mare; she was patient and willing. I came to the sea at Sibari and started on the road that follows the coast to Taranto. Here I fell in with a mounted party traveling to Bari for the day of the saint, and in their company my fear of robbers was much less. They were Italians from Crotone; in order to avoid questions I affected to speak only Norman French, and in this pretense my tallness and fairness helped me.

With this, the worst part of the journey was over. We came through the hilly, thickly wooded country in the south part of Apulia, and reached the sea again two days' journey from Bari. And so I arrived at the town in good time; next day was the second Sunday of May, the day of the miracle, when the uncorrupted body of the saint exudes the holy oil. The town was packed to bursting with pilgrims from every corner of Europe, many with the hood and staff and satchel of those who had traveled weary leagues on foot; some had come from as far away as Scandinavia and the lands of the Slavs, and had been months on the road. All degrees jostled together in the narrow streets and along the wider way that ran by the sea.

First I saw to the mare, which had served me so faithfully and well. To cope with this great annual swelling of the town, and with all the travelers from the east who arrived during the year at the port of Bari, there were wooden lodging houses of three stories, built round a courtyard with stables. I had to pay for the stabling at least three times what it should normally have cost. This was the King's money, but there was no help for it, it was not my fault but the fault of those who had agreed on this crowded place for my meeting with Lazar. Naturally, here I could not use the King's authority or his seal to impress or browbeat; here I was a pilgrim among pilgrims, I could do nothing that might draw attention to myself. I took a bed space that was screened with boards on either side, and this cost me more than a place in the dormitory, where there were no beds, only straw from wall to wall, but I reasoned I would be of better service to the King if I had good rest and refreshment.

I was dirty and verminous after these days on the road; I had slept in my clothes, a thing I greatly disliked doing. Keeping my body clean has become more important to me over the years, as has fresh linen next to my skin and clothes as good as I can afford. It is only dress, but I have come to feel it is the truth of me. I was not familiar with Bari, but I knew that it was for long an Arab town and that many Arabs lived here still, though naturally there was little sign of them in the streets at this time of Christian pilgrimage. Where there were Arabs there would be clean water, hot and cold; with great intensity of desire I was looking forward to an Arab bathhouse.

I found one in a street that lay at right angles to the line of the shore, saw at a distance and with joy the domed roof pierced with apertures like an inverted colander so as to catch the light, always so important to Moslems, as anyone who enters a mosque will see. Unlike everything else in the town, the price of admission had suffered no swelling. I left clothes and purse in one of the metal coffers set in the wall and got the key to this, and towels and slippers, from the keeper. Now began a period of bliss. To say truth, in that steam I lost all reckoning of time, going from the hot room to the cooler

one, where the basins are and the attendants wait with their bowls
to throw water over you, warmer or colder according to desire, then
back to the heat again, feeling the start of the sweat on face and
chest.

I found a bench in one of the recesses set round the room, where
it was a little cooler, and lay here in a trance, watching the trails of
steam rise slowly up toward the perforations in the dome high
above me, break into shreds and glow briefly as they were trans-
fused with light, then quiver and curl very delicately as the air of
outside touched them. Some words of a song came into my mind, a
song of the troubadours popular at that time in Palermo. *Your hair
will be tied with silk for the dance, you will grace the dance with the
beauty of your hair* . . . These were words for gentle ladies, ladies of
the court. She shook out her hair like a savage, fiercely. That glass in
her navel perhaps not smooth as I thought then but cut into facets
to make it glitter the more. The art of mosaic is the art of catching
the light. Light is splendor, light has no boundaries . . .

These, or something like them, were my thoughts as I lay there
between sleep and waking, watching that climbing and curling of
the steam. In my languid state I felt a stirring of excitement at the
memory of that ornament nestling at the center of Nesrin's being,
flashing its message. It must be kept in place, I thought, kept resting
in the dimple, by those thin chains of beads that lay across her hips.
Mirabile dictu, no swirl or ripple of the belly disturbed that glittering eye of glass.

This, which should have been a matter for wonder, not lust, nevertheless made that stirring more definite. I was glad for the towel
that lay athwart my loins. If there had been women there to do the
massage, as in some of the bathhouses of Palermo, I might have
taken one and paid her to do the things they know how to do, taking

care, of course, to use my own money for this. But this was a place of
strict Moslem observance; the sexes were kept apart. A man's hand
on me I did not want, except only those of a barber.

I made for the outer room again, had cold water thrown over me,
dried my subdued flesh with the towels that they bring in from
Egypt, very thick—nowhere in Italy can they make them like this.
Then I dressed and drank a juice made from apricots, very delicious, and afterward went to the room where the barbers had their
tables and found one to wash my hair, which he did with yolk of
egg, rinsing it out and scenting it with attar of roses. Then he took
the hair off my face, applying first some yellow-colored paste that
must have been an invention of his own, spreading it with a wooden
spoon and taking it off again, and the hair with it, using the edge of
a mussel shell. And all this without breaking the skin anywhere! I
do not know why we Christians have not adopted this use of the
mussel shell for shaving; it has a keen edge and is light and easy to
manage. But no, we go on scraping with knife and pumice stone. It
is a mystery, when we have borrowed so much else.

I felt a different man when I emerged. I was dressed in the clean
things I had carried with me and wore the hooded robe of the peni-
tent over them. The clothes I had traveled in I left in a bundle there,
in the yard. There were Arab cook shops and sweet shops adjoining the bathhouse, and I had a square of rice jelly sprinkled with
ground walnut, eating it as I stood there, with the little spatula they
give you. It was already evening and the light was beginning to fade
as I set off back toward my lodging. There were some acrobats performing in the square, and one of them was very good—he walked
on his hands and kept his legs very steadily upheld, and one of his
fellows put coins on the soles of his feet and they did not slide. As I

turned to go on my way, I glimpsed a face in the crowd that I thought resembled Mario's, even to the mark of the scar, though my eyes had moved away before this resemblance struck me, and when I sought the face again, though it was only moments later, I could not find it any longer among the people there, and so thought I had been mistaken, a mistake perhaps caused by the fact that I had wondered about his disappearance, and this wondering had kept his face present to my mind.

The illusion was brief, dispelled almost at once, as acrobats and spectators were scattered now by a party of mounted knights and their ladies, whose people ran before them, clearing the way. The knights were armed with sword and mace and dressed in cap and vest of mail and long surcoat, the ladies wore silk gowns and their faces were freshly painted and their hair threaded with gold. Tomorrow these riders would be nameless, on their knees in cloak and hood, part of the penitential throng. I thought that perhaps it was the knowledge of this that brought them out now to parade their wealth and power. I was angry to be jostled and pressed back so they could pass. But below this, irrepressible, was the bitterness of envy for that very wealth and power, for the weapons and the armor and the richly caparisoned horses and the look of calm indifference the men wore. In my heart I felt that I belonged in their number.

Close by there was a stall selling badges and emblems of Saint Nicholas. Such stalls were all over the town and doing a brisk trade, but I had not paused at one before. Now, however, perhaps seeking distraction from this culpable envy of mine, I stopped and looked, and the stall keeper began at once to tell me that these goods of his were of a quality much superior to any that could be found elsewhere. Some were made of tin, some of plaited straw, and some of pottery. I took up one of those in tin and looked more closely at it. It was circular in shape with a pin behind, and it was painted in blue and red and showed the saint with satchel and staff—a clever thing, this, as it made Saint Nicholas too into a pilgrim. "What are you asking for this one?" I said.

The vendor was a short, fat man with hair that grew in curls and the kind of arching eyebrows I have noticed to be common among dishonest persons. "I leave it to the faithful and the pure in heart to set their own price on these sacred images," he said. "As we know, in truth they are priceless."

"Two *kharruba*," I said.

"You are joking," he said. "At least I hope so, for the sake of your soul."

"We do not measure souls in *kharruba*." I held out the money to him. "Here, take it."

"Nine, I will take nine. These fashioned in tin cost more to make and so are more costly to buy, but you thereby do more honor to the saint."

"So this is the way you leave it to the faithful and pure in heart," I said. "Do you think it matters to Saint Nicholas whether his likeness is fashioned in tin or in straw? He is in heaven—he is a soul in bliss. I will give you three."

"You are one that would haggle with Saint Peter over the terms of entry," he said, taking the money, which I think he was pleased enough with, it being a full third of what he had asked.

"You will not get so far as the gate, if you continue thus," I said, and I went on my way, solaced to think I had had the better of this exchange, and relieved from the bitterness I had felt on seeing the splendor of the mounted knights. I had been a good custodian of my master's money; I had shown that stall keeper that I was a person of consequence, no mere ignorant bumpkin to be taken in by his lies. I kissed the image before pinning it to the front of my cloak and uttered in my mind a prayer to Saint Nicholas, humbly asking for his blessing and protection through the days to come.

IX

NEXT MORNING I made my way early to the church. I had no idea when Lazar would arrive there or whether he had yet arrived in the town. I had decided to station myself at the entrance to the crypt and wait for him there.

My way was impeded because of the thronging in the streets. It was now for the first time that I saw Russians, the men stocky and heavy-bearded, in hats trimmed with the skin of animals, the women in black shawls and shoes such as I had not seen before, shoes that came right up over the ankles. Oddest of all, to my mind, were the hats of the German women, shaped like tall crowns, with a strap that passed below the chin. As we neared the church many people fell to their knees and shuffled forward in this fashion, which made it more than ever difficult to pass.

When I finally reached the basilica, I took up the position I had decided on, near the steps that led down to the crypt, a little to one side. Here I was jostled and there was a press of bodies round me, but it was aside from the main movement of the pilgrims, which was toward the top of the steps, and so it was possible to stay there without being dislodged and borne away. The closeness of people was oppressive; there was not air enough, but I could see no help for it. I felt a renewal of anger against those who had chosen such a place. I suspected it had been Lazar himself.

A confusion of voices carried to me from the crypt, and I understood that the priest had begun to extract the holy oil. This set up a new conflict within me. I knew I should remain here, at my post, waiting for Lazar. To meet Lazar, to make my coming empty-handed significant to his mind, and so inspire him with purpose, this was what I had been assigned to do, it was what I was there for. The Kingdom of Sicily was in grave danger. Unlikely as I felt it to be that a clandestine conversation in a corner of Apulia between two men without great power or influence could do much to change events, it was my duty to follow instruction. It was what I had always done, and I took pride in it. But Lazar was nowhere to be seen and I was standing near the stairway that led down to the tomb of Saint Nicholas, and a miracle was taking place there and even just the witnessing of this, without partaking in the oil, might redeem some of my sins, if not all, and turn God's favor toward me, because this oil was a balm for the soul as well as for the body. The voices from the crypt were sounding in my ears and I knew that I might never have such an opportunity again. There was a burden of sin on my soul, a burden of rage and envy, visits to Sara not confessed and now this plunge of appetite for a pagan dancing girl.

The struggle was brief. The cries came up to me, seeming louder. I edged my way to the stairs and began to make my slow way down along with the throng of the faithful. Reaching the foot, I struggled against the crowd until I could set my back against one of the thick columns that ran close to the walls.

The priest was standing with his back to the altar, facing the people, who had fallen to their knees, so that now there was no sound among them and those on the stairs behind were halted there and obliged to wait. Behind the priest was the tomb of the saint, its marble panels open at one side. He raised his voice in a chant that filled all the space and seemed to come from all directions, from walls, from ceiling, from the stones at my feet: *Holy God, Father Almighty, have mercy on us!* And the kneeling folk made reply in wavering chorus: *Lord have mercy!*

I became aware of other voices, these too seeming to be everywhere at once. It was the pleading of beggars, who I saw now were stationed against the walls, some blind or seeming so, others with missing limbs. The priest and the people and the beggars made an antiphon of voices:

Glory be to the Father and the Son and the Holy Spirit!
Alms for the love of God!
Lord have mercy!

Pressed back against the column, assailed by the voices, I felt my obdurate soul loosening, I felt the descent of grace, I heard my own voice mingling with the others: *Lord have mercy!*

The priest raised his hand in blessing and the chanting of the people ceased, though the beggars continued unheeding with their pleas. Then the raised hand turned from blessing to beckoning, the kneeling people began to shuffle forward, and there was a strange sound to replace the singing, the sound of knees dragging across the stone floor. And now I saw there was another priest, who had been hidden from sight behind the tomb but who now came briefly into view before prostrating himself and entering with almost the whole of his body through the open panels to gather the manna from the imperishable body within. For some moments all that was visible of him were his shoes and the hem of his robe. When he emerged he had in one hand a silver beaker and in the other a little rod of glass, and as the people came up to him they raised their faces, ordered in this by the first priest, and he dipped the glass in the beaker and gave each one a little of the holy oil, letting a drop fall onto the lips of the face raised to him. After this they moved aside and stood and mounted again to the basilica by a stairway that rose from the far side, beyond the tomb.

When I saw this a great longing came upon me to be joined with these people in common devotion and the hope of heaven, and feel the touch of the miraculous oil on my lips and be forgiven my sins. I lost sight of my mission and fell to my knees and joined the others who were moving forward. I was drawing near, I was raising my face in preparation, when among those who had taken the oil and were retiring I saw a face I knew, luxuriantly bearded, narrow-eyed, with a high, smooth forehead. Lazar had not changed one whit since I had seen him last. The sight of him, the disagreeable sense that he was my associate even in this, ruined my moment of receiving the manna, took away all my bliss in it. The glass was raised, the drop fell, and I felt it on my lips, but I could think of nothing but how I might dispel any idea in Lazar's mind—for I was sure he had seen and recognized me—that I had been selfishly concerned with my own salvation when I should have had my royal mission in the forefront of my mind. It was not for my own sake—I did not much care what Lazar thought of me—but for the sake of the King, so that his purposes would not fall into disrespect through the failures of his servants. I decided to tell Lazar that I had joined the kneeling penitents in order not to seem conspicuous.

I followed him at a little distance behind until we were out of the church and in the street again. Here he drew on his hood and I did the same. He led me to a narrow square with a small, dark wineshop at the end of it reached by a steep flight of stairs. We found a table to sit at and ordered red wine.

"Well," Lazar said, "now that we are purged of our sins we can speak truth together, like children, like brothers, little brothers in Christ."

I had not been drawn to Lazar from the start and these present words of his recalled the reason: it was as though his long habit of subterfuge had ended by making him seem to cast doubt on his own sentiments even as they fell from his lips. Also, at our last meeting, in Tirana, he had told me that he wrote poetry and this had not struck me as a good sign in one who wanted to lead a rebellion.

"It is well that we speak so soon after," he said. "Sins can soon again start infesting the soul."

"The reason I decided to join them—"

"Yes, I know, it was the same with me: I felt it was unwise to stand apart like that, safer to go down on one's knees and—"

"There was no sign of you. I thought you might be down there."

"That was good reasoning. In fact, I was down there."

"Why did you go?"

"I thought you might be down there."

"This wine has been watered," I said. "It looks like horse piss and tastes like it too." This was not language appropriate to my mission, but I was angered by the way Lazar made us seem so similar in conduct when I was clearly superior, and so I blamed him for the wine, because it was he who had brought us here.

He compressed his lips and nodded several times. "True," he said, "it is not of the best. Why do we always speak ill of the piss of the horse? It is the same among the Serbs as it is among the Greeks. Is it worse than that of other animals? Is there some intrepid soul who has compared?"

This too I remembered about him, that he would fall easily into digressions, speaking on any matter that came into his head, and I believed that this was to disguise his eagerness for the gold; it was his notion of dignity. "We are more familiar with the horse, that is the reason," I said, a little soothed now by the thought that this time at least no gold would be forthcoming. I would have to choose the right moment to tell him this; it must not seem vindictive or any cause of satisfaction to us, but solely a matter of the King's justice.

"You may be familiar with the horse, as a person of good birth and sufficient means. But what of the swineherd, what of the shepherd? For them it would come more naturally to speak of pig piss or goat piss."

"We have not come here to talk of piss," I said.

"True." He reached for my hand across the table. "It is good to see you again, Thurstan." He had eyes that could take on a melting look, and they did so now. "More than two years, old friend," he said. "Much has happened in that time. We are on the brink."

"We have seen little sign of this in Sicily," I said, and I asked him to give me an account of the progress that had been made. He embarked on this readily enough, but it soon came to seem as lamentably thin and threadbare as the report he had given me two years before. As on the former occasion, he tried to make up for the lack of substance by slipping back into the past, speaking of twenty years before, when the valiant Serbian rebels under their leader Bolkan had joined forces with Steven II of Hungary in resistance to Byzantine tyranny.

"Our people were encamped beside the Danube," he said, "close to where it joins with the Nera. The Byzantines crossed the river secretly and fell upon us without warning—the cowards would not risk meeting our fighting men face-to-face. We were pinned against the bank . . . it was a massacre. Those of us who survived were driven from our homes and forced to settle in Asia Minor, led in chains to a land not our own. We Serbs do not forget these things. We are a proud people and we do not forget."

This at least I knew to be no less than the truth; the grudges of centuries, large and small, are stored in Serbian heads. "Well," I said, "fortunately you yourself were not led away in chains. You are free, and able to work for the freedom of your country. We know you Serbs have good reason to hate the Byzantines, and it is the policy of our King Roger to support you in this, to aid you in your lawful desire for independence. But we are interested in the present, not the past. Hungary has a different king now, the Serbs have different leaders, he who rules in Constantinople is Manuel, not John."

"We are on the brink, on the very brink," Lazar said. "The Hungarian cavalry is massing on the border."

I had heard these words before. I could not for the moment remember where. Perhaps it was no more than imagination on my part, but his eyes seemed to stray more frequently to the level of the table, which was also the level of my waist, where the bag of gold dinars would be, nestling under my cloak. "The train is set," he said. "A spark is all that is needed."

I had it now: they were the very words Yusuf had used in sending me forth: it must have been Lazar who penned the report. That he should use the words again now was an offense to intelligence. Did he think I was so gullible?

"Pardon me," I said, "the Hungarian cavalry has been massing on the border for a very long time now. Who can remember a time when they were not massing on the border? They were massing on the border when you and I last talked together. Also at that time a spark was all that was needed. My King has grown weary of waiting for this spark. Until it comes, you will see no sparkle."

I was pleased with this witticism, which had come to me on the spur of the moment, and I let this pleasure show on my face. "No spark, no sparkle," I said.

"What do you mean?" Lazar's eyes were melting no longer. They were as hard and bright as jet stones.

"No shine of gold, in other words. We have disbursed money from the royal coffers for five years, so far without any result that we can see. The time has come to call a halt. Our hope in this is to make you see the gravity of the matter. So far we have paid for promises. Now we will pay only for results. But we will pay well, better than before, if you can raise the people in numbers great enough to turn Manuel Comnenus from his designs on Sicily."

He was scowling at me now in such an ugly fashion that I eased well back in my chair so that I was beyond the sweep of a knife. I did not think it likely he would make such a move—he was a man in hiding—but it is better to take precautions; I once saw a man slashed across the forehead in this way, over a dispute at cards, without the assailant even rising from his chair.

"So that is all it means to you," Lazar said. "Our Serbian blood will flow in streams so that Manuel Comnenus might turn his eyes from Sicily."

"You knew this already, do not pretend otherwise now. Our interests are not the same, but they come together here. Your freedom is our safety." I was already regretting my forthrightness. He knew it; yes, none better. But our stated reason had always been friendship for Serbia. "We must have something to show for the money we have spent before we spend more," I said.

"Holy Mother of God," he said, and he banged his fist on the table. "It is madness to deny the money now, when we are on the brink. Only two weeks ago our people assassinated a provincial governor."

"Yes, word of it came to us. A knife between the ribs in a remote region near the Bulgarian border. He was not killed for patriotic reasons. He was killed because he had come to enforce the collection of taxes. That is your idea of a spark?"

Lazar stood up abruptly. "I have come all the way from Belgrade only to hear my people insulted."

"I too have traveled far," I said.

"I will report this to my council. I will report your words and manner. This betrayal of us will seriously delay the rebellion."

With this he flung away from me and disappeared down the steps. As a parting shot it was not effective—the rebellion was seriously delayed already. But I had no satisfaction in this thought or any other that came to my mind as I sat on there after his departure. I had lied about my reasons for joining those kneeling penitents, I had lied with the oil fresh on my lips, and Lazar had anticipated me in the lie, thus associating both of us together in it. Contrary to my instructions and my own resolutions, I had shown pleasure in refusing the money and even smiled at my own poor joke; I had spoken sarcastically of the Hungarian cavalry and the killing of the tax collector, and too openly about the King's reasons, always a mistake, even when they are known on every hand. Yusuf would not have approved of my conduct, had he witnessed it—and he would get Lazar's account if the reports from Belgrade continued.

But it was not fear of Yusuf's displeasure that troubled my spirit now. Dislike for Lazar, yes. But as I stared before me with the sour taste of the wine still in my mouth, I was aware of a deeper dislike— for the stranger who sat alone here, and for the work he did.

X

THERE WAS NOTHING now to keep me in Bari. I did not relish the prospect of that long journey back over land, and there was no need for it now. I decided to ride only as far as Taranto and take ship from there. But before leaving I wanted to see the Madonna of Odegitria, which Stefanos had told me of, he being very devout and full of knowledge. He had said she was kept in a chapel behind the Church of San Sabino, which was now being re-built after damage suffered during the wars with the Saracens. I wanted very much to see her, since it is the truest likeness anywhere to be found, both in face and form, having been made from a draw-ing of her by the Apostle Luke, which he did in the time before the Crucifixion—she did not allow any more drawings of herself to be done after, because of her great grief.

However, I was destined not to see her likeness that day, and in fact I have never seen it. I asked twice for the way, but the streets that led to the church were narrow and meshed closely together and to a stranger's eye they looked all alike. I took a wrong turn and found myself at a market of vegetables and fruit, with roofless stalls that took up most of the short street, and beyond them a sight of the sea. I was about to ask one of the stall keepers for the right way when I was caught up in a throng of pilgrims who suddenly appeared from I know not where, I think from the direction of the harbor, they were jubilantly singing as if in joy at having landed safely. There was a sound of piping among them and a jingling of bells, and it seemed that all the dogs of Bari had joined them, barking and cavorting in a state of great excitement. Added to this were the angry shouts of the stall keepers, whose trestles were in danger of being overturned.

I was swept some way on the loud tide of these pilgrims and then, to get free of them, turned into a street on my right-hand side that led away from the sea. This brought me after some time to an open space, where there were the ruins of a fort, or perhaps only a fortified house, I could not tell. Not much was left of the walls but there were two low, rounded arches and some fragments of a floor mosaic. In my search for the chapel of the Madonna I had climbed higher than I knew. Beyond the walls and a narrow waste of thistle and wild oats the sea was visible, but it lay well below.

The jingling and the singing and the barking died slowly away and were succeeded by a silence that settled round me. The sea was unmarked, there was no wind, no movement in the grasses of the open ground. This calm, after such turbulence, was strange, rare in a town the size of this one. It seemed like a blessing, a visitation. I went through into the square of ground where the building had stood, stepping over the walls where they were low enough. There was a scutter of lizards on the sun-warmed stone, and a cat the color of cinnamon walked slowly along the wall on the side farthest from the sea.

How long I stayed alone there I do not know. A sort of dreaming state descended on me, as if I had passed through some narrow gate and found sanctuary here. My mood, which had been somber since the meeting with Lazar, lightened now, and I began to think more kindly of myself and the part I had played. There was the picture that acted on my mind like touching a talisman, and I summoned it now, the shining silver of the King's barge, which I was helping to keep afloat on the dark water.

I was standing on the broken pavement, breathing deeply in this peace surrounding me, trying to make out the fragments of mosaic; there was part of a peacock's tail, the curving stem of a plant. I heard the clatter of hooves and looked up from my scrutiny to see a small company on horseback approaching. They were three, two of them women, the other, who led the way, a groom in livery of green and red, richly turned out from his hose to his plumed hat, and wearing a sword. They were in file, with the younger of the women coming close behind the groom. She was dressed differently from our Norman ladies in Italy, and differently from her companion, though this was a confused impression of mine—all I saw as she drew nearer was the Saracen style of the hat she wore, a white turban set back on the head, allowing the fairness of her brows to be seen and the pale gold hair that curled round them.

They drew level, the ladies sitting straight-backed and not sparing me a glance, though the groom eyed me carefully and slowed his horse to a walk—I supposed the better to do so. He was a broad-faced, handsome man, in middle life, and he had not the bearing or the glance of a servant. They would have passed thus, in silence, but at the last moment before they did so I thought I knew the younger lady's face and her name, and this broke from my lips almost without my willing it. "Alicia," I said. "Lady Alicia, is it you?" My throat tightened as I spoke, for fear I might be wrong.

She reined in her horse and looked at me, and this made me think she was who I thought. Her expression was not cold, but there was no recognition on her face. Certainly my clothing did not help her; I was wearing still my rough cloak of a pilgrim, open because of the warm weather, to show nothing beneath but belted tunic and dark leggings. But the cowl was thrown back, my face was uncovered as I looked up at her. The groom turned his horse now to place himself between me and the lady, and I spoke as he came forward. "Do you not know me? You knew me once."

For some moments longer she looked closely at me, then her face broke into a smile of surprise—and of pleasure too, as it seemed to me. "Thurstan," she said, and my heart expanded because after these many years she still remembered my name. "You have grown tall," she said, still smiling.

She turned to her companion and spoke my name to her, though not my father's name, which I supposed she did not remember, then told me that the lady was Catherine Bolland and related to her by marriage. I made the best bow I could and heard Alicia explaining that she and I had known each other as children, that we had both been sent to the court of Richard of Bernalda to learn manners in our different ways. She did not say that we had been sweethearts, that she had filled my mind for two years, the first one ever to do so, that we had both wept when she had left at fourteen to be married. These were not things to say in the hearing of a groom and an attendant lady—I knew from the tone Alicia used with her that she was this, knew it from the way she was asked now to go forward some distance and wait.

This she did, the groom following her, leaving Alicia there before me, though I knew she could not remain there long. How could she linger, even had she been so inclined? She was accompanied, richly mounted; I was on foot, poorly dressed, alone. To meet like this, and then have no time to talk together! My breath came quickly. I felt like one drowning in a sea of things unsaid. "Is it Bari where you live now?" I asked her.

"No, I am recently arrived in Italy. I have come from Outremer, from Jerusalem. I am staying with my cousin here in Apulia. I am only in Bari for the day of the saint. And you?"

"I am leaving for Palermo later today." I heard the sound of voices and laughter from somewhere farther along the street. "We will go our different ways," I said, "and we will never—"

She glanced once over her shoulder, then spoke quickly, in lower tones. "If you are leaving later today, you might want to stay somewhere close by so as to be early on the road tomorrow. There is a house of the Hospitalers, a hospice for travelers. It is where the road from Bari comes to the first houses of Bitonto. The monks hold the land in grant from a neighbor of my cousin, William of Sens. If you go there, speak his name to them and they will look after you well."

With this she urged her horse forward and moved to join the others, and at that moment the people whose voices I had heard came into view. They were country people, on holiday from their fields for this day of the saint, talking and laughing together. When I looked back to the way the riders had gone, there was no sign of them and no sound of hooves, and for some moments I could hardly believe that the encounter had taken place.

There was no longer room in my thoughts for the Madonna of Odegitria. Alicia was marvelous likeness enough—to herself, to the girl of fourteen I remembered loving. I had one sole object now: to recover my horse, pay for stabling and fodder, and start on my way to the house of the Hospitalers. She had not said she would be there, but she had lowered her voice, she had not wanted the others to overhear, she had wanted it to be something between us. And this caution had been familiar to me, like a secret remembered across the gulf of years, recalling the backward glances and whispered tones of our courtship, when we had schemed to contrive a brief time together in some corner of the castle that was not overlooked, a game of conspiracy, but one that we played for our own pleasure, when so much of our play was striving to please others, our elders.

The sun was setting when I reached the hospice, and the bell of the cloister was sounding for vespers. The monk on duty at the gate came to let me in, and I used the name Alicia had given me and asked for lodging. There were beds in the dormitory, but I offered to pay more for a separate place to sleep, and this was agreed. My reason for it was the rule of curfew for guests in monastic houses, those in the dormitory being required to be in bed with lights out after the office of compline, whereas I wanted to keep my freedom of movement in case Alicia came and we could talk together. I was shown to my place, one of a row of cells on the ground floor, with no furnishing but a narrow bed, a water jug, and a chamber pot. I left my few belongings here and came out again into the courtyard; I wanted to be where I could see the gate, have the first sight of her— if indeed she came.

There was an ancient walnut tree in the courtyard and a fountain with a ram's head carved in stone. When we wait with heightened feelings in a place that is strange to us, this very strangeness can sometimes make a deeper mark on memory than the sights of every day. Even now, after all that has passed, those overarching branches and the shadows they cast, the docile head of the ram with its dripping mouth, will come back to my mind unbidden and carry me back to that time of waiting.

There was some coming and going of travelers in the yard, but not so very much. It seemed likely to me that the hospice would always be more frequented on the eve of the saint's day, when many would arrive after dark and seek a bed here rather than continue to Bari so late. Alicia had made a good choice for me—and for herself, I was hoping.

Dusk was falling, and they lit lamps at the gate and on the walls of the yard, and the white crosses of the hospitalers who carried the lamps stood out on their dark habits. And suddenly my waiting for her and not knowing if she would come was like the many times when we had plotted to be together but could not be sure of succeeding because of some claim that might be made on us, some errand or task that came at the last moment to disappoint our hopes.

I had not noticed her at first among the other girls. She was seven when she came and I was eight—I had been there a year. I saw her every day without remarking her at all; we boys spent much of our time in the women's apartments on the third floor; while the girls were learning sewing and embroidery and singing, we were waiting at table, setting up beds, attending the lady wife of our overlord and striving to meet her every wish. Alicia was like the others, anxious to please, homesick—like all of us. But she was not fearful, as I was to learn later, and this made her different: submissive in behavior, yes, as she had been taught to be, but I never found fear in her, only caution, by no means the same thing. For my sake she was ready to risk disgrace, as I was for hers.

It was only when I could see her no longer that I missed the daily sight of her. And this makes me think there must have been some earlier signs between us that the stronger feelings of later overlaid.

When I was twelve my voice began to break, and the strange croaking I sometimes made meant that I was approaching too close to manhood to stay among the women. I was moved down to the second floor under the tutelage of the baron himself, and his seneschal and his constable and his chamberlains. Here there were different lessons: riding and the care of horses, exercises with the sword, and, later, as my strength grew, on horseback with the lance. We saw the girls rarely now; we slept below on beds that were set up in the great hall of the donjon and they remained with the lady, sleeping in the hall above, which was kept guarded—someone was always on guard at the door that led from the spiral staircase in the donjon wall. We saw each other on court occasions, at dinner when there were guests, at hunting parties, and at the lists, when the girls and women together watched the jousting from their balconies. But occasions for speech, for private words, were few. Glances came before words. When was the first time that we exchanged glances and knew?

I was seeking to trace in memory this elusive moment when I heard a mailed fist strike at the gate, saw the gate open, saw them pass through, three men-at-arms with Alicia in the midst of them. A serving woman came behind, but of groom and lady attendant there was none.

I had thought to go forward and greet her, but I faltered when I saw her so surrounded, and stepped back into the shadow of the tree. She was beautiful as she passed under the light. She wore no turban now, her pale hair was dressed with silver threads and she wore a veil across the lower part of her face, in the fashion of Moslem ladies, but very thin, the red of the paint on her cheeks glowed through it. And perhaps it was this too, this beauty of hers, that made me draw back, the gleaming threads of silver in her hair, the rose glow of her cheeks through the delicate veil: I had been absorbed in thoughts of her childhood face, the lustrous pallor of her skin, the long hair parted in the middle and gathered behind, without ornament.

I remained where I was while the horses were seen to and the party conducted within. I counted the moments as I waited there. The serjeants would be allotted beds in the dormitory; for the lady Alicia a chamber would be provided, the best they had, with a place close by for the serving woman so she could be within call. The courtyard was overlooked by a short gallery with a balustrade, roofed but open at the side, and after a while I saw the two women pass along this, led by a monk who bore a lantern, holding it high to give more light. A door was opened for them and they passed from view.

She would come down alone, she would know I was here, she would ask, no doubt idly enough, if a man traveling alone had given the name of William of Sens, she would guess I was waiting here, in the courtyard.

The time passed and it seemed long to me. Then I saw her pass again along the gallery, without her servant now, and descend the steps. She entered the yard and paused there, as if in doubt. I saw she no longer wore the veil. I stepped forward from the refuge I had taken in the shadows, and we regarded each other at a distance of some half dozen paces, smiling, not speaking in these first moments.

"I thought you might not come after all," she said, drawing nearer to me. "I thought you might decide to ride farther on your way, being Thurstan Beauchamp and not afraid of the dark, not afraid of anything, as you would tell me."

"Was I so boastful? I have learned to be fearful since. Did you really think I would not come, when you had counseled it? When I thought that you—" I stumbled here, aware of my clumsiness, afraid of offending.

"That I intended to come myself? Well, so it was. But whether I so intended before our meeting or only after, it is more modest in me not to say. You will understand, we can talk only here, in the open."

"Of course." I glanced up at a sky that seemed throbbing with stars. "It is a good place to talk. Any place would be good."

"So long as the company pleases."

"If there were no limit but that, I would stay in this courtyard forever. I will ask them to fetch chairs for us."

She laughed at this and her laughter was low and pleasant to the ears, but I could not tell whether this quality of her laughter was a thing remembered or a thing discovered only now.

"I see you are more used to inns than to the houses of Saint John," she said. "Where would they find chairs? They have benches in the refectory, they have benches in the chapel. In no other place do they ever sit. The master will have his chair, quite a grand one, but I cannot believe he would give it up very readily."

"Not to me, certainly."

"In any case, their chairs would be like their beds, made for penance, not comfort."

It was the tone of one who had traveled, one acquainted with luxury. She came from Outremer, where the beds were said to be soft. Thinking this, I was in sudden thrall to an image of her lying naked in one. The demon of lust is an agile climber, he can make himself thin, he can enter by any chink or cranny. It is Peter Lombard, as I believe, who first spoke of this thinness in the second book of his *Sentences*, that devoted to angels and demons and the fall of man.

"If you will deign," I said, "there is a muretto that goes round the fountain there, broad enough to sit on. And we can rest our backs against the wall, if we so choose, one on either side."

"Yes, let us do that. You were always resourceful. The ram will not mind; he has seen and heard everything by this time."

"The resourceful one was you," I said as we took our places there.

"Why do you say that?"

"You always found good reasons." I paused here, wanting to say how much I had admired this courage and cleverness of hers, this steadiness in deceiving those set over us, when she knew full well what disgrace the discovery of our trysts would mean for her. In this respect there had been no comparison between us; I would have been punished in some manner, but for her it would have been an immediate return home with reputation tarnished. I could not see her well now, in the dimness of the yard—the lamps had been all extinguished, save only the one above the gate. I could see the gleam of silver in her hair when the thread caught the light, and the oval of her face, and the outline of her form in the long riding cloak, as she leaned back against the wall. "I will never forget how much you ventured for my sake," I said.

I saw her smile. "Venturing made the kisses sweeter. There was the excitement of it—the time together was short, so it was precious."

"As it is now."

"We are not children now. We can have more time, if we want it."

"Tonight? Tomorrow?"

"I was not speaking of tonight and tomorrow," she said. "I hope our future will contain more days than that." As if to forestall any reply I might make to this, she said quickly, "You risked for me too."

"You were worth any risk, a hundred times over."

"And you were not? There were windows that looked down over the exercise yard. I used to watch you at practice. I saw you hurl the darts at the target. I saw you do the cut and block with the other boys. I saw you dash down the straw men with your lance. I thought you so splendid. Where you were the sun always seemed to be shining."

Such was my pleasure at this that I was driven to shift the subject for fear that some quiver in my voice would betray me. "Well," I said, "if we shared the risk, now let us share the credit, because it is the fact that we were never found out."

This again brought laughter from her. "No," she said, "but we came near to it sometimes. Do you remember that boy, he who was made the chamberlain for the women's apartments? He was a page still, younger than you. He watched me and followed. He found us sitting together on some stairs, do you remember? We bribed him with the honey cakes my mother used to send me."

"I remember him, yes. His name was Hugo. He fell ill not long after and was sent home and never came back. It was a disorder of the stomach—everything he ate he vomited up. We never learned what became of him."

"It was providential. He would have betrayed us in the end, the supply of honey cakes was not regular enough to prevent it."

"He would have asked for more than cakes from you. They always ask for more. Hugo watched the boys as well as the girls. He was only ten, but spying and extortion came naturally to him. He was the first of that kind I ever knew. There have been a good number since."

I had spoken with a bitterness that I at once regretted; it was a note too harsh for this enchanted occasion of our meeting. For a moment or two she was silent, then she said, "I do not know what your life has been, but your face is that of the boy I knew."

This was very gently said, and it acted on my soul as if a gate had been opened to let out trapped water, because she who sat there close to me, though half obscured now in the dimness of the yard, had still the face I had loved when my hopes were high, when everything had seemed possible. I told her of my disappointments, of my father's decision to retreat from the world—she had heard nothing of this, she said, having been away all this time in the Kingdom of Jerusalem. I told her—and my voice shook on it a little in spite of myself—how sick I was of carrying the purse and counting the coin, how I longed to live in the light of day. I told her what I had told no one else: I spoke of the figure I kept with me like a talisman for my spirit to touch, the shining silver of the barge, the glory of majesty that made the King so dazzling to the eyes as he rested on the dark water, the creatures below the surface that kept the balance.

She said little, but I could feel the closeness of her listening. And when I had done she attempted no easy words of comfort but in her turn told me of her fortunes since the time when, soon after her fourteenth birthday, she had left to be married to Tibald of Langre, an acquaintance of her father's, a man of thirty-four whom she hardly knew, who had amassed money in the wars with the infidel and wanted to settle down. He had a fief in the Holy Land, as a vassal of King Baldwin, also estates in Sicily.

"We had no issue," she said. "He blamed me for not giving him an heir and I took the fault for mine, as it is always considered the woman's fault. But Tibald had other loves, and made no secret of it, and none of them bore him a child that I know of. So I do not know if I am barren, I have not put it to the proof except with him." Her face was turned toward me as she spoke; there was not light enough to read her expression, but I felt she had spoken these words for me, and my heart was stirred.

He had died the year before while taking part in the siege of Ascalon, not of wounds but of a seizure. "He always ate too much and drank too much for the climate there," she said. "He was like many of them, he saw no need to change from his habits in France. He drank wine for his thirst, and he ate fat meat. It was pork that killed Tibald, if I have to find one word for it. One evening, after a day in the saddle, when he tried to rise from his chair where he was sitting among the others, he fell back and could not move and lost his power of speech. They carried him to bed but he died that same night, without finding his voice again."

There was no trace of sadness in her voice, or even of much regret, except perhaps for Tibald's habits of eating; she might have been talking of any man's death. If she had wept for him the tears were long dry. It surprised me a little that she did not affect sorrow even if feeling none, because such is the practice of the recently widowed. Then I understood that she was paying me the compliment of frankness, and I remembered suddenly that she had been the same in the days of our courtship, deceiving others but never me, never pretending reluctance, never requiring to be persuaded or cajoled, not disguising her eagerness any more than I disguised mine.

Since Tibald had died without issue, the land had come to her, both that in Jerusalem and that in Sicily. She would return, or such was her purpose at present. She was used to the life there and liked it, but she had wanted to see her parents, who lived in retirement on their lands near Troina, in the Val Demone. She had been accompanied from the Holy Land by her brother Adhemar, a knight in the following of Raymond, Count of Tripoli, who had given him leave.

But she had come to Bari without kinsfolk to partake of the holy oil and give thanks to Saint Nicholas for bringing her safe to Italy. On the morrow she would return to Borsora in Apulia, where her cousin Simon of Evreux had his lands. She would stay there two days more, then return to her parents. Her father wanted her at home. How long she would remain in Sicily she did not know; she had made no plans.

"To say truth I am enjoying the freedom that has come with my widowhood," she said. "I suppose it is wrong to say this, even to you, but I cannot help feeling it. There was always someone's permission to seek. Now it is only a pretense. I defer to my father and my brother, but it is only for the sake of manners. And this is because I have come into possession of Tibald's lands. They are in my grant. I am Alicia of Bethron. Of course I must marry again, and before too long, my estates in Jerusalem will need a man to manage and defend. Ascalon and Jaffa are close, and they are still held by the Moslems. But I will never be given away again. I will choose. I have vowed it."

I saw a hand stray to her throat but could not see what lay there. For a short while there was silence between us. When she spoke again it was in a tone much lighter. "There is no doubt of it, more is permitted to a widow than a wife, much more. Otherwise, how could we two have sat here in the dark so long?" With this she rose. "It is late," she said. "You have a weary way to go tomorrow."

"Thoughts of you will make the way seem lighter." I rose and took some paces toward her, following the curve of the muretto. "All these years, and I have never forgotten you," I said.

She moved forward a little and stopped, as if hesitating. I thought she might come close to me, close enough for me to take her in my arms, but she did not. Two paces more, and I could have touched her, laid my hand on her hair or her cheek. Some grace in me conquered this impulse, kept me standing still there.

"Nor I you," she said, "my splendid Thurstan, my valiant boy at the lists."

She was turning away. "And tomorrow?" I said. "Will I not see you tomorrow?"

"We will leave not much after daybreak."

"I will be waiting here, by the fountain, if it be only for the sight of you."

"Well," she said, smiling now, "I hope we can greet each other at least. It is not many hours away—we have talked long. Good night, Thurstan Beauchamp."

"Good night, my lady, and a sweet repose to you." I watched her move to the stairs that led to the gallery, saw her mount them and pass briefly under the lamp that lay over the door of her chamber. The door was opened and closed, and she passed from my sight. I stayed there some time longer, gazing up, as if by not moving I could somehow prolong a sense of her presence. The words of a song came to my mind, one from Provence, which I had sung sometimes: *To console me for her loss, I think of the place where she is . . .* I heard no voices from within and thought that perhaps Alicia had not wanted to wake the woman who attended her, who would be sleeping now. She would undress and prepare for bed unaided, and this consorted with what I felt to be the kindness of her nature.

I will confess here, since I am resolved to confess everything, that for a little while, as I stood there, I put to use that faculty of speculation I have spoken of before, encouraged in me by Yusuf but I think already there in strong enough measure, and I began to picture this undressing of hers but did not go far with it. She was all marvel to me, not flesh. She was my lady found again. And I was her splendid Thurstan, not a spy, not a lecher.

I was there at my post at daybreak, having slept very little for fear of sleeping too much. But our time together was brief. She sent her people to wait beyond the gate, except for one of the serjeants, who held the horse for her while we walked about the yard. The bleak light, the presence of others, the imminence of our farewells, all this constrained us.

"Take good care on the road," she said. "You are returning to difficult times."

"How can I see you again? But perhaps you do not want to?"

"Yes, I want to. I will come soon to Palermo, very soon."

She glanced up at me as she spoke and my heart lifted at the promise in her glance and in her words. "Angels guided my steps in Bari," I said.

"And mine. Now I must be on my way, and so must you."

There was still no touch between us. She looked once more at me, then turned toward the man who held her horse. He would have dismounted to assist her, but I went forward and took the bridle from him and brought the horse to her. I knelt in the dust of the yard and made a stirrup for her with my hands and lifted her thus into the saddle and wished her Godspeed. I felt the touch of her hand on my head and the murmur of her voice above me, "Thurstan, my knight," or so it sounded—her voice was very soft. Then they were gone with a clatter, and one of the hospitalers was already closing the gate.

XI

HER FACE of the evening and the morning, her voice and her smile and the touch of her hand on my head, stayed with me all through the journey to Taranto. I went over the circumstances of our meeting again and again, how I had blundered by purest chance into that deserted place, with its weed-grown terrace and broken walls and vestiges of mosaic. I remembered the sense of relief that had come to me there, with only the cat and the lizards for company, the peace and self-pardoning after the ugliness of my talk with Lazar. It had been like a stage, a place prepared, swept clean for our meeting by kindly spirits . . .

But on boarding the ship I had news that put her image out of my mind, at least for a while. It came from a man I fell into talk with, a bailiff, as he told me, on the royal lands at Castel Buono. "Well," he said, "the times were not easy before, but they will be worse now."

"Why is that?" I asked him.

"There is only William left, and the King has no wife." He glanced now more closely at my face. "You have not heard?"

"I have been long on the road. Has some ill befallen Duke Roger?"

"He died eight days ago."

"But there was no illness or weakness in him when I left." I was staggered by the suddenness of it, so much so that I could scarcely credit the man's words. "How could such a thing have come about?"

"He died of a fever—or so it was given out."

"What do you mean?"

"It cannot be natural," he said. "I have been in the King's service for near on twenty years now. When Queen Elvira died, he had five sons born in wedlock, all in good health. Then Tancred died, then Alfonso, then Henry, and now Roger, the eldest, the heir to the throne, the one he pinned his hopes on. Four strong sons, with the blood of the Hautevilles in their veins, gone to their maker in a space of ten years. And not one of them died of wounds. It cannot be natural."

I was deeply distressed by the news of this death and needed time to ponder it in private. But Yusuf's teaching was always strongly present to me. *Let the one you talk to think he knows more, so you will find out what he thinks and so you will find out what he knows.*

"You don't believe someone had a hand in it?" I said.

"It is the Germans," he said, "and I am not alone in thinking this. They should not have been allowed to come so close to the throne—our King's Confessor is a German now. I don't speak of him, but there are those who work for Conrad among them, those who would like to see the Hohenstaufen get his hands on Sicily and bring it into his empire of the Romans, as it is termed, though there is little of Rome in it that I can see. He is Emperor of the Germans. And let us not forget, the Pope has not consented to crown Conrad."

"That is true."

"What has Conrad promised him in return for the imperial coronation? That is what a good many of us would like to know."

"Well," I said, "you will not know it. Nobody will, not for certain. You can be sure it was not set down in writing." I thought again of Hugo the page boy. What honey cake had Conrad offered Pope Eugenius? A Sicily with a different ruler, one more submissive to the demands of the Church?

It was not until some time after this conversation, when I had retired to consider the news on my own, that I realized that Alicia must have known of this death. She had been with her parents near Troina; they would have had word of it soon after. She had said nothing, and my heart gave full approval to her for it; she had done, I thought, as I myself would have done, she had allowed no intrusion into that charmed talk of ours, nothing to mar the brief time we had for ourselves. Perhaps only then, at our parting, it had been in her voice, when she spoke of difficult times ahead . . .

I half expected that some difference in me might be remarked upon when I was back in Palermo, so much did I feel myself changed by my meeting with Alicia, as if there were a light about me. But if this was noticed, nothing was said. And as the days passed and my usual tasks were resumed and I heard nothing from her, this light began to fade into that of common day.

The King was said to be unconsolable in his grief for his first-born, and he kept to his apartments and saw no one. I could not make my report to Yusuf immediately, because he was closeted with others of the Curia Regis in matters arising from Duke Roger's death, speculation as to who might take command in Salerno, interminable discussion of the merits and defects of various possible brides for the King—it was obvious to all that he must marry again, and soon.

While waiting for Yusuf's return to the diwan I asked Stefanos to fetch one of the palace tailors. "Red and silver and black are the colors I want," I said. "Both for the dancers and the two who play the instruments. I want him to bring the stuffs with him so we can choose." As Purveyor it fell to me to see to the appearance they made who came by my arrangement to perform before the King. I had decided that the men would wear red tunics and black pantaloons and black turbans with silver stitching, and that the women would repeat these colors but in a different order—black bodices and red skirts and silver girdles. This I thought would be tasteful and sumptuous at the same time. "These palace tailors think they are princes," I said. "He is to make careful note of the time he spends and the cost of the materials. He is not to exaggerate in anything, because we will infallibly find him out."

Stefanos nodded. "I will see he is told this, but it is time wasted, these warnings make no difference." He smiled saying this, a smile of regret and resignation mixed. Stefanos was a gentle soul, but he was shrewd. He had been many years a bookkeeper in the Diwan of Control, and he was old now—I thought he must be fifty at least. His hair was scant, and poring over the accounts had given him a stoop, but his brown eyes had the glint of irony and humor in them, and little escaped his notice. "They add the warnings to their costs," he said. "It goes down on the bill."

"All the same, it lends us an advantage to have warned him when the reckoning comes."

Stefanos smiled again. "A moral advantage, you mean? We might feel that, but will he?"

"I will see that he knows it. They are housed well enough, the people?"

"Yes, they are close to the guardhouse at the west gate, the one near the outer wall, where the stables used to be until the yard was found too narrow and the horses were moved. There was some trouble at first with one of the dancers."

"That would be the younger one."

"Yes, how did you know? She is difficult, that one, certainly." He paused a moment, shaking his head in mild perplexity. "A beautiful girl," he said, "in her face and in her movements also. But very excitable. She shook her skirts about as if there were rats underfoot. She said she was not a horse, to sleep in the stable, she had two legs, not four. Shapely legs they are, what I saw of them."

I could see he had been taken by Nesrin, even in the midst of this flagrant misbehavior of hers. "She is perverse," I said. "She is one who sleeps by the roadside, but walls and a roof are not good enough."

I had spoken more eagerly perhaps than met the case, and I felt Stefanos's eyes on me. He said, "I explained to her, as well as I could—her Greek is limited—that they are not stables now but chambers, and I pointed out to her the swept floors and the clean straw that had been put down for them, with the cotton quilts to lay over. Then she said she would not share the space, she wanted to sleep alone. We had thought one room for the men, another for the women, but this turned out to be a mistake because the others are in couples, a man and a woman together."

"All this no doubt they discussed among themselves in their own tongue, loudly and at length."

"So they did. Now they are occupying three stables—rooms, I mean—and for the present they are content."

"Well," I said, "if she is by herself she will have only herself to quarrel with. Let us bring the tailor and make a start with dressing them. I foresee difficulties at every stage with these people, but time is on our side, though gained through misfortune—the King will not want to see dancing so soon after the death of his son."

I had scarcely finished saying this when one of the eunuch slaves employed as messengers came to tell me that Lord Yusuf had returned and required my presence as soon as possible. I went immediately, bearing with me a written statement containing details of all the monies disbursed in the King's name in the course of my mission. These he would have to approve and sign. Among them was no mention of my stay with the Hospitalers of Saint John.

I recounted the purchase of the birds and the hiring of the dancers. Naturally, I said nothing about the difficulties and irritations that had been attendant on these transactions. Yusuf listened, with his eyes on my face, but made no comment of any kind; birds and dancers were after all my responsibility, and I would have to answer for any shortcomings in either.

"And Mario?" he said suddenly, cutting me short. "What became of Mario?"

"So you were informed of it? I was coming to the mention of him."

"If I had been in your place, and rendering this account, I would have begun with that. It is unusual. The other things are not unusual, neither the herons nor the dancers."

"Not unusual?" I said warmly. "They are amazing. They can move their bellies in a way never seen before."

"Thurstan, Thurstan," he said in a lowered voice, as if in pity for me.

He said nothing more for the moment. The midmorning light came through the tall window where we were standing together, as generally in these colloquies of ours, and fell on his white turban and robe with a brightness that perplexed my eyes a little, and just for a moment I was reminded of my visit to Mohammed, his form as he rose to greet me and the way he had seemed to become a shadow of himself, a white shadow. But Yusuf's face was clear and familiar, and there was a look of kindness for me in it.

"You should always pay attention to the unusual," he said. "A guard may get drunk and cause trouble, he may wound or kill someone in an affray, or be wounded or killed himself, he may rob someone or rape someone. These are usual things, unfortunately; the people we employ are of poor quality and not enough provision is made for their wages. But this Mario, he vanishes into thin air, in Calabria, far from home—he is Sicilian, of Palermo, that much we know, though it is all we know, for the moment at least."

I made no mention of that fleeting impression of Mario's face among the crowd of pilgrims at Bari, convinced as I was that I had been mistaken. "He may have met the woman of his dreams," I said. "Who knows?" This was frivolous, deliberately so, but I was suddenly weary of the lecturing he gave me, a weariness I dared not show openly but which I had felt more often of late.

As I had expected, he did not waste words on a reply. "And Lazar?" he said. "How did he take it?"

"He was far from pleased to go away empty-handed, and he made his displeasure plain. Perhaps he will do more for us, perhaps he will change sides."

Yusuf regarded me with his usual expression, quizzical, slightly sardonic. "If his friendship does not help us, his enmity cannot do us much harm. He is not necessary."

"Yet we have been paying him."

"The money was set aside for that purpose. If we spent only

when we were certain of return, our coffers would be always full. With or without Lazar, the Serbs will rise against their Byzantine masters—they make restless subjects."

I knew Yusuf was fond of me in his way and that he spoke with no unkind intention, his aim being always to instruct me in the realities of the palace administration. But it was not he who had made the difficult and dangerous journey he now dismissed as pointless. Adept at concealment when he had ends to serve, he took no pains to conceal from me that I was a means of serving those ends, that money and bearer had the same weight in the balance. A sudden resentment rose in me and I spoke to him on the spur of it. "Restless subjects, yes," I said. "Not like the Saracens of Sicily."

Nothing changed in Yusuf's posture but it was a different face that looked at me now, and before he spoke I felt the chill of his displeasure. "So you make our patience a reproach to us?"

"No, I did not mean that." Already I was regretting my temerity. "The rule of our King Roger is merciful and just, unlike that of Manuel Comnenus, and so there is no cause for his subjects to be restless, whether Moslem or Christian or Jew."

But this came too late. "You talk loosely, Thurstan," he said, "and that is because your mind is loose. My people have been loyal to the Norman King. This shows lack of spirit in your view? We should emulate the Serbs?"

"Lord, I did not think you would make this application of my words."

"A man should always think before speaking. How many times over how many years have I tried to instill this simple precept into you?"

"I meant only that the Serbs—"

"The Serbs are a fractious people. If they had no overlords they would fight among themselves. It is this quality in them that might make them useful to us in turning Manuel's thoughts from the invasion of Sicily. My people are different. Our ancestors took this island from the Greeks by conquest, and it was by conquest that our fathers lost it to the Normans. My father was still young when the last Arab city surrendered, Noto, the city of his birth. I was born in that same city five years later, born subject to the Norman rule. What is the experience of the father is in some sense the experience of the child. It is in the minds of all of us that we have been dispossessed. How could it be otherwise? But in these sixty years since the taking of Noto, not once have my people risen against the Christian ruler. You are a Norman, half of you at least. Do you think the Normans have more right to rule here than we had, that there is something in the soil or the soul of this island that makes it more suitable for Christians to reside in and govern?"

His eyes had taken on a light I saw in them rarely. "Answer me," he said.

"No," I said, "no," and this was a lie, for in my heart I did think so. "My lord, do not speak loudly. There are always people ready to listen." I was alarmed because he had raised his voice, a thing I could not remember him ever doing before, in this place of corners and corridors where listening people could hide, where anyone— domestics, attendants, messengers, guards—could be a spy.

"Not once," he repeated. "The King's Saracen foot soldiers are the most steadfast and loyal troops in the army. He knows it well—it is not for nothing that he forbids them to convert to Christianity. He trusts them more than he trusts his fellow Normans, he uses them in battle against his Christian vassals—these it is who rise against him, not us. This town you have just come from, who was it that defended the citadel of Bari against the combined forces of Pope and emperor for four weeks, when all others had deserted the King's cause? Was it the Christians?"

"No, lord. I was young when this happened, not yet twelve, but news of it came to us at Bernalda."

"Four weeks, fewer than five hundred men, all Moslems. Every man of them was hanged when the citadel was taken."

His hand had strayed to the cube of embroidered leather at his breast, where he kept the scroll with the names of God in it. "Not once," he said again, more quietly now. "And what is our reward? The land is given to the Christians."

"Some new allocations of the land there must be, when new rulers come," I said. "Our King respects the rights of all his subjects."

"You repeat the words you hear others say. There is something in you that persists, and it is endearing but also foolish, a wish for comfort, a wish to believe. Here in Palermo our people are privileged. The King has grown up among Arabs, he speaks our language, he prefers our company to that of the Frankish nobles, whom he finds boorish and ignorant, which, let it be said between us, they are. But who are these Arabs that surround the King?"

I took this for a rhetorical question and so attempted no answer. He was regarding me with less animosity now and I breathed more easily for it; he was formidable in his anger, there was such threat of harm in it.

"They are artists and philosophers and men of science, people of the court. I am not questioning the King's justice. He is just, unjust things are done in his name—is it so difficult for you to bring these things together in your mind? Go to Butera or Randazzo. Go to Noto, where I was born. See the colonies of Lombard emigrants there. Their numbers are swelling from month to month. They build their houses, they take over the land. They are encouraged in this by some who stand close in counsel to the King. The Arabs become serfs on the land they owned."

I did not reply at once to this, knowing that the Arabs kept slaves long before the Normans came, but it was as if Yusuf read this thought in my mind, for he said now, "There was oppression of Christians in the days of Arab rule, I do not deny it, but a Christian could still have title to land, legal title that was respected. Without the right to hold land, a people is reduced to nothing."

He fell silent and looked away from me, and I saw the rise and fall of his breathing. I looked down over the courtyard that lay below the window and saw a man in the royal livery of scarlet and gold with a hunting mastiff on a chain. It was a boarhound and half as high as he was. It was straining at the leash and the man's arm was wrenched with the force of it as he tried to lead it where it should go. Then two palace Saracens in bright green robes and turbans came out from the portico. They spoke with their faces close together and they were laughing and the silk of their robes gleamed in the sunshine. With their fluttering gestures they were like birds of paradise. It was the same courtyard where I had encountered Glycas, not long ago if one counted the days, but it seemed like another life—between that time and now lay my meeting with Alicia.

"It will not be so," I said. "The King has always dealt justly with his Moslem subjects."

"Do not deceive yourself. We are hated here. The failure of this crusade, the humiliation of the Franks in Syria, has made the hatred worse. Before many years there will be no land owned by Moslems in Sicily. I should not have spoken so to you, but your words provoked me, coming at a time when the wrongs suffered by the Moslems were uppermost in my mind. While you were away a cousin of mine by marriage, the son-in-law of my mother's brother, was killed at Vicari, on the land he used to own, by the son of the Lombard who now owns it. The connection with me was not close enough to prevent the expropriation, but it was close enough for them not to throw him off the land altogether—he remained as a bailiff. Seeing a Moslem serf being badly beaten by a son of the new owner, he protested and the young man stabbed him to death. I am applying to the courts but without much hope of success. The father is related to the Lombard clan of Sclavus and so very close to the Lombards in the Office of the Vice Chancellor. They will bring it in as self-defense. He never went armed, but of course they will find the weapon."

He looked directly at me and I thought I saw a suspicion of moistness in his eyes. "Five years ago," he said, "such a crime would have been punished, whoever the culprit. If the courts give us no satisfaction, what can we do? We must find other ways." There was no threat in his voice, only sadness, but it seemed to me that this young Lombard was destined not to survive his victim long. Yusuf was right in any case: five years ago the Lombard faction would not have dared to touch a man related to the Lord of the Diwan of Control, however distant the relation.

"How long can it last?" he said. "If they take the right to ownership of land, all other rights will go with it. Our King is beset with bad counselors. He rules a land where many races live close together. And with his crown he inherited the knowledge that the peace of his realm depends on the acquiescence of non-Christians to Christian rule. If he fails to keep that rule within bounds that the Moslems can accept, there will be civil war in Sicily. We too will become restless subjects like the Serbs." He was looking at me very closely now. "The Moslems cannot win such a war, it would be the end of us. But it would be an end long in coming—we would be a thorn in the flesh of the Norman kings for many years to come. You can help to prevent this, Thurstan. If the King makes me Lord Chamberlain, I will strive to advise him well, to nurture respect for the claims and the rights of all. You will help me, we will work together. We will take more Christians into the diwan, Latin and Greek, until no one can say it is one thing or another. Our scribes will copy in Latin and Greek as well as Arabic. You have a good head on your shoulders, when you care to use it, and you have a good heart. You will prosper if you keep by me. It is a mark of trust that I speak my mind to you in this way."

Indeed, he had never spoken to me in such a way before, and this in spite of the fact—but I was not to learn this till later—that he knew of my talk with Béroul in the tavern, knew I had kept it from him. I wonder now if he had some presentiment of evil that came masked as good: the Devil is well able to play such tricks. As he spoke he reached forward to take my hand, and I was moved by this, which I think he saw. If we had stopped there, I would have carried the warmth of it away with me. But even as our hands were still clasped together he said, "That is why I chose you. That is why I brought you here."

As I returned to my office, these words echoed in my mind. That was why he had picked me out, to be a representative Christian in the spectacle he was putting on—his douana, a model of races and creeds living in harmony. He was the lord of the douana: it was he who was the Purveyor, not I. It had not been my knowledge of Arabic or the good reports of my teachers; it had been my looks, my Norman ancestry, my Roman religion—attributes of the rulers . . .

No doubt I did him an injustice: he had appealed for my help in good faith, he had made me the hearer of dangerous words—a signal mark of trust in such a man. But I could not rid myself of the feeling that I was no more than an instrument to him, that I lived and breathed and was Thurstan Beauchamp to serve his advancement. And I forgot, in the injury to my pride, that his advancement meant also my own. The truth was—and this I knew even then—that the need for dignity was more present to me now that I had felt Alicia's hand on my head and heard her murmured words above me.

Stefanos was not there when I returned, and I supposed he was still engaged with the tailor. I sat at my table and began to busy myself with the papers there. These were royal renewals of privilege, originally written in Greek with a version in Arabic attached to them. It was my task to ensure that the translation reflected the meaning accurately. This was not so difficult as it might seem, since I had read a good number of such orders for renewal in my time at the Diwan of Control, and the form of words was always the same. Nevertheless it required some concentration, as the scribes occasionally made errors. And concentration, this morning, was lacking. I stared down at the first one, following the *arenga* with which they always began:

Since it is beholden on us zealously to guard the rights of the holy churches and keep them in peaceful state, we therefore order that the rights and privileges of the Abbey of San Filippo in the district of Corleone be renewed and tended for scrutiny so they may be confirmed by the power of our sublime Majesty . . .

My eyes lost sharpness, the words swam together; out of them, like a reflection of cloud on water, gathering and thinning and gathering again, came Alicia's face as I had seen it on the morning of our parting, the clear look of her eyes, their readiness to meet mine, as they seemed to do now from the page, the long fair hair falling loose about her face. Hair made even fairer, she had said, by the sun of Outremer, though she had allowed no touch of that sun on her skin, where the pure lily mingled with the flushed rose—no, that was wrong, a single flower, a pure white rose with a flush at the tips of the petals. Perhaps I could set this into verse, find an air to sing it by . . .

I was interrupted in this train of thought by the return of Stefanos, who told me that the tailor was waiting in an anteroom across the passage. We went together to see him, since he had more space there for the showing of his fabrics.

He had a boy with him to carry the pieces he had brought us to see—he would not have dreamed of carrying anything himself. Tailors in the palace employ were highly skilled in their trade and much favored. The King had a corpulent and imposing figure, and he spent freely on his dress and on those who fashioned it, and in this he was followed by the people of the court. All this had given the tailors an exaggerated idea of their own importance. They dressed in the height of fashion themselves, as if they were perambulating advertisements for their own handiwork, and put on all manner of airs and graces. This one was dressed in green velvet with an embroidered shirt that came high and was stiff in the collar so that it forced his chin up, giving him a look more condescending than ever. Seeing him thus, I surmised that this high neck would be soon the general fashion and I resolved to have two such shirts made for me. The tailor was inclined to be sulky, having learned from Stefanos who his clients were; it was clear that he felt it beneath him to make clothes for a band of ragged nomads.

Naturally, I paid no attention to this nonsense of his. I had clear ideas by now of what I wanted them to wear. I looked at the quality of the pieces he had brought, and their colors, and found both good. I explained to him the combination of black and red and silver I had in mind. I went into detail with him, particularly in regard to the women. They were to wear a close-fitting bodice of black sarsenet and a fine crimson damask for the long skirts, and these must be very low at the hips and cut in a curve, so as to expose the abdomen when they whirled to unwind the silver sashes. They would not be wearing undergarments and the lights would be set in the wall behind them, so that the lower parts of their bodies would be easily glimpsed through the thin stuff of the skirts. Then, if they went backwards onto their hands, as the Greek trader had seen them do, Holy Mother! I felt a loosening in my nether parts. My unruly imagination had brought about in my own loins the very stage of exaltation I was hoping to elicit in those of my royal master. And this so soon after my pure and worshipful musing on the Lady Alicia!

The shame of this did something to restore me to order, but I was glad when the interview with the tailor came to an end. He went to return his pieces to the storeroom, promising to take the measures that same afternoon, and I returned to my desk.

XII

However, I was not destined to go further with the royal renewals that morning. I had hardly returned when the doorkeeper came to announce a visitor, a man by the name of Leonardo Malfetta, who came on urgent business, or so he said. The doorkeeper was that same Sigismond who had caused trouble on the ship, but he smiled on me now and inclined his head. I asked after his family and told him to come to me if he heard anything about Mario and he said he would do so.

This Malfetta was a merchant, a Genoese, and he was already known to me slightly, because he had once done, or attempted to do, a favor to us by introducing some acrobats and rope walkers that he had brought from Naples. He had even parted with a sum in payment of their passage and their maintenance in Sicily. His idea had been to gain a favor in return from our diwan; he was seeking a concession to export the cotton and hemp that are cultivated at Giattini. He had failed in this, as the trade was in the hands of a company of merchants from Amalfi and there was a charter already in existence. His Neapolitan acrobats never appeared at court, and this had been by my decision. They were accomplished, certainly, but the time was not opportune, because Negro acrobats from Africa had performed for the King not very long before, and they had made a human pyramid of twelve persons and had also been rope walkers, so Malfetta's people had nothing new to offer. If they had been allowed to perform, even though he had met with refusal in the matter of the concession, Malfetta would probably have said nothing about the money he had spent, regarding it in the light of an investment for favors in the future. But in the circumstances he had felt justified in making a claim on us for reimbursement. This had been met but in part only, because the claim had been greatly exaggerated—one would have thought he had lavished a fortune on these poor acrobats from the streets of Naples. There had been dispute at the time, and at first I thought he had come to renew this and my heart sank.

Certainly he had dressed with care for the visit: red tiara-shaped silk cap with a jeweled clip, pale blue wide-sleeved silk gown slashed at the shoulders to show the embroidered linen of his tunic below. But this finery served only to emphasize the grimness and stiffness of his face, with its small, deep-set eyes and long nose and a mouth that was like a thin cut in a lemon. His two attendants he left outside the door, and came stalking in, no less arrogant for having been required to consign his sword to Sigismond before entering. He eyed Stefanos haughtily for a moment or two, then said, "My words are for you only, Signore."

Stefanos left without waiting to be asked, without glancing at Malfetta, saying to me that he had matters to attend to.

"Well," I said, "how can I be of service to you?"

"You permit a great deal from your clerk. He did not so much as give me good-day."

I said nothing to this. After a moment Malfetta allowed himself a smile, and a truly calamitous smile it was: he had a face not constructed for smiling, the features seeming to resent the call made on them, cracking painfully only when they could resist no more. "It is a trifling matter," he said. "I hardly like to trouble you with it, but I thought your help might save me time that could then be spent on more important things."

"Please be seated," I said, and I waited while he took the chair on the other side of the desk.

"Some months ago," he said, "I had occasion to borrow a sum of money. It was a time of temporary difficulty, from which I am now happily recovered. However, this man, this moneylender, is making trouble for me."

"What was the debt?"

"Five hundred ducats."

"Full silver?" I asked, and he nodded. It was a sizable sum. "A Jewish moneylender?"

"No, a Berber. His name is Zenega Waziri. Perhaps you know the man?"

"No, I do not know him." In fact I knew little of the Berbers of Palermo, other than that a good number had taken refuge here in recent years, having been driven from their lands by the Arabs.

Malfetta seemed disappointed. "If you knew him you would know what a scoundrel he is. He has that thick-lipped, flat-nosed look that some of them have. Negro blood there, without a doubt. He insists that I have not returned the money, when I have friends, men above suspicion, men of *rank*, who are ready to come forward and swear that they saw this money being handed back, principal and interest."

"And the paper, the contract that you drew up together at the time of borrowing the money? Waziri must have returned this to you at the time you repaid the debt. He should also have given you a note, dated and signed, to acknowledge the repayment."

"There is the rub, you see. I suppose I was distracted at the time. I must have had my mind on other things." He paused, shaking his head. "A man cannot be thinking about money every moment of his life, can he? Of course, Waziri, being a man without religion, does not understand this. We humans are midway on the ladder between angel and beast, so we are told. But it seems to me that there are ladders for every kind, and they each have their scales. Just as one beast may be superior to another, so it is with men. I would put Berbers on the lowest rung, along with Negroes. Let them fight, and let the loser fall down among the beasts."

It was his second reference to Negroes. He was a vindictive man and I wondered if the greater success of the Negro acrobats in outshining his Neapolitans had turned him against the race as a whole. His dislike for Berbers was easier to comprehend . . .

"So Waziri still has the contract, and you have nothing to show in proof of repayment?"

"That is so, unfortunately, yes."

"And now he is pressing you for the money?"

"He has no shame. He is hoping to get the money twice over."

"Well, I see the plight you are in, but I do not see how we can be of help to you. It is a matter for the courts."

Malfetta leaned forward. "That is precisely why I have come to you. The Douana of Control has the ear of the judges, everyone knows that—especially in cases to do with contested wills, disputed debts, and so forth. Now judges are as various as other men. There are some with a very barren notion of justice, basing everything on scraps of paper, not admitting as relevant the excellent witnesses, *Christian* witnesses, that a man of my standing is able to bring forward. There are others with a broader view, who will accept the word of a man of honor against that of pagan Negroes. The trouble is, we do not know whose court we will end in. I thought you might steer my case in the right direction."

I remained silent for some moments, not quite knowing how to reply. I had no intention of doing as he asked and squandering what influence we had on such a case. Five hundred ducats was a very considerable amount of money. This Waziri would be a man of substance if he could lend money on that scale. The Berbers kept together, there might be a family strong enough to cause trouble.

The pause had been long enough for Malfetta to work up a degree of virtuous indignation. "Think of it," he said. "It almost defies belief. A judge, professing to be a Christian of the Roman liturgy, will find in favor of a godless immigrant, ignoring the testimony of his own co-religionists! But it cannot endure long. This generation of vipers, these corrupt judges, will be swept away. People of the Latin rite are more and more numerous in Sicily, every day sees greater numbers."

"But surely these are immigrants too."

"Holy Mother of God, what are you saying? They are not immigrants, they are settlers. They are members of our community, people like us, people you can trust—in fact, I never have dealings with anyone else."

"Except when borrowing money."

"Our religion forbids the breeding of money. We leave that to baser creeds."

Malfetta was attempting smiles no more. His face bore a look of great sincerity. But sincerity is not to be trusted, I had learned that in my time at the Diwan of Control if I had learned nothing else: a man is never more sincere than when he earnestly wants to be believed. What would Yusuf do? He was still my model. He would engage Malfetta in discussion of a more general nature, reach some accord of opinion, part on amicable terms so that his good offices would be taken on trust without his needing to make assurances, then do nothing.

"In the Sicily of today," I said, "a judge should be of all religions or none. But I do not believe it is primarily a matter of religion. Judges are attentive to documents because documents have material existence and the law does not, so they save themselves from nullity by grasping one, like clutching at a straw in a sea of abstraction. It can be anything, a witness, a weapon, a wound. And proceeding from this . . ."

What had begun as a means of distracting him ended by engaging my interest: there was paradox in it, this importance of the object in a system so codified. "Even proof itself is thought of as weight or mass," I said. "We speak of the burden of proof, *onus probandi*, and this comes from the law of the Romans, which we have inherited. The weight of proving a controversial assertion falls on the shoulders of him who makes it. I would be interested to hear your opinion on this."

"It is Waziri who is making the controversial assertion," he said.

"No, excuse me, it is you. Waziri is simply demanding that you fulfill your agreement."

"But I have fulfilled it."

"Listen," I said, "a document is not a controversial assertion, and Waziri has the document."

"Ah, so we come back to that."

I think he saw that he was not getting far with me, for he now played what he clearly felt to be his winning card. "You owe me something, your douana."

"How is that?"

"Do you mean to say you have no memory of it? I hired a group of acrobats of phenomenal skill and brought them here at my own expense, thinking they might give entertainment to the court. I was greatly out of pocket in that business."

"Excuse me, you were not out of pocket. Your expenses were re-paid in reasonable measure. In the end, as I remember, you pro-fessed yourself satisfied."

"Well, one doesn't want to haggle, a man of my standing. After all, one is not a putter-on-of-shows."

I had not been greatly sympathetic to his cause before, but it was these last words that set me against him. So ill natured was he that he would belittle even the one he asked for favors. I said, "Was it you or another who haggled till we were all out of patience?"

"It is the pains I went to," he said. "I did not mind the losses to my purse."

"You suffered no losses to your purse."

"It was not the money that was important to me, it was the desire to be of service. That is all I ask in return, a gesture of goodwill. Of course, I would be ready to show my gratitude. Should we say one twentieth part of the debt?" He tried his smile again. "Depending, naturally, on the outcome of the hearing."

I now began to be heartily sick of this conversation. Why was I endlessly taken up with venal persons and malodorous concerns? How had it come about? The image of Alicia came to my mind. I thought of that moment of recognition, the moment she had looked at me and pronounced my name. If she could see me now, involved in this squalid talk of debts and favors, would she still think me so splendid?

"Malfetta," I said, "our diwan cannot be of practical help to you, but I can offer you some advice. It would be most unwise of you to let this matter come before a court. The judge will find it difficult to understand why you did not obtain the document of release from the creditor. He may well find it puzzling that you went accompanied by a number of friends when you repaid the debt. It is not common practice, is it?"

"I asked them to accompany me for fear of being robbed on the way. I was carrying a large sum of money."

"He may also think it strange that, if you were so accompanied, none of those with you thought to ask Waziri to render up the contract, they were all in the same state of distraction as yourself."

Malfetta was looking at me narrowly. "I do not like your tone," he said. "You appear to be doubting my word."

"No, what I am saying is that the judge is likely to doubt it. If he finds against you, you will have to pay the cost of the hearing as well as the debt, and any you call as witness will cut an extremely bad figure. You made a mistake in not making sure the contract was annulled. A man must pay for his mistakes."

Malfetta got to his feet. He was looking at me now with scowling displeasure, an expression much better suited than smiling to the general cast of his countenance. "Who is this judge that finds everything strange?" he said. "Is he a Berber? He does not exist, he is an invention of your own, you hide behind him to avoid doing me a service."

This was too much. I rose in my turn and stood looking across the table at him from my greater height. I said, "You think unwillingness to offend derives from fear? It is so with you because that is all the manners you have. But it is not so with me. Do you doubt it?"

He was silent; he would not go so far. Perhaps he was surprised by the fierceness of my looks and words. But I was ashamed now at having borne with him so long, and it was shame that kept me angry. I wanted to provoke him to a quarrel. "I have listened with patience to this tale of yours," I said, "but I will not tolerate your insults."

But he would not take me up on it, even under this imputation of falsehood, though there was murder in his eyes as he looked at me. "You will pay dearly for this," he said, and with that he went from the room, leaving me, after that rush of anger had abated, far from satisfied with myself. Once again I had failed to bear myself with the restraint that is proper in a servant of the state. I had made an enemy of Malfetta, and a bad enemy he might well prove to be. In fact, all I had succeeded in doing was to make the world more dangerous for me.

I felt the need to be alone for a while, in a place where no one would look for me. I went quickly down the stairs and out into the narrow uncovered passageway that follows the line of the outer wall and leads to a gate on the south side of the palace not much used and guarded by one man only, who raised the grid for me. I followed the bank of the rivulet that flows alongside the street of the Benedettini. The current ran fast still, though May was all but over, and there were martins flying low over the water. I came soon within sight of the Church of San Giovanni degli Eremiti, and I entered by the western door. It was cool inside and the light was muted. There was a scattering of people in the nave, some sitting, some kneeling. I went into the presbytery and from there entered the little courtyard, which also belongs to the mosque that adjoins the church, and which was a favorite place of mine. It is the only church in Palermo, and perhaps in all Sicily, that is joined in this way to a mosque. Our King had ordered it to be built alongside the mosque and ordained it so that Christian and Moslem could pass freely and without hindrance each to his own place of worship, and in this he had shown the wisdom and spirit of tolerance that made me proud to serve him. It was for this reason that I loved this church best of all those in Palermo. On the other side of it, that farthest from the mosque, there was an abbey of the Benedictines.

There was no one in the courtyard at this hour, and I sat in the shade of the portico for a little while till the peace of the place had worked on my spirits and Malfetta's baseness had receded to that region where such qualities had their dwelling, a region I always tried to feel was far distant, though knowing full well that it lay round any corner.

With recovered calm I began again to think of Alicia, of our meeting and our talk together. Thoughts of her came always in the same way, from a misty surface, the mist rent asunder by little shocks of memory, and always with a sense in me of pleasurable helplessness, of being subjugated by the detail of it, her eyes, her smile, a gesture she had that I had known in the girl and found again in the woman, a way of touching her hair at the temple above the right ear, very lightly, as if she were herself, for that moment, distracted by some thought from the past. To these memories of her that were real, I added others that could not be so: the shape of her foot, the texture of the skin at the nape of her neck, invented memories, but they did not come accompanied by desire, they were elements of her wondrous existence, they seemed like the proof of it. The more fully I could create her in my mind, the more of substance I could give her, the more I could believe that we would meet again.

Did she wait for this with an eagerness equal to mine? I wanted to believe this, but how could I know? I knew she had loved me once, I could not be wrong in that. At fourteen she had loved me, she had lived for the stolen times of our meetings, as I had, the clasped hands, the kisses that stayed warm on our lips, the longing to touch more closely, always denied. I would have braved any danger for her, gone forth to confront dragons or seek a new Grail.

That was a fever we shared. But it was long years ago, and much had changed. Then we were equals, children of noble families sent away to learn what we needed to learn for the maintaining of our station. She was born to wider estates than I, so much I already knew. But as a knight I could have hoped to become rich; for one who was bold and skilled in the lists there were prizes to be won; an opponent unhorsed in single combat would forfeit to the victor charger and trappings and armor. There were merchants who dealt only in these and would pay well for them. Some years of traveling from tourney to tourney and I could have amassed enough wealth, taken service with a great lord, been granted a fief to add to the dowry lands of my bride, my Alicia . . .

So I sat there, mazed in that eternal contradiction of humankind, regret for the loss of what was never possessed. Tibald had come and carried her off to Jerusalem. When I was still two years from knighthood and the triumphs of the joust, she had lived as his wife in the fabled land of Outremer. Now she was free, but we were not equals now: she was an heiress, her family was among the richest in Apulia—and I, what was I? Thurstan Beauchamp, a man of public spectacles and private bribes, living on a palace stipend. What had I to offer? A man could not go to a lady such as she with for only quality the need to be rescued.

These things I knew. And yet, perversely, sitting there on my narrow stone bench against the wall in the deserted courtyard, I felt the stirring of hope within me. I was not yet thirty years old. If Yusuf rose in the King's favor, I would rise with him. He wished me well, he would not forget me; there was every chance that I would come into his place at the Diwan of Control. This too was a way of amassing wealth, though not the way I would have chosen.

But hope is a hound that once unleashed can change its nature even as it leaps. Perhaps there was another way. If Alicia and I could find again the feeling that once we had, perhaps we could recover the selves we once had too and the prospects that had belonged to those selves. We could help each other in this. There was no bar to my knighthood—I was descended from the Norman nobility of England; nor was there any bar to Alicia having the man of her choice. Then I could offer more than my need of rescue: I could be a rescuer in my turn. When she had spoken of Ascalon and the need to defend the land she held against the infidel, I had seen myself on a war horse, in full splendor of arms, at the gallop. Of course, Yusuf, on whom I so much depended, was an infidel too . . .

At once exhilarated and confused by these thoughts, I rose from my bench with the intention of retracing my steps through the church and returning to the diwan and my scrutiny of the royal renewals. But even as I got to my feet I saw a man in monastic habit come out into the courtyard just as I had done. After a moment I recognized him. It was Gerbert, a Benedictine, who had come recently to Palermo as abbot at the Monastery of San Salvatore. He waited there some short while and was joined by another, whom I knew slightly better, having met him on occasion, a Lombard of the minor nobility named Atenulf, a chamberlain in the Royal Diwan, of considerable influence, as it was said. The two men took some paces, then stopped and stood together in what seemed close conversation. They glanced across the courtyard from time to time, but I was still in the shadow of the portico, and standing close against the wall, and so I think they did not see me.

Since I had not come forth from my place at once, I was unwilling to do so now because of the seeming closeness of their talk. They would think I had been hiding there so as to observe them, and this suspicion would not have been unfounded; the palace service made spies of all who worked within it, and there was something in this colloquy that roused my curiosity. I wondered whether they had met by chance, and what might have brought them here. I thought Gerbert might have come to visit the Benedictine abbey nearby. Perhaps Atenulf came to this church for his private devotions. But it had not looked like a chance meeting . . .

They stayed in talk for some minutes, then withdrew once more into the church, the Benedictine entering a little earlier than his companion. I waited some while longer, then did the same. There was no sign of either man in the body of the church.

Speculations about this meeting continued in my mind as I made my way back to the diwan, but they did not long survive my arrival there. Stefanos was waiting for me, and the tailor, very peevish-looking now, was at his side.

"They will not have it," he said.

"Who is it that you are speaking of?"

"They, the dancers. They will not let themselves be touched.

The tailor went there to take the measures. He says that if he had not started back she would have clawed him."

"Who? No, no need to tell me, I know who. That one has been a source of trouble to me since I first set eyes on her."

Immediately upon saying this I was conscious of some slight confusion, which I did not myself altogether understand, and it was not lessened by the knowledge that Stefanos had his eyes closely upon me. He is a mild man, as I have said, but there is not much that escapes his notice, and he is fond of me, as also his wife Maria, and that makes him notice all the more.

"Indeed, yes" was all he said now, but I seemed to detect some extra significance in the inflection of his words.

"She was the worst," the tailor said, "but they were all three much the same, ridiculous creatures, I could not get near any of them, they seemed to think I wanted to put my hand up their skirts, what an idea, I have better things to do. The men just laughed."

"Perhaps they did not want to give the men cause for jealousy," Stefanos said. "They are simple people."

"But the worst one," I said, "she does not belong to either of the men."

"Does she not?"

"You know quite well she does not." I had a sudden memory of the white birds, that strange desolate wailing, Sigismond's face as he fought for breath, Nesrin's eyes on me, attentive, dispassionate. "She wanted a chamber for herself, did she not?"

"I would like to say that I should never have been put to such a task," the tailor said. "I am His Majesty's second wardrobe attendant and the first is old now, his hands shake, it will not be long before I am stepping into his shoes. I tried only at the shoulders and waist, I did not embark on the hips or bosom, and would not do so now for any inducement, even if you promised me an armed guard."

"We will have to get a woman to come and do it," I said. "We cannot let them appear in the rags they are wearing now."

It was a practical solution, but it overlaid a vast astonishment on my part. These women had tramped the roads of Asia and Europe, dancing for men who clustered closely round them. Time and again they had revealed their bodies to strangers, either openly or by enticing suggestion. Yet they would not permit a tailor to lay the lightest of touches on them. Could this fierceness be called chastity? A challenge it would be for a man to soften it . . . "This our world is full of marvels," I said to Stefanos. "You find a dressmaker. I will have to go with her, I suppose, to calm things down."

When I got there with the woman it was to find all five of them grouped together outside their quarters in what had been the stable yard, talking eagerly together in the sunshine. Nesrin was in the midst. It had been almost a month since I had seen her last, but it seemed a much shorter time, though I did not know why this should be so.

Before the seamstress started her work I wanted to speak to them, to tell them that they should not be troublesome or difficult as they had been with the tailor, but should try to help things forward, as this would make everything easier and work to their advantage. They would be performing at the court, before King Roger himself, and this would be a great honor, one they would be able to relate to their children in time to come.

I spoke slowly, in Greek as simple as I could make it, and they listened, or appeared to, though how much they understood I could not tell. Only Nesrin looked at me as I spoke; the others kept their faces turned from me, both the men and the women. They wore the expression I remembered from before in my dealings with them, somber and brooding, not defiant or even indifferent, simply the look of their faces in repose. She, on the other hand, looked continuously and intently at me, but not really as listening to my words, more as simply watching me while I talked, and this was strangely unsettling to me and impeded the ordering of my thoughts. Twice she smiled, not broadly but sufficiently to show the edges of her teeth, and I wondered even as I spoke what she did to keep them so white in the wandering conditions of her life, and these thoughts too made me falter a little in my speech, as did the fact that her smiles did not come at points that were intended by me to cause mirth—nothing of what I said was intended to cause mirth—so I had the feeling that it was something in me, in my face or person or manner of speaking, that caused her to smile.

However, I said the words I had in mind, stressing the need for obedience and good behavior, adding as further inducement that in addition to the very generous payment they had been promised they would be allowed to keep the fine and costly clothes for which they were about to be measured. Then I gestured to the dressmaker to begin with her measuring rule.

I had intended to quit the scene immediately after making my speech, but now I decided that it might be better to remain for a while so as to assure myself that everything proceeded in a proper fashion. Nesrin was the first to come forward and present herself—in all my experience of her she was always first or last or loudest or quietest. But I was not prepared for the way she behaved now.

As she turned this way or that, or held still, in accordance with the wishes of the dressmaker, she continued to look at me, sometimes full in the face and boldly, sometimes glancing over her shoulder with a stately movement of the neck. Sometimes she presented her back, turning her head from side to side with a luxurious shrugging movement of the shoulders, as if, though for the moment she could not see me, she was well aware that I was seeing her. This taking of the measurements she turned into a sort of dance, not for my entertainment but for the entertainment of the others, a mockery of my solemn words of earlier: she had smiled, now she danced, and both meant the same thing.

And the dance was protracted, for she sometimes went contrary to the wishes of the dressmaker, though without once stepping beyond the reach of the woman's arm. Sometimes, as I watched, she performed movements in that stained and tawdry dress of hers that no dressmaker would ever dream of requiring, a subtle sway of the hips, an eel-like wriggling motion, a proud pressing back of the shoulders that brought into prominence the shape of her breasts, other, slighter motions, a slightness almost miraculous in view of the charge of suggestion they carried, at least to the sinful soul of the Thurstan who watched them, who knew full well by this time that he should not be lingering there.

No, I should not have stayed to give countenance to this insolence of hers, but I was captivated, enthralled. There was defiance and self-love and comedy and provocation in this dancing, and it held the attention of all: even the kneeling dressmaker, though impatient at first, was smiling now. The two men made low-pitched exclamations and laughed together. Some laughter came also from the women, but for all that they were both watching me closely, and under this combined regard of theirs I knew myself suddenly for the victim of a conspiracy. The women were leagued against me and the men enlisted as spectators. I was being mocked for the secret desires of my heart and the pompous words of my mouth. And even as I felt this mockery and saw the way she swayed her body and glanced down at herself, clear as it was that she sought to tease me and ensnare my eyes and make naught of the words I had spoken, even so I could not prevent a heat spreading through me, seeing her suppleness, thinking what it might be like to lie between her thighs. I felt the heat in my face also and was put in a sudden fear that it might betray me, so without more ado I left, taking care to keep a grave face and avoid all appearance of discomfiture or haste. In spite of this, I thought I heard laughter continuing behind me.

Yes, to my shame I will confess to this consuming carnality and at such a time—it was the untimeliness that made it shameful. I was young, venery was often in my mind, my member was unruly—I would not have taken myself to task for any casual rearing-up. But this had come so soon after my high resolve to be worthy of Alicia, to be her knight, with the knighthood she had conferred on me through that lingering touch on my head. Twice already that day I had failed her, and it was only midafternoon. There and then, as I started back to my room, I resolved to visit the Tiraz that evening and spend some time with Sara, thereby achieving peace of the senses, for a while at least. Fornication was a sin but it was also a practical solution, and I was inclined to regard it as true of ethics what Cicero said of mathematics when he praised his fellow Romans, as opposed to the philosophizing Greeks, for confining themselves to the domain of useful application. Though this of course dismisses Greek philosophy almost in its entirety, which could hardly have been Cicero's intention. Besides, though I had found no doctrine to support me, I felt in my heart that, knowing how strong was the element of fire in me, God would be less offended by my sin than by that of one who sins coldly. He would know that I aspired to the good, that my true nature was worshipful. He would not want me to be tormented by unchaste thoughts about a little wildcat from Ararat who did nothing but make game of me.

XIII

As it happened, I did not return to my desk that day after all. The afternoon was well advanced, and I felt a certain reluctance to face the questions Stefanos would be likely to ask about the way the measuring had gone. I decided on another visit to the Royal Chapel. The mosaics always drew me, and I had not seen Demetrius since leaving for Calabria; we had parted on strained terms, and I wanted to mend the friendship between us. Next day was the fortieth after Easter, the day of our Lord's Ascension. There had been word that the King himself would be attending the liturgy, which he was accustomed to do on that day, to mark his own ascension to the throne and give thanks for the divine grace and favor by which he had been appointed God's deputy on earth. It would be his first appearance in public since the death of his son and would come after twenty days of mourning, during which no one outside of the royal apartments had looked on his face. He would come early, as was his habit, with the rising of the sun to dress him in splendor, and the chapel would be made ready for him.

It was an afternoon of bright sunshine, cloudless, with none of the haze yet that would come with summer. The sun was low in the sky and its rays shone directly into my eyes as I approached the chapel; I could hardly make out the guard at the entrance but he knew me and let me pass. Inside, at first, I could see nothing. Sight was restored in glimmers and flashes: the glint of gold in the mosaics of the apse, the light that gleamed on the tresses of the Magdalen and made a glory around her head. As I drew nearer to the Sanctuary, an errant ray ran down one column of the Virgin's throne and a shaft like a spear pierced the palm of Christ's hand. The Magdalene's head was joined in glory by this radiance to the hand of the Pantocrator, and I took this as a message to me, because she was redeemed from her sinful life by the compassion of Christ and in this I saw a promise that I would be given the grace to transcend such unbridled thoughts as those of earlier that day during the dance of the measurements.

My sight was fully restored now, and this I felt to be owing as much to my hope of salvation as to the habituation of my eyes. I could feel the gaze on me of other eyes, eyes from the dome where Christ looked down on me, the eyes of the angels and archangels that encircled him, set in their disk of gold with the words of abiding power wreathed among them: *The sky is my throne, the earth my footstool.*

I heard a series of light tapping sounds from somewhere ahead of me, which I supposed were caused by someone at work there, though they ceased suddenly and were not resumed. There was no sign of Demetrius, but two of his people were working together on the arcade of the nave on the north side; they were on a platform slung from the ceiling, and they had a lamp on either side and mirrors arranged to give them a stronger light. They were working on the lowermost coil of the Serpent and the base of the Tree where it widens. In the lamplight the Fruit glittered red and gold and it was easy to see why God's wrath was risked for it. By a trick of reflection from one of the mirrors I saw, in a narrow band of light, the cheated Esau stretching his bow to shoot a white dove.

Both of the men working there glanced down at me at the same moment, perhaps hearing my steps or seeing some movement of my shadow, but now I myself heard steps, and as I came into the crossing I saw Abbot Gerbert, whom I had watched earlier that day in talk with Atenulf, emerge from the southern chapel, and with him two others unknown to me, both in monastic habit. As they came into the Sanctuary they made shadows that shifted in a way that seemed strange to me without my knowing why, but this I took for some trick that the light was playing; mirror reflections and shadows were shifting constantly there.

In any case it was an impression that passed quickly, because Gerbert paused to greet me and I was both surprised and gratified to discover that he knew who I was, a churchman of such rank—there were those who spoke of him as soon to be appointed Rector of the Papal Enclave of Benevento, and he must therefore have friends at the Roman Curia. It was the more flattering as he had not been long in Palermo and as far as I knew had had no dealings with the Diwan of Control, though of course there were some who came there without my knowing.

He spoke in German to his companions, mentioning my name and, as I supposed, also the place I held, and they inclined their heads. "These are two from the community of Groze on the Moselle, where I spent many years as a monk," he said. "I brought them to see the wonderful work that is being done here so they can tell their brothers of it when they return, which is soon now. They had hoped to celebrate our Lord's Ascension in the royal presence before leaving, and I had obtained permission for them, but it was not to be."

"Why is that?"

"You have not heard?" He looked at me with raised eyebrows. "There has been a change. His Majesty will not be attending the liturgy. He leaves early tomorrow for Troina, where there is a dispute over the investiture of the Bishop that urgently needs his presence. You were not told of this?"

"No."

"We knew of it some hours ago. Perhaps the douana in which you serve omitted to inform you. You should come to work for us in the Office of the Capellanus, we would know how to value you."

It was said lightly enough, and the words were accompanied by a smile, but there was something disquieting in it that remained with me after they had passed and moved away down the nave toward the west door. He had taken good care to let me see his surprise . . .

Still thinking of this, I took some steps forward. I was standing now at the center of the Sanctuary, looking toward the northern chapel at the arched alcove of the King's loge, set high in the inner wall, where he sat when he came to hear the liturgy, screened from the view of those below by the marble wall of the balustrade. None would see him arrive here and none would see him leave; he came from within the palace by means of the covered gallery that led from his apartments. Once again I tried to bring the King's life to my mind, and this time, perhaps because I was alone there and close below his viewing place and surrounded by the emblems of his glory and majesty, I succeeded better. He would approach by the covered passage, which was narrow, too narrow to admit anyone to walk at his side—those favored would walk behind him. Once seated there, he would see the images of his kingship on every hand. I raised my head to look up at the vault as he would see it, the scene of the Ascension, the Apotheosis of Christ, to which his own destiny as earthly ruler was linked. Glancing to his left, toward the eastern wall of the chapel, he would see the standing figure of the Virgin and Child, Guardians and Protectors. Looking straight before him across the nave toward the southern chapel . . . But here my attention was distracted. I was again aware of moving shadows on the south side of the crossing, a rapid flitting that passed over the marble of the floor like a bird's wings or faint ripples on the surface of water.

So strong was this sense of movement that I turned to look back down the nave, as if in expectation of figures approaching, but there was no one. And in that brief time of looking away all had again become still. The shadows lay over the marble, unmoving; all was calm and golden. Then I was lost amid the paths of light and stood there for a time I did not measure. It was the sound of hammering that roused me from this: there was a man standing on a plank laid across two trestles and driving a nail into a joint of the wall on a part of the nave arcade where no mosaic had been laid yet, so as to make a firm base for the mortar. I called up to the two who were working on the platform above me, asking them where I could find Demetrius, but the hammering was loud and they did not hear. I thought that if he were anywhere there at all he would be in the workshop alongside the chapel, and it was here that I found him, supervising the preparation of the mortar that was to be applied to the section of the wall where the man was driving in the nails.

He greeted me in friendly fashion, with no sign of ill feeling. I asked him if he knew that the King's plans had changed and he said that yes, he had been told, not more than an hour before. "It was because I learned of this," he said, "that I set the fellow on to drive in the nails. Otherwise there is too much dust, and it takes too long for the air to clear, and the dust clings to the pieces and takes from their luster. I did not wish my lord the King to have a bad impression of our work when he came to hear the liturgy."

I seemed to detect something almost of sarcasm in his tone, though I might have been mistaken in this. "The man driving in the nails," I said, "is he one of the newcomers?"

"He is one of those that have come now, but he is only employed to make the frame."

"You will lay the mortar this evening then?"

"Yes, we will have short hours of sleep tonight. We must have the bed ready for the setting of the pieces by early morning. It is the scene of the building of the Tower of Babel on the arcade of the nave. We will take it by stages, as always; tomorrow will be the beginning. Since the King will not be present, we have leave for our work to continue through the day."

"It will take many days, will it not? I am happy to think that you will stay in Palermo for the time that is needed."

"Well, there are figures in it, and that needs more changes of color in a lesser space. There are the workmen at their tasks of building, there are people watching, grouped together." He smiled and widened his eyes as he did so, a habit I had always found engaging in him, seeming to hint at an exciting prospect suddenly perceived. "It will be the last thing before we go. To be frank with you, now that I have had time to reflect, I will not be sorry to leave Sicily. We are not welcome here. The moment I step outside these walls, I cease to be Karamides an artist in mosaic, I become Karamides a

Byzantine sailor taking part in the siege of Corfù, an island formerly belonging by divine right to the Byzantine empire, now by divine right belonging to the Kingdom of Sicily."

"It should surprise no one that there is hostility to the Byzantine," I said, "in view of the imperial edicts you send out from Constantinople denigrating our King." These words came stiffly from me in spite of my wish for ease between us; I had not liked the way he spoke of divine right as if it belonged to both and therefore to neither, when anyone who looked at a map could see that the possession of Corfù was necessary to Sicily for control of the Adriatic.

His smile had gone now, and he shook his head as he looked at me. "What edicts are these that I send out from Constantinople while fully occupied with the mosaics in Palermo?"

"The latest was only some months ago. Our good Roger is called a dragon belching fire, the common enemy of all Christians, an illegal occupier of the land of Sicily."

"And what is that to you or me? How do we enter into it? Thurstan, think what an absurd and terrible thing it is to blame a whole people for everything that is done or said in their name. By that reasoning, I, Demetrius Karamides, am to blame for the miserable failure of this latest crusade, because the Emperor of the Byzantines did not provision the Franks generously enough in their passage through his lands, and the country people of Konya charged too much for their chickens or hid away their grain, whereas the true blame lies in the arrogance and stupidity of the crusaders themselves."

Outrage came to my rescue at these scornful words of his, diverting me from the suspicion that I was having the worst of the argument. "I am not surprised you find the streets of Palermo dangerous," I said. "If these are the sentiments you give voice to when you go abroad, you are lucky not to have been hanged from the nearest tree. The Crusade was blessed by the Pope, it was preached by that great man of God Bernard of Clairvaux. Those who took the cross were ardent to defend the holy places."

"Ardor comes in various forms." His dark and heavy-lidded eyes were regarding me with a patience that seemed almost sorrowful, almost like martyrdom, and this annoyed me further. "You know well," he said, "that many were possessed by ardor of a different kind, and that was to get their hands on as much land as possible. But however that may be, blessing and preaching and ardor do not save us from stupidity and arrogance in the conduct of wars, nor do they save us from defeat."

I could find no very convincing argument to counter this: that there had been a defeat, and a catastrophic one, was undeniable. "It is true that nothing much was achieved," I said.

"Nothing at all was achieved and many thousands died in the course of not achieving it. For a disaster on that scale, someone to blame must urgently be found, and they found it in the Empire of the East, a vast extent of territory counting many peoples and languages."

It was obstinacy now that kept me arguing with him. "You cannot deny that you formed an alliance with the Turk against your fellow Christians."

"I did not ally myself with any Turks—I do not know any Turks. I was here in the Royal Chapel, working on the Pentecost vault. Fellow Christians, did you say? It is not two years since your King Roger took Corfù. What was the first thing he did after taking it? He raided Thebes, a city inhabited by his fellow Christians, and carried off hundreds of silk workers to help the silk industry of Palermo."

Hearing this, I thought of Sara and her welcoming plumpness, and I felt some shame that this was all that the ravishment seemed immediately to mean to me.

"After that it was Corinth," Demetrius said. "A prosperous city, densely populated with fellow Christians. Corinth was sacked and all her treasures taken back to Corfù. It was obvious to Manuel Comnenus—it was obvious to everyone—that Roger intended to use Corfù as a base for the further raids. It was fear of this that drove Byzantium into the arms of the sultan. Now tell me, if Manuel betrayed his fellow Christians, what did Roger do? Which is the enemy of Christendom? Or, putting it another way, who has most right to Corfù?"

He smiled again and reached forward with his left hand and took the forearm of my right. "The same question, the same answer," he said. "We are friends, we can speak frankly. You have a soul, Thurstan. I have seen the way you look at the mosaics. I am older than you by a dozen years, but we are the same, though you may not know it yet. We do not live by the words of kings or emperors. I am Demetrius Karamides, I made the mosaics in the Royal Chapel of Palermo, those of the apse and the Sanctuary and the crossing and the chapels. There are no mosaics more beautiful anywhere. I did not make them in homage to your king. They will still be here when Roger and Manuel are dust, and all the generations of their descendants. Why should it matter to me who owns Corfù?"

I looked at him in silent wonder for some moments. He was not joking; he was not speaking with the defiance of one soon to leave. He really did not care, and this was something I could scarcely understand, not to put first, before all other things, the loyalty to those set in authority over us, not wish to see them triumphant and so to triumph with them. I remembered now his contempt for those who would take his place, but it had been for their skills, and because he was being supplanted, not because it was Franks who were ousting him. He would not change his style of dress or the cut of his beard so as to pass unnoticed in the streets, not out of patriotic feeling as I had supposed and always admired in him, but simply because these were things that belonged to him, they were himself—he brought everything back to himself. He did not care who owned Corfù, he did not care whose banners flew there! He had no devotion, no spirit of service. I felt pity for him at that moment, as if he lacked some limb and was condemned to hobble through the world instead of walking. But this pity lasted scarcely longer than the time it takes to draw a breath. The demon of envy that lies always in ambush struck me and pierced me and I thought suddenly of that Filippo who in the twelfth year had set his face against the waiting ship, and then I thought of Nesrin and how she turned in the dance. I strove to put these thoughts away, because I knew them for corruption. "You are wrong," I said. "We are not the same, you and I. I serve the King my master and hope for his greater glory. Corfù belongs to the Kingdom of Sicily by lawful title."

He shrugged slightly but said nothing, and I saw that this too, our sameness or our difference, did not matter to him one way or the other. He reached and took up a handful of the tesserae that lay on a trestle beside him. They were small cubes of silvered glass and when he let them fall again into the tray, pouring them from tilted palm, they caught the light in falling and made a cascade that seemed unbroken. "Silver is used for the light that comes from Christ," he said. "It gives white reflections of great intensity. It is used for the arms of the Cross, and for the halo. Angels also may have silver halos, but no other figure may have them. Silver pieces can be used for the shine of weapons, they can be used to heighten the effect of other colors, especially the blues and grays." He took up another handful and let it fall again. "Yes, silver has various uses. Without the silver our work would show much less. But in my palm, or in the tray, the pieces are all the same. No one can see the form that will be by studying the pieces, no, not if he spent all his life in the study."

It was hot here, in the long narrow rectangle of the workshop. The shutters were open but the walls were of brick and held the heat of the day. There was a slight vapor in the air: the resin that was to form the first layer of the bed had been heated to make it more adhesive and easier to spread. Dust from the powdered stone they were to use to strengthen the mortar hung in the air between the beaten earth floor and the raftered ceiling. Looking up, I saw a flutter of wings: some small bird that had entered through a window and did not find the way out.

"You will come to it, sooner or later," he said. "There may be some, even many, who fulfill their own needs by serving another's, but you are not of that company. Take the lesson from the mosaic. There is one true assembly of these pieces into the shape that is needed. Whether they are gold or silver or marble or glass or mother-of-pearl, they will be set in such a way as to have a meaning in the form and to catch the light. And that will be their only setting, because the one who puts his thumb on the pieces and sets them into the bed will tilt them just a little this way or that; no one can ever repeat the thumbprint, no one can ever catch again the same effects of light, not even the one who set them. Who can remember all the marks of his thumb?"

It was on this note we parted, amicably enough, though without my being able to utter the words of reconciliation I think he was hoping for. He was like Yusuf: he wanted always to be teaching, and to hear the thanks of the student. Mohammed also. Perhaps there was something about me, something of which I was not aware, that brought this out in them. I promised to come to the chapel again soon to see the progress that was made on the Tower of Babel. Some of the things he had said that afternoon seemed unnatural and perverse to me, and even contradictory: he too served an exacting master, more exacting than the King. But his words about form and light and the look of his face as he poured the silver pieces from his palm, these lodged in my mind. They are there still.

XIV

THE KING'S DEPARTURE meant that the Anatolians I had brought from Calabria had to be kept longer than expected— we were to have asked permission for them to perform as soon as the clothes were ready. In fact, the King stayed away from Palermo for more than a month, journeying on from Troina to Messina and after some days taking ship for Salerno, where a long-running dispute as to the status of the Papal Enclave there and the prerogatives of the Pope in ecclesiastical appointments had now broken out more violently. Relations between King Roger and the Roman Curia were far from cordial at this time. Our King was insisting on his right to appoint bishops and so questioning the Pope's ecclesiastical jurisdiction in Sicily. Until this issue was settled, there was no hope that Pope Eugenius would give his formal recognition of Roger's kingship.

During this time of the King's absence, I saw little of the troupe, either the men or the women; in fact, I saw them only twice. They had been given leave to go out into the town, but strictly forbidden to dance or play in public: it was essential that the court should be the first to see them, essential that the element of newness should be kept. This I made clear to them. Unthinkable, I said, that our King Roger should come second to some idle, gaping folk at a street corner. They had money enough, they could come and go as they pleased, with only this one condition; if they disobeyed in this they would be sent packing and this great opportunity lost to them forever.

In making this speech I took good care to keep my eyes turned away from Nesrin, feeling sure she would seek to undermine my words in some way. Still on my mind was the discomfiture of the previous occasion, the dance of the measurements, the way the men had laughed together, something steady and noticing in the regard of the two women. All this confirmed me in the belief that there had been talk of me among them, talk of a certain kind. And this in its turn made me feel sure that my weakness had been noticed, that my face had given me away.

If true it was a serious lapse on my part, or so at least I regarded it, not just a weakness of the flesh. It had been my training, and it was required in much of the work I did, to remain impassive in my dealings with people, not to give any indication of feeling. This principle of concealment Yusuf had patiently schooled me in—he was himself a perfect example of it. In his kindness he had persisted, though I was not a good pupil, I was too quick-tempered, it was always too easy to read my feelings by the look of my eyes and mouth. It was a fault in me, and I was conscious of it, and I felt that my composure had not been proof against that triple assault, the mockery, the seducing movements, the scrutiny of the others. And besides, whatever my face may have shown, certain it was that I had stayed there, I had watched her . . .

The truth was that the girl still ran in my mind, as she had done from the beginning, not just the movements of her body in the dance but the look of her face, the cheekbones that lay so close below the skin, the narrow eyes with their upward slant, the suffering of the mouth, a suffering dissolved in mischief when she smiled. And this despite all my hope in Alicia, the wonder of our meeting, my resolve to prove worthy of her and of the regard in which she had once held me. But owing to some defect of nature in me, the higher thought did not cast out the lower. It may be as Guilbert of Nogent somewhere asserts, that the reviewing of our faults, an activity we feel to be virtuous, can sometimes be a snare laid for us by the Evil One, who tempts us to think we are resolving to make amends when what we are really doing, under cover of piety, is dwelling upon the pleasure of the sin.

All this was very present to my mind as I spoke to them, as I avoided meeting Nesrin's eyes. I repeated everything several times, speaking slowly and emphasizing the words. They could go out and see the wonders of Palermo—and wonders they would be, I told them, after the wretched places they had seen up to now. They must keep together as far as they could and they must promise not to dance or make music—I kept coming back to this. To my mind they were primitive people, living the days as they came, not looking far ahead; I was afraid they would yield to the passing lure of coin.

"Naturally," I said, "we will trust your word. But to make sure you do not forget, you will be accompanied by a man of trust from our diwan. Do not try to elude him, because we would take that to mean that you have broken your promise, and in that case you would not be allowed to perform before the King, you would not receive the gold dinars, you would not be permitted to keep the new clothes."

"This one with us is man or woman?"

"Why, a man, of course," I said, finally obliged to meet her eyes.

"And he follow us everywhere?"

"Yes. Well, of course, not when—"

"He follow us into the bushes?"

Everyone laughed at this. Seeing this laughter, and Nesrin's falsely serious face, I had a sudden strong impulse to laughter myself, which I overcame for the sake of dignity, but only in precarious fashion—so much so that I judged it better to retire without adding more words.

On the following day something happened that drove all other thoughts from my mind. It was midmorning when Yusuf sent for me, at a time when Stefanos and I were engaged together on the tax registers of the Royal Demesne in western Sicily. It was a secretary of Yusuf's who came with the summons, a palace eunuch named Ibrahim. I found Yusuf in his private cabinet at a littered desk, and he motioned me to be seated across from him.

"We have had a request of an unusual kind," he said, and he looked at me with his head tilted a little to one side, as if he were considering me in some new light altogether. "It has come from the Diwan of the Lord Chancellor. They have asked that you be given leave to join a hunting party at Favara."

"But how can that be?" I said, made stupid by amazement. "It must be a mistake." Favara! It was a place of resort for the King himself, or those in his favor, or for visitors he wished to please, not for servants of his administration. I had ridden past the gates of the palace of Favara, but I had never set foot inside.

"I do not know how it can be," Yusuf said. "I thought it possible you might know. But there is no mistake, the invitation has been confirmed. It is for the middle days of July." He was looking at me intently and rather coldly, as I thought. The dark eyes, luminous and unblinking in that narrow face, had long been trained to note and question; they were difficult to meet with composure now, because in this brief interval of time it had come to me like a shaft of light who it was that might have brought this invitation about. "But the King is away from Palermo," I said, more to gain time than for any other reason, so as to master my quickened breathing and keep it from his notice.

He waited before replying, his eyes still upon me. "That is what makes it even more unusual. It seems that this was arranged in advance, before the King left. The hunting party is headed by Bertrand of Bonneval."

This was a nephew of the Count of Conversano. I knew his name and parentage but little more, beyond the fact that the family had ties with Robert of Selby, the King's Chancellor.

"Do you have any acquaintance with this Bertrand?"

"No, none at all."

"We have no list as yet of those who will be making up the party, but we will have one soon. I have set Nicholas to find out."

I nodded. Whenever there was anything of this sort to unearth, Nicholas Langen was assigned to the task. He was adept in it. He lingered in chanceries on feigned errands, he gossiped with grooms and porters and serving women. He was open-faced and friendly in his ways. He never failed.

Yusuf permitted himself a slight smile. "So far, we have two names only, Bertrand of Bonneval and Thurstan Beauchamp."

"I have not exchanged one word with him in the whole of my life," I said, and I knew these words of mine came with too much emphasis, as I had already denied the acquaintance, but the knowledge that I was concealing something from him made me unsure of being believed even when I spoke the truth, and this unsureness was made worse by my feeling that he sensed it and perhaps misunderstood it. It was not that I thought he disbelieved me; he trusted me to the limits of his capacity for trust. But suspicion was never entirely disarmed in him. And there was something here he did not understand.

"Can you think of any reason why you might have been included in this Norman hunting party?" he said.

I took care to avoid any appearance of haste in my denial, shaking my head and meeting his eyes firmly. I had never spoken to him of the Lady Alicia, not of our meeting in Bari and the time we had spent together there, not of the passion there had once been between us. I could have spoken of her now—so much would have been spared us had I done so. But I did not. To protect her name from any loose association, my first duty as her knight? To protect her from Yusuf's investigations? She was not his to inquire into. She was not there for his knowledge. She was mine; she belonged to my life of before the diwan, when the air was pure and the ground clear before me. She could help me to recover such a life. In protecting her, I protected myself also. Was that the true reason? How can such questions ever find answers? It was the first time that I had lied to him, and it was like a stone dislodged from a bankside, there was to be a heavy fall after it.

"Well," he said, "if that is so, there can be only one reason, or at least the reasons must all be of one general character. They will want to find out some weakness, they will want to learn something from you that can be used to damage our diwan and turn the King's favor from us."

"They will not succeed through me."

He was looking at me more kindly now. "Not by your intention, I know that well. But you will need to be vigilant, because you are not made of one piece. If we think of a man as a wall with joints that make cracks for a bar to be inserted and so bring it down, my wall has no cracks in it. I am an Arab of Sicily, born of parents who were Arabs of Sicily. I can trace my family in a continuous line to the Fatimid Caliphs who ruled here two hundred years ago. We have always held public office. One of my ancestors was vizir to the Emir Jafar, he who built the palace of Favara, which was a resort of pleasure long before the time of the Normans. When I entered the King's service I was following in the path of my forebears, and I have followed in that path ever since. Such facts tell us nothing about a man's true nature or his innermost desires, but they make a singleness that is difficult to attack. Your wall has joints in it and these have made cracks where the bar could be put in. You are of mixed birth, you come from another land, you have gone from squire to guardsman-in-training to purse bearer and Purveyor in the *Diwan al-tahqiq al-ma' mur*. These are momentous changes. An enemy could seek to use them against you, by dividing you against yourself."

"None of these changes was by my choice, you know that well." I raised my head and straightened my back to say this. His words had wounded me, seeming to suggest I was inconstant of purpose and uncertain in my loyalties. Nor had I liked being compared to a cracked wall, though I could tell Yusuf was pleased with the figure:

the lines of his mouth were normally straight and thin, but a slight curve of relish visited them when he had made a comparison he felt to be felicitous. "You know why I had to give up my hopes of knighthood," I said. "And as for the Household Guard, it was you yourself that took me from it." *For your own sake you took me, not for mine,* I could not help saying within me, and I felt the return of resentment, thinking how he had employed me for his own advancement.

"That is true," he said. "I was taken with you, I was struck by your abilities. In the midst of learning to kill or maim your fellow man, which for the Norman is the only essential training, you had learned to read and speak Greek, and even some Latin. You were destined for better things than the Guards, Thurstan. I have never regretted bringing you here. What I said was not meant as a reproach to you, but as a warning, so that you will be on your guard when you go there."

At these words my resentment was forgotten and my heart expanded with joy: after his questioning of me and his close looks I had begun to fear that he would forbid me to go, which it was in his power to do. "Lord," I said, "I promise that I will be careful."

"These are difficult times. The King has enemies on all hands, both at home and abroad. Your co-religionists will try to make you believe that the threat to his life and throne comes from his Moslem subjects, this so as to have no one close to the King but themselves. But their words are not true. There are those of the King's own faith who hate him—who hate him in secret, you understand?—because he took no part in this crusade, because he resists the Pope's claims to overlordship. They would like a king of Sicily more friendly to these claims. Now, of five princes, there is only William left. Before the year is out the King will marry again, but until his new Queen gives him male children, all who love him should be concerned for his safety and that of the realm. We must be on our guard. While you are at Favara, keep your eyes and ears open."

"I will do so."

"In particular, you will report to me on what is said directly to you or deliberately in your hearing, anything you think is designed to sway you. I want the words said and the names of those who say them."

I earnestly undertook to do this, and only then did Yusuf's sternness abate altogether. He smiled and said it would after all be useful that I should go; it was unaccustomed company and there was much that we might learn. He even joked a little, his usual joke about my clothes, about the *sorcot* and the *chainse* and the *chauces* I would need to wear to make a good figure among these Norman nobles, giving the French words an exaggerated inflection. He had himself been to the palace of Favara several times, he told me, together with other high officials of the Royal Diwan, to sit in council with the King. "I was never invited to a hunting party, however," he said, still smiling. "Once, I remember, there was some hawking. You will like Favara—they have enlarged the gardens since I first went there and extended the lake: the water encircles the palace now. There are strange devices in the grounds but I will not spoil the surprise by speaking of them now. I am sure you will enjoy your time there."

I felt sure of this too, if what I suspected proved to be true. And what other explanation could there be? Only when I got back to my desk and made pretense of continuing work on the land registers was I fully able to savor my good fortune. There would be a list of course—the tireless Nicholas would furnish one—and until I had scanned that I could not be certain. This I tried to keep in mind so as to guard against disappointment. But my hopes ran ahead of me. I remembered the words we had said, the looks she had given me, the touch of her hand. I knew her name would be there.

There was also the joke against Yusuf to add to the pleasure. He had been quite mistaken in seeing such dark motives behind the invitation. So grave he had been, so ponderous with his suspicious looks and his talk of plots and machinations. He saw conspiracy everywhere. It would never occur to him that it might simply be a lady's contrivance. True, considering my office, it had been in a certain way unwise of Alicia to bring me into this lion's den of the Norman aristocracy. But then, she did not know the nature of this office, I had not spoken of it much and she was recently from Outremer—how could she know the rivalries and divisions that governed our lives here in Palermo? And then, I thought, there was a lady's caprice in it: she had wanted to see me, she had wanted to find circumstances in which we could be together without hurt to her good name . . .

Thus the edifice rose glittering before me, founded on no more than wishes and desires. I began from that moment to count the days to my going to Favara. In my chamber at home and in what intervals I could find at my desk, inspired by thoughts of Alicia, I returned to an earlier practice of mine, of late years abandoned: I began again to write verses for singing. My model for these were the Provençal songs that were now popular at court, but I used the Italian vernacular, not knowing well the language of southern France. I did not try to devise new melodies, for which I had no gift, but sought to fit my lines to melodies that I knew, sometimes the Latin *carmina* I remembered from my student days, sometimes a folk song, sometimes a dance tune that I had heard in the streets. I tried to emulate the great Bernard of Ventadour, whose song about the rising lark was heard everywhere now, and compose three-line stanzas without repeated phrases.

I was occupied with this on a morning three days after my talk with Yusuf when I was alone in the room, Stefanos having gone to see to the fitting of the dresses for the dancers. I had begun with the subject of my meeting with Alicia and the joy of love remembered and the hope for love renewed, but my imagination was too carnal, the lines that came to mind were not always true of my experience, though I hoped they might be. *The memory of her kisses, the fragrant warmth of her mouth,* these were true enough, but *the dazzling whiteness of her breasts* went too far and had to be excluded. I tested the shape of the words by singing them, which was the only way I knew, keeping my voice low so as not to draw attention to the fact that a man was here singing who should be studying the document before him on his desk, which concerned a plea, written in Latin, from the Monastery of San Giorgio di Fragalà for a royal grant to extract salt from the mines of Castrogiovanni. *In my heart a secret joy I tell no one, this joy devours me,* no, *consumes me,* no, not strong enough, *burns me, mi brucia,* yes, that was better, *d'amor lo cor mi brucia, I tell my heart to hope, to look upward* . . . But if the joy was secret, was it necessary to add the fact that I told no one? And could the heart look upward?

I was still puzzling—and still singing—when Stefanos entered, accompanied by the dressmaker. The Anatolian women would not wear their skirts without an underskirt, and since I had said there should be nothing it had been thought best to refer the matter to me.

At a stroke all higher thoughts were driven from my mind. "What is their reason?"

"They will not agree to wear the skirts without an undergarment that reaches to the knees," the dressmaker said. "I cannot argue with them, I cannot understand them even when they do not shout."

"It is for reasons of modesty," Stefanos said. "They say the stuff of the dress is very fine, it is damask, without an underskirt the lower part of their bodies would be too plainly visible." He paused for a moment, looking at me in his usual mild and slightly peering fashion. "Even as high as the fork, she said."

"Who? No, no need to tell me."

"She is headstrong. She is like my older son, Matteus, who will have about your years, who would be a sailor whatever one said to him, and a sailor he is." Stefanos always spoke of this self-willed son as if in deprecation, but in truth he was proud of the young man, who was now master of one of the King's ships. That he should have made this comparison at all was a sign that he approved of this girl in spite of everything. "Her name means 'wild rose,' " he said now. "She told me that without my asking, perhaps as a way of making it known to you."

"Why should she want to do that?"

"She might think it of interest. It is a beautiful name in the sound."

"Well, the thorns are there, but I do not see the petals." I felt suddenly weary, and in some way discouraged. My words had been a lie. The petals displayed I could see well enough, those hidden and enfolded I could all too easily imagine. I did not feel able to confront these people again, to find the eyes turned from me, somber and indifferent-seeming, except only hers, and she looking only to find weakness and finding it, as if she saw something within me that was beyond my own power to discover, but it was an illusion, it was only her presumption, she knew nothing but dusty roads in summer and muddy roads in winter, and the dance of the abdomen.

"I cannot talk to them now," I said. "They would wear down a stone. With the lights in the walls behind and no lights in front it would have been a spectacle indeed, it would have given delight and we would have acquired merit."

"She says their bodies are made like the bodies of other women. Millions and millions of women, she says. It is their dancing that makes them different, not what lies between the legs. She is outspoken, that one."

"In any case, it is useless to insist. Tell them we agree to a petticoat. It can be as long as they like, but it must be made of some thin material. Otherwise, all the King will see of their lower parts will be a swaddled-up bundle. He will not be gratified much by that, will he?"

"I will tell them." Stefanos blinked mild brown eyes. "I will go back with the dressmaker and explain it to them. I have found that they misapprehend things and get easily excited, but if one speaks calmly to them they quickly grow quiet again."

"This is the behavior of children. Nesrin, she grows quiet too?"

Stefanos smiled indulgently, but whether the indulgence was for Nesrin or for me, I could not be sure. "She especially. That is, when she does not feel called upon to do battle. She does not need to fight me, I do not matter."

"And me? Are you saying this little savage is hostile only to me?"

"I did not say she was hostile."

"Stefanos, spare me these subtleties. I am not in the mood for them. Have there been any complaints from the one that escorts them?"

"No, he says they have behaved well. They go to the markets, they buy little things, trinkets, scarves, belts set with beads. The men have bought knives—they say the knives are good here, so far they have not found much else to praise."

"Did they go to the bathhouse?" This was a question that came with a leap—it was out almost before I knew it. "I think she mentioned that they might do that," I said after a moment.

"I do not know. They did not speak of it." He frowned a little as if perplexed. "I can find out."

"No, it is not important. Just tell them what we have decided about the skirts."

He left on this errand and I was glad to be alone for a while. But I made no further attempts at writing songs that day, why I do not know.

XV

THE LIST CAME, her name was there, and strange it was to see it so indifferently mixed among the others when it sounded with golden trumpets and the voices of angels when my eyes came to rest on it. Day followed day till that one came, the much awaited. I rode out of the city while it was still early, before the sun grew too hot. The sky was clear, the larks were singing, my heart was high with anticipation. The waters of the Oreto sparkled as I crossed it by the Admiral's Bridge, as they call it, a bridge of many arches that was made on the orders of the Emir George Antiochenus, the same who afterward raided Thebes and carried off the silk workers, among them my Sara. Before long, I thought, I will free myself from these silken strings; one last present, in gold, a keepsake; then all my heart and homage for Alicia . . .

This thought raised my spirits further, and as I left the river behind me I lifted my head and broke into song:

Lady, my heart,
the best friend that I have,
I leave in your keeping,
till we can love with all our bodies

I ceased, however, not feeling the words to be fitting, as I passed by the Church of San Giovanni dei Leprosi, which lies not far beyond the river. This church was built by our King's uncle, Robert Guiscard, on the very spot where the Norman army first encamped before Palermo, which was then still in the hands of the Saracens.

The outer gates to the palace were reached by a roadway with forest on either side. I announced my name to the guards and they knew it without needing to look at any list, something of extreme rarity in my life up to then. I was conducted by one of them, who walked alongside, holding my horse, this also being far from common in my experience. I wondered whether I might in future take my father's title and call myself Thurstan of Mescoli.

We came to the lakeside and the arcaded front of the palace rose before me, set amid groves of orange trees. There was a causeway, built up with stone, that led across the water to the gilded gates of the palace itself—the only way to reach them by land. Passing over this, I saw a ripple and a flash of gold as some great carp turned near the surface. There was a strange, sudden impression of extended distances and doubled perspectives, as if the lake itself, the sunlit waters and the dark-leaved trees and the interleaving arches of the palace were shifting and receding as I drew nearer.

It was a confusion of the senses very fleeting, ceasing as I came before the gates. Glancing aside before entering, I saw a group of men and women walking together at the borders of the lake, dressed in light-colored clothes. I wondered if one of the ladies might be Alicia, but it was too far for me to see clearly. In the open courtyard beyond the gate, my guide was replaced by a groom in the same colors of dark red and pale blue, who took my horse's bridle and held her head while I dismounted, keeping close in case I needed help—servants trained to this perfection do not distinguish people by their seeming young or old or fat or thin. He led the horse away, having first handed my saddlebags to yet another liveried attendant, who went before me across the courtyard and delivered me to a chamberlain waiting in the hall, dressed with sober richness in black velvet. Never before that I could remember had I been greeted on arriving anywhere by so many persons, one after another, before even setting eyes on my host. To live in the open and be known, to bear your own wealth and be careless in the display of it, to have knightly title and a lady of birth at your side, to be surrounded by care and attention. Not just for a day, but every day of your life!

The chamberlain conducted me to my room, which was on the floor above and had a high-vaulted ceiling carved intricately in wood in the Saracen style, and a broad window shuttered against the sun. All this was splendid enough, but it was the bed that caught my eye: it was big enough for four Thurstans, canopied in green silk. In the wall opposite the bed there was a niche tiled in dark blue with a design of red flowers at the base. It seemed to me that this must be one of the finest sleeping chambers in the palace—certainly I had never slept in one so fine. Outside the door, some few paces along a passageway, there was a privy, which the chamberlain pointed out to me. It was for my use only, he said. I nodded and strove to make it appear a commonplace in my life that I should have a privy to my private use—it was one of the privileges I hoped to inherit if I succeeded to Yusuf's place at the diwan.

Having waited to assure himself that all was satisfactory to me, the chamberlain bowed and took his leave. I opened the shutters and immediately a low sound of running water came into the room: below my window there lay a courtyard with a marble fountain, and tiny streams carried the water from the basin of the fountain into lower basins until all the water flowed into a small pond, and there were white lilies floating on the surface of this.

A serving girl came with towels and a ewer of scented water for me to wash and refresh myself after the journey. She was followed shortly afterward by an armed retainer—he too in the same livery— who bore throwing lance and long dagger and hunting horn, but of these I had no need, having brought my own. At this season it would be the hart that was hunted, not the boar, so it was useless to carry a sword. I had hunted hart as a squire in the service of Hubert of Venosa, and since then sometimes in the woods of the Conca d'Oro with companions from the palace administration. My horse was not notably spirited, but she was steady. I was confident of bearing my-self with credit, and I had brought with me hunting clothes specially made for the occasion, which I thought suited me admirably well, a high-waisted doublet with slashed sleeves, and leggings that did justice to the shape of my legs, the whole in matching colors of wine red and pale yellow. It had cost me half a month's wages.

The chamberlain returned to ask me if I would be pleased to de-scend. In the main hall my host and his lady awaited me, and they responded very affably to my bows. Bertrand of Bonneval was a very tall man—taller than I—broad-faced and fair-bearded, with blue eyes so clear and direct as to seem childlike. The Lady Isabelle seemed low of stature beside this stout lord of hers, though I think she was of middling height; she was delicate of feature and not much given to smiling and very brightly painted.

"I knew your father," Sir Bertrand said. "A very valiant knight. We were companions-in-arms at the siege of Salerno in the summer of 'thirty-four. Now making his peace with God, as I hear reported. Admirable, very admirable. Even if it were only for the father's sake, we would be glad to welcome the son."

I made some confused reply to this, expressing appreciation on my father's behalf and on my own. The exact words I have forgotten. In fact, the confusion was caused by what I felt to be some ambiguity in his remarks. Did he mean that I had been invited for my father's sake? Surely not—I did not believe he had known my father so well. He must have meant that there were reasons in addition, reasons he was too circumspect to mention, in spite of those guileless eyes, or one reason at any rate: Alicia had found some way of recommending me to him. It had not occurred to me before, not fully, so delighted had I been, how difficult it might have been for her to press my name, to show her interest in a way that was consistent with her honor. Perhaps she had enlisted some third party to act as go-between . . .

We were joined now by others, introductions were made, we moved all together, not into the main courtyard through which I had come on entering the palace but across the hall, then across a second, smaller one, and so out into the rose gardens behind, where there was a marble pavilion in the style of a Greek temple, but with an arcade of slender Saracenic columns. Within this, shaded from the sun, there were people already sitting at a long table laid for a meal and decked with vases of roses white and red.

As we drew nearer I saw that Alicia was among those seated and I felt the blood leave my face. I could give no sign of recognition unless she did; I did not know whether she had spoken of our meeting or wished to keep it secret. But she looked up as I came to the table, our eyes met and she smiled. Never had fire warmed me as that smile of hers so openly upon me—a smile for all to see. She spoke in turn to the men on either side of her, one of whom looked of an age with me, the other older, tonsured and wearing the dark gown of a cleric. I knew she must be speaking of me, as both looked toward me and nodded a greeting. On the spur of this I went to where they were sitting and made my bow to them and they stood to return this bow and I heard Alicia say my name and those of the two with her. The younger man was her brother Adhemar, who had accompanied her from the Holy Land, the other her uncle, Abbot Alboino. He was recently from Rome, she had said. Adhemar had his sister's fairness and her level brows. He smiled readily and his manners were easy and pleasing. The abbot, by contrast, smiled hardly at all, but he addressed me in friendly fashion and said that his niece had spoken well of me. He was round-faced and well fleshed, but his eyes seemed to gainsay this air of well-being: sadder eyes than his I could not remember seeing in any man's face.

These civilities over, I returned to the place allotted to me, guided in this by the lord's steward. Water was brought in silver ewers and poured over the guests' hands, a second servant following behind with towels. Grace was said by our host, and the first courses were brought in.

I remember the meal as excellent, but at the time I scarcely paid attention to what I was eating, or to the words exchanged with those sitting next to me, so enraptured was I by the knowledge that Alicia had spoken of me to these members of her family and that they, far from thinking me unworthy, had seemed pleased by the acquaintance. She would also have spoken of me to her parents, I thought, on her return to Troina. They too had not been displeased by the connection; otherwise, how could the brother have shown such friendliness toward me? From time to time, more frequently perhaps than was decorous, I glanced down the table at her, eager for anything of her that my sight could register, her hands, the set of her head, the movement of her throat when she drank. Sometimes our eyes met, and then her look lingered on me.

When we rose from the table my first thought was to join her immediately, but she was borne away by those in attendance on her, I did not see the way they went, and spent a time that seemed wearisome to me looking in courtyards that led to vestibules and antechambers that then opened to other courtyards, with no one in sight but servants who bowed to me silently. At last I came out by the lakeside and stood there, gazing down at the water, wondering where to look now for her, and whether there was someone I might ask.

There were reflections of clouds in the water, faint shreds and curls of cloud that I had not known were there in the sky until I saw them thus reflected, and also of foliage, the sharp-leaved foliage of the orange trees and the golden fruit. And now again there came that sense of shifting and displacement that I had felt earlier while crossing the causeway. There was no wind to stir the water, the surface was calm, yet the clouds and the leaves and the bright globes of the oranges stretched and shifted, and it was strangely difficult to see where the borders of the lake ended. I looked up at trees and sky with some vague idea of finding an explanation there, but these too for some moments seemed to stretch away from me, and their confines melted into distance. I had a feeling of threatened balance, as if the ground under my feet was not firm. Through the trees, in that part of the island farthest from the palace, I saw a flash of brilliant light that remained for some short while, then ceased. I walked toward this, passing beyond the trees into terraced gardens and pergolas of jasmine and honeysuckle, very sweetly scented. The flash of light came again and the pergolas multiplied strangely.

Then, coming once more into the open, I saw the cause of it: raised on brass pillars to a level above my own height was a disk of polished tin greater in diameter than the span of a man's arms, and it was turning, very slowly, through a wide angle, and catching the sun as it turned. No slightest sound came from this great weight of metal. I saw it stop at the limit of the turn, and pause, and then begin the slow swing round to its former position. As I came closer, I saw that there were two dwarf Saracens of brass, identical in every respect, bearded and dressed in turbans and robes, suspended on chains below the turning mirror at a distance one from the other, and that each held a long-handled ladle with a deep bowl. By means that I could not determine—perhaps by conduits passing under the ground—the lake water was brought here into a pool, and then in some way invisible to me forced upward, compelling each of these brass water men in turn to dip his ladle and fill his bowl. When one bowl was full the weight was enough to swing the mirror, but even as it did so the water in the bowl poured itself away, the other bowl dipped down and the mirror began its return.

How long I stood watching this I do not know. I could not look long at the gleaming surface of the metal because of the blinding flashes that came from it and because it made the mind dizzy, turning earth and sky and water into a medley of wheeling forms and fleeting colors, that had no bounds, no confines. But the Saracen water men fascinated me, their movements continuous, relentless, not smooth as human movements are but marked by infinitesimal intervals, as if they might cease, rebel against the water that governed them, but they did not—they were condemned to labor forever. I could not see by what cunning means the water of this calm pool could master them so. Somewhere hidden, I thought, a pump, a pressure that mounted by pipes, but in that case . . .

"There is another," a voice said behind me. "Another mirror, exactly the same, on the other side of the island."

I turned to find a man regarding me whom after a moment I recognized: it was the groom who had ridden before Alicia in that street in Bari, where we had met. He was not in livery now, but in a long surcoat of undyed linen. I had not thought at the time that he had the air or the glance of a servant, and I did not think so now, from the way he was regarding me.

"You walk softly," I said.

"A careless step can cost a man dear." This was an Arab saying, though he spoke in Italian, and he smiled as he uttered it. He was a handsome man, with a good forehead and a high-bridged nose and eyes of a color between green and hazel. "Yes," he said, "one catches the reflections of the other, between them they invert the order of earth and heaven. Our good King's Saracen engineers fashioned them in the fifth year of his reign, at the time when the improvements were made here. The Saracens have no match when it comes to the harnessing of water. There is a gardener here whose sole task it is to keep the surfaces polished and remove drowned insects from the pools."

"You have come to tell me this?"

"I have come at the Lady Alicia's bidding to lead you to where she awaits you."

"You are the lady's groom?" I asked as I went with him.

"Her groom, her bearer, her messenger, her man-at-arms when she has need of one. I came in her following from Jerusalem. My father was in the service of her father, Guy of Morcone."

"So you have known the family long?"

"A good many years, yes."

"And your name?"

"I am called Caspar."

A thought struck me now that made me pause briefly in my walk. "If your father was in that service, you must have known the Lady Alicia as a child?"

He had stopped with me but did not look at me fully, glancing away as if tolerating these questions rather than welcoming them. "I would not say 'known,' " he said. "I was a stable boy in the castle when she was born."

I had a mind, as we resumed our walking, to question him further; anything concerning Alicia was of absorbing interest to me, and this Caspar must have seen her grow up. Not only that: if he had come with her from Jerusalem, it seemed likely that he had gone with her there when she left to be married to Tibald. But he stopped and pointed and said, "She is there, you will come upon her if you follow the paved way through the gardens. There is a gate and beyond it a walled yard with a fountain and a small pavilion."

With this he inclined his head and withdrew, leaving me with the impression that he quitted me thus abruptly, and while still at some distance from where Alicia waited, so as to curtail this talk of ours and forestall further questioning. But the anticipation of seeing Alicia drove all else from my mind, and I walked on eagerly until I came to the gate he had spoken of, which was low and tinted with silver and surmounted by arabesques.

Passing through this, for a fleeting moment I thought that the enclosure was peopled, then saw that there were shrubs of some dense-growing sort, which had been very skillfully cut into the shapes of animals and birds, and these cast shadows on the walls, which had been whitened with lime, so that the figures were repeated there.

Among these shapes and the shadows they cast there was at first no sign of Alicia, but then I made out her form above me, inside the pavilion, saw the pale color of her gown first, then her face. She heard my step and turned and saw me but remained in the shade of the pavilion. This had a balustrade with short marble pillars set very close together in it like bars. Now this is strange to relate, but as I began to climb the marble steps toward her, I thought I heard somewhere in the distance that wailing sound of the herons, *wulla-wulla-wulla*, and a memory came to me, brief as the flicker of an eye, of mounting to the deck of the ship and looking across the white birds in their cages at Nesrin.

Then Alicia came forward and held out both hands to me and I took them in my own and would have kissed her, because this was a different kind of being together now, we were no longer wayfarers amazed at a chance encounter, wanting to talk and remember, we were meeting in private, by assignation, by a summons of the lady. I would have kissed her on the mouth, but she held back, though it was gently that she did so, and she still remained close.

"We have little time," she said.

"All the more reason." My breath came quickly. The nearness of her face, face so much dreamed of, confused my sight. As if seen in a dream now, the level, fair brows, the candid blue of the eyes, the mouth full but well formed, half smiling. "All the more reason, if the time is short," I said, in a voice not quite my own, and I leaned and kissed her and felt the answering warmth of her lips, but then she drew away a little and half raised a hand as if to stay me. "This evening at supper we will have more time together. We are to sup at the lakeside, they will make fires. Then, with the dark and all the movement and the boats, it will be easier for us to escape notice."

The promise I felt in these words went to my head like a strong drink. I pictured this retiring together, away from the firelight, into the darkness of the woods . . .

"Do not look so," she said. "I meant that we will be free to talk together and make plans, without attracting any particular attention."

These words too were delightful to me, though in a different way. To make plans was to talk of a future shared. I felt my whole being brim with joy. When I spoke my voice came huskily. "Lady Alicia, let me tell you my gratitude—"

Gratitude, I was going to say, and which I felt from a full heart, for her existence in the world and for the pains and care she had taken to contrive our being together in this way. But she laid a finger on my lips to prevent my continuing, and I kissed it with the passion of my gratitude, but when I looked into her face I saw something of distress there, in the eyes and the mouth, something I was at a loss to understand. "What is it?" I said. "What is it troubles you?"

"No, it is nothing," she said. The look had left her face as I spoke. She hesitated a moment, as if uncertain, then said, "It is Adhemar. He is always watching me. Even here . . ."

"Adhemar? But why should he watch?"

"He has his own ideas for my future, and you have no part in them."

"What ideas? He seemed so friendly and full of smiles . . ."

"Yes, he can smile, but he has a strong will behind the smiling. There is one he favors as a future husband for me, a fellow of his in the service of Count Raymond of Tripoli."

This came as a blow to me, all the heavier for the joy of the promise that had gone before. How could her brother behave with such a degree of friendliness when all the time he was regarding me as a possible adversary, an impediment to his plans? There was an element of treachery there that went beyond the necessary, and I felt the chill of it even in that shaded warmth of the pavilion.

"Take care not to show him that you know this," Alicia said. "Do not change in your behavior toward him, return his smiles. So he may be lulled into thinking that he will have his way, and cease from pestering me with praises of the wealth and prowess of this knight."

"And will he? Will he have his way?"

"Can you ask me that after the way Providence has brought us together again, after the words exchanged between us? This friend of my brother's means nothing to me. It does not matter to me if he is wealthy and well famed. I have had my fill of my family's friends— Tibald was one such. It is as I told you that night at the hospice. I am free to choose and I will choose at the bidding of my heart. This I promise you."

These words, and the look she gave me as she said them, went far to solace me for the double blow of Adhemar's perfidy and the existence of another suitor, but did not altogether heal it. My rival was rich, it seemed. Before I could reply there came the loud sound of a hunting horn from somewhere closer to the palace. "They are calling the Assembly," she said. She raised her face to me and kissed me lightly. "You must go to hear the huntsmen. I will follow more slowly. I will not join you there, I do not take part in the hunt—this one or any other. I do not enjoy the sight of the bleeding stag."

I did as she bade me, leaving her there still in the shade of the pavilion. As I made my way toward the gate, I saw how the shadows cast by the effigies onto the walls crossed and overlaid one another, making strange, deformed shapes. The lion was a jawless crocodile, the tall flamingo had a camel's hump.

XVI

THE PLACE OF ASSEMBLY was an antechamber of the palace, adjoining the main hall. Here Bertrand and his lady—who it seemed would join the hunt—awaited their guests in company with two huntsmen. Adhemar was there already and he smiled at me and I returned the smile, but I knew him now for an enemy. Of Alboino there was no sign.

When all who would take part were gathered, the huntsmen began to advance their separate claims. Each had followed the spoor of a deer with his bloodhounds and discovered the harbor, or resting place, of the beast and marked it for the morrow. They spoke in turn and earnestly: he whose deer was chosen would be paid in coin and receive some share of the meat. It was for this reason that, even though his punishment would be severe if the company was disappointed, a huntsman sometimes overpraised his deer, and so the questioning had to be careful. Neither man had viewed his quarry, but they assured us, from the height of the traces left by the antlers, that each was a hart of ten. On this point they were very definite and for the reason we all knew well: with less than ten tines on the head a hart was not judged ready to be hunted with dogs.

This discussion of the relative merits of the deer was elaborate and protracted as always, and as always it was conducted in French. No matter how long the Normans had lived in Sicily, they used the language of their forebears when talking of the hunt. Each man, by courtesy of the host, was allowed a question if he so chose. Bertrand did me the honor of inviting me to ask the third question, after his own and that of the favored guest, and this was a knight of very high estate, a nephew of Count Theobald of Blois. This courtesy I put down to Alicia's commendation of me—it could hardly be due to my own standing in such a company as this. My question, fortunately, was already prepared. I inquired into the depth of the impressions made by the feet and knees when the beast rose from its bed—an important matter, this, as it indicates the weight. After I had thus played my part and showed myself no stranger to the business, I regret to say that I began to lose interest, especially as we now entered upon a long discussion concerning the width of foot, each huntsman eagerly showing, with fingers laid side by side, the flattening of the grass where his beast had trod.

There was a line of pillars along the side of the room opposite the entrance; they were of the kind known as serpentine, very slender, with a rope of marble winding from pedestal to capital, so that the whole pillar took the form of a twining snake, this too the work of Saracen masons, perhaps made, I thought, in the days of Yusuf's ancestor, he who had been vizir to the Emir Jafar, who built this palace and was the first to make a lake round it. And as I followed these snakes of marble up to the Arabic characters inscribed in the capitals, then down again to the low pediment, in sinuous, unceasing lines, I remembered Yusuf's face as he spoke of his forebears, the pride and sorrow in it, and then I remembered his anger when I had compared his people to the Serbs. He had spoken on a tide of feeling, something very rare in him; he had spoken of rebellion and civil war, dangerous words for any man to speak, however highly placed . . .

I drifted from this to thoughts of the guileful Serpent twining round the Tree, and the honeyed words that had brought our first parents to exile and sorrow till Christ came to redeem us from that sin and hold out to us the promise of eternal life. The hart was the symbol of this, because God gave to the hart the ability to renew itself. When it has lived for thirty-two years it is driven by its nature to seek out an anthill, which it then destroys by trampling upon it. Below this anthill there is found a white snake, which the hart kills and devours. It then goes to a desert place and throws off its flesh and becomes young again, and this signifies the soul's discarding of the body as it enters into purgatory and so prepares for eternal life.

I was roused from this half-dreaming state by being asked my opinion as to the merits and defects of the excrement of the two animals. The huntsmen had brought specimens of these *fumées*, as they were called, and we gathered wisely round a table to compare them. This also requires a great deal of study, the points of comparison being in the thickness of the turd, its length, and the hardness of its consistency. The palm was finally awarded, the defeated huntsman took himself disconsolately off, and the victor was told to have his lymers ready for the next day.

After this I set off again to look for Alicia but did not find her, and supposed she would be resting; she would not venture much into this hot sun of afternoon. I thought of her fairness, the pale brows: she had taken care to keep her face from burning in Jerusalem, and so she would do here.

I found my own chamber very sweet-smelling when I returned to it; in my absence they had come and strewn the floor with dried mint, and I think other herbs mingled with it. I lay on the bed and thought of the events of the day and became drowsy as I did so, so that impressions were jumbled together and lost all order of sequence, the turning mirrors, the servitude of the brass Saracens, the false smiles of Adhemar and the sad eyes of the abbot, the strange distortions of the shadows on the walls, Alicia waiting for me in the shade of the pavilion, the kisses we had exchanged—I seemed to feel them still on my lips. I remembered the change in her face as I tried to speak my gratitude, and how for a moment she had seemed at a loss, perhaps unsure whether she should confide in me. She had seemed afraid as she spoke of her brother and his spying. But that brief look on her face, when she had raised her fingers to my lips to prevent me from speaking, that had been more like distress than fear. Pale hands, pale as ivory . . . some words that might be the beginning of a song came to my mind.

Her honor and her good shall be my care.
I am her liege man and her lover.
Wherever I may be . . .

Her liege man and her lover, her lover and her liege man. Which had the best fall? The first was more lyrical, the second had more weight on the end syllable . . . Before this problem could be solved I drifted into sleep and lay lost to the world while the sun waned and sank and the evening came and the light softened. There were already the first grainings of dark in the air when I descended, and I saw that fires were already burning on the farther shore of the lake.

These fires it was possible to reach in one of two ways, I was informed by the chamberlain, who seemed to be permanently stationed in the hall below: I could leave the island by means of the causeway, then make my way on foot round the edge of the lake until reaching the fires; or, if preferred, there were little pleasure boats, I could paddle across. I said I would prefer the latter, and a gardener's boy was summoned to show me where the boats were. Only three now remained, moored at a little landing stage, though this sometimes stretched away and the boats were multiplied, according to the swing of the mirrors, invisible from here, the sunlight no longer betraying their presence. If one lived long on this island, I thought, one would lose forever the capacity to trust in anything, even in one's own senses. Or perhaps one would simply become wary as to where he set his foot. There were zones that were free from these bewildering reflections, like the gardens surrounding the pavilion and the pavilion itself, but it was not possible to know where the borders were. One step farther and the world stretched and yawned and the distinction between the one and the many was lost.

The paddleboats were built for calm water, with gilded prows and cushioned seats. They were small, yes, but quite big enough for two, and it was now that a certain idea came to me: if I could make myself master of one of these boats and prevent it from being taken by anyone else, it might provide the means of having Alicia to myself for a while, and defeating Adhemar's vigilance.

With this thought in mind, I did not paddle my boat directly to the mooring posts on the opposite shore, but tied it to a waterside tree at some distance away, then scrambled ashore and made my way on foot through the trees to where the fires were burning and the people were gathering. Tables had been set up and there was a smell of roasting meat. I took a place, and bread was brought to me, and soon after a cut from the breast of a duck was brought on a dish, and this was very tender and good, the bird had been well chosen and turned long on the spit. The wine cup came round to me, made of silver and very deep in the bowl so that it was heavy and had to be raised with both hands. I drank and passed the cup to my neighbor, a knight I had met that morning and who had been at the Assembly. We spoke together for a while about the clearness of the night weather, the promising starlight, and the prospects for the hunt next day. As we were speaking a minstrel came forward and sat facing us, with the firelight on his face. He struck some notes on his viele and began with a song of King Arthur, singing in French, a good strong voice and perfect in the words. My neighbor told me that this was Renart the Jongleur, the famous singer who traveled and performed in many places and was welcomed in the houses of the great, and could sing in Breton and Provençal and Latin with equal ease. He had been brought here by our host for this occasion. Now I too knew many songs and could accompany myself on the viele; I listened carefully to this singer and it seemed to me—nay, I knew it—that my own voice was the equal of his in its range and tone. "He has a good horse and a full purse," my neighbor said. "He goes from one court to another. If he complains of mean treatment he brings shame to the one he complains of, and so he is always treated well."

"Well," I said, "generosity is a virtue, however it comes about."

I was constantly looking around for a sight of Alicia but did not see her. This distraction made me a little inattentive to the young knight's words—he was younger than I, he looked no more than twenty. He was speaking of Bertrand's patronage of him and how this had advanced him and how Bertrand believed that those of Norman blood should be united, since only if they spoke with one voice would the King see their loyalty and devotion, and bring them closer to him, and send away the false counselors that surrounded him.

I answered him as best I could—these were views I had heard before. After a while longer, with some friendly words about our riding together next day, he quitted the table. I was rising to do the same when Abbot Alboino came and took a place on my other side, obliging me to resume my seat.

He asked about my activities of the day and listened and nodded with head inclined, in the same kindly but very serious manner I had noticed in him that morning. I did not speak of my meeting with Alicia in the pavilion, and if he knew of it he gave no sign. "I was hoping to have some talk with you," he said. "As I told you this morning, my niece has spoken of you in very high terms. You were childhood friends, were you not?"

He was looking closely at me as he spoke. Once again I was struck by the sorrowing expression of his eyes. I could not tell if this was feeling in them or an accident of their setting. It was as if they testified to a life quite different from the one that was lived by his body—he had twice my years but he was robust and confident in his bearing. It came to me that he was inviting my confidence, while at the same time knowing more than his words suggested. "I was heartbroken when she left to be married," I said. "I was sixteen, no longer such a child." I took care to smile and say these words lightly, so that it could still seem an extravagance of childhood.

"Well," he said, "you are a fine upstanding fellow now, and so you must have been at sixteen. But the dangers that beset the soul are greater now."

He was still regarding me with the same attention. I saw his mouth draw together as at some sharp taste. Perhaps it was this impression of bitterness in him that made me think by contrast of Hugo the Spy and his taste for honey cakes. "Children know wickedness too," I said. "But I suppose the temptations are fewer and more simple."

"That was not my meaning. I was speaking of you, your situation."

For a moment I thought he might be referring to the attraction that Alicia had shown for me. He could not but know that she had exerted herself to have me invited here. He had eyes in his head, he had watched, he must have seen the glances we exchanged. And in any case he must have wanted to take a look at me. It might have been for this that he had come to Favara—he had not been at the Assembly, so did not intend to take part in the hunt. There was power in him, both when he spoke and when he was silent; it came from him like an emanation. Alicia too must feel this power . . .

"Lord Abbot," I said, "I have no ill intentions in regard to your niece, I beg you will believe this." A lump had formed in my throat, and I paused before speaking again to swallow it down. "If it rested with me, she would be kept safe forever."

"I have no doubts of that," he said. "Though it is true that Alicia causes me concern, as she does also to her brother. She is self-willed, but she lacks guile or even great caution in bringing her ends about. This could be used to her harm."

It seemed to me he judged her wrongly; guile and caution she had possessed in large measure already at fourteen, who should know that better than I? " 'Used to her harm'? You mean by others?"

Darkness had fallen as we talked. Behind us men came with armfuls of dry tinder and heaped the fires so that they blazed up, and in this stronger light I saw the abbot's face half turned away, the high brow and firm mouth and strong chin. Despite the sad look of the eyes, it was the face of one who knew his way through the thickets and marshes of this world.

He had left my last question unanswered. After a short silence, during which the voice of the jongleur still sounded, though now from farther away, he said, "No, I meant your situation at the douana, the fact that you are at the orders of a Moslem, you rub shoulders with Moslems, day by day you are subject to the influence of their religion."

For some moments it seemed to me that he might almost be joking, so very gentle and equable was the voice he used. But the face he turned to me now had no joking in it. "No one of good Christian family can find that acceptable," he said.

"But I am not subject to the influence of their religion. I do not discuss religion in my work at the . . . diwan."

"Does not Yusuf Ibn Mansur quote passages from the Koran? Does he not use the name of his god in your hearing? Do you think a human soul is lost at one stroke? Day by day, the touch of wrong, so you become habituated, you grow callous. That is what destroys the soul."

"But he does not quote from his book more than we are accustomed to quote from ours, or name his god more than we."

"Young man, what are you saying? I see that already there has been a deadening of the soul. Do you put them on a level, his blasphemies and our Holy Writ? So one doctrine is as good as another, so long as there is faith? Any noxious plant can grow so long as those who tend it are devout? Do you not know that devotion can pervert the soul if the object of it is mistaken?" He turned his face from me and remained for a while in silence, shaking his head slowly. "The weeds spread and choke our garden," he said, in a voice hardly louder than a murmur, as if speaking only to himself. "We cannot live with Islam. We must root it out. It is a pernicious weed in our garden."

He turned to look at me and said in a stronger voice, "Our garden is Christendom, Thurstan, this great movement of our Latin Church that has grown in power for a century now, to bring salvation and peace and order under the spiritual authority of the Pope, who unites us in bonds of faith. That movement, that authority, knows only one truth, not several living side by side. In our garden of Christendom all compromise is corruption."

For some time I could find no way of answering him. I felt myself in the grip of dilemma. Our King chose Saracens for his companions, preferring them to Normans for their learning; he trusted his Saracen troops to defend him and they had proved loyal, much of the Royal Diwan was in the hands of Saracen officials. It seemed to me that if the King kept this balance it was because he recognized more than one truth, and knew that the security of the realm depended on this recognition, it kept him afloat on his silver barge, and I, as his faithful servant, was bound in duty to uphold this view. But I could see that any talk of balance or silver barges or strife below the surface would not be welcome to Alboino, and I was afraid of offending him, afraid that he would speak ill of me to Alicia, and so incline her away from me when I was not there to speak in my own defense.

"My Lord Abbot, I will ponder the matter" was all that in the end I could find to say.

"Ponder it well. And ponder also this: If the Saracen is our enemy in Syria and Palestine, how can he be our friend in Palermo? Is it not the same beast?"

I promised to add this to the things to be considered. Then, in order to change discourse, and remembering that Alicia had said he came from Rome, I asked him whether his coming had been recent and whether he would stay long. And with these questions of mine he relaxed the severity of his manner and seemed glad to tell me something of himself. He belonged to the Cistercian order and had spent some years at the Papal Curia, where he had been sent at the behest of the head of the order, Bernard of Clairvaux, to work for the moving of a new crusade, against Byzantium now, whose treachery was blamed for the loss of Edessa and the failed siege of Damascus. But the King of the Germans, Conrad, had shown a lamentable lack of Christian fervor and declined the venture, and in view of this Pope Eugenius had abandoned the idea and sent Alboino to Sicily, recommending him to King Roger, who had appointed him head of the Monastery of the Trinità in Palermo.

All this was interesting enough, but it left one question unanswered. Why Sicily? King Roger might be asked to furnish ships and provisions for a new crusade, but no one would want him for an active partner, it would be too dangerous: he still laid claim to the Kingdom of Jerusalem, through his mother, Adelaide. Something else had induced Eugenius to send the abbot here, and I was casting about in my mind for some way of discovering this when I suddenly saw Alicia, in the company of her brother, standing near the fire that was farthest from us; it seemed to me that they had come through the trees from where the minstrel was singing. At once all thoughts left my head save only one, and that was my strategy with the boat.

The darkness of the trees was behind her, but she was full in the firelight and clearly visible to me, from the gold net in her hair to the slender feet below the hem of her red gown. This suddenness of her appearance by the fire and the not seeing her approach took my breath for a moment, making her seem like an apparition summoned by my desire, the dwelling of my mind on her.

They came toward us and we rose to greet them. I spoke the polite words and returned the smiles, and we stood there, the four of us, talking together—though to say truth I spoke very little and have no memory of the words. I had reached a stage of awareness of Alicia's presence that made me scarcely dare to look at her when others were by, for fear the force of my feeling would create some material sign: a bolt of light or a burst of flame that would envelop us.

I could not long remain where I was, in any case; my presence among them was the chief impediment to my hopes; while I was in Adhemar's company I certainly would not succeed in seeing Alicia alone. So after some further talk I made as if I were retiring, bade them good night, and walked a little way off toward the place where I had left my boat.

I did not go far, only into the darkness of the trees. From here I could watch without being seen, as they were still in the light of the fires. Servants with lighted lanterns were waiting at the little jetty where the boats were moored, which made me fear that people might be returning to the palace before long, and Alicia with them, constrained by her brother and uncle. I waited there and watched and hoped—it was all I could do. For some time they stood talking together. Then—miracle of miracles!—the two men withdrew together, though they did not speak any farewells, or take definite leave, as far as I could tell; it was as if they were intending shortly to return. I thought perhaps they had gone to relieve themselves. Alicia remained alone and took some steps toward the moored boats and some steps back toward the fires.

It was my chance, the only one I might have. I went through the trees toward her. I came into the open and Alicia saw me and paused a moment, then walked in my direction. I took a lantern from one of the men waiting there, and holding this in one hand I held out the other to her. When I would have led her into the cover of the trees she held back, but I told her that the boat was there, not far away, and I begged her to give me her company, if only for a little time, to let me be with her when no one else was by, and at these words she resisted no longer but followed behind me as I held the lantern up to show the way.

The place where I had left the boat had not been well chosen: there was no secure stepping place onto it from the shore. I had to bring it close and help her onto it while holding up the lantern so she could see where she was setting her feet. In order successfully to achieve this I was obliged to go over my knees in the water and she was concerned and said that now I would be wet and uncomfortable and it would be her fault. But her hand was on my shoulder and mine rested a moment against the small of her back as she got on the boat, and I felt heat not chill, and this I told her and she laughed and said my name in a tone that lay between remonstrance and tenderness, and my heart expanded to hear her say it thus. Nevertheless, I was thankful that it had not befallen at a time when I was wearing my new hunting clothes.

The boat had two narrow benches. She took one and sat facing me while I seated myself on the other and took up the paddle, which had only one blade and so had to be used from side to side.

The lantern we set between us. There was no breath of wind; the surface of the water was still and dark, no faintest tremor on it as it stretched away across the lake. The ripples and rings of earlier, when there had still been light, insects skating on the surface, fish rising, were gone now. The light from the lantern was cast upward over her bosom and face, and white moths came out of the shadows of the bank to flutter against the flame.

I paddled out into the open water, taking the moths with us, aware of nothing for the moment but her face before me and the need not to shed a single drop of water on her as I crossed the paddle from one side to the other. As we moved out toward the middle of the lake, I had the feeling that together she and I were entering a territory altogether new, a place from which we would not emerge unchanged. I brought in the paddle and the boat drifted round, following some current of the water imperceptible on the calm surface.

I began now, as my exhilaration subsided, to see some disadvantages in this boat. I could only look at Alicia; I could not touch her. At the most, leaning forward, I could have laid my hand on her knee, but such a gesture could have had no sequel, would moreover seem grotesque, as if I were about to offer some ponderous advice, like a wise elder. Closer than that, without much care on my part and extreme docility on hers—and it was too soon for that—I could not get, without risking to send us both overboard, the boat being too light and shallow, too easily overturned. Always, always, there was some impediment. The time was short, there was a journey to make, Adhemar might be watching. And now this closeness and farness of her . . .

As the boat moved in its slow arc I saw the turrets and domes of the palace outlined against the sky and the cluster of lanterns at the landing stage. The fires must have been replenished, the light from them lay red across the water, reaching almost to the opposite shore. A boat with a lantern at its prow was crossing the water and it passed through this reflection of the fire, and the lantern was not reddened but silvered by it.

"We must not stay long," she said, thus unwittingly adding to my discontent.

"When will we have time for ourselves," I said, "without someone watching, someone waiting?"

"Soon now, my love. We must be patient."

This came in the deeper, surer tone of the woman she had become, but the soft endearment and the ceaseless need for patience before the tyranny of time had all the essence of our early love, and memories of this came flooding back to me now and it was as if nothing had changed: the night that surrounded us, this boat in which we drifted on the dark water, seemed no different from an obscure corner in the castle of Richard of Bernalda, one of the many where we had met and kissed and made our promises. I spoke words of love to her now as I had then, and now, as then, the fullness of my heart made the words stumbling. I vowed my service of patience to her. I was her knight, I said, she had made me so by her touch on my head. I would show my service in patience. Was not patience in devotion the quality of a true knight?

"You will be my true knight before the world," she said. "You will be my husband, if you so desire. When next we meet it will be to exchange our vows and make our betrothal known. Now we must return. I must rejoin my uncle and brother. They will be wondering what has befallen me."

So calmly uttered had these words been that I had obediently taken up the paddle before the promise in them came fully home to me. When it did so I could find no words but those of adoration, and these came in a rush. As I swung the little boat round and headed for the fires that were still blazing at the lakeside, my exultation knew no bounds. I blessed the sky and the water, the very night itself, for my good fortune, and as I did so, at that same moment, we crossed in our boat some invisible line and entered the territory of the mirrors: the leaping fires and the lanterns clustered at the landing stage and those on the boats returning to the palace and the shifting reflections of all these on the water and even the drops from my paddle that were caught in the starlight, all began to wheel and tilt and multiply and stretch away, rank upon rank, into a distance that seemed infinite, the heat haze above the fires shimmered over the water and a multitude of boats trembled in this heat and the ripples of it played like a soundless music on the turrets and towers of the palace, and suddenly, between one thrust of the paddle and the next, I saw an exact copy of Alicia sitting behind me, somewhere on the water, her bosom and face illuminated.

An exclamation of wonder rose to my lips at this celebration of my happiness—for so I took it to be. But it was never uttered, because Alicia had made no sound at all and her face had not changed, nor her posture on the seat, and so I knew that she could not have seen this spectacle, only I had seen it, it was I who had my face toward the turning mirrors.

It may seem strange to one who reads this, as it sometimes seems strange to me when I recall it, that I made no mention to Alicia of the tricks my eyes played me. I could have done so, though briefly, as we drew nearer to the fires. Perhaps I was unwilling that such a difference should be declared at a moment when all else united us in joyful thoughts of the future. And then, there was so little time: this riotous breeding of images was short-lived, we were soon again in the world I knew. I would tell her another time, I thought: I would tell when we were next together. Once we had made our vows public, we would have more time together and more freedom in our talk.

I did not bring the boat as far as the jetty but grounded it higher up on the shore, and this time it was an easy step from the boat to the land and so I got no second wetting as I helped her out. I would have walked with her and lighted the way but she did not wish it. "There is light enough," she said. "It is not far." She turned to face me, still in the shadow of the trees. She raised her hands and brought them together in a gesture that seemed at first like prayer. "I leave you my ring," she said, "as an earnest of my love, until the time we can be together."

I slipped the ring from the little finger of my left hand and I swore my love and service to her and we exchanged the rings.

"I told you true when I said you are splendid," she said in low tones. "You will always be so. You will always be my splendid Thurstan."

She came into my arms and kissed me and her body pressed against mine and somewhere in my stomach I felt a movement like a fish leaping. Then she was gone through the trees to where the boats and lanterns waited.

XVII

ALL THROUGH THE HUNT, from sunrise when we rode out, her image stayed in my mind. The time passed as in a dream, when the thoughts and feelings belong only partly to what is before our eyes and there is an attendant life that runs along beside us. While we waited for the finding and unharboring of the hart, while I held myself in readiness for the chase and listened for the baying of the scent, while we followed the ruses and doublings of the quarry as he ran back on his own tracks to strengthen the scent then bounded sideways to confuse the hounds or entered and left the streamlets that run through the woods so as to break his traces, while I galloped with the others and followed the sound of the horn and shouted with all the power of my lungs and ducked the low branches, amid all this hullabaloo and headlong career, I still drifted on the dark lake, still heard the words of love and promise she had given me, still felt the ring where it lay threaded against my breastbone. And when this splendid animal was worn down at last and lost its faith in flight and turned to confront the dogs, when Bertrand, as Lord of the Hunt, brought his mount forward and lifted his bulk in the saddle and plunged his lance through the shoulder and pierced the heart, my pity for it and my admiration for the stand it had made were deepened by memories of Alicia's words and glances, her face bright-eyed in the light of the lantern, and the beauty of the hart's slaying was the beauty of her hands as she raised them in the dimness of the trees to take off her ring.

It was late when we regained the palace; there had been much to do—as generally in a hunt that is well conducted—in the flaying and butchering of the hart and the rewarding of the dogs. And here again Bertrand showed me his favor, as he had the day before at the Assembly. When the hart had been laid on its back and the scrotum and testicles removed and the skin of the throat slit up the length of the neck, and we had sounded the death on our horns and the dogs had bayed the death and been granted a brief time to tear at the throat, so as to remind them that the hart was their true and noble quarry, when the skin had been well and neatly peeled away by the huntsman and his varlets, Bertrand, whose prerogative it was to make the first cuts of the jointing, turned courteously to me and graciously asked me, before all that company—and her brother Adhemar among them—to assist him in it. Bertrand of Bonneval, whose mother's brother was the Count of Conversano. And he allowed me to use his severing knives from his own scabbard, with handles made of ebony inlaid with gold. With our sleeves rolled up to keep them from the blood, we worked side by side, he very elegantly cutting out the tongue and I slicing the smaller muscles of the shoulder. And glad I was for my time as squire to Hubert of Venosa, when I had learned the unmaking of the hart under his exacting gaze.

So it was with a great sense of well-being and satisfaction that I returned, bearing in my pannier some delicate morsels I was hoping to offer Alicia when we feasted on the venison that night, in particular those tender muscles the Normans call *fol l'i laisse*, meaning he is mad who would leave them. But I had scarce had time to wash away the stains of blood from forearms and hands when there was a tapping at my chamber door and it was Caspar, come to tell me that his mistress had left in the morning, being worried for her father, who was ill and needed care.

The surprise of this made my disappointment all the keener. I remembered now that she had spoken once before of her father's ill health. But she had said nothing to me of her intention to leave so early, on the very day of the hunt. Perhaps it was only this morning she had decided to go. Otherwise, surely, she would have told me . . .

Caspar must have read my feelings in my face—it was always Yusuf's reproof that I allowed too much to show there. "He is asking for her," he said. "The messenger came early, soon after you set out. She left me here to inform you of it and to give you her regrets for this sudden departure."

"What is the nature of the illness?"

He paused a moment before replying, then shrugged slightly, a gesture that would have been insolent in a servant but in him, with the special place he appeared to enjoy in Alicia's regard, it seemed natural enough. "Well, it is no secret. He is losing the powers of his mind. So it has been for some three years now. He does not remember the happenings of his life, he does not recognize faces that once he knew well, and this grows slowly worse, though he is still strong in body. The Lady Alicia was always his favorite, he knows her and he listens for her voice and her step. None can comfort him as well as she."

He fell silent here, as if awaiting some reply, but I could find none to give him. "She is very devoted to her father," he said.

"She left no other word for me?"

He hesitated for a moment, his eyes upon me. Once again I was struck by his handsome looks and the independence of his bearing. "She asked me to assure you that this changes nothing."

On this he bowed slightly and withdrew, and I had to be contented with it. Neither Adhemar nor Alboino was present at supper, so I supposed they had left at the same time. The venison lacked savor without her, though I had an honored place at the table and was listened to when I spoke of the events of the chase. With the hours that passed I grew reconciled to her departure and even found good reason in it. She was the only daughter, only she could give her father solace when he felt distressed in his darkness. It seemed to me entirely natural that any man, father or no, would call to her in his need. And I had her ring in my keeping and her promise in my heart.

These were the feelings that remained uppermost in my mind on returning to Palermo, and there now began a period of happiness for me as I waited to have word from her. Whatever in my work might have seemed tedious or distasteful before now came lightly to me. I looked forward to the time when Alicia and I would be man and wife and I would return to the life I had been intended for. She had not said how long it would be before we exchanged our vows, but I was content to wait on her wishes and her sense of propriety. Indeed, this very waiting was a fulfilment of the vows of service I had made her on our parting, in keeping with the order of chivalry I would soon now be joining. My years at the Diwan of Control, my purveying of pleasures and all that this had masked, all the unworthy acquaintance, in my new life these things would dwindle in memory, almost as if they had never been. No more lies, no more deceivings . . .

The King had returned from Salerno and we were finally able to offer him the spectacle of the Anatolian dancers. This was done in proper form by Stefanos through the Office of the Seneschal. The Dance of the Belly, the first time ever in the King's domain—so we gave it out, saying nothing about their wanderings in southern Italy, letting it be generally inferred that they had been wafted, by means more or less magical, from the Taurus Mountains.

The royal summons came sooner than we had expected. King Roger was to entertain a company of notables from Germany, among them Otto of Zahringen and his son Frederick, whose active help he was eager to obtain in fomenting revolt against Conrad Hohenstaufen. His widowed daughter-in-law, Elisabeth of Blois-Champagne, was to join them—it was her last appearance at court before returning to France.

It was late in the afternoon that he sent notice, either on the spur of the moment or because Sir Stephen Fitzherbert, the chamberlain in charge of the kitchens and all matters concerning the seating at table and the serving and the entertainments, whispered in his ear. This service Stephen had sometimes done before and claimed a fee from our diwan—or a gift, as it was called, to remove the notion of payment. Naturally he would expect a gift on this occasion too, since whether or not it had been his doing no one could say.

There was very little time; they had to change into their new clothes immediately. The King would dine early, as his habit was: often, after taking leave of his guests, he would go on working far into the night, attended only by his notary, Giovanni dei Segni, one of the very few who enjoyed his whole trust. While he was dining we would wait in an adjoining anteroom. When we were sent for I would lead them into the Great Hall, make my bow to the assembled company, then return to the anteroom and await them—there was no place for me in the hall; I was neither guest nor performer.

It only remained for me to give them instructions as to how they were to bear themselves in the King's presence. It was the first time I had seen them since Nesrin had made us laugh with her talk of going into the bushes. I was as aware as ever of her presence there among them, and strangely glad for it. But I took care to address the group as a whole without letting my eyes rest too long on anyone. They were to follow me in file, the three women and then the two men. The dancing space would be lit by torches against the wall; they would see it there before them. I would make my bow and leave. They would form a line facing the King and his guests, and they would all bow together, bending the knee and holding the body low.

Fearing they might not have understood my words, I gave them a demonstration, not thinking, in my eagerness to have everything done properly and in order, that I might look ridiculous, inclining my body in this fashion, all alone there and without an immediate reason. "Keep this bow and hold yourselves still while you count to ten. Count slowly. One—two—three—four. When you come to ten, straighten up. Try to do it so that you all straighten up together. Ozgur and Temel will then seat themselves with their backs to the wall. They will start playing and so the dancing will begin."

There was a prolonged silence among them after these words. They had not followed their usual practice of averting the gaze while I spoke, but watched my movements closely as I bowed and counted and straightened up. Now they were regarding me with a certain fixity of expression that I took at first to mean they had not understood. I was supposing with some weariness that I would have to go through it all again when I realized that the look was not one of failure to understand but of wary curiosity: they were regarding me as one might regard a creature of unusual shape encountered in an unlikely place.

This was disconcerting and made it difficult to know what to say next. I essayed a smile. Of course, they were not civilized people, the practice of bowing would seem strange to them. "Time is short," I said. "Perhaps we could practice it a little?"

A hand went up and it was hers. I was not deceived for a moment by the expression of serious inquiry on her face, not for a moment . . . She looked beautiful in her new bodice and skirt with the silver sash round her middle. Her black hair was untied, it lay loose to her shoulders. I noticed now for the first time that it was not quite straight but had a curl or wave in it that I supposed must be natural. But perhaps not—perhaps she had made it with curling tongs. I had a sudden sense of her life as it might be in private, when she was alone. And for a moment she seemed indeed alone, there was no one else there, we were looking across an empty space at each other. I felt my smile faltering. "What is it?" I asked.

"They hear the counting, they will laugh."

It seemed to me that she spoke the Greek words with a better accent now, and more easily. But it was clear that the spirit of mockery was not changed in her. "You must count inside your heads," I said, tapping my own head with a forefinger to drive the point home.

But this was a mistake on my part because Temel now repeated the gesture, but in a more rapid and violent way, and he was followed in this by Ozgur. They were signaling that they thought me mad, and this angered me because they were savages and had no idea of polite behavior, and made this ignorance into a virtue. "Well, whether you like it or not," I said, "if you want His Royal Majesty's favor, you will have to make your bow and do your count. Otherwise you will disgrace yourselves and me."

At this they fell to talking among themselves, all but Nesrin, who did not join in but stood apart from them. I hoped this might be a sign of sympathy with me but could not be sure—I was not sure of anything about her except that she was beautiful.

There was no time now for any more discussion; we had to set off immediately in order to be in attendance when the call came. We were escorted to the royal apartments by two household guards in their plumed hats and silver braids. As they clattered and jingled along beside us I wondered how I could ever have wanted to become one of them. Higher things awaited me now.

When we were ensconced in the antechamber not much more was said among us and I took this to mean they had agreed among themselves to follow my instructions. The call came from one of Fitzherbert's stewards, who stood at the door and beckoned. I followed him, and the Anatolians followed me in the order I had prescribed. We reached the dancing space and I stepped forward to make my bow. I had a confused sense of the spectators seated close to me, lower down in the hall, and of the King at the high table with his guests. It was the same confusion I always felt in his presence, as if I had come suddenly from some dusky place into a fullness of light that bewildered my eyes and prevented me from seeing him clearly. There was the gleam that lay on the circlet of gold over his brows and on the gold brocade at the shoulders of his robe—more than this radiance I did not see. I bent my knees and inclined my body low and began my count.

The Anatolians were at my back and ready to bow in their turn, or so I thought. But before I was halfway through my counting I heard voices and laughter behind me: they were calling to one

another in their own tongue, just as they had on the night when I
first saw them, just as if these courtiers before them now were the
same gaping boors that had surrounded them then! I heard the clatter of the women's shoes as they shook them off onto the stone
floor, then the quick tapping of the drum and the first plaintive
strains of the long-necked dulcimer. They had not formed a line,
they had not bowed, they had not counted. In the royal presence
they had shown no slightest mark of deference or respect!

My throat had tightened. I could not have spoken to them, even
if they could have heard. I felt the touch of a swirling skirt, like a
breath. I turned to see Nesrin swaying close behind me. The music
grew louder. There was nothing for it now but to leave in the best
order I could and let things take their course. I would no longer
have my place as Purveyor after this gross breach, so much was certain. I would be lucky to escape prison.

I turned and took two paces toward the door we had entered by.
But I was not able to get farther. Nesrin took some dancing steps
across my path and seized my hand in her own much smaller one
and held it tightly—so tightly that without unseemly violence I
could not free myself. I thought for a terrible moment she wanted to
bring me into the dance, but it was not this, because as soon as she
had my hand in her own she stopped dancing; she stood still and
looked at me and I saw that she wanted me, for some reason of her
own, to stay there, to be present while they danced.

A great swell of laughter came from the assembled company to
see my escape cut off, to see us standing hand in hand there, while
the music sounded and Yildiz and Havva turned slowly in the first
steps of the dance. At the laughter—and this seemed almost the
strangest thing of all—I saw Ozgur and Temel, who were sitting
back against the wall with their instruments, nodding and laughing

together as if sharing a joke. After a moment I realized that they were not laughing at me but at the spectators, and I felt that they were my friends and never afterward lost this feeling.

But still I could not move. Nothing like this had ever happened before, through all the succession of jugglers, buffoons, strongmen, and acrobats that I had at different times introduced into the royal presence. Nesrin's eyes were on me, bright and unwavering, neither timid nor bold but with something that seemed like trustfulness in them. Quite suddenly I knew what I should do. I did not know why she wanted me there but I knew what I should do—or better, I knew what I should not do: Thurstan of Mescoli was not a man to slink away with laughter in his ears. I smiled at Nesrin and nodded, and she released my hand and turned away from me, back into the dance. I raised my head and walked with a pace neither fast nor slow to the nearer wall, and I stood against this to watch the dancing. And in doing this I turned my face from the King.

For a while it was little more than strolling, as the women snapped their fingers and Ozgur began a crooning song. Then he struck the drum sharply with the heel of his hand, exclaiming loudly as he did so, and the women echoed this exclamation, and then they were dancing.

Yildiz was first to quicken pace, turning her back on the people in the hall and facing Ozgur, who seemed both to lead and follow the rhythm of her steps with quick finger-tapping at both ends of the drum. She raised her arms to shoulder height and shivered them and the loose copper bangles ran along her arms and glittered. Then the others quickened too, and they too faced away from those watching, dancing for one another, or so it seemed, making their arms shiver in the same way, a shivering that seemed to come from the arms themselves and not from any effort of the shoulders.

Then all three began turning upon themselves and the scarves fell away, leaving their middle parts bare.

When that shuddering of the body came that precedes the dance of the belly, there was complete silence among the people there, though they were flushed with wine and had been loud enough before. And then, with the shudders ceasing and the ripples of the belly beginning, every eye was on the shining pebbles of glass set in the dancers' navels, and the rolling movement that caused the dimple of the navel to close on the glass and dim it then open again to reveal its shine. Nesrin raised her arms to the nape of her neck as if to lift her hair, but she kept them there motionless and looked down at her own movements, watching herself with a pride that excluded the spectators only to involve them more.

Watching, I forgot my disgrace. I was moved by the beauty and wildness of the dancing, and I saw, I think for the first time, that the beauty of it lay in this wildness. It was the dancing of outcast people, rebels. They obeyed nothing and no one. They made no attempt to match their movements one with another. They made no smiles, they did not seek the eyes of those watching. None gave a glance toward the high table where the King sat. And yet, on that night of moonlight and firelight when I had seen them first, Nesrin had danced before me and looked me in the face. And even now, as she turned this way and that, setting her feet with that grace and care I remembered, even now sometimes our eyes met.

Unexpectedly, in the midst of my trouble, I was attacked by self-reproach. How could I have expected these lawless wanderers to bow and count? When I thought of all the bowing and counting I had done in my life I could not feel satisfied with what it had brought me. I forgave the Anatolians in my heart for all the trouble they had caused me in the past and all that they were likely now to bring upon my head. And in the particular case of Nesrin I extended this forgiveness to include the disturbance of my senses and the distraction of my thoughts that she had caused me from the first moment of seeing her.

The dulcimer fell silent now and the beating of the drum came in alternate rhythms. The dancers went back, back, arching over until their heads came close to the floor behind. Bodies arched thus, legs slightly spread, faces looking upward, they repeated that raising and shivering of the arms. It was an astonishing thing to see. I remembered now the words of the Greek trader, made poetic by his desire of coin. *As if inviting the love of a god* . . . I had eyes only for Nesrin, who was between the others, for the slightly parted knees, for the toenails reddened with henna. Failing a god, why not Thurstan of Mescoli? So whispered the slumberless demon of my lust.

There was dead silence in the hall as they came slowly upright again. Then the King's voice sounded, a single shout of bravo, the supreme mark of royal approval. It released a great storm of applause that seemed to rebound from walls and ceiling. Coins began to clatter on the floor but not one of these people, who had bargained with me so stubbornly for two ducats at the inn, made a move to pick them up, and I was pleased at this because I was in their midst and felt for that moment that I belonged with them, pleased that these homeless strangers, born to poverty as I supposed, did not give any there the satisfaction of power, to see them scramble for the coins and thus feel the restoring of a supremacy that might have been put in doubt by the talents of the humble.

The plaudits were continuing. The Anatolians were standing gravely there, a dew of sweat on the brows of the women. Some words passed among them and all looked at me as I stood against the wall. Then Ozgur gestured toward me, a movement strange to my eyes as often the gestures of these people were, bringing the palm of his hand toward his chest with fingers splayed, in a manner that seemed fierce almost, as if he would strike himself. I understood then that he wanted me to come forward and join them. But I still had not moved when Nesrin came to me and again took my hand and brought me to stand among them, she on one side and Havva on the other, and the applause continued, with shouts and even some stamping of the feet—indeed, it seemed to me that the sound grew louder as I came forward. And after some moments of confusion I found myself gratified by this tide of applause, more than gratified: I felt warmly immersed in it, as if it were my natural element. And this was in a way strange, as I had never before heard approval of me shouted by numbers of people at the same time—the nearest I had come to it was at the age of fifteen, with shield and lance, on occasions when the lord brought his guests to watch us practice at the lists.

In short, the Anatolian dancers were a great success, and this it was, I believe, that saved me from the King's displeasure at their failures of courtesy. I had done well in the past with some dwarf jugglers and an Armenian who could lift enormous weights and two Italians from Modena, a man and a woman, who could tell stories without words, only by movement and gesture and changes of face, so that one could understand everything. These had been some of my successes, but they all paled by comparison with this one. Besides, I had not been present at those times, not had this experience of being lifted up and borne along on a warm tide.

Before we could leave the hall, Fitzherbert came down to us—in person now. Not to order my immediate arrest for lese majesty, but to inform me that by immediate command of the King this company should hold itself in readiness to appear again before him on the following evening. Fitzherbert, who is haughty and cold in his usual manner, smiled upon me and congratulated me on the finding of such dancers. And in this courtier's smile of his I read the King's pleasure. The coins that had been thrown were gathered up for us, and this turned out to be a great advantage, as more were added in the process, and it was a heavy purse that lay in my palm by the end.

There was more to come. Orders had been sent through to the kitchen. We were escorted to the lodge that forms part of the gatehouse at the entrance to the inner courtyard, and a table was set up on a trestle in a room there, and before long there came servants with trays of food: roast venison in a juice of grapes and garlic, fish cooked in wine and dressed with sage and parsley, the bread they call gastel, made with brown flour and olive oil and honey. These were dishes from the King's own table! And with them came flagons of raisin wine, as they make it in the eastern parts of the island, wine that was clear to the bottom of the cup and delicate in taste and deceiving in this delicacy, as it mounted quickly to the head.

We feasted together like lords, and afterward with the wine still passing round, I emptied the purse on the table and shared the coin among them. I made the division in five parts, but it was the women who took charge of the money, making bundles with the scarves they had discarded in the dance.

"This is only the beginning," I said. "You have pleased the King greatly, you have also pleased his very important guests. He will not delay in showing the marks of his favor."

I was exhilarated by the wine and by the success of the evening and my rescue from opprobrium, for which rescue I now felt deeply grateful to these people, altogether forgetting, in the exaltation of my spirits, that it was they who had caused the risk of it in the first place. I decided that it would be fitting to make a speech at this point and got to my feet. I said that this had been a very brilliant and unusual occasion with a good many first times in it, the first time there had been such great applause, the first time anyone had been engaged for the succeeding evening, the first time food and drink had been sent, at least in the years I had been purveyor of pleasures at the Diwan of Control. And from the King's own table! Above all, it was the first time that I had stayed to watch and been included in the applause. The idea of including me might have been in all their minds, but it was Nesrin who had come and taken my hand, so it could be said that it was her doing. I looked at her as I spoke. Her hair was tied back with a red ribbon now and the upper part of her stomach, below where the bodice ended, was still uncovered—she had tied the scarf, with its knot of money, round her waist. Under that scarf, I thought, there would be the glittering pebble in her abdomen, temporarily eclipsed. Whatever I noted in her looks came always as a surprise to me, even when I had looked at her only shortly before, it was still surprising, even though familiar. I am well aware that this is a statement lacking in logic. In this my account I labor to serve truth; logic I leave to the schoolmen. She was smiling at me now and there sprang into my mind the unruly notion of yet another first time, and I stumbled in my discourse, saying I was not sure why they, why she, had wanted me to stay but I was glad that I had done so and would remember this evening for a very long time to come. I could think of nothing further to add to this, but only to thank them, which I did, with a full heart, and I raised my cup and drank to them and wished them luck.

Then Ozgur got to his feet and he smiled and looked at me fully, which I could not remember him doing before, and began speaking in his hesitant and strangely accented Greek. They had all wanted me to stay, but it was certainly Nesrin who had taken my hand and she had decided this herself, why he could not tell, it would have to be asked of her. He was only a man, what did he know? There was laughter at this and Nesrin looked aside, but not as one displeased. In any case, Ozgur said, it was something only she among them could have done. But they all felt glad I had stayed and they thanked me for bringing them here and making their fortunes and they would never forget me.

Still on his feet, he glanced around him and said some words in a low tone, and the others rose and they all moved from the table and formed a line before me and they bowed all together as I had shown them how to do and they began counting, but aloud and in their own language. They did it exactly, perfectly, the bowing and the counting and the straightening up. And every one of their faces had a smile for me.

I was greatly moved by this because I knew it for an expression of friendship and respect and because by making a joke of the ceremony in that way they were seeking to show me that I had been in the wrong when I tried to compel them. And I had thought them savages. No doubt it was the fault of the wine, but I felt some start of tears and thought of making another speech but decided to give them a song instead. I chose one written by a great hero of mine, the troubadour Bernard of Ventadour, born the son of a castle servant, whose talents won him honor in many courts and made his name famous.

When grass grows green and leaves show forth
And trees are bright with blossom,
And lark lifts up his voice,
Such joy it gives me,
Joy in my lady, and in myself joy . . .

As I sang I looked often at Nesrin and I saw by her face she was held by my singing, and this brought more tenderness and joy into my voice.

There was much applause when I finished and they asked for another song and would not be satisfied till I agreed. This time I chose one I had composed myself, very different in mood.

The one I most desire
Is cold toward me.
She does not summon me now.
Why is she so changed?
If she love me not with her body
At least let her show me kindness . . .

The heartbreak of this and the abjectness of it, and my heightened feelings, and Nesrin's attentive face before me, combined to break my voice a little as I sang—it was sometimes a fault in me when I sang before others that I allowed my feelings to come too close to the words I was singing and so the even tenor of the voice was threatened.

I did not sing more, though they wanted me to and loudly asked it. I could tell from their words and faces that my singing had moved them, the more so perhaps as they had not known of this talent of mine and so had been taken by surprise.

"This night stays in our memory forever," Temel said, and he raised his cup to me and I touched it with mine and we drank together. I saw how they all enjoyed the wine, though the women drank less. I made some joking remark about the Prophet's forbidding of it, and they said they were not Moslems but Yazidis. This was a religion quite new to me, and I was about to inquire into the tenets of its faith when it occurred to me that it was a question I might put to Nesrin, if ever I got the opportunity to engage her in talk when no one else was by.

The opportunity came sooner than expected. It was growing late, the gathering had been a happy one for all of us, and when we began to bid one another good night it was in friendly and affectionate fashion, both the men and the women reaching to take my hand and the men also patting me on the shoulder.

I do not know exactly how it came about, this was a night of blessings. I waited for the others to pass first, Nesrin hung back a little, and so it happened that we two found ourselves alone together at the door and standing rather close. The time was very short if I wanted to keep her there—a matter of moments. I wished only to delay her, to delay the parting a little. I had no other thought. The Yazidis would not serve as a topic: this proximity had come by chance, it was not a moment for discussing religion. My slow-wittedness makes the blood rise to my face now, as I remember it and confess it. In my dumbness I nearly lost her, nearly let her leave in silence and rejoin the others, who I thought perhaps might be waiting outside. She herself said nothing. She looked at me briefly, then looked away. After a moment she made a movement toward the door . . .

"How did you become such a dancer?"

She smiled a little and I had the feeling that she was relieved that I had found some words. "My mother . . . she also was a dancer. She teach me when I am a child, tall like this." She raised her hand to show me the height from the floor. "I start to dance when I start to walk."

"Your dancing is beautiful." *Everything about you is beautiful,* I wanted to say, *your eyes, your throat, your hair.* But I did not find the courage. It was the first time she and I had ever been alone together. I had often wished for this and imagined how it might be. But in that wishing I had always been ready of speech, at my ease, masterful—even lordly. I had not been this present Thurstan, tongue-tied, woefully lacking in address, gazing at a dancing girl with a nude stomach as if she were a princess in a courtly fable.

She waited a moment longer, then passed through the door out onto the cobbled space before the gatehouse. There were guards at the gate and two lamplighters with their ladders against the inner wall, but there was no sign at all of the other Anatolians. It was a warm night and the moon was nearly at the full. In the gentler light beyond the range of the lanterns at the gate we paused again. Even more strongly than before I wanted to keep her with me.

"There was moonlight when first I saw you," I said. "Moonlight and firelight together. Why did you take my hand tonight? Why did you want me to stay?"

I saw her shake her head a little as if perplexed. "You do not know? It cannot be one of the men because men do not take the hand that way. It cannot be Yildiz or Havva because they have their men with them, it is not a proper thing for them to take your hand. And so it is left to me because I do not . . . because there is no one . . ."

I was obscurely disappointed by this explanation. Was it no more than that? I began to move in the direction of the stables where I had left my horse. "You do not tell me all the truth," I said. "You speak as if all of you had decided on it and you were the one chosen. But that is not so. I was there, I was watching. The others were already dancing and playing. You decided without them to come and take my hand. You decided alone."

She stopped at this and turned to me and tossed her head at me like an impatient pony. "I tell you what is true," she said. "I say what is in my mind. Thurstan Bey, you are important man and pass your days in a palace, but there is much you not understand. I do not say who decided, I say why the others could not do it." There seemed to me a lack of logic in this, but her eyes had a light of battle in them and I did not feel equal to drawing her attention to this lack. And there was something else now occupying my mind. Absorbed as I had been in the talk between us, I realized only now that Nesrin was going the wrong way: instead of turning to rejoin her companions she had turned with me toward the stables. Did she know this? It was probably a mistake: she did not know the precincts of the palace very well, she might believe I was accompanying her when in fact she was accompanying me. Immediately I was beset with questions—always a weakness with me. What would a man of honor do? What would a man do who aspired to knighthood? What would Alicia expect of her splendid Thurstan? She would expect him to assume it was a mistake and point the mistake out with utmost promptitude. In that case Nesrin and I would part there and then, a thought I found difficult to endure. Or perhaps I could offer to escort her back to her sleeping quarters. But if it was not a mistake, what then? Nesrin would be wounded. Was it an ideal of knighthood to wound the weak and frail? It was not easy to think of Nesrin as weak and frail, but I tried hard to do so, and this is an example of how we force our thoughts to suit our wishes. In short, I said not one word. And with every step my hope mounted.

"I tell the truth to you," she said, and stopped again. "Yes, I decide alone. I choose you to stay, because I am free to choose. The other ones that watch me, I do not choose them. If they watch me or not, I do not care. I do not dance for them. But you, I care that you watch me. What is so difficult in that?"

We had started walking again and were drawing near to the stables. My heart was beating in my ears and my chest felt constricted. "I care that you listen to my singing," I said. "I was singing for you, that is the truth." We were close to the stable door now. The mare had heard my voice and step and she whinnied softly.

"That is your horse? She knows you."

"She is waiting to go home. I do not live in the palace. I live in the town."

"I know this. Stefanos told me."

"Did he so? I wanted to ask you . . . I did not know if you came here with me . . . if you had mistaken the way."

"Mistake the way?" Her eyes had widened with surprise. "How can I mistake the way? How strange man you are. All this time, while we walk together, you ask yourself does she mistake the way? One would only go with you if she mistake the way?"

"But you did not say anything."

"What should I say? I go with you, where is need to say anything? I wait for you to say if you do not want me."

"Not want you?" I said. "Not want you?"

For a moment she looked solemnly at me, then she gave me a smile that threatened to take away what poor breath I had left. "I do not mistake the way, I know the way," she said, and her voice was softer than I could have thought possible.

As we entered the stable the mare shifted but there was no other sound. Light from the lamp that hung outside the door fell across some straw bales piled against the far wall. There was the sharp smell of the mare, the smell of beaten earth and pissy straw. Smells of every day, deeply familiar, transformed into strangeness by the clasp of our hands together, the first kisses. I might have been a man at the dawn of creation, sniffing at a new world.

There was a loft above the stable where they kept feed for the horses. A wooden stairway went up to it. There were sacks of grain here and some loose hay. I made a bed with my riding cloak and surcoat and all the rest of my clothes, careless now of the finery I had donned with such care for this court occasion. My hands were impatient and clumsy and I made some wreckage of buttons and stitches as I tore and tugged at myself in the twilight of the loft—the lamplight did not reach here, but there was a barred window in the wall and the moonlight came through it.

"I must not hurt my new dress," I heard her saying. She was standing between me and the window and the moonlight fell on her as she undressed. I heard the rustle of her clothes, saw the movements of her arms as she raised the bodice over her head, saw the skirt fall to her knees, saw her step out and away from it. And all this was done with a deliberate grace, as if she was still dancing for me.

The moonlight lay on her hair and shoulders and flanks as she came toward me. Against these parts touched by the light, her eyes and the nipples of her breasts and the little bush of Venus made zones of darkness. Light was caught in the glass pebble at her abdomen, focus of my dreams, and in the thin chain that held it there, slung round the light bones of her hips. I was to think—not then, I was too stirred for thought, but later—that in these last moments before we were joined, as she showed herself to me, she was offering the beauty and promise of her body, an image on which love could rest, could guard itself through periods of separation in a way that memories of ecstasy, of bodies clutched together, cannot be guarded.

What she and I did I could not exactly say, in the sense of one thing following upon another. And since that night I have known for self-deceivers all those who claim a love was blissful and say *first we did this, then we did that,* as if there were one single track to the reaching of joy. It was no alleyway Nesrin and I entered together but a wondrous labyrinth, from the moment she came to me and with her nearness shielded the moonlight from me and brought me the feeling of darkness as our bodies touched, as if a band had been laid over my eyes. She came down to me and I remember—then or soon afterward or later—my sight restored to see her face above me, lit once more by the moon, and her face had a look of sorrowing and she made a long murmuring sound. Then the moonlight was streaked with fire and I closed my eyes against the glare. I must have cried out because the mare was startled and snorted—I heard the sounds she made but not my own. I kept my eyes closed, as if the fiery light and the throes of my body could not be endured together, but I still saw the glimmers of red against the lids. They were like sun streaks: it was like closing one's eyes against some ravishment of the sun. I swear it: there was cool and burn, moon and fire together, this first time we met with our bodies, as there had been on the night when we met with our eyes only.

XVIII

SHE WAS NOT THERE when I woke in the morning. On the floor, for only trace of her, was the red ribbon she had used to tie back her hair. The evening of that day they danced again, and according to Stefanos, whom I asked to go in my place, they enjoyed a success no less resounding. He had not been asked into the hall, he said; Stephen Fitzherbert, with his jackal's nose for the whiff of success, had taken the Anatolians into his custody and care, and it was he who had presented them.

I was glad to hear of this second triumph, but glad also that I had not been there to assist at it. I could not feel regret for what had passed between Nesrin and me; I could not cease to dwell on it and marvel at it in my mind. But the morning light had brought guilt with it, memories of the vows I had made to Alicia and our exchange of rings at the lakeside. She was so delicate and fine, a lady born, of noble family, all the best of my past was in her keeping, and all my hopes of betterment in the future. And in spite of this, so soon after our promises, I had been overmastered by passion for a vagrant dancer of no birth or breeding whatever and no knowledge of what it means to aspire to knighthood.

Made gloomy by these thoughts, I fell to thinking how much simpler our life on earth would be, how much more tranquil and dignified, if we could return to the time before the Fall. It is clear that Adam was meant to pour his seed into Eve's womb; we know it from God's commandment in Genesis to go forth and multiply. But at that time there was no disturbance of lust. Saint Augustine explains this to us in his *De Civitate Dei*—I think it is to be found there. He says that in the state of innocence those parts were moved by the same act of will by which we move our other parts, without the soul being snared by hot desire. Like raising an arm or winking an eye. I tried to imagine this blessed state, tried to imagine Adam's member as being moved in the same way as his fingers or his toes, but I could not. I believed it but I could not imagine it. Many men find their faith strengthened by what is beyond their imagining, but I am so constituted that the reverse is true of me—such failure makes the belief grow less. I began to wonder how Saint Augustine could have formed so definite an idea about these things, since he too had come after the Fall and his parts were moved in the same way as those of all of us—and not infrequently, if we can judge from the *Confessions*.

None of these speculations helped me to a state of grace or made me feel better about myself. I was resolved to keep away from the Anatolians as far as I could, since I was miserably lacking in faith in my fortitude should Nesrin and I by any chance find ourselves alone again; I did not even trust myself not to try to contrive this once I set eyes on her.

But there was no avoiding the farewells. On the afternoon of the day before they were to leave, our King Roger sent them by means of the faithful Fitzherbert a sum of 150 gold *tari*, a gift of unprecedented proportions. It was brought in a bag of soft leather and left for me to deliver to them. I went with it to their quarters and gave it to Ozgur and watched while it was shared among them. With the coin that had been thrown to them and the eight dinars from the diwan and now this magnificent gift from the King, they would be richer far than they could ever have dreamed.

"What will you do now?"

I spoke the words to Ozgur but the question was for all of them. Nesrin was there with the others, not in her dancing clothes now but in a simple linen gown, and this unaccustomed dress made her seem almost like a stranger, as if she had somehow anticipated the farewell, gone away from me already.

They would go home, Ozgur said, and I took it that he referred to them all. In the village of his birth, his share of the money and that of Yildiz put together would buy them a stone house, land for pasture and for tilling, sheep, two oxen. "Many sheep there," he said. "The land is good in the valleys. My father work for others, for the owner, the *mal sahibi*. But I work for me and Yildiz."

"And the music?"

"I play for my grandchildren. Yildiz will teach them to dance."

"We will stay in one same place," Havva said, and it was the first time I could remember her speaking directly to me. "No more road. We are tired of road." And she made a sudden grasp at her hip and twisted her face to show aches and pains, and everyone laughed because she was young and supple and graceful in movement.

Nesrin had joined in this laughter, but her face was serious again as she looked at me. And now, as by some unspoken agreement, the others went a little farther off and left us together. She stood there silent in her new dress, her hands by her sides. Would she go without a word to me? On an impulse of anger almost, not wishing, in the distress I felt at parting, that she should be the one to dictate the mood between us in these my final moments of seeing her, I stepped toward her and took her left hand where it lay by her side, and I said, "Farewell. Go with God."

She allowed her hand to stay in my grasp for a moment and looked me in the face with such a serenity in her regard as made me feel I was looking at her for the first time instead of the last. That taste of bitterness that lay on the mouth seemed less. Her eyes were darker even than I had thought them, almost black, like water that pools among dark rocks. She freed her hand and said some words of farewell. Once again it seemed she had gone from me already, as if, with her new dress and her newly acquired wealth she had embarked already on a future that held more for her than this scene of farewell. What she saw in my face I do not know. I did not look more at her, but made my last farewells to all of them together, feeling as I did so that I was parting from friends. Then I turned from them and began to make my way to my place of work in the diwan, where more renewals of the royal privilege were waiting for me to scan.

Before I could reach my room, while I was still in the passage that led to it, Yusuf's secretary, the eunuch Ibrahim, came quickly toward me from the head of the stairway. "I have been looking everywhere for you," he said, making it sound like an accusation. He was always hostile to me, as many of the palace Saracens were, though they dared not show it openly, because I was not of their race, they saw me as a friend to the Norman interlopers who threatened to usurp their place in the royal favor. "The Lord Yusuf wishes your immediate presence," he said. "Already he has been made to wait."

I was in the passage that led beyond my door to Yusuf's. Because of the impression of urgency, of being impatiently awaited, that Ibrahim had given me, I hurried past my own door, went quickly through the long room where the scribes were working, and entered Yusuf's cabinet without more than a light tap at the door. Entering thus abruptly, I had the sense of being somehow mistaken, of being in the wrong room. The figure before me, in these first moments, seemed like a stranger: no immaculate white robe, but silks of blue and scarlet and gold, a sheathed scimitar thrust through the broad sash. And he was standing close to the wall, and seemed to have been leaning down at the moment of my entrance, or just before that moment, as if to gather something he had let fall at the foot of the wooden paneling. But he had straightened and moved away before I was well into the room, leaving me to doubt the evidence of my senses.

For a moment he stood there, regarding me quite impassively. There was no displeasure in his face, but I had the impression that I had interrupted him in something. His eyes had their usual heavy-lidded look, and once again I thought how like a hawk's his face was, with the curved beak of the nose, eyes that blinked rarely but could easily hood themselves or widen as if adjusting to stronger or weaker light.

"Lord, please forgive that I entered with so little ceremony," I said, "but I knew from Ibrahim that you had already waited some time for me and I felt to blame because I was not there at my desk to obey your call at once."

"Where were you?"

"I was sharing the King's gift among the Anatolians, those whom I found in Calabria and brought here, as my lord will remember. And I was making my farewells to them."

Yusuf nodded, and the movement brought glints from the diamond he wore where the folds of the turban crossed at the center of his forehead. There was a sapphire on a thin band at his throat, and the handle of the scimitar was set with sapphires and opals. "One in particular you were sorry to lose," he said, with the slightest of smiles.

I felt a leap of surprise at this. I had never spoken of her to him, never mentioned her name. I know now that he intended me to feel the shock of it, he wanted me to know that he had sources of information other than myself, and this not because he thought Nesrin important—he cared nothing about her—but because he wanted to warn me. This I realized later; at the time I was concerned only to deny him the sight of surprise on a face he had often told me showed too much, to deny also the suggestion of his smile and defend Nesrin from it. I have not much to be proud of in regard to Yusuf, but I am proud that I succeeded in this small rebellion.

"Yes," I said, "I was sorry indeed to part from her. The man who wins her for his wife may count himself lucky." How had he known? Had he set someone to watch? Had someone followed us that night, stood below, heard the sounds we made? I thought it probable enough. Trust between us was much impaired; both of us knew it. I had kept too much from him, and this mainly because of Alicia. In relating my time at Favara, I had not spoken to him of Bertrand and the favor shown to me, or of my talk with Alboino, or the vows Alicia and I had exchanged. And now, in the considered manner that was characteristic of him, he had just given me proof that he did not depend on me for his knowledge of my doings, that he had other sources. He was so much more powerful than I, so much richer; the jewels and silks he was wearing I could not have bought for a year's stipend. I knew from them that he had been riding in cavalcade through the city, as he regularly did, in company with his fellow Saracens of high office, to show through their splendor that greater splendor of the King, a splendor veiled these days—His Majesty was rarely seen now in public.

"Well," he said, "you will be wondering why I have sent for you."

"Yes, lord."

He began, as was always the cautious way with him, by telling me what I—and most of Palermo—already knew. After the failure of the crusade and the headlong retreat from Damascus, Louis, the King of the Franks, had stayed on in Palestine, remaining there through the winter and visiting the shrines of the Holy Land.

"Those with him there say he prostrated himself at each shrine," Yusuf said. "He does not touch the ground only with knees and forehead, as do we, but with his whole body. He is very pious, but the god of the Christians did not come to his aid in Syria."

"He does not blame God for the failure, he blames the Byzantines."

This made Yusuf laugh, a thing not at all common with him, though I did not see why—I had not intended it as a joke. "Well," he said, "blame must be laid somewhere. King Louis set off for home last April and after many mishaps he is expected to land on the Calabrian coast in these next days. He will wait there for Queen Eleanor to join him, and then the royal pair will make their way to Potenza, where our King Roger will be waiting to greet them. They will be the King's guests there for some days before resuming their journey to Paris." He paused for a moment, smiling. "A fruitful meeting on both sides, as all are hoping. Every effort will be made to encourage Louis in his belief that it is the Byzantines who are to blame. Rather than God, eh? Byzantium is our enemy too. Those who join us in enmity are our friends. An alliance with the kingdom of the Franks would be of great value to Sicily in these troubled times."

He looked at me for some moments, and the smile faded. "So much is general knowledge. Now we come to a thing that is not. A request has reached us from the Curia Regis, under the seal of the Lord Chancellor's Office, that Thurstan Beauchamp, our Purveyor, should be sent to Potenza in advance of the royal party, in order to help in the preparing of entertainments for their majesties. First Favara and now this. You are in great demand, so much is clear. What is less clear is who is demanding you."

"But it is for the lord of Potenza to arrange the entertainments. He must already have done so. How can I be of any help in it, going there so shortly before the royal arrival?"

"You are right, you cannot be of help."

"And so?" I was bewildered. "There must be some mistake."

"No, there is no mistake. Under cover of this you are to carry money to someone there. A sum of five hundred *tari*. It will not come from the Royal Exchequer even though the request for your services has come through the Curia Regis. The money is to be issued by our diwan and entered in the usual way, though without any words as to purposes—there will be no declared destination for it. I am being asked to grant permission without knowing for what purpose the money will be spent, without knowing who it is destined for. All this is highly irregular, Thurstan Beauchamp, would you not agree?"

"They are seeking to divide us, they are seeking to destroy the trust between us." In this they were succeeding, I knew it as I spoke, knew it from the look in his eyes, the tones he used, above all from this ironic use of my full name, which once he had used like a father when he wished to cajole or persuade me but was now a cold reminder of my Norman blood.

"Why should they wish to do that?" We were standing in the embrasure of the window, our usual place when we talked privately together. As he spoke he reached a thin arm to my shoulder, but in no friendly fashion—there was a surprising strength in the tightness of his grip. "Why should they wish to do that?" he said again, and I felt the danger in him, as I had sometimes felt it before, inspiring not fear exactly but a sense of what it might mean to become the enemy of such a man.

"Lord, I do not know," I said. "How should I know? You can refuse to send me."

He took his hand from my shoulder and smiled and shook his head. "This request comes under the seal of the third power in the land. It may well have the blessing of the King himself. It would not be politic to refuse outright. Moreover, it would not be fruitful. Refusing, I would not learn the reasons. This is a question of money, and money reaches into many corners and has many uses. It was money that took us out riding today, for our wealth to be seen, by our display to reflect the glory of the King, who is unseen."

I nodded at this but could not feel in full accord. The Franks who were coming in ever-increasing numbers, and in particular the Norman knighthood, whose ranks I aspired to join, did not understand this Arab notion of kingship, indeed were hostile to it. Roger was a Norman, one of them, their feudal lord. They detested the Saracens for keeping him from them, for hedging him about with divinity. I said, "When Moslem and Christian go riding in company to honor the King, that will be the time of greatness."

"You are right, we should work for that. I had hoped you and I would work together for it, but now I am less sure. In any case, it will not be soon. There is hatred on both sides. Those I ride with are men who have come to riches by their merits, by their service, not by accident of birth. Many were brought here as eunuch slaves. They have no family, no land, no power outside the palace. They know that only the King can protect them from the hatred of the Christians, and so they do everything they can to keep him apart from them. Only with God's help can hearts be changed." He took me by the arm, but gently now, and began to lead me away from the window. "There is no God but God," he said, "and on Him do we rely. They will send for you soon, those who have picked you out for this mission. You will go to the place of meeting, you will listen to them carefully. You will require to know the name of the person for whom the money is intended, and the reason it is being paid. If they refuse to tell you this, you will refuse to go and I will support you in this refusal. Five hundred *tari* is too great a sum to be consigned without knowing who or why."

I promised to do as he ordered me. "And if indeed I go to Potenza," I said, "everything that happens there and everything that is said to me will be faithfully carried back to you."

"Yes, I will expect your report." The words were uttered indifferently, without great conviction, and it came to me that he would not now be relying on my report alone. I was no longer trusted; someone else would be there at Potenza, someone whose duty it was not only to watch the proceedings but to watch me.

He kept his arm through mine as he went with me to the door. "Ah, Thurstan, Thurstan," he said at parting, no more than that, but I felt the regret in his tone and it echoed my own feelings of loss.

The summons came four days later. The attendant they sent

from the Chancellor's Office led me to a stone-flagged chamber closely adjoining the shelves of the chancery archives. The archivist was waiting for me here, a monk named Wilfred of Aachen, very pale of face and peering, with lips that seemed almost bloodless and hair of a reddish color. After a while we were joined by the Lombard Atenulf, whom I had last seen in close conversation with Abbot Gerbert in the courtyard of San Giovanni degli Eremiti. All men with German for their native tongue . . . There was a recess with a low doorway leading directly to the archives, where Wilfred did his work of collating and annotating and copying. Also kept there were notes on the people of the palace administration, a fact well known to all. Somewhere among these shelves, recently dusted and referred to, there would be details of my own life, origins, parents, all my history since arriving in Sicily at the age of six.

A table and chairs had been set in the recess, and the three of us seated ourselves. Atenulf was a thick-necked man, full of face, with small eyes the color of raisins, a quick voice, and a frequent habit of showing his teeth in a half smile of superiority. I knew something more of him now—I had taken some pains to know more. He had come from Austria a dozen years before, a younger son of Arnulf of Tostheim. He enjoyed the protection of the Vice Chancellor, Maio of Bari, though I had not been able to discover why this was so. He had made his fortune by the founding of a new chancery, which he had named the Office of the King's Fame and which concerned itself with the way King Roger was seen by the people under his rule and by states abroad. He sent men noted for their gift of speech among the people to explain the King's actions and set them in a favorable light; he had a say in the appointment of ambassadors, speaking for those who would be most skillful in justifying the King's policies; he also advised the King on the manner of his public appearances—it was said to be on his advice that Roger had taken to wearing a canopy of red silk over his head to veil the light on him, in the manner of the Fatimid rulers of Egypt. By these various means Atenulf had gained much favor at court.

He greeted me cordially enough, as cordially as his looks and manners allowed. These were disdainful even when he wished, as now, to be friendly, and I thought it strangely incongruous that one who had made his name by setting our King in a favorable light should present himself in one so little attractive.

He began by telling me what Yusuf had told me already. I was to go in advance to Potenza, where the meeting between the two monarchs would take place. My reason for going—the reason that would be given out—was to assist in preparing the entertainments.

"It is reasonable," he said. "It carries belief. After all, you are the King's Purveyor and have good fame as such. My congratulations, by the way, on the success of the Anatolian dancers—I was there and I saw them. Also, you are trained in arms, and so would strengthen the guard on the King's person."

"Our diwan has no duty in the protection of the King's person. We deal only with the dues from his demesne."

"But were you not trained for knighthood till the age of sixteen? Were you not soon to be admitted to the Household Guard when Yusuf Ibn Mansur took you into his douana and had you sent to Bologna to study Roman law and the keeping of account books?"

It was as I had surmised; they had studied the course of my life. I had sensed some intention of belittlement in his last words, something almost involuntary, as it seemed to me, habitual to him when addressing those he thought inferior.

"You know so much," I said, "yet you do not know that there are no courses in the keeping of account books at the School of Law of Bologna."

An ugly expression flickered over his face, but he sought to disguise it with a smile. "No man can know everything," he said.

"It is enough that a man should know where to look," Wilfred said, a view natural enough in a keeper of archives. He got up from the table as he spoke and went to the door and opened it and gave a quick glance this way and that, down the passages between the shelves.

"You will be expected," Atenulf said. "You will be received and shown to your quarters. You will wait until a certain person makes himself known to you. He will tell you that he comes from Avellino, so you will know he is the one. You will answer that you have a cousin there. To that he will say it makes you a neighbor. Not much more is required of you. You will hand over the money; the sum has been agreed. He will give you something from his person, a badge with a bird on it, in token that he has received the money. You will bear this back to me. You need know nothing more about it. It will be in your usual line of duty, after all, nothing out of the ordinary, that is why you are sent. You are the purse bearer, is it not so? When you are not the purveyor of spectacles and shows."

The sneer was back in his voice but it was not this that swayed me. Even without Yusuf's orders I was not disposed to be treated thus lightly and kept in ignorance. It was a question of dignity— once again I felt the eye of Alicia on me and remembered my vow to be worthy of her. She would not want me to be ingratiating toward this arrogant interloper. He was of higher rank than I, but he was acting under instructions, I felt sure of that, though why I was so sure I could not have said. Because of this he would not want anything that might appear as a mistake on his part, anything that might make him open to question.

"You speak as if I had no choice but immediate acceptance of this mission," I said. "But that is not so. It is not a mission that comes within the tasks and duties of my diwan; otherwise we would have had the notice ourselves and arranged the matter in the usual way without this naming of me from outside. I will need to know more before I can agree to go."

"Agree to go?" he said. "Harken to this young cockerel, Wilfred. Your office has agreed to this interview and that is tantamount to acceptance of the mission."

"Animus promptus consensum valet," Wilfred said.

"That may sound like wisdom but it is not, in Latin or in any other language," I said. "Willingness to consider does not imply readiness to agree, either in law or religion. One need not be versed in logic to understand so much. The greatly revered Peter Abelard, in a letter of reply to Bernard of Clairvaux, draws attention to these quite separate states, the one exemplifying the separateness and even loneliness of each individual soul, the other leading to the unity of all souls in Christ. No doubt you are familiar with this text?" I was by no means certain that the source was to be found in Abelard, and was relieved to find that neither of them knew enough of the matter to dissent. Taking advantage of the silence that followed, I said, "Who is this man that I must meet? What is the money for? How can I return and present a report to the lord of my diwan with this information lacking, particularly as the money is to be accounted through us? He would never accede to it, he would protest to the Curia. With all respect, Excellency, if it is the case that you are not authorized to answer these questions, you must seek the authority."

"It is permitted to me to say more, at discretion," he said coldly. "But this obduracy of yours will be made known. The man is a Neapolitan. His name is Spaventa. He has a mark in Constantinople."

"A mark? You mean a quarry? He is an assassin then."

"He is presently under our orders."

"I see. I suppose he is one who will be under orders to any, if the pay is enough. And who is marked out for him?"

"I will explain it to you. Corfù has fallen to the Byzantines, as all of us know to our cost. Only by treachery could this have happened. They had provisions for a year and fresh water in plenty. It is a well-known fact that the citadel is impregnable. For the Greeks it was like shooting up to the sky—they could never have taken it. Someone opened the gates to the enemy. In the dead of night, someone lowered the drawbridge, pulled the bolts from the gates, leaned over the battlement above the gateway, and sawed through the chains."

I was discovering in Atenulf an accomplished storyteller. His eyes held mine, he had lowered his voice for greater effect. I could begin to see now the reason for his success: building the King's fame was also a kind of storytelling. His recounting of such sustained and deliberate treachery had brought horror to my mind. I saw the Evil One crouched at the side of the traitor while he filed and sawed at the chains. "He must have had accomplices," I said.

"That cannot be known now. But the captain of the garrison, where is he?"

"How should I know?"

"I will tell you. He is in Constantinople, enjoying the protection of Manuel Comnenus, who has granted him the post of Commander of the Imperial Guard. No need to look further, would you not agree?"

"So this Spaventa . . ."

"He will be the executioner of this foul traitor. It will be known to all that no one betrays our King and lives to profit from it."

"And he can be trusted not to talk?"

"A man who has made killing his trade does not talk, either about his failures or his successes. He would not last long if he did. You must know this yourself—you have carried money to assassins before, have you not? This Spaventa is very experienced and very careful. It is because of this that he is so expensive—the money you are taking is only the first half of his hire, the second will come when the work is done. He is gifted, very gifted. He can make death look like an accident or a suicide, he can make it a public spectacle or a private disgrace. He is an artist, a shaper of circumstance, he is one who understands the importance of the symbol."

His harshness of demeanor had quite gone, melted away in the warmth of his praise. He had spoken as one master commending another, a man after his own heart.

"So," I said as I rose, "in Constantinople it will be the public spectacle?"

"The precise manner of it will be left to him. He must make it notable, memorable. Such are my instructions to him—I am entrusted with the fame of it, the mark it makes on men's minds. Perhaps this recreant will be found hanging upside down in some public place with his testicles in his mouth, perhaps he will be wearing women's clothes, or a false nose and jester's cap. Perhaps only his head will be found, mounted on a spike. Something men will remember and be warned by. They will know the power and scope of our King, who can reach a long arm to be revenged on those who have played him false."

"And the name of the man to be killed?"

"Enrico Gravina."

I took my leave on this, satisfied that I had prevailed upon them to give me the information I demanded. I did not myself believe that these orders had come from the King; he was at a level high above. It seemed to me that this Spaventa, and those who had thought of hiring him, and Atenulf who was entrusted with the fame of it, and I who would carry the money, all belonged with my friend Mohammed, creatures feasting and fighting below the surface of the dark water on which the King's silver barge rode serene, enveloped in light. Yusuf's words came back to my mind: *He is just but unjust things are done in his name* . . . But this was not unjust. The traitor deserved to die. Would it not be a worthier thing to abduct him, bring him to trial in the King's court before the people he had wronged? This would not be beyond the power of resolute men. But it was not our King Roger who decided—he had no knowledge of it. It was the creatures below the surface. Why did I labor so to keep the knowledge of this death that was planned from the King's mind, to keep him sheathed in brightness? And why, to my faltering spirit, did the labor seem always greater?

XIX

THAT SAME DAY I went to Yusuf and gave him a full account.
"So Wilfred sought to settle the matter with four words of
Latin," he said. "That is very typical of the Roman clergy. For them,
Latin is the magic formula. No matter what the problem, by expressing it in Latin you have solved it before you reach the verb.
And this faith is founded on the very thing that should give them
pause, the fact that so few words are needed. Latin is excellent for
inscriptions on tombstones, where space is lacking. But no one
should dream that such conciseness serves the interests of truth—
rather the opposite is the case: truth is obscured because no room is
left for doubt. The Arabic language is far superior; it is looser and
more ample. We do not see truth as a dead butterfly to pin down—
we follow the path of its flight through the fields and forests where it
lives."

He was silent for some moments while the pleasure these comparisons had caused him faded from his face. "Wilfred of Aachen,"

he said. "Wilfred of Aachen was for some years a monk at the Monastery of Groze on the Moselle. Among the community there was Gerbert, who has had great advancement since and is soon to become the Pope's Rector at Benevento, a very important post, which is in the grant of the Roman Curia but usually given to an Italian, not a German."

"Perhaps in his native place there are those to recommend him."

"Yes, perhaps so."

I had not told Yusuf of my meeting with Gerbert and his companions in the Royal Chapel, not thinking it of any importance, but I had told him of seeing Gerbert and Atenulf in close conversation together in the courtyard of the Church of San Giovanni, and I think this was in his mind now, though he made no direct mention of it. "Perhaps it is so," he said again. "We will try to learn more of this prelate. I have the feeling that he will repay our scrutiny, also the archivist. It may be no more than chance, but there is the form of a triangle in it, and I have found that rarely comes by chance."

"A triangle?"

"Gerbert and Atenulf, Atenulf and Wilfred, Wilfred and Gerbert."

It seemed to me more in the nature of a circle, but I did not say so. "I see, yes. Well, as I have told you, lord, they were very unwilling to explain their purposes."

"Of course, you made it a matter of your own dignity, you did not declare you were acting on my orders."

"How did you know this, lord?"

"I did not exactly know it, but I know you, my fine fellow. Well, it makes no difference. They were expecting you to insist, whatever the reason. They would have been disappointed if you had not."

I stared at him. "Disappointed?"

"They knew well that Yusuf Ibn Mansur would require to know these things before releasing money through his own chancery."

"But if they knew it, why play these games?"

"It was not exactly a game, or at least not one that is played for amusement only. Think, Thurstan, my young man. Must I be forever giving you lessons? These years with me and still lacking in suspicion? Or is it that your mind was on other things?"

As I looked at him now in silence, at a loss as to how to reply, it came to me that my mind had indeed been on other things and that this was something useless to speak of to Yusuf, he would never understand because he would never be seduced by his imagination. Perhaps Atenulf was cleverer than I had thought, cleverer than he wanted known. The gifted and versatile Spaventa, the demon-led traitor sawing at the chains, the King in his silver barge . . .

"You are full of duty," Yusuf said, "and you are careful to fulfill orders, and you are brave, but you are too open, too sunny—you must cultivate the flower of suspicion, which is a shade-loving plant. Many qualities serve us who serve the King: intelligence of deduction, instinct of the creature, wisdom of experience. But two things are essential above all others, and they are faithfulness and suspicion, and no amount of the one can make up for a lack in the other. Why the delay, why the reluctance? Come out of the sun and think."

"Yes, of course. By their seeming unwilling I would be the more likely to believe."

"Exactly. In this our world a readiness to speak is taken for the mark of the liar. You had paid a price, you see. You had asserted yourself against Atenulf's greater authority, you had insisted in face of his displeasure. We always value more what we have paid for, is it not so? And the conclusion of all this?"

"If they wanted me so much to believe it . . ."

"It is the less likely to be true, yes. Good, we are coming closer. But we must not fall into the opposite error of supposing it to be false. It is in accord with Atenulf's care for the King's fame. We must simply keep in mind that the reason they have given may not be the true one."

"Then the money may be intended for some other purpose?"

"It is possible, yes. And since the payment is to be made through the accounts of our office . . . you see?"

"Yes, I see well. We may be held to account for the use to which it is put."

"There were two of them. Why was Wilfred needed? As I understand from you, he did not take much part in it. But the oaths of two weigh against the oath of one, if it comes to swearing. We can be sure no one else has made public mention of this money or this mission. So it might in the end be made to seem that the purposes were ours from the beginning. And since we cannot know for certain what these purposes are . . ."

He paused at this and narrowed his eyes and thrust out his hands with the palms upward, as if to receive some blessing or guidance from above. "Only God sees equally the hidden and the revealed. There are those who work against us, who would wish to see me discredited. We are watched by famished eyes, Thurstan, the eyes of wolves. They want me dead, but it is not only that: they want this diwan. They would fall on it, dismember it, tear it limb from limb, sharing out the powers and prerogatives that belong to us and gorging on them. The Royal Diwan is not a monument, it is not like a castle with strong walls, it has no defense but the King's favor. Chanceries are born and die, they unite and divide, they come into being or cease to be at the will of the King—and those close to him.

If our enemies succeed, the *Diwan al-tahqiq al-ma' mur* will exist no more, not even as a memory. We must judge it safer now to break this money into smaller sums and find entries of an innocuous nature for them. Then silence will wrap round the money. Silence is golden, as the proverb says. In this case not even the clink of the gold will be heard."

He smiled as if pleased, but his eyes rested on mine and I felt he was watching for the effect of his words. My faculty of suspicion, woefully inadequate as he had deemed it, was well roused now. Not Atenulf's powers of narration had lulled my mind: it was he, Yusuf, who had done it, by appearing to take seriously—even to be angered by—their withholding of the information only to tell me on my return that he had not believed in it from the first. Why had he disarmed me thus in advance? To make some use of my ignorance that I was still too stupid to see? Once again I felt used by him, tricked by him. Why was he telling me what he proposed to do with the money? It was rare with him to confide his intentions in this way. He ran no risk—the accounting would be skillfully done as he knew well how. If he thought I had new masters, would he so confide in me? Perhaps he was testing me, perhaps he wanted me, for reasons I could not fathom, to make known to others these intentions of his.

Even as I smiled and nodded with a full air of comprehension, playing the part still that I had always played, of favored pupil, the questions twisted through my mind. Amid all perplexities, however, one thing had become very clear to me: I, Thurstan Beauchamp, was the one who would bear the purse and run the risk; there would be no record of the money anywhere, no one would admit to any knowledge of it; if anything miscarried while it was in my possession I would be in serious trouble. There and then, still meeting Yusuf's gaze with what firmness I could, I resolved that if I succeeded in delivering this money, from the moment of handing it over I would deny all knowledge of it in my turn. I would lend my name to no statement made by anyone about it, including Yusuf. I would be in Potenza as the King's Purveyor, and for no other reason in the world.

Thus I denied my loyal support to Yusuf even before he claimed it. And when I remember that denial now, I cannot but think that it played its part in what came after. Not much more was said between us. As was his way, he warmed to me at parting, said he had heard of the great success of my singing coming after the great success of the dancers. "A night of successes," he said, and there was slyness in this, but no ill nature. "And the *sorcot*," he said. "Another new one? And the *chainse*?"

Later, when I drew the money, we spoke together again and he wished me Godspeed, but I have no recollection of his face on that occasion, or of what we said. What I remember now is the refuge we both took in this habitual topic of my clothes, the look of amusement and guile he wore when he teased me about them, and underlying this the unspoken knowledge of the hurt we had suffered, not something gone but something spawned by the air we breathed every day, the air that nurtured the shade-loving plant he had spoken of.

These are memories that return now. In the days that followed, while I waited for the order to leave, there was one event only and it filled my mind, eclipsing all else. It was Caspar who brought the message, and he came to my lodgings to deliver it, led upstairs by Signora Caterina, who always made her wheezing more audible when there was a visitor, in the hope of a gift either from him or from me. It was a note written on parchment, secured by two strands of cord with a seal of red wax to join them, and on the wax the imprint of the ring I had given her, a circle with a tiny scarab in the center. Rarely can so few words have given such delight to any mortal man. She would come to Potenza in the King's following, accompanied by some members of her family. We would announce our betrothal before them and before the King himself, and by this act our vows would be made binding. *My beloved, I count the hours.*

Caspar had waited there while I read it. He was only a servant, however elevated, and I strove to remain impassive under his gaze, with what success I know not. My joy was almost equaled by my wonder. To contrive to be included in the King's retinue at such short notice, and on a visit of state! It was barely three days since I had learned that I myself would be going. Once again it came to me how great must be her family's influence at court, though it could not be her father to exercise this in person, lost as he was in the darkness of his mind . . . "Tell your mistress I shall not fail," I said.

He bowed and would have retired, but at the last moment it occurred to me to ask him how he had found me, how he had known it was here that I lived. He looked at me without expression for a moment or two, as if slightly at a loss, taken aback by my simplicity in asking such a question. Then he said, "We made inquiries. My lady thought it better her note should be delivered in private." With this, he bowed again and withdrew, leaving me, as always in my dealings with him, a prey to some wonder as to the nature of his duties and his standing in Alicia's household.

We went by ship from Palermo to Salerno and thence overland to Potenza. There were eight of us in this advance party, the others all being members of the King's household, sent ahead to help in the preparations for the royal arrival: a wardrobe mistress, two serving women who kept very close together at all times, two Norman serjeants-at-arms who made attempts to separate them, a Sicilian stable master, and a cellarman of Stephen Fitzherbert's, whom I knew slightly, a Greek named Cristodoulos, rather womanlike in his ways and modes of speech but very strong in the arms and chest from hefting barrels.

A mixed company—in normal circumstances we would not have had much to say to one another. But the arrival of King Louis on our shores had released a flood of gossip in Palermo and it formed the topic of our talk through much of the journey, though I said little myself, content for the most part to listen.

I learned nothing that was new to me, but I was made aware, yet again, how ready the humble are to rejoice at the mischance of the great, and how easily one kind of error is confused with another, as if they all belonged in the same box. Errors of one sort or another there had been in plenty in the calamitous two years that had elapsed since King Louis set out at the head of his Frankish army through Bavaria on the Second Crusade. He was twenty-six at that time, famous for his piety but not for much else—certainly not for strength of character or military capacity. Traveling with him was his wife, Eleanor of Aquitaine, the niece of Raymond, Prince of Antioch, the greatest heiress in France and as resolute—some would say willful and some among the present company did—as her husband was hesitant. Already, according to some in their following, there was strain and ill humor between these two.

The miserable story of the French king's vacillations and failures of judgment, culminating in the disastrous decision to commit his force to an attack on Damascus, was known to all, as were the terrible losses suffered in the retreat. What interested my traveling companions more were the months prior to this fiasco, in particular the time that the high-spirited and beautiful Eleanor and the devout and lugubrious Louis had spent in Antioch.

"We have to remember the troubles she had been through," the wardrobe mistress said. "We must not judge her too harshly." She was of those who, under the appearance of understanding and pardoning, insinuated strong disapproval for the queen's behavior. "She had nearly been killed by those heathen Turks," she said. "She had nearly been wrecked at sea. It is no wonder that she was glad to reach Antioch and fall into the arms of her uncle, Prince Raymond."

"It was not only his arms she fell into," the stable master said. "She fell into his bed."

On this issue the company was divided, there being no evidence that Eleanor had slept with her uncle, but the majority thought it probable on the grounds that she had sought his company and made it no secret that she preferred her uncle's to her husband's.

"Incest is incest," one of the serving women said, "but as men there is no comparison. Prince Raymond is a proper man, he is handsome of face and well made and brave in battle, and he knows how to talk to a woman. I like that same type of man myself."

There was general agreement as to these advantages of Raymond's, though none of us had ever set eyes on the prince. "And a great commander in the field," one of the serjeants said, "which no one can say for King Louis."

"In my opinion, it was his endless praying and prostrating himself that set her against him," the stable master said. "It wore her down."

"She would have stayed there, she would have stayed in Antioch with her uncle," Christodoulos said. "She didn't want to go any farther. Louis had her dragged to the ship by force. She won't forgive him that. I wouldn't, if it was me. Well, would you?"

As I say, I took little part in these discussions, except to put in a few words now and again so as not to seem to be assuming airs of superiority—otherwise, they would not have talked before me. By virtue of my office I knew some things they did not yet know. I knew that Eleanor was seeking a divorce. I knew that her beloved uncle, abandoned by Louis, had been killed some three weeks before in what many regarded as a suicidal assault on the Turkish host—he had attacked Nureddin's army with four hundred knights and less than a thousand foot soldiers. I knew that his skull had been sent in a silver box to the Caliph of Bagdad as a proof that this great enemy of Islam was truly dead. And I knew that Eleanor had recently learned these things and been grief-stricken, and that she laid the blame on her husband, who in his jealousy had denied to her uncle the support of the Franks in defending Antioch.

None of this presaged well for the marriage, and I was privately convinced that the two would not remain much longer together, though it was rumored that one last bid was to be made: after leaving Potenza they were to journey to Tusculanum, where Pope Eugenius was currently residing, and ask for spiritual guidance. The outcome of the Holy Father's advice was of concern to me insofar as it might affect the prospects of an alliance between France and Sicily, but I did not think it could touch on my personal fortunes, not then.

By the end I was weary of the journey and of the company and of the incessant howling of wolves in the hills around Potenza, and I was relieved to see the donjon of the castle before me on its rise of ground. It was early evening, still light. The watchman on the wall saw us as we came up to the stockade, the bars of the gate were unfastened and we passed over the drawbridge and into the gatehouse, where the iron door had been raised for us—it was a sliding door of very new invention that could be raised or lowered by a winch above. I noticed that the men-at-arms at the gatehouse, in addition to ax and javelin, carried steel crossbows, a weapon that had been expressly forbidden by the Lateran Council of ten years before as being too powerful and murderous; in the hands of one who knew how to use it such a bow could kill a man at a distance of four hundred paces. This was the castle of Vincent de Faye, Lord of Potenza, who held his fief in vassalage of King Roger—only the strongest barons could so soon flout the interdiction of the Church. But I did not believe that a weapon so effective could be suppressed for long, and thought it likely that another decade would see it in general use.

At the gatehouse we separated, some going through into the courtyard beyond. I was led away from the others and taken by a little stairway to a room in the wall itself. It was small but I was pleased with it because it had a narrow aperture in the wall on the side that looked over the town and a short bench below this so that one could sit in the light. I have always hated rooms that have no daylight reaching into them; one of the things I had most coveted and most hoped to inherit was Yusuf's window.

There was a stout oak bar on the door, always a welcome sight to a purse bearer, and this I set in place before turning my attention to anything else. The bed had been made up for me and I saw with approval that side rails were fitted, so that the ends were braced and the covers and mattress prevented from slipping off, no matter how much I should thresh about in my sleep; in fact, on closer inspection the practiced eye of Thurstan the Traveler noted that there were several mattresses, not just one, and they were all padded and the top one stuffed with feathers. There was an oil lamp, a bronze candlestick with a good wax candle, a small rug rolled against the wall, a thin plank on trestles with on it a basin and ewer, and a towel hanging from a hook in the wall. The water in the ewer was clean, and the ewer was closed at the top so as to keep the water fresh; the towel also was clean, and sweet-smelling.

Everything was in good order. It was no more than the usual care for a guest but at once I thought of Alicia—perhaps it was her doing. I wondered which room had been set aside for her. As a favored guest she would be in an upper story of the tower, some distance away, not easy to reach without being observed. But if it was true that she had sent orders for the preparation of my room, perhaps she had been able to arrange for her own to be nearby, just a few steps away . . . It was not long to wait, King Roger was expected from day to day. I would take her in my arms, press her to me, feel her warm and breathing presence. It seemed long now since she had walked away from me through the trees at Favara, briefly seen against the firelight then lost among the shadows at the landing stage. I felt the need, not now to revive or restore our love, but to keep it firm in our life of the present, where my hold was precarious and my knowledge of her less. To keep her before me in the times we were apart, I fell back on memories of her when we were children, growing up together and loving as we grew.

This castle of Potenza was larger than that of Richard of Bernalda: the donjon had three stories and there were outbuildings. But all was familiar as I stood there, the gleam of light on the worn stone, the smell of the rushes that had been laid on the floor, the sounds that came from outside, clatter of mailed men moving on the battlements above, barnyard sounds from the kitchen courtyard, the distant whinnying of horses from the corral inside the stockade. I was taken back to the years of my childhood, when these sights and sounds had been at first the marks of my loneliness, in the early time, away from home, then the sounds of home itself, deeply familiar, accompanying my first successes with javelin and lance and the light of love I saw in Alicia's eyes. Here I had stood, those years ago, with beating heart, listening for her steps. And here it was fitting we should exchange our vows, the *verba de praesenti et futuro* that in the eyes of the church would bind us in the sacrament of marriage.

At the approach of darkness a manservant, elderly and slow in movement, came with supper for me on a tray, grilled fish and boiled vegetables and a pint of new wine. My room was a good distance from the kitchens and my servitor had taken his time, so the food was far from hot, but it was good, or seemed so to me—I had not eaten since the morning. The dining hall was being made ready for the royal visit, he told me—there was word that King Roger and his party would arrive the day after next in the morning. He lit the lamp, asked me if I lacked for anything, and slowly retired, with me at his heels as far as the door so I could bar it after him.

I was not sorry to be left alone. I was not much inclined to go abroad while I still had the money. And I wanted to take the time slowly and keep my hopes for these next days gathered warm around me.

I was reading the memoirs of Abbot Guibert of Nogent and had come to the events in Laon in 1112, when the merchants of the city were seeking to band themselves together into a commune and commute the dues they owed to the lords and the clergy. They had bribed the bishop to give them his support and free them from his jurisdiction, but when the time came he went back on his word and decided to keep the money and keep his powers too. However, the people rose against him. Besieged in his palace by the enraged populace, he dressed in the clothes of one of his servants and took refuge in the warehouse of the church, creeping into an empty barrel there. But he was discovered and dragged forth and in spite of all his pleas and promises very barbarously done to death with a sword stroke that opened his skull and spilled out his brains. Guibert describes this fearsome wound very vividly and also the mutilations and indignities inflicted on the body afterward, but what struck me most in reading were the things not explained in the text. What had betrayed the trembling bishop in his barrel? Who cut off the dead man's finger to take the episcopal ring? Did no one dispute his possession of it? The murderer is named, Bernard de Bruyères. And strange it seemed to me that a man's name would endure only for one cut with a sword when those whose lives are full of good works lie nameless and forgotten below the ground.

These questions were absorbing my mind when I thought I heard a tapping or scraping at the door, very light—a sound that might be made by drawing a fingernail across the wooden panel. After some moments it was repeated. All thoughts of the ill-fated bishop left me. That muffling of the sound, so like her secrecy and care. She was resourceful, I knew it of old—she had found an occasion to come early so we could have some time to ourselves.

In two strides I was at the door, had unbarred it, opened it wide. A man of medium stature, elegantly and expensively dressed in dark red, was standing at the threshold, who now took a quick step back as if put on guard by this alacrity of mine. He made no other movement but I saw how he looked first at my hands before he looked at my face and I knew who it must be and felt a fool for my eagerness. "I had not expected you so soon," I said, a mistaken thing to say but the first that came to mind.

For several moments we were motionless both. Then he smiled thinly and said in Italian, "Young man, this hasty opening of doors will bring you to grief. Take the advice of one who has lived longer. Always move slowly until you need to move fast. I am from Avellino."

"My cousin lives there," I said, moving aside for him to enter.

"That makes us neighbors." He stood in the middle of the floor, glancing round the room, at the walls and ceiling and embrasure of the window, as if to illustrate his own advice regarding slowness. He had eyes of a chestnut color set close together and a dark coloring of skin, but mainly notable in him was the beautiful molding of his head, which clearly he was proud of, as he wore his hair very short—it was like black mole fur. "But you were expecting someone," he said.

"I thought you might be someone else."

"I am never someone else. I am Spaventa. One who is sent to see Spaventa should not be expecting to see someone else."

There was a degree of menace in these words of his, and in the way his eyes rested on my face. I cast around in my mind for an explanation.

"I thought it was someone come to take the dishes away."

His eyes went to the tray where I had set it rather awkwardly beside my basin and ewer. "Why would he knock so softly? It is too early for sleep. And so much haste for a serving man?" He looked at me for a moment. "Perhaps not a man?"

I made no reply, judging it safer to let him reach his own conclusions—he would have more faith in those. "You were hoping she would stay a little, eh? Perhaps she had promised it—you are a fine young man. And she would knock lightly, of course. You open the door and before you there is only Spaventa."

"I have the money for you," I said. "It is in my pannier on the bed." I did not go for it immediately, however, but waited for his nod: with such a man it was advisable to explain the intention before making the movement.

The bag was heavy, I used both hands to take it to him. He sat on the roll of the rug, with his back to the wall and me well in view, and emptied the coins on the floor, on his left side, keeping them within the circle of his arm. I watched him count the money. His hands were steady and very neat in their movements as he laid one coin on top of another in piles of ten, each pile then returned to the bag and the tally kept with the point of his knife on the stone floor—the knife he kept close by him, on the right side. His fingers were thick and they looked very strong. I was reminded of my days of training for knighthood, when we strengthened the grip of our hands and the muscles of the forearms by squeezing together metal bars on a spring. By the look of his hands and wrists Spaventa had spent much time on this exercise.

I was not afraid of him exactly, and in any event it was not in his interest to harm me, I had to return to Palermo with his token of payment. But I will confess to a feeling of awe as I watched him put the last coins back into the bag. And it was one I had experienced on occasion before when delivering money to assassins. He would travel to a far city, he would track down a man whose face he had never seen, against whom he had no grudge, and he would take that man's life in whatever manner was required. And he would regard payment for this as no different in kind from that of any other undertaking where the balance of the money depended on a successful conclusion, as with a mason, for example, or a water diviner, or an advocate.

He took something small from a fold at the neck of his coat. "Bear this back with you," he said, "in token that I have received the money." He held it out to me from where he sat, obliging me to cover the ground between us. It was of blue enamel, oval-shaped, with a pin at the back, and it corresponded to Atenulf's description, having some kind of hawk in red, very small, at the center.

The knife was still there beside him, within reach of his right hand. Nothing showed in his face, but I knew he would trust me less now that I had his token. I had thought he would leave at once now that the money had been paid, but he showed no disposition to do this. Evidently he was in a mood for talking.

"Well," he said, "so we try again."

This I did not altogether understand, though he seemed to think it clear enough. There had been no previous attempts, to my knowledge, to put an end to the former commander of the garrison at Corfù. Perhaps he was referring in general terms to the need for renewed efforts in an enduring battle . . . "Yes," I said, "determination and tenacity of purpose are much needed in our service to the King."

He gave a short laugh. "I see you are a joker," he said. "We will serve him well on Mount Tabor."

At this I passed from uncertainty to bewilderment. It seemed that he was responding to what he thought was my joke with a joke of his own. But there was no laughter in his face. Yusuf's counsels, and my years at the diwan, now came to my aid. *Seem to know, nod the head, wait to learn more.* This I did, but he added nothing, though looking still at me. The silence lengthened and I deemed it wiser now to find some new topic of talk between us. "It is a lot of money," I said—and indeed this was true, it was far more than I had ever known paid for a killing. "Tell me, what would there be to stop you walking away with the money and going no further in this thing you are charged with?"

He gave the same narrow smile as before. "Walk away? That would be very dangerous, my friend. Those I had betrayed would seek for me. They would set people on who are clever at such seeking, well versed in it. I would outwit them, naturally. I am Spaventa. But after these many years as the hunter, I would not take well to being hunted. Besides, there is the second half of the money. We must honor our agreements. What kind of world would it be otherwise?" He smiled again. "Why do you ask me questions, master purse bearer?"

There was that about him that drove one to speak in haste. I answered with the first words that came to me. "It is enjoined on us. The Gospel tells us we must love our neighbor. Obviously implied in this is that we must seek first to understand him, since love cannot be exercised in ignorance and still keep the name."

"You are wrong, my young friend. It is only in ignorance of our fellow man that we can love him. The words of our Lord contain no previous conditions, no injunction that we should seek to know a person before loving him, I mean in the sense of knowing or understanding him in the workings of his soul. And there is a good reason for that. The more knowledge we have of him, the less possible it becomes to love him. For Spaventa it is only necessary to know which way the duck will fly."

I saw some refuge in this argument from the oppression of his presence, and I went on with it. "I cannot agree. In his Sermon on the Mount, in the Gospel according to Saint Matthew, Christ tells us that we must love not only our friends but our enemies too. Clearly, in order even to make this distinction, in order to know who our enemies are and what makes them enemies, we have to see our fellows in their difference, not in their sameness. In sameness there are neither friends nor enemies."

For the first time since he had entered the room his face lost its half-smiling expression. His mouth tightened and his eyes narrowed in obvious displeasure. "Young man," he said, "be warned, I do not like contradiction. Friends, enemies, it is all one, it is like the ocean, all one salt. Do you search for sweet water among the billows? You are young, take the advice of Spaventa. Do not trouble yourself with such useless distinctions. They weaken your eyes and spoil your aim. Know the flight of the duck and where to wait for its passing."

I could well understand why he did not want to trouble himself with differences. All men were strangers to him. A stranger might or might not be easier to love, but he would be easier to kill. However, the spirit of dispute worked within me, I would not give ground. "It belongs to our dignity to make distinctions," I said. "As it also does to argue against a man if we cannot accord with him, and more particularly so if he warns us against it."

"You talk like a lawyer."

"I was a student of Roman law at the School of Law of Bologna."

"Were you so? Well, I will tell you something now about Spaventa, and why he does not like to be contradicted in matters of theology. Listen now and mark me well. I have taken to you, and for this reason I confide in you. Before I found my true path in life, I was intended for the priesthood. My sainted mother wanted this for me, may she rest in peace. But it was seen otherwise by our Father in Heaven. One evening at suppertime I fell into dispute with a fellow student at the seminary in Viterbo where we were preparing to take holy orders. The subject of our talk was Saint Anselm's proof for the existence of God, that which they call the ontological proof. I was pointing out to my friend, who was sitting opposite to me, that it is possible to conceive of a being that cannot be conceived not to exist and that this is greater than one that can be conceived not to exist and hence, if that than which nothing greater can be conceived can be conceived not to exist, it is not that than which nothing greater can be conceived. And he, instead of recognizing the truth of this and complimenting me on the coherence of my argument, contradicted me and derided my logic. He laughed in my face. The blood rose to my head, there was a carving knife on the table, in one motion I had seized it and in one stroke severed his jugular."

He paused on this. A glisten had come to his eyes. "That was the end of my hopes of ordination. It was almost the end of me altogether—I was forced to flee. But the talent was there already, sleeping within me till it woke that day. In that fraction of time, of all the blows he could have struck, Spaventa chose the fatal one. And it turned out for the best. As a priest, I would not have made a great figure in the world. Is there by chance some wine remaining? If so, we could drink a cup together and toast this great enterprise of ours."

"Yes, there is some." I went to the jug and poured wine for him into my water cup. The cup I had used already I filled again for myself. He took the cup and waited and watched me and I understood he was waiting for me to drink first in sign of good faith. When I had done so, he raised his cup.

"Render unto Caesar."

It seemed a strange toast to me, but I thought his mind was still running on the Gospels. "And to God what is His," I said.

The movement he made on hearing this was of the slightest: he leaned back against the wall and raised his head to look more fully at me as I stood there before him. But with that small movement the whole posture of his body had changed, become tense and gathered. His eyes were bright and without expression, or none that I could read. There had been something in the first moment, before that involuntary gathering of the body, some leap of surprise masked immediately. My reply to the toast had been the wrong one, not the one expected.

"But of course," he said softly. He set his cup, still with most of the wine left in it, carefully down beside him, restored the knife to his belt, took up the bag of money in his left hand, bearing the weight of it quite effortlessly, and rose to his feet. While I still had not moved he took three quick steps to the door, unbarred it, and was gone.

XX

I SAW NOTHING MORE of Spaventa during my stay at Potenza. Perhaps he left that same night. To this day I am not certain by whose contrivance he could come and go so easily; at that time I assumed there was someone in the castle under orders from Atenulf to assist him. With the money delivered my heart was lighter; there was nothing before me now but to wait for the arrival of the King's party and the sight of Alicia.

In the afternoon of the next day, in the gardens that lay between the inner and outer walls of the castle, I saw among a group of French knights who had arrived that morning in advance of their king a man I thought I knew from the days we had both been squires, when we had met on several occasions, bearing the shields and tending the horses for our respective lords at tournaments. I was not sure of it, the years had passed, we had changed; moreover, he was white-faced and haggard-looking, as if he had been through some illness. But when I came closer and asked him if he were not

William Clermont, he knew me and greeted me by name and seemed glad to see me. We drew apart from the others and walked together, descending through the terraces until we came to a small loggia with benches inside where we could sit in the shade.

We talked about ourselves, about the things that had happened to us. His story was very different from mine. He had been knighted at the age of nineteen by his godfather, the Lord of Montescaglioso, and had recently returned from the Holy Land, where he had taken part in the crusade. I asked him why he was in company with the Franks when he was as Sicilian as I was, more so, since he had been born on the island, descended from a family who had come with the invading Norman army under Robert Guiscard, our King Roger's uncle.

He had been desperate to take part in the crusade, he said, and his smile twisted with the words as if there was a bitter joke in them. "I wanted it more than anything," he said. No crusading army had assembled in Sicily as King Roger had declined to take part. So he and his father and some others in the following of Godfrey of Enna had crossed over to France. They had gone to the Assembly at Vézelay in March of 1146 to hear Bernard of Clairvaux preach the crusade. Never in his life had he heard such preaching.

I noticed now that William's hands had begun to tremble slightly, though he sought to disguise this by pressing them against his thighs, and that his eyes had taken on a fixed look as he spoke, as if he were reciting a lesson learned by heart.

Such preaching, he said, there was so much power in him. Edessa had fallen, the holy places were falling to the infidel, the Franks had been slaughtered by the barbarous hordes of Imad ed-Din Zengi, their women sold into slavery. The crowd was vast, there were too many for the cathedral, they had put up a platform in a field outside the town and Bernard had spoken from that, promising remission of sins to all who took part.

"We began to cry out for crosses," William said. " 'Crosses, give us crosses!' The cloth they had brought was all used up. Bernard tore off his outer clothes to be cut up for crosses. Men fought over the scraps of his robe." He raised an unsteady hand and produced from within his bosom a scrap of dark cloth, frayed and ragged. "I have kept it," he said, and he laughed a little, though his eyes lost nothing of their starkness.

I was becoming uneasy now at his manner, and particularly the change in his voice, which had been lively enough when he first greeted me but had fallen now into a droning monotone.

"I have kept it by me," he said.

"To remember the crusade?"

"To remember the time before, when we did not know, when we were shouting for crosses. Everybody was shouting. I could not tell the difference between the shouts in my ears and those in my throat. 'Crosses, give us crosses!' "

He again pressed down upon his thighs, staring before him as if hearing these shouts again. He had not looked at me since beginning to speak of Bernard's preaching, but I felt now that I had been the unwitting cause of his distress, that the surprise of our meeting had jolted him, set him talking in this vein.

He had taken the cross that same evening, among the lesser nobility, after King Louis and his brother Robert, Count of Dreux, and Alfonso Jordan, Count of Toulouse, and Henry, heir to the county of Champagne, and William, Count of Nevers. "Immediately after these, the royal vassals," he said, and I saw how, even in the midst of his disorder, he took care to list these illustrious names, and showed satisfaction that he had been in such company. Everard of Barre, the

Grand Master of the Temple, had also joined them with a body of knights from his order, and many great ladies had accompanied their husbands, Eleanor of Aquitaine, the countesses of Flanders and Toulouse . . .

The recital of the names had steadied him a little, and lifted his voice, but this was short-lived. There was nightmare in his face when he began again, a nightmare two years old but as fresh to his mind as if it had been yesterday. The German army, under their Emperor Conrad, had gone before, leaving Nicaea in October. "We did not know what had become of them. We were told they had won a great victory over the Turks, but the corpses we came upon were German, not Turkish. When we reached Nicaea we discovered that they had been massacred at Dorylaeum by the Seljuk cavalry, and that Conrad had fled the field. We kept coming on the bodies as we went forward, more and more of them, men and horses all piled together, one great smell of rotting flesh. We did not breathe air, we breathed death."

For the first time since he had started speaking William turned his face to me, and I saw the dew of sweat on his brow. "So many bodies," he said. "We knew the Germans were ourselves. We were looking at our dead selves, we were smelling our own decay."

Then the arrival in Jerusalem and the Grand Assembly at Acre. He launched again on the recital of names and titles: King Baldwin of Jerusalem, the Patriarch Fuller, the archbishops of Caesarea and Nazareth, Conrad's half brothers Henry Jasomirgott of Austria and Otto of Freisingen, Frederick of Swabia, Welf of Bavaria . . .

He knew the names like a lesson learned, and it gave him some comfort, as before, this litany oft repeated. But his hands still pressed down on his thighs as he went on. And what did they decide, he asked me, these princes and prelates? He attempted a laugh. Never was there better illustration of that verse in Isaiah, *Take council together and it shall come to naught.*

The folly of the decision to attack Damascus was well known, as was the greed for land that had led to it. What no man could know unless he had lived through them were the sufferings of the retreat toward Galilee. "A year ago, almost to the day," William said. "Hot like this, much hotter. You think of the desert as light-colored, sand-colored, like the sand of our Sicilian beaches. But that desert was hell-scorched, dark gray. The heat from it burned your face like a flame if you looked down, and the wind blistered you when you looked up. We had no order in the retreat—we were massed together, an easy target. These Turcoman riders are not cavalry as we Normans understand it. They are mounted archers, and they move fast. They hung on our flanks, mile after mile, pouring arrows into the mass of us. The way was littered with corpses, men and horses." He raised one hand and took my arm above the elbow. "You understand?" he said. "It was prefigured. The same bodies, our bodies, the same stink. I smell it through my sleep, it wakes me."

I could feel the tremor of his hand on my arm and I was swept by a rush of pity for him, though at the same time I felt dismayed that a man should so exhibit his weakness who had been schooled to conceal it. "These things will pass," I said.

"You could not tell, it was like bolts from heaven. You would be riding alongside a man and see the arrow strike. You would hear the whistle of it and the thud as it struck. My father was killed; he took an arrow through the nape of the neck. He had taken off his helmet because of the heat. I was beside him. I heard the arrow strike." He paused and opened his lips and drove out his breath between clenched teeth, making a sound like the rising flight of a strong bird. "The arrow went through his throat. I saw the head of it come out below the chin. He rode on with his throat pierced, then blood came round the head of the arrow and he pitched off his horse. I left him there to rot—there was no time—he was left in the open, in the sun, like all the others. In the night I smell it, the stench of rotting men and horses and my father, and I cry out for the time before the greed and the rivalry and all the death, to the time when we were calling for crosses."

He stopped and his hand moved away from my arm and silence fell between us. I would have liked to say words of comfort to him but did not find them. It seemed to me better, far better, to be alive, even in the grip of a nightmare that would not fade, than to be feast for crows in that hellish desert, but I could not say this. I wondered whether, in William's place, I would not have felt in my heart, amid all the horror of it, some gladness that another man had been struck and not myself, even if it was my father. But naturally I could not speak of this either. It seemed strange to me, and passing all understanding but God's, that William, who I did not suppose lacked for courage and had entered eagerly on the war, should now be so white-faced and trembling when others who had ridden at his side showed no mark of it in speech or bearing. Strange too, though in a different order of strangeness, and very disturbing to me, that while I longed to resume my dream of knighthood he should cry out in the night for refuge from the nightmare experience of it. I would have spoken of this, perhaps protested or even rebuked him, that he should cast such a shadow over my hopes and call into question the disappointment I had lived with through the years since he and I had been *scudieri* together. But when I would have spoken I saw that color had returned to William's face and his shoulders had straightened and his eyes lost their staring look, and I understood that this telling of it to one who had not been there acted as a cure for him, quelled the demon, though not driving it out. So the wound he had dealt me I kept to myself, and we parted amicably enough, promising to spend more time together at supper. This was served in the hall of the castle, where I in company with the party of Frankish knights made a number great enough to occupy a table. But on this occasion William sat silent and morose, a little apart from the rest of us. His companions, all of whom had been on the crusade with him, ate and drank and laughed together, and paid no heed to William, which made me think they were accustomed to this behavior of his.

The evening passed in wine and talk. I was in good spirits, looking forward to the morrow, when King Roger and his party would arrive, Alicia among them. For this reason I was sparing with the wine, wanting to have a clear head and clear eyes when she and I met. This was fortunate as it turned out, because a quarrel rose among us that, had I drunk more, might have had bloody consequences.

It happened in this way. The talk passed to the life lived by the Franks of Outremer, which all of these men had seen at Antioch and Jerusalem. Since they had seen these wondrous cities and I had not, it was very natural they should seek to impress me with descriptions of them, and they vied with one another in this. They were rough men for the most part; many of them were landless knights who fought for pay and keep, and they were used to hardship and the discomforts of life in their native Normandy, wearing coarse wool next to the skin and washing seldom. Now they were divided between wonder and censure as they spoke of the luxury of life in the Frankish East, the houses with their carpets and tapestries, dining tables inlaid with ivory, mosaic floors. Dinner was served on plates of gold and there were even dishes of porcelain brought from

Persia and Cathar. The rich had water conducted by pipes directly into the houses and it could be heated while still in the pipes. The ladies of the house had baths and elegant chambers, their beds were hung with damask, the linen well laundered and soft. Whether my companions had themselves set foot in these chambers—which was the impression they sought to give—or whether they were merely repeating what others had told them, it was not possible to know. But it was this mention of ladies that changed the course of their talk. They began to speak of the eastern style of dress of these ladies, their veils and turbans, their jewels and silks, their absence of petticoats, the languor of their movements, their mincing gait. From this it was a short step to the looseness of their morals, and one man in particular grew loud and forthright in this regard. They took lovers as a matter of course, he said, they took them to bed in their own houses, no one thought anything of it, the husband least of all because it left him free for his own amours. "I tell you," he said, "a lady of good Norman blood, two years out there, and she becomes little better than a whore."

He was a red-faced, flaxen-haired fellow, a few years older than myself, with blue eyes made vague now by the wine he had drunk. "Not two, no," he said. "The more virtuous may resist so long, but most will settle to their venery sooner."

"You are speaking of the generality," I said. "What you say may be true of some of them, or even many, I know not. But it is not true of all, to my certain knowledge."

"What knowledge is that? You have not been there. I say they are all the same, wife or maiden, ready to open their legs to any man that takes their fancy."

My rage rose at this but I kept a rein on it. He was looking belligerently at me now, scenting a quarrel. Like all his kind, he had a keen nose for this, fuddled or not. "A man should bridle his tongue when he cannot be sure of his company," I said. "I say there are ladies who have lived long in the Holy Land and are as pure and virtuous as I trust your mother is."

He brought a fist down on the table. "Do you speak ill of my mother?"

Where this might have led I cannot now be sure. I felt I had right on my side and was ready enough to take the thing further in defense of my lady Alicia and in rebuttal of the aspersions this loose-tongued fool had cast on her. But before I could answer him another intervened, an older man sitting farther down the table. "Come, sirs," he said, "let us not mar the occasion with reckless speech. Subjects of King Louis of France and a subject of King Roger of Sicily are met here tonight, two of his subjects, I should say"—this with a sideways glance at William. "If we quarrel here it will not augur well for a good understanding between our masters tomorrow." Murmurs of agreement came from round the table. He rose from his place and came to lay a hand on the shoulder of his companion. "No offense to you was intended," he said, and as he spoke he looked across at me and smiled a little and gave a nod, as much as to say, *Now it is for you to speak.*

"I intended no disrespect to your lady mother," I said.

The man hesitated a little, but he was not proof against the hand on his shoulder and the feeling he sensed from round the table. He said, "There are always exceptions, so much is true. I would not question the honor of any lady vouched for by you, wherever her dwelling place."

It had not come easily, but with the words once out his face cleared as if only they had been needed to restore his good humor. This suddenness, both of dark and light, I had met before in his fellow countrymen—by his accent I knew him for a Breton—and I was glad of it now and I reached out my hand to him and he took it and I repented that I had thought him a fool when it was only that he was drunk.

The man who had intervened to restore harmony among us seemed of higher degree than the rest, and possessed some authority over them. I noticed that they paid attention to him when he spoke, though the inflections of his French were different from theirs, he was of the south. Certainly he had gifts as a peacemaker, as he had proved already and was to prove again now.

"William has told us you are a notable singer," he said. "He told us of the meeting between you after all these years and said how he recalled your singing, how it gladdened men's hearts. Is it not so, William?"

"Yes, it is so," William said—his first words of the evening. "He was known for his singing."

"Will you favor us with a song now?" the older knight said, and his words were at once echoed by others round the table, among them the one with whom I had quarreled.

I did not need much persuading. My heart was light with thoughts of next day and I was gladdened that the good fellowship had been restored among us. First I sang a Neapolitan song that was popular at that time, in which the singer compares his sweetheart to an April day, beautiful in her smiles, changeable in her moods. It was a pretty, lilting air, without great range in the notes—easy to sing. And while I sang, taking me quite unawares, thoughts of Nesrin and the moods I had known in her came pressing upon me, her face in rage and in mockery, in laughter and in promise and in ecstasy of love. My Alicia, my intended bride, had one face only to my mind, reposeful and beautiful. Our knowledge of each other would grow with time . . .

Next I chose a song of my own composing with words that were at the same time sorrowful and sweet, and I sang it to an air that I knew from my student days.

I will not raise loud lament
To make her guilty for my hurt.
I am steadfast in my love.
If I suffer, should I need her consent?

This was greeted with much applause and I thought I saw tears in one man's eyes. Encouraged by this, I went on to give them several more songs. When we finally rose from the table every man of them came to praise me and thank me. Particularly warm in his commendation was the older knight who had first asked me to sing. "You have a talent far out of the common," he said. "Believe me, I have some knowledge of such matters. It is interesting to hear troubadour songs in the Italian tongue, a thing not so often met with. Can you play on any instrument so as to accompany your voice if need be?"

I told him I could play on the viele and the mandora, and he nodded and looked at me in a considering way but said nothing more, and soon after we went our separate ways to bed.

The couriers came early next morning to announce the impending arrival of the King and his party. I mounted the stairway that led from within the gatehouse up to the parapets. From here I could see the road they would come by. And here I waited, above the curtain wall, among baskets of rocks, and stakes with fire-hardened points and other weaponry for defense against siege. And through all the years of my life since then, when I remember that waiting, there comes to my mind those instruments of hurt, the jagged rocks, the blackened stakes, the great cauldrons with the bar through them for tilting the blistering oil.

With the news of the royal party's approach, the gates were opened, the portcullis was raised—the creak and grind of the chains as they drew it up was to my excited senses the music of Alicia's arrival. As I stood there—joined now by others who had mounted the walls—I felt a need for the sight of her that was almost painful. To see her was to believe again in my own life. She would come and she would redeem my life and join the past together, broken as it was, like a fractured limb that she would bind up and make whole, bone and blood and tissue. Only later was it to come to me how grossly, in my concern to mend my own life, I had failed to take into account that hers too might be damaged, broken. That day, as I stood waiting there, such thoughts were far from my mind. In the time of our first love I had thought of my life and hers as pure, unmixed. There was one aim, one course of action, everything was in keeping: a knight's son, a knight's daughter, the same class, the same thoughts for the future . . .

There was a light breeze, and the pennants on the battlements fluttered. Glancing up, I saw a pair of hawks, high in the sky, in lazy flight. Something must have alarmed or enraged the fowl in the kitchen garden, because there was a sudden outcry from there. When this died down I heard the hooves of the horses on the road and saw the dust from the mailed men that were riding ahead of the King. I saw them pass through the stockade gate and heard the clatter they made on the lowered bridge. The King came next behind, mounted on a white horse with a silver harness, as on the day of his coronation twenty years ago, when my father had lifted me up to see him. But I had not seen his face then, and I did not now: he rode beneath a canopy of scarlet silk—Atenulf's invention, as it was said. I saw nothing of him but the grip of his legs on the horse's flanks as he covered the space from the stockade wall and disappeared in his turn below the overhang of the gatehouse. My eyes went eagerly to those following. I saw them enter in twos and threes, saw them reach the bridge, heard them pass into the gatehouse. They rode in order of rank, the Cardinal Bishop of Santa Rafina, Gilbert of Bolvaso, Master Constable Designate, with his lady; and behind these the King's notary, Giovanni dei Segni, and the Provost and John Malaterra from the Vice Chancellor's Office, and others whom I did not know. But the face I was searching for I did not find, and my breath came short and I felt the skin of my face draw together with the quick flight of the blood. She was nowhere among them. She had not come.

XXI

THE DISAPPOINTMENT WAS TOO KEEN to be borne in its full-ness. I snatched at hopes: she had been delayed, she would arrive later. But the hours passed and she did not come. In the afternoon the French King arrived, his wife at his side, escorted by Saracen troops from the garrison at Brindisi. I saw the Queen's face as she passed below me, and she was beautiful and held her head very proudly, but the sight of this much-celebrated Eleanor of Aquitaine meant little to me at that moment, my heart was heavy, my last hopes of Alicia's coming were ebbing away. No one in King Roger's following had sought me out with a message from her, there was no one I could ask. Something had happened to prevent her, something sudden and unforeseen—if she had known of it in time she would have sent word. I thought of her brother Adhemar and what she had said about his hostility to our marriage. Perhaps there were others, acting in concert with him . . .

My misery increased as the day wore on, and to darken my mood even further was the fact that I was not among those invited to the royal banquet in the Great Hall that evening but had to be content to sup in a much smaller room, ill lighted and farther from the kitchens, with for company the serjeants-at-arms I had taken ship with from Palermo, a number of lesser palace officials who had come in the King's party, and some Pisan merchants who had nothing whatever to do with this meeting of monarchs but were seeking trade concessions from the Lord of Potenza. I tried to keep myself apart as much as I could, eating little, not sharing in the talk. I knew with bitterness that if Alicia had come and our intention to marry had been declared I would not have been treated thus; at that very moment I would have been sitting in the light, among the nobility, with my betrothed by my side.

Of the talk among us at table I can remember almost nothing. As I say, I took small part in it. One of the Pisans, too coarse-grained to notice my dejection, spoke to me about the great benefits to commerce brought about by the Crusades, benefits to which the recent defeat, he said, made no smallest difference but rather the contrary, creating a market in Europe for luxury goods from the east, bringing closer the trade links with Constantinople and the Byzantine Empire. "And those that are settled there," he said, "the Frankish states in the Holy Land, they are in need of weapons and supplies. Constant need, you understand me? And what is the best way to transport them, these weapons and supplies? I will tell you, my friend. The best and safest way is by sea. We of Pisa are well placed."

As I was about to rise from the table, the knight who had saved the peace among us the previous day entered the room and came to me. Seeing that I had finished eating and was ready to leave, he asked if he might have some words of talk with me. I had no desire for this, I wanted only to retire to my chamber and nurse my unhappiness there: I was too cast down even to feel much curiosity as to his purposes. But it would have been churlish to refuse, especially after all his courtesy toward me.

We walked for a little while together on the cobbled stretch of ground between the inner wall and the postern gatehouse. He had come from the royal presence, he said, from the hall where they were banqueting; he had obtained leave from King Louis to come and speak to me. "I praised your singing to him," he said. "To the King, not to Queen Eleanor, she knows nothing of it, and there is a design in this that you will understand in a moment."

The night was dark, there was only the lantern set in the postern gate to see by, and this gave hardly light enough for us to make out each other's faces. From somewhere close by, up toward the battlements, there came the hooting of an owl, a sound that seemed, in my present wretchedness, to pour mockery on me and my singing both. "I did not think King Louis had a taste for songs," I said.

"Nor does he, unless they are sacred in character and preferably sung in church. To say truth, he does not have a taste for anything that lifts the heart or raises the spirits. No, it is she that is the lover of music."

The darkness seemed to press upon me. The desire of solitude grew stronger. I said, "Sir, I am not in the best of spirits tonight, and my understanding is slow. I cannot find meaning in what you say."

"Bear with me a while longer and I will make all clear to you. I am speaking now in confidence, which I know you will respect. I am Robert of Talmont and I am the Queen's man, not the King's—I have spent most of my life at the court of Aquitaine. I was present when they married in the Cathedral of Bordeaux, and I was in her following when she accompanied Louis to Paris to reign as queen. You will know that things are not well between them—there has even been talk of a divorce. There are those who would wish this, for the sake of some private advantage. But any who have the peace and safety of France at heart will want this marriage to endure. I have thought that in a small way—but small things can lead to great ones—you might help in this."

This seemed such an extraordinary idea that it distracted me for a moment from my gloom. "Help in it? How in the world could I help in it?"

"Queen Eleanor loves music. She grew up in her father's court and heard when still a child the songs of Cercamon and Marcabru and other troubadours of like gifts. Her husband does not care for such things but he wants to please her, he wants to save the marriage. I have suggested to him that he should make a gift of you to the Queen, and he has very graciously consented."

"Make a gift of me? In heaven's name—"

"You would have great success in Paris. The Queen would like you and so would the court. You have a voice of rare quality and range, and you know how to put feeling into the words, which is not such a common thing. Also you have a fine presence, you are tall and handsome and have the look of the north about you, which makes you different from the singers of Poitou and Aquitaine that people are used to."

I almost felt inclined to laugh, it was such an absurdity, coming at such a time. My head and trunk and arms and legs, all the ties of my life in Palermo, all the hopes I still had, in spite of everything, in Alicia, bundled together into a packing box, tied up with ribbons, and sent off to Paris! "I am grateful for your good opinion of my singing," I said, "and I hope for a better understanding between their majesties, but what you are asking of me is quite impossible. To be frank with you in my turn, my life is about to change, but not in such a way as that. I am soon to be married, and my bride and I will be leaving for the Kingdom of Jerusalem, where we will live on our estates."

He was silent for a while and I saw him nod his head. "That will be the lady you so stoutly defended yesterday. A pity—with your gifts you could make your fortune in France. Well, I see the time is not right, which is often the case with causes that are otherwise good. But the offer is there still. If for any reason you should change your mind in these next weeks and decide to come to Paris, remember my name, Robert of Talmont, ask for me and I will make sure you are well introduced."

I thanked him for his kindness and promised not to forget his name, and he wished me good fortune, and so we parted. The encounter, and the unexpected proposal, had helped to turn my mind from the disappointment I had suffered that morning, and once back in my room I began to think what it might be best to do. She would not come now, so much was certain. There might be some word from her waiting for me at Palermo. I had delivered the money to Spaventa and I had his token. No one here would care whether I stayed or went. I decided to leave with first light, whether or not I found company, even though some parts of the way were dangerous for the solitary traveler. In the event, I was fortunate: the Saracen troops from Brindisi, their escort duties concluded, had a period of leave that they were spending in Salerno, and it was in their company that I left the castle.

The return journey has left no mark on my mind. I was hoping to find some message waiting for me, but there was nothing. It was late at night when I came to Palermo, and I was exhausted—from the haste of the journey, from the tumult of my feelings. This must still have shown on my face next morning, as Stefanos remarked with concern on my drawn looks, and he was the only man, of all those I knew, who would be concerned for me in this way. Yusuf might see, but he would not speak. My father did not see my face, nor I think any other, except perhaps the suffering one of Christ Crucified.

I had intended to make my report to Yusuf immediately, and in particular relate the circumstances of my meeting with Spaventa and the words we had used; these I had memorized carefully so as to give him an accurate account. But he was not in the diwan, so Stefanos told me, nor in his townhouse, where I might have sought admittance; he was at his mansion in the Conca d'Oro, host to a party of Arab dignitaries from Spain.

I busied myself during the day with the documents that had accumulated during my absence. When we were making ready to leave, Stefanos asked me if I would like to accompany him home and sup with him and his wife, Maria, something I always enjoyed because of the warmth of their welcome and the attention they gave me. Maria was an excellent cook, far surpassing Caterina, the Amalfitanian woman who kept house for me. This time, I knew, the invitation was not planned: Stefanos had asked on impulse, out of kindness, seeing the dejection I was in. I accepted gladly and we went together to his house in the Cala, where Maria greeted me with evident pleasure.

In the company of these good people, whom I had known and trusted for a good many years now, my heart was eased and my case began to seem more hopeful. She had been prevented from coming, and from sending word. Something had occurred, some unexpected obstacle. But she would find a way to circumvent it. I had her love, she had shown it when still hardly more than a child and now again as a grown woman. And she was resourceful, I knew it of old—how often, in my thoughts of her, I found comfort in this resourcefulness, proved over and again in the stratagems of child-hood.

"But you have lost weight, you are thinner, even your face," Maria said. She was stout of figure and broad-cheeked, with a high color and luxuriant eyelashes and very lustrous black hair, often in some disorder. She believed in feeding as a means of solving all problems, whether of heart or mind or spirit. She had used this method with her three sons, she was fond of saying, and they had all grown up to be full-bodied men and were making their way in the world. It was extraordinary to listen to her and look across at Stefanos and see how lean he was.

She had not had time this evening to prepare a wealth of courses, but what she served was plentiful and delicious. We had chicken on the spit in the Greek style, flavored with cumin and garlic, a great platter of minced cabbage and lentils and beans in the pod, wheat cakes flavored with honey and the sweet pastries she had learned to make from Arab neighbors—in this region, on the south side of the Cala, Arab and Greek lived happily enough together. With the meal we had the red wine that comes from the slopes of Mount Etna, and it was good and fresh, only recently fermented.

Under the combined assault of food and drink and warmth of friendship, I came very close to unburdening myself to them, con-fessing my feelings for the Lady Alicia and the difficulties we were encountering in the course of our love. I did not do so, whether from caution, care for her name, the habit of reticence, I do not know. I have wished often enough since that I had spoken of her then. Stefanos's position in the diwan was not exalted, he was in the third category of the administration—but he had been there many years and heard many things, and he was observant and shrewd and retentive of memory; he might have known something, remembered something, perhaps only a scrap but it could have changed everything.

Instead I asked about the things that had happened during my absence. In this way I learned that Demetrius and his Byzantines had ended their work at the Royal Chapel and were gone from Palermo. I was sorry to hear this, though it was no more than I had expected, and I could tell that Stefanos, who was of the Greek faith, was sorry too. The new people who had come were Lombards and northern Italians, he said. Some spoke only German. The King would come to the chapel for the Feast of the Transfiguration on the Sunday after next. It might be the last time he attended in single state to hear the liturgy: he was soon to marry Sibylla of Burgundy.

As he spoke of the Transfiguration—a feast day formerly more celebrated among the Christians of the East but gaining much in importance also in the Latin Church of late years, though Rome had not yet established a date for it—something tugged at my mind, something heard or witnessed, something quite recent. But it eluded me, and Stefanos's next piece of news distracted me from it: old Glycas had died, his monumental task of proving the existence of Sicilian kings in remote antiquity still uncompleted. "He died as he lived," Stefanos said. "Pen in hand, at his writing table, between one phrase and the next."

"So the work will be abandoned. If such a scholar as he, after so many years . . ."

"Abandoned?" He surveyed me across the table, the usual gleam of irony in his brown eyes. "There is another already appointed to continue the work. It is just this continuing that matters most to our King Roger. So long as the search continues, the thing sought for can be said to exist. If it did not exist, it would not be sought for."

I had my doubts of this on the plane of logic, except in the negative formulation that it could not be said not to exist. But I knew better than to take him up on it; he was subtle and quick-witted in argument like many Greeks, and very tenacious for so mild a man; an issue of this sort could occupy the rest of the evening, and I was likely to have the worst of it. "Well," I said, "however that may be, to abandon the quest is to admit defeat, and so our good King is right to continue in it."

"There is something else you may not have heard—good news this time, a reprieve. That evening of the day you left Potenza word was brought to the King that the Serbs have risen in revolt against the Byzantine yoke. They are supported by Hungarian mounted archers, who have crossed the border in what is said to be large numbers. Whatever the numbers, Manuel Comnenus will be forced to take action to quell the uprising, and by the time he restores order—if indeed he succeeds in doing so—winter will be upon us, the seas will be rough, all thoughts of invading Sicily will have to be abandoned, for this year at least."

"That is good news indeed." I thought of Lazar's face as I had last seen it, in the tavern at Bari, full of rage at being refused the expected payment. I remembered my self-contempt as I sat on there after he had left. Whether this rebellion was his doing could not be known for certain. But he would claim the credit, there was little doubt of that. And with the credit, the reward. Another journey for Thurstan the Purse Bearer, more clinking of coin. But of course, if my hopes were realized I would be Thurstan the Purse Bearer no longer . . . "Our work has borne fruit at last," I said.

There was a pause while I resisted Maria's urging to eat more of the pastries, her third or fourth attempt at this; I wanted to please her but had no space left in me even for a crumb.

Stefanos passed the wine. "There is not much else to hearten us in recent events," he said. "This failure of the Crusade has brought much harm in its wake. Conrad Hohenstaufen, who calls himself the Emperor of the Romans and claims title to Italy, cut an execrable figure, having lost his entire army and only saved his own skin by fleeing the field. This has called into question his God-given right, as he sees it, to be the sword and shield of Christendom in the West. And now here is our King Roger, who took no part in the Crusade whatsoever, putting himself forward as the champion of Christianity, in alliance with Louis of France. Conrad has always hated our King as a usurper of his ancestral lands. He will hate him all the more now as a usurper of his imperial prerogatives. Such hatred cannot bode well for us. Then there is the change in the situation of the Arabs, you will have seen that yourself."

I thought for some moments. Yusuf had spoken of this, with a passion unusual in him, but he had been speaking of a gradual process of loss and subjection. Other than this, what was there? I had been so much concerned with myself of late—first there had been Favara and the exchange of promises, then the presenting of the dancers and the turmoil of my feelings for Nesrin, then Potenza and the waiting and the disappointment . . . "No," I said. "As you know, I have been away a good deal lately."

"Perhaps it is also because you live in a better neighborhood." Stefanos smiled, saying this, to take any suspicion of grievance out of the words. "I mean less mixed," he said. "Here we live cheek by jowl with Arabs, we see them at the markets, we chat together sitting outside our houses in the warm evenings, we use the language of the Cala, which is also mixed—like the people. We bought this house with Maria's dowry and we have lived here for thirty years, since before King Roger was king at all. But now friendship is more difficult for all of us."

"Why is that?"

"The failure of the Crusade, the manner of its failure, was a great humiliation for the Franks, as you know. They cannot avenge that defeat in Syria, where it happened, because they lack the power and the will, at least for the moment. But they can avenge it in a hundred small ways on the Moslems who live among us, who have lived side by side with us all their lives, and know nothing of the Holy Land."

"But that is unjust. Any cases of insult or violence should be reported to the officers of the Royal Diwan and brought before the King's Justiciars."

Stefanos smiled, and there was much affection for me in this smile. He shook his head. "Thurstan, I will say this to you, and it is something I have often thought before and not permitted myself to say because you are in greater authority at the diwan, but you are young enough to be my son and I wish nothing but your good, so you will not take it amiss. You are too straight a man for the crooked ways they make you walk. It is not that your mind is simple, but you are not pliable: you are too frank in your feelings and open-hearted, you have too much need for belief in those you serve. The need for belief is a mark of innocence, and those who are truly innocent will always remain so, in despite of experience. It would not be different if you stayed another twenty years in the palace service, except that you would grow always more unhappy as belief became more difficult to maintain."

"And you?"

"I have never had this need, not since the days of my childhood." A trace of the smile still remained on his face, but his eyes were serious as he regarded me. "The King does not see what happens in the streets of the Cala—should I decline to serve him on that account? Should I lose my stipend and be reduced to beggary because the

King closes his eyes? Even if he saw he would take no heed. Why should he? Does it threaten the peace of the realm or the safety of the throne?"

He paused for a moment and lowered his head, as if taking counsel with himself. When he looked up the accustomed light of irony had returned to his face. He said, "The world is changing, and the King's justice must keep pace. He is always just, naturally, but his justice is exercised on varying objects. Just now it is directed to appearing as the champion of Christendom at home and abroad, strengthening the ties with France and gaining the goodwill of Pope Eugenius so that his rule may be recognized in Rome. It does not consort with the King's justice at this present time to show clemency toward the Moslems or defend their rights. Rather, he will wish to show himself severe toward them."

I was taken aback by these words of his, coming as they did from one who had spent his life in faithful service to the King. He had never spoken in such a way before, some recklessness had come to him, perhaps, I thought, released by his frankness about my qualities of character. I took no exception to this last, because I knew he was swayed by affection for me, though I privately thought myself more sinuous of mind and more versed in the ways of the world than he gave me credit for. But he had spoken of the King as one might speak of any mortal, his tone had verged on disrespect, almost he had impugned the King's constancy . . .

And now, as I hesitated over my reply, he went even further. "As for these reverend Justiciars," he said, "they will look grave and purse up their lips and put their fingertips together and then proceed to deliver the judgment that their royal master desires."

"We have known some like that," I said, speaking in haste to forestall more words from him, "but I believe them to be a small number. I have been wondering about the Anatolians. I suppose by now they will be well on the way toward home."

"Well, yes." He was looking at me now with a different expression, as if there were a joke contained in my words. "All but one, that is."

"What do you mean?"

"You did not know? I thought she would have told you she was intending to stay." He smiled suddenly and broadly. "She is a law unto herself, that one. She saw no need to speak of it and so she did not."

A number of feelings contended within me on hearing this news, which was both welcome and not. I felt my life to be difficult enough just at present without Nesrin returning to it. Despite myself, however, an obscure excitement began its climb toward my throat. It was halted, at least for the time, by the sudden memory of her face at the moment of bidding me farewell, that look of absolute composure. Of course she was unmoved—she had never had any smallest intention of leaving! Thinking of this, the effrontery and obstinacy and self-containment of it, and the hidden glee, I felt the cramp of my anxiety loosen and dissolve, and a laugh of pure amusement came from me, the first for many days. "As you truly say, she is a law unto herself. She has been here all the time then? Where is she? What is she doing, dancing in the streets?"

"She is living here, in Palermo. She has taken a room near the Church of the Ammiraglia, above the bottega of the saddle maker. No, she is not dancing. She is living on her share of the money they received. She has enough to last a year, so she tells me."

"You see her then?"

"I see her four times a week."

I stared at him. "How is that?"

"She comes for lessons in Greek."

"Early in the morning," Maria said. "Before he leaves for the douana. He wanted to ask only a little for the lesson but she found out the price that is paid and made him take it. How she found this out I do not know. She comes on foot through the streets. I make an infusion of mint and honey for her and she has a little bread or sometimes a piece of the cake with cherries and walnuts that my mother taught me how to make. She does not eat enough, she is like a bird. I tell her to take another piece of the cake but she will not."

"She asked me not to tell you about the lessons," Stefanos said. "I am not sure why. Perhaps she wanted to surprise you. Well, I have told you now."

"So it is quite some time that she has been coming?"

"Since the King left for Salerno and the dancing was delayed."

I remembered now that I had noticed an improvement in her Greek the night we had lain together, when we were talking beforehand, but I had not remarked on it, being too much taken with desire for her.

"She learns quickly," Maria said. "Stefanos has taught her the alphabet, already she can recognize some words when she sees them on the page. Sometimes she stays here after he has gone, she helps me in what I am doing and we talk together. She has had a hard life. Her parents also were wandering people, they died when she was still young. She is a beautiful girl, do you not think so?"

"Yes," I said. "Yes, I do." I felt the eyes of both upon me, and a spirit of rebellion rose in my breast. "A beautiful dancing girl," I said.

"When we practice the forming of questions, she asks many questions about you," Stefanos said. "Also when we are not practicing anything she does the same. Your habits, your work at the douana, your life in the past. She takes great interest in all this."

These were not words that a man finds it easy to reply to. In fact I did not attempt any reply but after a moment reverted to the subject of the King's forthcoming nuptials. It was clear to all that after fourteen years as a widower he was driven by the need for legitimate heirs, there being only William now left alive of all his sons. It was felt generally that Sibylla, a sister of Otto of Burgundy, was a wise choice: she was young and the stock was good.

From this we went to other things and the evening passed without further mention of Nesrin, for which I was thankful. I had noticed the care Stefanos took to tell me exactly where she was living, but even before I rose from the table I had resolved to avoid seeing her. I had betrayed Alicia once with her, but that had been an accident of proximity and circumstance—or so I told myself. I had been flushed with wine, with the success of the dancing and my singing, we had found ourselves alone together, she had shared in it. But now to go and seek her out, saying nothing of my betrothal, that would be a wrong indeed, out of keeping with my fealty to Alicia and the knightly Thurstan I wanted to be—wanted still to be.

XXII

I DO NOT KNOW if this resolve of mine would have held. I like to think that it would; it was truly felt and there was respect for Nesrin in it, as well as for myself. In the event it was not put to the test—or at least only very briefly, for the next eight or nine hours of my existence, in fact. The following morning, as I issued into the street on my way to the diwan, I found Caspar waiting for me at the corner, holding his horse by the bridle. His face was more somber than I had ever seen it. "You must come with me at once," he said. "My mistress is in sore distress."

I needed no more than this to accompany him. Ever since Potenza the shadow of some disaster had lain on my spirit, and it had grown darker through the hours of hearing no word from her. I tried to elicit something from Caspar as we rode together, but he would not speak other than to tell me our destination, which was the Monastery of the Crocefisso, three miles or so outside the city walls in the foothills of Mount Pellegrino.

Here we were met by a monk in the dark habit of the Benedictines and I was led through the cloister to a narrow chamber adjoining the chapel. Caspar did not accompany us. From that moment I never saw Caspar again.

I waited a little while, then the same monk came for me and brought me down a short passage to a stout oak door. He knocked and opened and bowed me in, closing the door soundlessly behind me. This was a much larger room, high-ceilinged, with frescoes going round the walls. Before me stood two men that I knew: Abbot Alboino and Bertrand of Bonneval. Even in this moment of uncertainty and apprehension I was struck by the contrast they made, the sad-faced abbot in his monastic habit, the huge Norman in a long white surcoat, with his blue-eyed stare and bushy eyebrows. Of Alicia there was no sign.

"How good of you to come with such promptness," Alboino said. "Please sit. May I offer you a cup of wine? It is excellent. I can recommend it; they make it here in the monastery. Many things are said these days against the Benedictines, but no one questions their skill in the making of wine."

Whatever I had expected, it was not this. He spoke as if I had not been brought here, as if I had decided from courtesy to make this morning visit. I sat in the chair he indicated and waited while he poured the wine and brought it. Bertrand also seated himself, though without speaking. His broad and ruddy face wore an expression of deepest seriousness, reminding me strangely of his look when engaged in the delicate task of cutting out the hart's tongue. Alboino too remained silent for a while, and this silence made a tightness in my chest after I had been led here on such an urgent summons.

"The Lady Alicia sends you her greetings," Alboino said at last.

"She is well then? I was hoping to find her here. Her man gave me to understand—"

"Unfortunately she cannot be here." He paused and hesitated, as if about to say something more in explanation, then glanced toward Bertrand, who said, "We would be happy indeed to have her here with us."

"Has some ill befallen her?"

"Not exactly that. Not yet at least." Alboino sighed, a strangely heavy sound in that silent room. "I find myself in a position of great difficulty," he said. "Perhaps more so than ever in my life before. How much easier it would be if our temporal rulers followed the example of this great man depicted here." He made a gesture almost of benediction toward the fresco on the wall to his right, where a man richly attired and wearing a gold coronet was presenting a scroll to another, who was dressed in episcopal robe and miter. "That is Constantinus, donating the Roman Empire, in perpetuity, to the Vicar of Rome, subordinating the temporal power to the spiritual. If only that legacy had been honored! There would now be one supreme and unquestioned authority, the Holy Father, heir to Saint Peter. Instead Christendom is divided, princes professing the same faith war among themselves, this our well-loved King Roger disputes the Pope's right to appoint bishops and surrounds himself with Saracens, people of a false and corrupt religion."

"Not only that," Bertrand said. "He gives them positions of influence and power in the land, to the detriment and loss of his Norman peers."

It seemed to me that there was some quality, not of reproof exactly, but at least of admonition, in the glance Alboino gave him. But

I was too concerned for Alicia to think much about this. "I beg you to give me news of your niece," I said. "You must have remarked the closeness of the attachment between us."

"Certainly, yes, but others have remarked it as well as I. Alicia is so guileless, so open and frank in her nature, it is not in her to practice deception or concealment. Reports of this feeling between you have come to the ears of the Roman Curia. Even your childhood love is known to them."

"How can that be? I have spoken of it to no one, and I am sure that Alicia would not. Why should she? It concerns no one else."

"I cannot say how they came by this knowledge. Perhaps someone there at the time, someone who watched you and remembered."

Hugo, he of the honey cakes: perhaps before illness compelled him to leave he had boasted of his knowledge . . .

"There is always someone," Alboino said, as if reading my thoughts. "You were watched at the hospice, it was seen that you talked together alone through the hours of the night. This was made known to them by one of the hospitalers, as was the manner of your parting in the morning. The time you spent alone together at Favara was noted, your meeting in the pavilion, and then later, in your boat on the lake. All this was observed and word sent to Rome."

"Who it was that played the spy I do not know," Bertrand said. "Someone among the guests or perhaps a gardener or a servant of the house. I wish I had the dog between my hands, he would rue the day."

"She is being held," Alboino said.

"Against her will? On my account? But that is absurd. I knew of course there would be opposition. I am not rich, I have no title. But my birth is good, I am loyal, and I have a strong arm. With her help at the beginning I could become someone to reckon with. Besides, the lady is free, she disposes of her own life and fortune."

"There is more yet to tell you. What a vale of tears is this world! How difficult it is sometimes to understand God's purposes and try to fulfill His will! Three separate pieces of information are in the hands of my brothers in the Curia, each of them useless without the others. There is your love for Alicia, there is your position of trust in a douana headed by a powerful and ambitious Saracen who seeks still higher office, and there is the fact, remoter in time but no less important, that Alicia's father, Guy of Morcone, was a close associate of Rainulf of Alife, Duke of Apulia, and played a part in the latter's uprising against King Roger in 1137. You will remember that Rainulf died before the King's vengeance could reach him, but several close to him were put to death when the rebellion failed."

"Yes, I remember learning of it." The King's wrath had been terrible. Some details, recounted then, had lived in my mind ever since. After subduing Troia, where Rainulf was buried, he had forced the townspeople to break open the tomb and remove the putrefying body. A rope had been fastened round the corpse's neck and it had been dragged through the streets for all to see, then taken to a foul stagnant ditch outside the town and weighted and sunk there. Certain knights that had been his followers were forced to do these things on pain of blinding and maiming . . . "It was in that year that Alicia left for the Kingdom of Jerusalem to be married," I said.

"Not by chance, though Alicia did not know this. Her brothers, Adhemar and Arnulf, went at the same time. It was judged safer to put them beyond reach of the King's wrath, or at least the consequences of his suspicion. The father stayed where he was, living in retirement on his estates. The evidence of his involvement was kept, and it ended in the archives of the Curia, where many such things end. It was kept in the hope that it might someday prove useful."

He paused and the sorrow of his face deepened into grimness. "Those were troubled times," he said.

"Better to have rooted the traitors out like a nest of vipers," Bertrand said. "That was my opinion at the time and it is my opinion now. Not the young ones, of course, they had nothing to do with it."

Alboino looked at him for a long moment. "We are speaking of the husband of my dear sister, who has been dead these many years," he said. "Our zeal must take account of family affections."

Bertrand maintained his open, staring look, not seeming at all affected by the rebuke. However, he remained silent. There was an alliance between them; it was strained, congenial to neither, I saw that; nevertheless, alliance it was. Why else was Bertrand there? What purpose did his presence serve? Nightmare has no moment of beginning, we are launched on it before we know. Perhaps it was now that it came to me, not doubt exactly, but a growing sense of anguish: the things I was hearing and seeing did not match together, did not correspond among themselves; some element was lacking and there was horror in this lack.

"Where is she being held and by whom?"

Nothing changed in either of the faces that were regarding me. "The whereabouts we have not been told," Bertrand said. "Would I be sitting here if we knew?"

"It is not needful for us to know," Alboino said. "We are intermediaries only. We are promised that no harm will come to her if you comply with their wishes."

My feeling of anguish deepened. "What wishes are those?"

"We will come to it, have patience. As to those who are holding her, they are not the King's people, but they are his friends, did he but know it. As I say, the evidence was kept for a time when it might be needed. Now that time has come. My brothers at the Curia are worthy men, true servants of Holy Church. God has placed a sword in their hands for the furtherance of the faith. I am asked to be their spokesman though playing no direct part. As uncle of Alicia, and friend, as I hope, to you. It is of first importance in the eyes of the Curia to prevent Yusuf Ibn Mansur's further rise to power, it is necessary to . . . stop him. In order to do this they have brought to danger of death for treason Guy of Morcone and any of his family who are taken with him, and that includes my niece and the one brother who is here, Adhemar."

"But they are guiltless."

Alboino nodded. "That is so, in the strictest sense of the word. But in the eyes of those who rule us, to be in a certain place at a certain time can constitute guilt enough. Would King Roger visit his wrath on the father and leave the children to thoughts of vengeance? No, with the father would go the children, consumed in the same fire."

"Her father is in the twilight of his life, his mind is gone, the head that he laid on the block could have no treason in it."

"Young man, I understand your distress and I share it, but we must not let our judgment be clouded. Will the King consult the doctors before he passes sentence? Twelve years ago Guy of Morcone's mind was clear enough."

"The King is just, his justice is known to all." The words came from me without conviction, born only from a need to delay the words of theirs, already heard, already sounding within my anguished heart, the words that would tell me what was expected of me. "He does not revive old hatreds," I said. "Past and present, races and creeds, he keeps the balance on which our state depends."

"It is here that the King has erred, and we thank God he is coming now to a better state of mind." For the first time there was harshness in Alboino's voice. "We have no need of balance," he said. "Balance is anathema. There can be no counterweights, no scales. This Sicily is a Christian kingdom, it belongs in the universal congregation that we call Christendom. Do you know what Christendom is? Do you know what it means?"

My mind went back to the darkness at the foot of the steps below the chapel, the hooded figure that waited me there. "That same question was asked me by Maurice Béroul when he was sent to bribe me."

"Was it so? And who is this Maurice Béroul?"

It seemed to me that the second question came a fraction too late after the first. I looked at the two as they sat there before me. They had seemed so different in my first impression, one from another. But it was a difference of the surface only. The Roman prelate and the Norman noble. One serving his church, one serving his class, both bent on ousting the Saracen, both eager for the power and privilege that emanated from the throne. Perhaps something showed on my face. I saw Alboino's nostrils draw down a little and his mouth tighten with arrogance or disdain. It was only a moment, like the briefest twitch of a mask. But in that moment I knew he felt himself above any judgment that one such as I might make of him. "Alicia's life is in your hands," he said. "It is only you who can save her." He drew from the folds of his habit a scroll tied with a thin cord. "They have appointed me to be the bearer of this."

Bertrand cleared his throat, a sound of startling loudness. He said, "My part is to guarantee your safety and the protection of your peers, as they will be—I will myself confer knighthood on you, and you will take your place in the rank you were born to. I know this has been your dearest wish. It is also within my power to grant you a fief, which you will hold in vassalage to me. Naturally also there will be a sum in gold, sufficient for the furnishings you will need. If you want to try your fortunes in the Holy Land, I will see that you are recommended. The Lord of Tripoli is my half cousin. Once we have your signature on the document we can obtain the Lady Alicia's release. You will wait for her at the palace of Favara. You will have my seal for your admittance. She will join you there. I give you my knightly word that no harm will come to her or to you. Now you will need time alone to consider."

They came with me, one on either side, in a ceremony of escort that belonged also to nightmare, back down the passage to the room where I had first waited. Someone had been busy: there were quills and an inkstand on the small table against the window. Here I seated myself while they withdrew. Here I unfurled and read the document they had given me. It was a declaration that Yusuf Ibn Mansur, Lord of the Douana of Control, taking advantage of his position of authority, had on various occasions and over a course of several months, dates and times being specified, sought by bribes and promises of advancement to convert me to Islam, assuring me that this my conversion would be kept secret until the day that accounts were settled and the wrongs of the Moslems avenged in blood.

XXIII

T HE SILENCE I experienced in that room was the most terrible of my life. At first my mind was muffled by it, as by some soft wadding, keeping me from clear consideration of the words before me. But as the moments passed and the starkness of the choice became clearer, the oppression of the silence grew upon me, the wadding was stretched into strands of a web, and I was caught in it, a traitor already: for remaining there, for considering.

Every moment made the wrong more grievous. And yet I could not rise from the table. To do so was to abandon her to the jailer and the executioner. Perhaps it was not true that her life was in danger, or her father's life either, perhaps it was merely a subterfuge, to dupe me into betraying my benefactor. But if so, why had she not come to Potenza, why had she sent me no word since? No, she was being kept confined somewhere. Perhaps they had lied, perhaps Alboino knew where she was. As her uncle, he would have been able to use her trust in him to lure her away to where she could be kept under guard, at least long enough for me to be persuaded to sign the document. In that case, she was in no danger, there was no treason, it was all a tissue of invention designed to frighten and coerce me. But how could I tell, how could I be sure? My mind crawled around like a fly inside a jar, seeking an exit. I had no one to turn to. And there was no time. I had to emerge from this place with the document signed or not; I had to abide by the consequences. How could I take the chance of it? How could I play at hazard with Alicia's life, when she had given me her love, promised to share that life with mine?

Her image came before my eyes, memories of our childhood meetings, snatched with such joy from the supervision of our elders and all the duties that beset us. I remembered her steadfastness and her trust in me and her loyalty—she had risked disgrace for my sake. The mind in travail will select one single image among many to cling to. There was a gown she wore that I remembered, very simple, a linen gown, pale blue in color, gathered at the waist, with a high neck and a collar of white lace. The color brought out the blue of her eyes . . . Then came the face and form of the woman she was now, who had returned to my life and filled it with promise, the marvelous moments of our meeting at Bari, her look of delighted recognition on that charmed ground as she came riding toward me, as it seemed from the spaces of the sea that lay beyond. Had that encounter too been observed, reported back to the Roman Curia, as had her voice and laughter in the dimness of the courtyard, the touch of her hand on my head as I knelt before her, the kisses we had exchanged in the pavilion of Favara? If by signing I would save her, by signing I would also stand before her on equal terms: did I not have Bertrand's promise of knighthood, and a grant of land, and gold for my horses and my armor? It struck me now, with a bitterness that twisted my mouth like a physical taste, that all the honor I had striven for and despaired of, the fidelity I would have vowed my life to, could be purchased now by the slightest movement of my right hand in an act of betrayal. *I know this has been your dearest wish.* By what means had he discovered this? They must have found out and questioned the companions of my boyhood; one talked freely then of hopes and dreams.

As I look back on it now, the matter was foregone. It is true that I suffered. But the arguments I conducted with myself were not real arguments, they were only the motions of the fly in the jar, which cannot accept that there is no escape and will not keep still and die, but dies while still searching. One attempt I made to save myself, at least from falsehood. I left the room, went back along the passage, tapped at the door and entered. I found Alboino and Bertrand sitting silently together in the same positions in which I had left them, as if only by my consent could they be set again in life and motion.

"I have heard Yusuf complaining of the treatment given to Moslems," I said. "I have heard him denounce the increasing influence of the Latin clergy and the Norman nobility. I have heard him say that civil war will be the result if the Arabs are denied ownership of land. To save Alicia and her family I am ready to sign to that effect, if the document could be written in a new form."

Thus basely did I try to save an appearance of virtue, even as I offered to play the part of traitor. I knew it for ignominy even as I spoke, knew at the same time that it would not suffice for them. Whether they possessed the power to change the document I had no means of knowing. But even if so they would never have agreed to such terms. Yusuf had been incautious—he had trusted me—but there was no real disloyalty to the crown in his words, and the words themselves were too common among Arabs, and too general, to make a strong case against him.

"No, no," Alboino said. "What are you thinking of?"

"It would be enough to remove him from office."

"No, you are wrong, it would not be enough for that. Yusuf is quick-witted and agile of tongue, he would find a way of twisting the words and cheating the King's justice. No, it must stay as it is worded in the document."

"Cheating the King's justice? There is no question of justice here. The document contains nothing but lies."

Neither made any reply, and in this silence of theirs a terrible suspicion came to my mind, one that I immediately struggled to suppress. "It is a capital charge," I said. "The new law that has been introduced by the Council of Justiciars defines attempts at conversion to Islam as tantamount to high treason."

They were the words I had used with Béroul as he sat opposite me in the reeking tavern. But Stefanos had added his own to them since then. *They will deliver the judgment that their royal master desires.*

Bertrand was smiling. "Is it only this that gives you pause? Do you think that the King, whom Yusuf has served so long, would exact the extreme penalty? Come, come, use your knowledge of the world, use your knowledge of our great King and his gratitude and his gracious favor. Yusuf will be stripped of his powers, his career in the palace service will be over, but that will not be such a tragedy in his case. He is no mere palace Saracen: he has lands in his own right, he comes from an ancient family."

It was my only attempt at bargaining, if such I may call this shameful offer. I returned to my table, to the silence and the knowledge of defeat. Still I delayed. Why now, after twenty years of his rule, should the King cause such a law to be made? Was there greater danger now from the encroachments of Islam in Sicily? How could that be, when it was the religion of the conquered and subjected? What Christian could desire, in Sicily now, to abjure a religion that was growing daily in influence and power?

I will not deny the truth or try to give myself the cloak of good reason. At the time I did so, but I will not do so now. I wanted to believe Bertrand's words, and for the few minutes that were necessary I succeeded in this—at least in holding off the doubt. But I knew in my heart that Yusuf stood to lose his life. And with this knowledge of my own heart there came a sense of what knowledge there might be in the King's, and I trembled at what I might have been serving.

It shames me now to remember how I wronged Yusuf in my thoughts so as to make it easy to wrong him by my actions. He had betrayed me, he had sent me on missions without full information, he had kept things from me, withheld his trust. Worse still, he had played games with me, appeared to believe while not believing; he had had me watched and followed, even to the stable where Nesrin and I had lain together. He had violated my loyalty. He had abandoned me, like my father . . .

The grief and rage were difficult to hold to, saner thoughts threatened. It was fear of these that guided my hand as I signed.

XXIV

On production of Bertrand's words and seal the outer gates of Favara were opened to me without demur. Once again I was met by a groom who accompanied me over the causeway, leading my horse; once again I approached the gate to the palace, saw the gilded bars and the arches and the water of the lake slip and stretch and lurch sideways then settle again as on the previous occasion.

This time there was no chamberlain to meet me in the hall, only one of the palace domestics to take my bag and lead me to my room, which was not the same as the one I had had before but smaller and darker, with one barred window high up toward the ceiling.

I did not much mind this, though noting it; I had reached a state in which such small comparisons and considerations counted for little; all my being was concentrated in waiting for Alicia. *She will be with you soon,* Bertrand had said as he gave me the pass with his seal. He had it ready to hand; there had been no doubt in his mind of the outcome. I had felt insulted at this, foolishly enough, though I had not been such a fool as to show it.

Soon could mean today or tomorrow. In that case she was not with her father in Apulia but somewhere closer at hand. Already, within minutes of my arrival, I was listening for her step. Deep within me, not fully acknowledged, was the feeling that I had purchased her life and rescued our love at heavy cost, and that I needed saving in my turn. Only by appearing now in all her graciousness and beauty could she lift the burden of the lies I had told for her sake. She would be, in the splendor of her person, my redemption and my reward. Everything but that would fall away; all the previous structure of my life would fall away like a rotting platform of wood, leaving me with a future in which there would be no lies, no deceit. When I was knighted and had gained my fief and had Alicia as my consort, I would ride abroad doing good, defending the dispossessed, redressing injustice, protecting the weak against the strong. We would go far away from the mire and miasma of Palermo. We would go to Jerusalem the Golden, the land that was promised, end of heartache, balm for sin. I would look into her eyes and there I would see not gratitude but the knowledge of what it had cost me to betray Yusuf, how abhorrent to my nature such treachery had been . . .

These and similar thoughts occupied my mind as I spent the hours of waiting, walking in the gardens that surrounded the palace or by the shores of the placid lake, where minnows chased in the warm borders and dragonflies made bright paths above the surface. From time to time—but never by design—I strayed into the zones governed by the turning mirrors, and then the world was strangely distorted, and until I found firm ground again it was not possible to know the true number and shape of things.

There were no other guests; the palace and gardens were deserted. I would come upon Arab gardeners, who straightened up from their work when they saw me and then bowed low. The guards who kept the gate would sometimes come in their spells from duty to take their ease among the trees by the water, where it was cooler, but other than an exchange of greetings we spoke no words together. The palace and all the wooded lands and the terraces and pavilions seemed held in the grip of a summer already waning but relentless. It was the time of year when decay seems to lie below the skin of things, not sealed away completely. Faint, sweetish odors came from the green scum at the edges of the lake, the split and oozing figs where wasps feasted. There was a feeling of weariness, the fatigue of too much repose, as if the world were longing for release from this thralldom of September. The peaches were falling and the crashes they made were startling in the still air, like presage of change that still did not arrive.

I revisited the places where she and I had spent time together, the landing stage, the little copse of ilexes where we had exchanged rings, the place where the tables had been set up for us, where Alboino had spoken to me of the touch of wrong and how day by day it destroys the soul, and where I had seen Alicia come out from the dark into the firelight, with her red gown and the gold net in her hair, and there had been my boat moored not far away and my plans laid to have her to myself for a while. The world around me was waiting for change, for release from the trance of summer, and I waited with it for my own release. She would come, she would bring new weather, a new quality of light.

When the first specter of doubt appeared I do not know. It did not come as a shaft or sudden visitation but like a companion that had been walking by my side, unnoticed, for a time I could not determine. Through the hours of that first afternoon and those of the next day and the next, as the sun crossed the sky and there was only the sound of the cicadas and the sudden violence of the reflections when I strayed into the zone of the mirrors, all the time he had been there, this companion. Perhaps it was the tranced, arrested nature of the place, the feeling of a void in which I was suspended, that bred the first suspicions. I thought again of Alboino and Bertrand and their different faces, which were the same face. How could they promise she would come, how could they convey the document to her captors, if they had no knowledge of her whereabouts? The document once secured, and no doubt countersigned by them both as witnesses, they would have all that was needed for Yusuf's immediate arrest. Perhaps they were not intermediaries at all, but the principal actors. In that case, why should they honor their promise to release Alicia? Why should they continue to conceal her father's guilt? Would they not seek to gain the King's favor by informing him of it?

The questions circled in my mind, they accompanied the wavering flight of gnats over the calm water, they leapt with the fish that snapped at flies on the surface, they were repeated and multiplied in the reflections that occasionally assailed me in my wanderings through the grounds. On the evening of the fourth day they were finally answered.

I was about to retire to my chamber, having lost hope she would come that day. The sun was close to setting, too soft to cast shadows. It was that time on a summer evening when with the approach of darkness a certain kind of paleness comes into the light, a blanched quality, when everything for a brief while stands out with peculiar distinctness. I was standing at the lowest terrace of the gardens; there was a bush of white roses close by me and in this spent light the white of the flowers was very full, incandescent, as if lit from within. I remember this luminous whiteness and I remember thinking how strange it was that it should presage the darkness soon to gather. The water of the lake lay beyond this, and there was a gleaming tide of light on the surface.

As I stood gazing here I saw the figures of men clothed in white robes and white turbans come suddenly into view from the fringe of trees at the border of the lake. As they approached I remained transfixed, quite without fear, though they were strangers: it was as if they could not be fully believed in, emanations, creatures of the blanched and deceiving light. Then I recognized the lordly swaying gait and portly figure of the man leading, and the darkly bearded face, and a sudden presentiment of ill came to my heart.

"Well, my Thurstan, *salaam*, greetings."

"Mohammed, is it you? But how did you come here? How could you persuade them to open the gates to you?"

"We do not stand at the gates of the Christian, begging for admittance. Many of those who work in the gardens here are my brothers in Islam. I know them, I know their names, I know the names of their wives and children. Their homes are outside. Do you think they use the main gates when they come and go?"

He had come to a stop some three or four paces away. His face showed no particular expression, but the tone was one he had never used with me before, cold and disdainful. His followers had gathered round him in close formation, one on either flank, one at his back. All three wore scimitars at their belts.

"The good news first," Mohammed said. "I am here to tell you that the lady will not come. You can wait for her till you take root and grow leaves, but she will not come."

"Why do you speak in this way to me?" But I knew, even as

I asked. "How have you come by this?" I said. "Why should I believe you?"

"I have come to tell you that you have been fooled and duped from the beginning, you have been led along like a little pig with a ring through its nose. It is a great pleasure to tell you this, my Thurstan. A greater pleasure even than killing you would be."

Some passion had entered his voice with this, and he paused briefly, as if to recover the impassive manner of earlier. "This Yusuf Ibn Mansur, who was arrested on your word, I have known him since we were children. Our fathers were friends and fellow tribesmen, he and I went to the same mosque school, he gave the name and the blessing to my eldest son. Let me tell you how this strumpet fooled you and led you by the nose and the words of your love were to her ears but the squealing of the little pig."

"You are very brave and free with your insults when you are four to one," I said. "Send your men farther off and we will see who squeals."

"What a fool you are. A traitor and a fool. You think this is a time for trial by combat, the rules read out beforehand, like good knights in the tilting field? You have published base lies about a man a hundred times your better and you prate of insults and issue challenges and put on airs of chivalry. How can you be insulted now? Mario it was who set us on, though he was far from wishing it. You remember Mario?"

"Yes, he deserted me at Cosenza, when I was buying herons for the royal falconry."

"No, he did not desert you. Yusuf was troubled by this disappearance of Mario, as he was troubled by anything that lacked explanation. He spoke of it to me. We lived in different worlds but we sometimes worked together. I had ways open to me that were closed to him."

"I did not know of this."

"Why should you know of it? It did not concern you. For a long time we found no trace of Mario. In the end we were helped by merest chance. The other who accompanied you, Sigismond, saw him in a street in Palermo. He was well dressed and he had grown a beard, but Sigismond recognized him and followed him to a house."

"Why was I not told of it?"

"By this time Yusuf no longer trusted you completely. You had kept too much from him. He had been obliged to set a watch on you. Sigismond was commanded to say nothing of it, on pain of the severest punishment. Once we knew where Mario lived, the rest was easy. We brought him from there and asked him some questions to which he was not able to withhold answers, not for long at least. Mario was in the pay of Bertrand of Bonneval, the nephew of the Count of Conversano, a powerful knight and very rich, already known to Yusuf as the leader of a faction of the Norman nobility set on destroying the Saracen influence at the palace and replacing it with a Council of Peers on the feudal model of the Franks."

I made no reply to this but into my mind there came a recollection of Yusuf's face and manner when he had told me of the invitation to Favara. Hardly surprising he was suspicious of me, knowing what he knew. I wondered if he had also known by this time of my meetings with Alicia. Alboino was associated with Bertrand, and Alboino was her uncle. Could she have been part of this Norman faction? Perhaps she was vowed to secrecy and for that reason had not confided in me. Was it this Mohammed meant when he said she had duped me? Was it only this?

"Mario did not desert you at Cosenza. On the contrary, he stayed with you like a shadow. He followed you to Bari. And there he and a man named Caspar Loritello, who was posing as a groom, tracked you through the streets."

He smiled for the first time, saying this. "Caspar had been seen visiting your house with some message. It was a man of Yusuf's who saw this. A watch had been set on your house by then. So when we had Mario in our hands we tested him with this name and it all came tumbling out." He smiled again. "As things will," he said. "Mario had no more to tell us but we made diligent inquiries and in time we discovered that Loritello was the name of Guy of Morcone's chamberlain, by whom the boy was brought up. He is a bastard son of Alboino, Alicia's cousin and one of her lovers in Jerusalem, one of several . . . She is a lady who gives careful study to her pleasure and her safety, and finds ways of serving the one and guarding the other."

As we had been speaking the first thickening of darkness had come into the air. The light on the lake was paler now, but Mohammed's turban and robe still held that luminous whiteness, making his face seem darker by contrast. Those with him remained silent and motionless.

"I do not believe it," I said. "You are lying. I will maintain her honor upon any that questions it."

"Sword in hand, eh? Before it was the pig squealing, now it is the donkey braying. Forget about the lady's honor—it was never in your keeping. Use your brain. But it is good you do not believe me at first, I like it better that you should resist, you will feel the hurt all the more. You have betrayed a man who was like a father to you, and you will get nothing for it, nothing. Those two fine fellows tracked your movements in Bari until they could bring you to a meeting with the lady, who waited very patiently for the right moment."

I had never doubted her. Her faith was beyond question, she had proved it forever in childhood. Why was it then that doubt sprang so instantly now? I have thought since that Mohammed's words served only to confirm a loss already suffered, that it was Favara itself that took away my belief, the lonely waiting, the cheating mirrors, the act of treachery that had gone before, the shame of it, destroying the sense of my worth, making of me a miscreant to whom no good could ever come. She was to have redeemed me . . . I thought back again to the moment of the meeting, the ruined house with its broken pavement, the fragments of mosaic, the peace that had descended on me in that place, broken by the clatter of hooves and the company approaching. Alicia straight-backed in the saddle, looking neither to right or left—it was indeed as if she had been given a cue, prompted in the moment, in that particular moment. Like a player coming onto the stage—players do not look at those watching. If I had not spoken, would they have passed by in silence? Or would she at the last moment have glanced at me, reined in her horse, assumed that same look of pleased recognition? But I had spoken, I had played my part. How was it that I, Thurstan, the purveyor of spectacles, had failed to see that this was a spectacle too?

My resistance was draining away, seeping from me, I could not hold to it, the vessel of my being was not stout enough. Would Mohammed have come here to lie to me, would he have taken such pleasure in lying? His pleasure was to inflict the truth. Nevertheless, I strove to keep him there, to prolong the talk between us, hoping still, when hope had all but gone, to find some falsity in him, provoke some unguarded words that might discredit what he had told me. With enmity for me in his heart, he was for these moments my only hope. My dread now was that he would leave me alone, with no company but the knowledge of Alicia's perfidy.

"And Yusuf knew of this?" I said. "He knew that the meeting had been contrived?"

"We told him what we had learned from Mario."

"He knew it and he said nothing. All through those weeks, all through the times we talked together."

"He did not know enough. He was waiting to know more. Some conspiracy there was, so much was evident. But what use they intended to make of you, that he could not be sure of. He did not think you would sell him to his enemies; he trusted to your loyalty in spite of everything. He was always a man to watch and wait. This time he waited too long."

He paused and glanced aside as if to assure himself that his silent followers were still in place. "I will not stay longer," he said. "I will not dignify you with more words from my mouth. You have been her dupe and so you will always be, as long as you live."

There was no other way of keeping him there but by inviting more hurt, offering more entertainment. "But why should she do it?"

"She belongs in the Norman party, which is also supported by her uncle Alboino and by some in the Roman Curia, as a means of extending the powers of the Pope in Sicily. Also her brothers are active in this. They will not return to Outremer. They know that the days of Frankish power there are numbered. Your Kingdom of Jerusalem will return to the possession of those to whom it truly belongs, my fellow Moslems. The future for families like that of the

Lady Alicia lies here, in Sicily, in the grants and favors they can exact for services rendered to their King."

"But this will be no service to the King. He holds Yusuf dear . . . Yusuf was his first choice for the post of Royal Chamberlain. Everybody knew this."

Mohammed made no reply, merely looked steadily at me, and this silence of his was more terrible than any words could have been. We sacrifice what we hold dear when there is a purpose we hold dearer. Had I myself not done so?

"You have played a vile part," he said, breaking the silence at last. "To have betrayed him with a truth would have been base enough. But to betray him with a lie, knowing it for a lie . . . you knew he respected the religion of others. Your presence there, in the Diwan of Control, was a proof of it. There were Arabs and Greeks and Normans in his diwan, as there are in the King's domain. That is why they hated him. He saw that this mixing was the only way to keep the balance of the state. You are the champion of balance, my Thurstan, are you not? It is a word often on your lips. Well, as you have helped to destroy it in the diwan, so you have helped to destroy it in the land as a whole. And for what? What stupid vanity made you so ready to believe in this Norman whore's love? You hoped she would bring you advancement, is it not so? You hoped to take his place at the diwan."

In the first moments the remnants of my pride held me back from answering this. Then I realized that he had no knowledge of the earlier love there had been between Alicia and me. Bertrand knew of it, and Alboino, but that was because she had told them—it must have provided the first idea of the way to ensnare me. But she would not have told anyone else—why should she? And if Mohammed did not know this, if he believed I had been led only by ambition, it was almost certain that he would not know of the conspiracy in which Guy of Morcone had been involved, would not know that I had signed to save her life.

He would never know it. Only this instant resolve enabled me to raise my head now and meet his eyes. "I will return to Palermo tonight. I will recant, I will retract my signature. Without that the case against Yusuf will collapse."

He was silent for a long moment. The dusk was gathering now, his face was indistinct, he and his men were no more than shapes of whiteness. But I saw him shake his head, as if in wonder. "Of course," he said, "you do not know, you have been kept apart here. He was executed yesterday at noon, though I did not know your part in it until today. The killing they gave him was a public one. On the orders of the King's Justiciars, among whom there are no Moslems, Yusuf Ibn Mansur was tied at the feet and dragged by a wild horse to a lime pit outside the city walls and what was left of him was burned there."

At this a giddiness came to me and I clenched my fists and made my body tense to help me keep my footing. His further words were made indistinct by this struggle of mine, and seemed to come from a greater distance. "They would not have allowed you to recant, they would have killed you if you had attempted it. They kept you out of the way for the time necessary—it is why you were sent here."

"Three days," I said, and my own voice too sounded distant.

"As you say, three days. Time enough when the result is preordained. The speed of the judgment is the one thing that lightens your guilt, though only a very little. His death was decided well before you put your name to the document. Tell me, Thurstan, devoted servant of your royal master, by whose will was this trial conducted in such haste? Why was no appeal heard, why was the execution of a Moslem of high birth and high position made into such a very public spectacle?"

"I do not know," I said.

"Yes, you know. I leave you now. Keep from crossing my path. You would be well advised to leave Palermo. There is no danger now. The names of the witnesses have not been published. Later, when you have grown accustomed to your baseness, when you have started to forgive yourself, then will be the moment for a visitor with a silk cord to give you the death we give to traitors."

He stayed a moment or two longer, looking at me, then turned and with his followers once more at his heels moved away from me, back toward the trees that bordered the lake. For some moments, as they retreated, I made out the glimmering of their white robes. Then they were gone, lost in the darkness.

XXV

HARDLY HAD THEY DISAPPEARED from sight when the nausea I had been fighting back rose into my throat and I leaned forward where I was and vomited.

Desolation followed on this. I could no longer bear to be in the open, now that the dark had come. I felt the need for the four walls of the room they had given me, where I could be alone, enclosed, in the light. I stumbled back to my room, lit the lamps, barred the door against the night and Mohammed's words and the gardens and the lake of this palace of Favara, which had delivered me a blow more grievous than any in my life before.

But there was no rest or relief here from the questions that pursued me. Over and over again I summoned to mind her words and looks, every smallest detail of her behavior since that meeting at Bari, until what was remembered and what was imagined mingled together in confusion. I still hoped to find something, even now, that would show this monstrous story of deception to be false. I still hoped to wake from it, from the white-robed nemesis that had come to me beside the lake. Accompanying this tormented quest, though bringing no sense of contradiction to my mind, was a sick amazement at my own credulity. How could I have believed that one such as I would be invited to this palace of Favara, to hunt on ground that formed part of the royal preserve, only on the word of a woman lately arrived from long years in the Holy Land, a woman with no consort and no great power? Bertrand it was who had the royal favor, not Alicia. And the courtesy he had shown me, the special place he had given me, how could I have imagined it accorded with my deserts, an obscure servant of the palace, Purse Bearer and Purveyor?

All this was sickness and confusion. But what brought horror to my soul was the cruelty she had shown me, the long-sustained, unfaltering cruelty to one she had loved—for she *had* loved me in those early days, of that I continued to be sure. She had used this love to fool me and betray me; she had watched me floundering. But of course . . . I saw it now, any but a fool would have seen it sooner: she had not changed, they were hers still, those qualities I had so much admired, the promptness to seize an occasion, the resourcefulness, the readiness to take risks to gain her ends.

My only respite from these bitter thoughts was to cling to a belief in the conspiracy in which her father had been involved. Mohammed had known nothing of it, but he knew little more than what he had extracted from the wretched Mario. It soothed me a little, it deadened the horror, to believe that the story Alboino had told me, of evidence in the hands of the Curia, of a dire threat to Alicia and her family, had been true, or if not true that they had made her believe it. This last was the version I preferred: she too had been duped, they had told her lies, it had been to protect her family and her own life that she had acted thus. I did not want to speak to her or look at her face or even hear the mention of her name, ever again. But it gave me some solace, through the sleepless hours of the night, to believe in this mitigation of her cruelty.

So the night passed, the worst night of my life. My chamber, at first a refuge, became a prison, and with the first intimations of dawn I left it and passed into the grounds, where I wandered aimlessly as the light strengthened. I wanted to leave and yet was curiously reluctant, as if I might turn some corner and find again the promise that had been here, in the woods and the gardens and the lake. Leaving was to brand myself finally as dupe and traitor and to stamp this land of marvels as a sham, when I had entered it in such triumph, Thurstan of Mescoli, with the lackeys running before me and the chamberlain, all smiles, awaiting me in the hall. It was a dream of recompense such as children have, when time seems something that can be gathered up again. But there was nothing here to recover: from the first moment every word of hers had been a lie, every look a cheat.

I stood at the edge of the water as the sun showed its rim over the horizon and pale colors of silver and saffron made spreading stains over the lake. There were clouds surrounding the sun, they shifted and thinned as it rose clear, and the surface of the water seemed to quiver in response to these changes, but the reflections of the trees were motionless, not a leaf stirring. I remembered how we had paddled out from the darkness of the bank into the open water. Then too there had been no faintest stir of wind among the trees. The reflections of the turning mirrors had splintered the world and mended it and I had felt we were entering together a territory altogether new, from which we would not emerge unchanged. *My prescient soul,* I thought bitterly—there had been change indeed.

The sun was still low when I made my way to the little pavilion where she and I had exchanged our first kiss. The shapes of birds and animals were as I remembered them. There was a gardener there, at work with long-bladed scissors, and he bowed to me and moved away, out of sight.

I mounted the steps and stood within the enclosure where we had stood together, out of the midday sun. Suddenly I remembered the wave of gratitude that had swept through me, a devoted gratitude for her presence there, for her return to my life, for the gift she had brought of a golden future. I had begun to speak this gratitude of mine but she had laid a finger on my lips to prevent me. For a moment she had seemed troubled, distressed, and I had not understood it. I understood it now. She had spoken of her brother Adhemar's spying in an attempt to explain her agitation and to distract my mind with alarm at his hostility. But Adhemar had not been the cause. She had felt a moment of pity for me, the poor dupe, stumbling out words of gratitude for having been deceived and tricked and ill used. Poor, pitiable fool . . .

This sense of her pity, the only tenderness she had shown, gave terrible pain to me. Worse than all her acting was this brief moment of truth, worse than all her pretended kindness was this true kindness of contempt. The hurt of it was so strong that I wanted to cry out. But I believe it was that moment that saw the obscure birth of my cure. The humiliation, my own abjectness, was beyond enduring; some escape from it had to be found. A dim prospect of this came—and only those who have not experienced such a blow to self-esteem will find paradox in it—not in heaping blame on Alicia but in reproaching myself. If I sought refuge in hatred I would never be free of her. That I knew her so little was proof of the neglect of her that had lain at the heart of what I called my love. She could not have so deceived me if I had not deceived myself; she could not have played me false if I had not aided her in it. I had fashioned her in the form of my desires, I had made her shining, lustrous from our childhood and the time of my hope, bright with the future when she would make that hope come true, a creature of light, not her own, bestowed on her. She had no light of her own . . .

I was standing at the head of the steps and the early sunlight was in my eyes. At this moment I again heard the wailing cry, *wulla-wulla-wulla*, that had come to me as I mounted these same steps toward the waiting Alicia and had brought Nesrin's face before me even at such a moment. Then I had thought it an illusion, some trick of the wind or human voices distorted by distance. This time there could be no doubt: it was the lament of the white herons, the same wailing that had come from the piled cages on the deck of the ship at Paola.

I went down the steps and turned in the direction of the sound. I had to follow the shore of the lake, from the farther side, passing the place where the fires had been lit for our supper on the first evening, going beyond this into a part I had not visited before, through trees thinly planted and then over an open space where the grass was tall and wasted with summer. Reflections from the turning mirrors confused my eyes and bedevilled my sense of direction. I was hunting for a sound that came no more, but I persisted, growing more intent as I proceeded. I have sometimes thought since that this intentness of purpose came to me through God's mercy.

At last, after much blundering, I came upon a wicker gate and a narrow path that led through trees to a row of bamboo cages, all empty save one, and this had the white birds in it, six of them I counted, all that were left, and as I approached they shuffled their wings and set up their wailing, and it was as if I were back in

Cosenza, before the meeting with Alicia, when I still had the trust of Yusuf, when Nesrin was filling my thoughts. There was nothing securing the door of the cage but a wooden bar. This I lifted off and held the door open. But the birds would not come for fear of me standing so close. So I left it open wide and began to make my way back toward the palace, feeling as I did so a lightening of the spirit—the first since Mohammed had come.

It was my intention to leave, and I was on the way to gather my belongings when I found myself in the courtyard below the room I had occupied on my first visit, which had delighted me so when I had opened the shutters and looked down. The sound of water was everywhere here, flowing from the mouth of the fountain into basins set one below the other and thence in covered channels to the pool in the center, which was undisturbed for all the little streams that fed into it, and I fell to wondering how this could be so, and marveling at the art of those who had made it. The respite I had felt since freeing the birds was still with me, and it was pleasant there, with the gentle splashing sounds of the water and the coolness it made in the air. The pool seemed deep to my eyes and I bared my arm to test it, but the water rose only to the elbow: the appearance of depth came from the blue tiles with which the pool was lined. The immersion of my hand and arm broke the surface, shivered into fragments the pale reflections of the clouds that still accompanied the sun that morning.

There are times after turbulence of emotion when a sort of emptiness comes to the spirit, and it was so now with me. I had been through a great deal since the morning Caspar had come with the summons. I had not slept, but felt no tiredness now, only this vacancy. As I still knelt at the pool, shadows like swift ripples swept across the face of it and when I glanced up I saw the six herons flying together very low, just over my head, saw them wheel and turn westward toward Palermo and the sea. And at once, unbidden, as I followed their flight, there came memories of other shadows, the sunlit afternoon in the Royal Chapel, shafts of light that entered from outside, contending with the light of the lamps, both together making a glory of light on the Magdalen's head and on the raised hand of Christ Pantocrator. Moving shadows everywhere within the space of the chapel, the two workmen high up on the wall with their lamps and their mirrors, they both glanced down toward me at the same moment, but this could not have been because of any sound I had made, I was standing motionless. Nor was there other sound, not at that moment, or I would have heard it. Some swift reflection passing across the mirrors they had on either side? But no movement from the ground could have caused such a reflection, the men were too high above. As high up as the Tree of Knowledge it must have been, or it would not have registered in the mirrors. Perhaps they had seen shadows moving over the wall before them, shadows of some unusual kind, to make them look away from their work . . . Then I had come upon Gerbert and his German companions, and there had been shadows like those the birds had made on the pool before me, swift shadows moving over the south side of the crossing, passing over the marbles of the floor like birds' wings or ripples on the surface of water.

I tried to concentrate my mind on the recollection of those few moments. The sunlight had entered from somewhere high up on the south side. I had been standing in the center of the Sanctuary, looking up at the mosaics, those the King would see from his loge opposite, the images to which his destiny was linked: the scene of the Ascension, with Christ borne aloft, prefiguring his own apotheosis as earthly ruler; the standing figure of Virgin and Child, guarding and protecting. Then there had been these flitting shadows. Gerbert and his companions could not have made them—the shaft of light had passed over their heads, it had come from higher up, from a window or aperture on that side. Someone had been moving up there, though very briefly. Someone had passed across the light. The next day had been that of Christ's Ascension, a very important day for King Roger and the Norman kingdom he had founded. It was known that he planned to attend the liturgy. His plans had changed, almost at the last moment, and the following day he had left for Salerno. Gerbert it was who told me of this change of plan. Gerbert, whom I had seen the day before in the cloister of San Giovanni degli Eremiti in close talk with Atenulf the Lombard. Atenulf, the student of dates and times and symbols, server of the royal power, faithful builder of the King's fame.

All this while I had been crouching at the side of the pool. These thoughts passed over my mind as quickly almost as the shadows over the water that had given rise to them, moments only—my arm was still wet from its immersion in the water. The reflections of the clouds on the surface had formed again, the shallow pool looked deeper than dreams could fathom. I rose to my feet, glanced up to the sky—the clouds looked less real than their reflections. The impulse was renewed in me to leave this place of cheating images, and I turned my back on the pool and began to make my way to my room.

This wish of hasty retreat was still with me on arriving there and I began immediately to put my few things together in preparation for leaving. As I did so I remembered the hopes with which I had come and I could not prevent thoughts of Alicia returning to my mind, how she had duped me and made a mock of me, and the terrible treachery there had been in her heart as she raised her hands in that gesture that had seemed like prayer and slipped the ring from her finger and uttered the words of promise to me. From the beginning it had been there, through all her smiles and glances, this deep well of her cruelty in which she dipped secretly, Satan at her side to hold the ladle, as he had been there with the saw at the side of the traitor Atenulf had spoken of, he who had cut through the chains of the drawbridge in the darkness of night and was soon now to die at Spaventa's hands.

These thoughts brought back the feeling of nausea, which was never far away during these days, and I paused in my movements about the room and stood still, taking deep breaths. And in this moment of enforced stillness it came to me that I had been in a certain way mistaken: the well of ill was deep indeed, deep beyond knowing, but the power of ill was limited, and this was true also of Alboino and Bertrand. In my misery I had seen conspiracy everywhere, but it seemed certain to me now that neither the one nor the other had played any part in sending me to Potenza—the time they disposed of had been too short.

It was Atenulf who had planned my going, and Atenulf was in no way connected with these two, or in any plot against Yusuf, whose words I remembered now as I stood motionless there. *There is the form of a triangle.*

Half mechanically, still with my mind on this, I began again to gather together my belongings. The line joining Wilfred and Gerbert was plain enough: they had been in the same community of monks. And that joining Gerbert and Atenulf? Could he have been associated with Atenulf in arranging my mission to Potenza? What had a prelate such as he to do with the King's fame? But supposing the reason for the mission had been other. The afternoon we had met in the chapel, he had come with his companions from the south side of the crossing, the side where the light was obstructed higher up, the side where the shadows came from. Next day the King was planning to attend the liturgy. It was the Day of Christ's Ascension . . .

A feeling of wondering surprise came to me. Why had Gerbert come there at that time? Certainly not to tell me of the change in the King's plans, and not to tell Demetrius—he already knew it. Somebody else then, somebody waiting there? But I had scanned the wall, I had noticed nothing. Some scaffolding, a curtain? I could not remember. It was possible: work was being carried out here and there inside the chapel, such a thing might well go unnoticed. Easy enough to leave a narrow platform there, screened from view so as not to offend the King's sight when he came next day to hear the liturgy.

Atenulf had sent me to Spaventa. Why should they wish to conceal the source of his payment if his mission was only to kill a traitor to the King? There could be no risk to paymaster or purse bearer in this. It was a question that had always puzzled me. Yusuf too had been suspicious of it, sufficiently to take pains to disguise the provenance of the money. But if Atenulf were serving some other master, if the quarry were another, if the consequences of failure were perilous to the sender . . .

It came to me now that I still had Spaventa's token—there had been no time to deliver it to Atenulf, and he had not sent for it, I suppose not expecting me to return so soon, and afterward not finding me at the diwan. It was where I had put it when Spaventa gave it to me, in the cloth pouch I wore at my waist; it had been reposing there disregarded through all the time since. I took it out now and peered at it, but the light was not enough inside the room, I could not make it out. A sense of urgency was growing in me. I was unwilling to pause and fumble to light the lamp. I went out of the room and down the staircase and passed outside onto a narrow terrace that looked toward the lake. Here in the daylight I held the token up to my eyes and looked closely at it. The bird was a hawk, just as Atenulf had described to me. The head only was shown, in profile; it was very small, but there was no mistaking the rapacious curve of the beak, the fierce eye, the flat head: it was the imperial eagle of the Roman standards, symbol of dominion. What had Spaventa said? *Render unto Caesar.* Who was Caesar now? Spaventa had thought I knew. He would have not lingered and boasted otherwise, not a man like that. Some message regarding my role had gone astray or been garbled.

The day darkened suddenly and I looked up to see banks of cloud, silver at the edges, drawing over the face of the sun. A rustling wind stirred the trees by the lake and there was a coolness in the air, a breath of relief, presage of rain. This long trance of summer was ending at last. What else had Spaventa said? Something about trying again. He had laughed at my reply, as if I had made a joke—he had not been suspicious then. What had been the first attempt? Once more I thought of those flitting, evanescent shadows, some movement unaccounted for, my vague sense that the light was broken higher up. There could be only one reason why a man should wait there, on the eve of the day of Christ's apotheosis and the King's, in the one place in all the chapel that afforded a clear view of the royal person.

I had not made the right response to the toast; he had understood his mistake, in circumstances more favorable he might have killed me for it. He had said something before this, before his suspicions were roused, something I had not understood. *We will meet him on Mount Tabor*—no, not *meet*, *serve. We will serve him well on*

Mount Tabor. Stefanos too had said something that puzzled me the evening we had supped together. But it had not been the meaning of his words; it was something else, something contained in them. He had been speaking of the Day of Christ's Transfiguration.

The knowledge that came was pure, it had been there always, waiting for the right touch, the touch of harm, the finger laid on my lips, to bring it forth. *After six days he leadeth them up into a high mountain apart by themselves.* Typical of Spaventa, once a novice priest, to cloak his secrecy in religion. That high mountain to which the disciples were led was Tabor, so it was believed. *And he was transformed before them.* The King was intending to be present for the liturgy on the Day of the Transfiguration. Was that to be the second attempt? Sitting in his loge on the north wall he would be inviolable, wrapped in majesty, invisible to all below. But not to someone high up on the opposite wall, someone positioned there would have a view across, would see the upper part of the King's body, above the marble of the balustrade. Twenty-five paces, perhaps less . . . A bolt from above to strike the King down. An iron bolt, from a crossbow. At that close range, it would transfix him. The perfect symbol, Atenulf's masterwork. Who could use symbols to build could use them also to demolish . . . A bolt from heaven, a judgment on the King's misrule, to blast him while he sat in state with the words of prayer on his lips.

The Sunday after next, Stefanos had said: by my hasty reckoning that was three days hence.

XXVI

HE SENSE OF SURPRISE persisted as I returned to Palermo, but now it was directed at my own obtuseness. If I was right in the suspicions that had only now come to me, all this while I had been confusing parties that were quite different in their aims, the one seeking to use me against Yusuf and so come closer to the King, the other seeking to use me for the King's harm. I tried to find excuses. Alboino and Gerbert were both churchmen of high rank; it was natural therefore to assume they had the same interest to serve, the same desire to expel the Saracens, increase the power of the Latin Church. And I had thought Alicia loved me and was working secretly to make our meetings easier and so had somehow contrived that I should carry the purse to Potenza. But she had used the knowledge that I was going there only to ensnare me further, only to build up my hope and dash it down again.

My misery was if anything deepened by these attempts at self-excusing; within them lay the proof—if more proof was needed—

that I was a failure, unfit for the world I lived in. Returning by the Admiral's Bridge I remembered my joyful expectations on the day I rode out to Favara for the first time and how, crossing the Oreto here, a song of love and promise had come to my lips. I was very far from singing now.

Once I was in the city all other feeling was swallowed up in the dread of being recognized. Mohammed had said that the names of those making depositions against Yusuf had not been published, but he might have lied to me for reasons of his own, or the names might have been made known only now, only this morning. It seemed to me that I could read accusation in every eye that met my own, as if there were a mark on my brow, a brand, plain for all to see. And all would think as Mohammed had thought, that I had betrayed Yusuf for my own advancement, on the promise of taking his place. I could not go to the diwan: the idea of encountering Stefanos, meeting his gaze, was unbearable. I could not go to anyone with my suspicions. How could I go to the King's Constable with a story of shadows and reflections and stray words? I had been the Purse Bearer, it might be thought I was one of the conspirators, seeking to betray my companions so as to gain favor. No, all I could do was wait for Sunday.

I made my way directly to my house and shut myself in there with orders that on no account should any visitor be admitted. They would disobey me if it was someone of rank or wealth, but it was all I could do. All that day my door was opened only twice and that was to Caterina, when she brought me first soup and bread and later some pastries of a kind I recognized. Stefanos had been, she told me, thinking I might be ill, and he had brought them with him. It occurred to me only now that Stefanos himself might be in some danger, through his long employment in Yusuf's diwan. My doing . . .

Something there might be among Yusuf's records, if I could come at them, something to give substance to my suspicions. I decided to make the attempt. I waited till after the supper hour, in the hope that I would find no one still working at the archives. If I saw signs of any presence I was resolved to retire immediately. I took a dagger with me, one with a short and broad blade, which I thought might be useful if I had to force a door.

The guards were at the gate by which I usually entered and they greeted me with no apparent difference of bearing and opened to me readily enough, supposing I had forgotten something or intended to work late into the night, a thing I did sometimes after an absence. All was quiet as I crossed the courtyard and mounted the stairway. I lit the lamp on the wall at the beginning of the passage and went down to my door. This was locked but I had the key to it. All was in order in my room, the documents on the table as I had left them. I went some steps farther down the passage, tried Yusuf's door and found it also locked. The room that the scribes and notaries used, which gave access to Yusuf's, had a door that was flimsier, and it was this that I had resolved to force, if I could do it with the dagger. But the door was unlocked, it swung open to my touch. While still on the threshold, I saw the reason: those who had been here had seen no need to secure the door because they had left little to guard. The room had been ransacked, drawers and shelves emptied out, a litter of parchment lay everywhere.

I crossed the room, my feet kicking against account books that had fallen to the floor and been disregarded. Yusuf's door on this side was closed with a latch only, easily lifted. There was a similar scene of desolation here. Everything had been turned out and scattered in some close search, for incriminating evidence against him, as I supposed—or against themselves. This, if they had found it, they had borne away. They had left ruin behind them, with documents spilled out of their covers and shed over table and floor. I walked over to the room beyond, his sanctum, where he kept his state when there were visitors, or private talks to be held. The heavy oak door swung widely open and there was the same devastation within, the same litter of documents, the cabinets gaping empty.

It was here, as I stood at the threshold of his inner room, his private self, that I truly felt his loss for the first time and knew that the grief and the blame would be with me always. His death was here, in this room. Before they had torn and mutilated his body they had violated the principle of order by which he had lived. Here was the tall casement where we had stood and talked together and which I had envied for the light and air it gave him; standing here he had given me the mission to carry an empty purse to Lazar—the mission that had been the beginning of his death. I remembered the delicate bones of his face and his hook of a nose and his eyes, always intolerant of dissent, always ready to show kindness for me. The sound of his voice came to me, the exaggerated accents of his French. *Is that a new* sorcot *that I see this morning?* Always the same form of words because he was fashioned so, never fully at ease when he was too close.

That I would not hear this voice again, no more seek to find some answer to his words about my clothes and my singing, only now came fully home to me. So far I had felt nothing but horror—at the violence done to him, at my part in it. Horror like a morass, a quagmire, leaving no ground to stand, no ground for grief. Now I felt the sobs rise in my throat and I choked and wept for Yusuf, whom I had blamed unjustly for my unhappiness when the reason was in myself. I had blamed my father also for this unhappiness of mine, and I wondered now, through my tears, what ruin of his world there had been that had taken him that day to the monastery gate.

It was here that I had known Yusuf and it was here that I mourned him, in the midst of this desolate litter that was all he would leave for memorial. I stood there until my storm of weeping was over and I was a little soothed and could see again. I was turning to leave when the memory came to me, like a message from him, of a day when I had come earlier than expected to his summons and found him in his finery, having just returned from a cavalcade with his fellow Saracens. I remembered the sumptuous silks he was wearing, the blue and scarlet and gold. He had spoken of this display of power and wealth as causing greater hatred for the Saracens and yet as being caused by this very hatred, in a circle that could be broken only by God's teaching. But by then he was back behind his desk. He had been close to the wall when I entered, bending down as if to gather something he had let fall below the wooden paneling. But there had been nothing on the floor and nothing in his hand as he moved away . . .

As if in obedience to some whispered command from him, I crossed to the place where he had been and crouched down to look. But there was nothing to see there, only the smooth face of the walnut they had used for the inlay. Still crouching there, I felt along the lower edge of the paneling, along the narrow line where the wood was inset. After some moments my fingers found an irregularity, a smooth boss of wood, smaller than a thumbnail. Pressing on this I heard the faintest of sounds and the panel swung open along the line of the join. Inside the opening thus made were loose sheets of parchment held between covers of stiffened cloth and secured with thin cord. They were numbered on the backs though without other distinction among them.

I took out the first and opened it and found details of sums paid and received with entries in Arabic against them. These would be irregular or unlawful payments of some kind, monies that had to be kept in a separate record, not passing through the official accounts of the diwan. The next one I opened was concerned with the providing of Moslem serfs in grant to Christian religious foundations in the region of Palermo. Such grants of labor, usually renewable after a certain term of years, were greatly sought after by monasteries, especially the richer ones with more land than the monks were able or willing to work themselves, and they had to be paid for in one way or another. There were no records of payments here, which I supposed was the reason that the documents were kept secret.

I might have stopped here, concluding that there was nothing of great interest, but I took up one more and opened it at random. These were not accounts but reports from various sources in Greek and Arabic and some few in Italian. A name sprang out: Wilfred of Aachen; after it another, marked off in parentheses: Rinaldo Gallicanus. So Wilfred the archivist had more than one name. I remembered his pale face and reddish hair and pedantic use of Latin. It had seemed to me that he kept a watch for eavesdroppers while Atenulf was explaining my mission to Potenza . . . I closed the door of the panel, heard that faint scraping sound as it fitted into place. I took the documents, still in their cloth cover, and bore them back with me along the passage to my room.

Wilfred's was the name that had caught my eye, and I began with him. It seemed he was not German, as all had believed, and as he himself had given out: he was the son of one Stephen Gallicanus, who had been a knight in the following of Rainulf of Alife and one of his closest supporters in the rebellion against King Roger twelve years before. Alboino had said that Guy of Morcone, Alicia's father, had also taken part in this rebellion, but there was no mention of his name here. It was this Stephen Gallicanus who had been singled out by the King and ordered to remove with his own hands his lord's putrefying body from the tomb where it was laid and to tie the rope round the neck of the corpse so that it could be dragged through the streets.

The feeling of horror returned to me, together with the nausea that always accompanied it. This desecration had been at the command of the King. And what of that done to Yusuf? It could not be more than a few weeks since he had compiled the information contained here. His own death had been designed already, by Bertrand and his fellow Normans, by Alboino and those in the Curia who had sent him, by Alicia and probably her brothers. This dragging of Rainulf in his grave shroud was a fearsome prefiguring of the end that was so shortly to be his.

Rinaldo Gallicanus was not much older than myself. He would have been barely twenty at the time of Rainulf's rebellion. Yusuf had inserted a question: *Did he witness the public outrage done to his father?* It was not known, but there was likelihood of it in the light of the young man's subsequent course of life. He had left his home in Apulia and traveled to Germany, where after some passage of time he had entered the Monastery of Groze on the Moselle, taking the name of Wilfred. Among this community was Gerbert, who subsequently served at the Papal Court and was soon to be appointed Rector of the Enclave of Benevento. These two had traveled to Sicily at an interval of some months, Gerbert to work for an extension of the Pope's prerogatives in the appointment of bishops, Wilfred to take employment as keeper of the palace archives. The report on Wilfred ended here, but there was a note in another hand stating that the post of archivist had been obtained on the recommendation of Atenulf the Lombard, Lord of the Office of the King's Fame, who considered the compiling and preserving of archives to fall within the province of this office. Yusuf had appended a comment here: *As also no doubt the altering or destroying of them.*

Further notes followed, also written by Yusuf, based on the material in the report, speculating in particular on the fact that all three of these men had come from Germany. There was the sketch of an equilateral triangle, with the three names at the angles and words of connection written very small and lines drawn outward from the sides of the triangle, these lines also with writing on them.

As I say, this writing was small, and I postponed the reading of it for a little while, turning to the sheets that followed. All the time I was looking for Alicia's name, feeling sure that Yusuf, once knowing that the meeting in Bari had been deliberately contrived, would have set people on to watch her and find out what they could about her past. But she was not here among these names: Yusuf had not made the same mistake as I—there was nothing to connect her with Atenulf or Gerbert or my mission to Potenza.

I found her in the entry concerning Bertrand of Bonneval, and more lines were given to him than to her. The long course of his efforts, public and private, to increase the Norman power at court and foment hostility toward the Saracens in the palace service, all was given here with details that went back over several years. Alicia had less than a page to herself. Those returned from the Holy Land who had known her there had been questioned and had testified to the dissolute manner of her life, her lovers, the lavishness of her spending, which was impoverishing her husband and the cause of much quarreling when he tried to curtail it. There were some who said that the manner of his death had been other than the one given out, that a stoppage of the heart can have various causes. But such rumors were too vague, Yusuf had noted, amounting to little more than gossip. Some lines were devoted to her father. Far from having taken part in any revolt, he had been Roger's firm and constant follower, with no slightest suspicion of disloyalty attached to his name. He had on various occasions given hospitality to his Norman peers at his castle in Apulia, among them Bertrand and his lady. There was no reference to the state of his health in the present or the past.

My last defense was stripped away by this reading, my last attempt to attenuate her treachery. There had been no threat to her life or to any member of her family, there had been no forcing of her. My bitterness returned, the sense of having been treated cruelly, like some tender-skinned creature that has strayed into a blistering light it is helpless to avoid and so can only wriggle and suffer.

To escape from these thoughts I turned back among the sheets until I found again the sketch of the triangle. Yusuf had drawn lines going out at right angles from the exact center of each side. I saw that these lines were designed to show connections between the three names written at the angles. Gerbert's name was at the apex, Atenulf's at the angle on the left. Along the line that came out on this side two things were written, one above and one below. I drew the lamp nearer and strained my eyes to read. The writing above the line related to Gerbert and gave a date of three months previously, when he had visited the city of Augsburg, where at that time Conrad Hohenstaufen was holding court. Below the line was a briefer note: *Tostheim-Augsburg 6 leagues*. Tostheim was Atenulf's birthplace, his father's lands were there—this much I knew. No date was given, but it was natural that a son should sometimes return to the home of his parents. A simple matter, in the course of one such visit, to travel those leagues. Departure and return would be scarcely noticed. Natural also that a prelate of high degree like

Gerbert, with his knowledge of the language and his experience of the country, should be chosen to bear missives from Rome to the King of the Germans . . .

I sat back, staring straight before me. These two events might have coincided—that must be what Yusuf had meant by drawing only the single line. That would mean that on a certain day in the early summer of this present year Atenulf and Gerbert had been at Augsburg together in the royal presence. *Render unto Caesar.* Who was Caesar now? I had asked myself. There was an answer here. He who hated King Roger with a mortal hatred as usurper of his lands and powers. He who had himself crowned King of Italy at Monza at a time when he still possessed no more than a German dukedom. He was Caesar and heir to all the Caesars, in his own eyes at least, grandson and nephew of emperors, bent on the Roman imperial title and the lands of Italy conquered and held in subjection by Charlemagne. *Conrad of Hohenstaufen.* Was it for him I had carried the purse?

XXVII

THERE WAS STILL NOTHING to do but wait. I could not go with
such a story to the Justiciars or the Curia Regis. There was no
definite evidence of a plot, no evidence that Atenulf had made the
journey from Tostheim to Augsburg or that Gerbert had sought an
audience with Conrad or that the times had coincided. If I made accusations now, my own part in carrying the money would come into
question. Moreover, the plan—if indeed there was one—would be
abandoned; some other means, some other time, would be found.

It was still no more than suspicion, but it was with me while I
measured out the time of waiting. It was a prospect of action, it
helped to save me from the misery of dwelling on the past—by day,
at least. At night it was otherwise; I was sleeping badly and would
wake sweating from dreams of gleaming water and looming, distorted shapes, and the nausea would return to me. Caterina brought
me food but I had no appetite for it. As the day approached a passion of desire grew in me that I should be proved right, that I might

recover a particle of self-regard as one who was not always duped, might even win some small degree of pardon from Yusuf, since these had been his suspicions too. It came to me in the fevers of my sleep that he and I were joined again, together again in understanding, and I had brief happiness in this, though we were united not in friendship but in suspicion, the common sentiment of the diwan.

When the morning came I rose at first light and dressed hastily. As I made my way toward the Royal Chapel, the dawn call to prayer was sounding from the minarets of the city, followed soon by the bells of the churches announcing daybreak. Groups of laborers with the tools of their trade strapped at their backs were gathering at street corners, waiting to be hired for building work. Familiar sounds and sights—the familiarity troubled me with doubts. Could there be an element of such astounding difference in this place known so well, in this pearly light of a summer morning seen so often before?

The doors of the chapel were open wide. There were women carrying armfuls of flowers inside to scatter in the aisles and transept, white lilies, in memory of the shining raiment of Christ on the morning of the Transfiguration. They had been gathered early—I saw the dew on them as the women went past me. The flowers were to honor the King's attending the liturgy, and I thought they must have been brought by order of the palace. This was confirmed when I went inside and saw an underchamberlain I knew slightly directing the proceedings, a man named Lupinus, who was employed in the King's household.

The flowers gave a scent of great sweetness, which filled the whole space of the church. I think that of all the moments that had elapsed since the shadows of the birds' wings on the surface of the pool at Favara and the vague birth of my suspicions, this was the one when the notion of a plot against the King's life seemed strangest. The bustle of the women, the air of importance Lupinus assumed as he directed them, the sweet odor of the scattered flowers, the daylight that entered through the open doors and filled the body of the church, it was all so much to be expected on such a day as this, an occasion of happiness, the one day before His death when Christ was imbued with the divine light and showed the divine nature, when God declared Himself well pleased with his beloved Son. Today the King would be present to bathe in this light, to share in it as God's deputy on earth . . .

I began to walk down the nave toward the Sanctuary. I could see nothing yet, the wall of the nave cut off my view. It was not until I had almost reached the crossing, close to the place where I had come upon Gerbert and his companions, that I was able to look up at the south wall of the transept. A platform there was, though it was not possible to see any scaffolding or planks that might be joined together because of a dark drapery that fell round on either side and was gathered below. However, I could see the ropes that secured the four corners; they rose through the canopy and were hooked together higher up, close to the ceiling. The covering itself was silk, by the look of it, and dark purple in color. It was so arranged that it allowed a parting in the middle, though this was closed now and I saw no way of opening it from below. There was a window directly behind, not visible in its shape but giving some faint light to the area enclosed by the curtain. I saw no sign of life or movement, no faintest shadow of a human presence, within this canopy. It hung there, directly opposite the King's viewing place on the opposite wall, a little higher than this.

I had stared up too long: a faintness came over me and for some moments I felt in danger of falling. This passed but I was still slightly uncertain of my footing as I walked over to Lupinus, the floor being made uneven by the strewn lilies. He gave me good-day but showed no gladness at the sight of me. By this time I was reassured that Mohammed had spoken the truth when he said my name had not been published, so I set down Lupinus's lack of warmth to a suspicion that I had come from the Diwan of Control to meddle in his work. To counteract this I fell to complimenting him on the beautiful appearance of the church, with the flowers strewn everywhere, but even as I did so I was reminded of the litter on the floor of Yusuf's rooms and the sickness and sorrow that had come to me, standing in the midst of it.

"That scaffolding and the curtain round it—will it not offend the King's sight?" I asked him.

He replied very curtly, muttering some few words about work in progress and permission obtained to keep the hanging in place. There was another platform, also with curtain, on the west wall, near the entrance, he said.

This was true certainly, but not much to the point, as there was nowhere on the west wall from which the King's viewing place could be overlooked. But I did not remark on this to Lupinus because it had come into my mind that if I had stumbled on the truth, if by these guesses that were my only logic I had discovered a conspiracy, then he might also, since he was here in the church, be one of the plotters and I would rouse his suspicions if I showed too much interest in this well-swathed platform.

However, perhaps from some resentment at the criticism implied in my question, or perhaps merely to add to his own importance, he now spoke some words that cleared him of all suspicion in my eyes. The orders for this drapery, he said, and for the lilies, had come from the Office of the King's Fame. He had heard this on good

authority—he was a man with friends in high places. He uttered no
names, there was no need: all knew that Atenulf was lord of this
douana; only the innocent would make reference to him when there
was no requirement to do so.

Boasting had released him from distrust. "Fresh lilies," he said
now. "White, they had to be white. The hanging is spun silk, it
comes from the altar to San Salvatore in the basilica of the cathedral. Bishop Leontius will conduct the liturgy, he who founded the
Cathedral of Gerace. The King's Chancellor, Robert of Selby, will
be in attendance, also Maio of Bari and the Lord of Lecce . . ."

He would have gone on, but a feeling of urgency pressed now on
me. Sunrise could not be far away. The King's habit was to attend
the liturgy early, making his way with the companions he had chosen, unseen by all others, along the covered passage from the royal
apartments to his viewing place. The women would be finished
soon with their strewing of the lilies.

I took leave of Lupinus without much ceremony and returned
along the nave to the west door, which was still open. As I came out
of the chapel and began to follow the outer wall on the south side,
the first rays of the sun came onto my face. There was a beggar, a
cripple, there in good time with his back to the wall and his bowl
before him, waiting for the great ones who would be crossing the
square to the chapel. I passed him without heeding his pleas, coming to a halt below the transept window. It had a deep ledge; it
would be easy enough for an active man to find lodgement here and
scramble through. I could see no means of climbing to it, but anyone doing so could have drawn a rope up after him. He would have
entered early, before there were people about, probably during the
hours of the night. The moment of greatest danger would be in
leaving, the deed done. Then he would have to rely on speed and

surprise. Once in the maze of streets on the eastern side of the square—and a score of running steps would take him there—he would not find it hard to elude pursuit. He would have looked at these streets already, planned the way he would run . . .

A sense descended on me that someone other was living out these moments of irresolution as I stood there below the window, someone not myself who yet was inhabiting my body, a person at odds with all the life around him, the voices and clatter of the wakening city, the people crossing the square, people with work to do even on this feast day, women with baskets and brushes on their way to the washing slabs in the via del Bastone, a sherbet seller with jug and cups on a tray slung from his shoulders, a group of Saracen soldiers talking together at the far end, perhaps waiting for a companion, or someone who would come to take command of them.

Some moments more I hesitated. Then I continued along the wall, moving quickly now. I rounded the apse and came to the workshop adjoining the chapel, where I had found Demetrius on the last occasion I had seen him. By great good fortune the door was unbarred. Inside there was a man who I afterward learned was in attendance on Lupinus. I saw two ladders, one lying flat, the other longer one propped against the wall. Whether the man was daunted by my suddenness or by my dress and bearing, or whether he knew me by sight, I know not. But he made no objection when I seized this longer ladder and bore it away.

Great care was needed now by the stranger inside my skin. I set the ladder against the wall, alongside the window, striving to make no sound as I lowered it into place. Then, step by step, I mounted. The sill was easily deep enough, as I had thought, for me to leave the ladder and lodge there on my knees, still without making any sound. But this same depth of sill prevented me from seeing immediately into the enclosure of the curtain, which was not set exactly before the window as I had supposed but a little to one side of it. I had to edge forward and insert my head and shoulders through the aperture before I could see inside.

He was sitting with his back to the window and there was a crossbow on the planks beside him. I think he had been peering through the join in the curtain, but he heard me now or sensed me there or perhaps it was that my body blocked the light, because he was turning already and his hand was at his belt. Even before I saw his face I knew him, that exquisite molding of the head, the short black hair like the fur of some mammal. He gave me now a fearsome demonstration of his promptness; the dagger was in his hand without my seeing the movement that brought it there. He turned as he drew it, still crouching, and the movement, the shifting of his weight, caused the platform to rock a little, he had to pause, to steady himself, before he could lunge at me.

This pause it was that saved my life, or so I think now. I was half in and half out of the window. My arms were confined—I could not get at my knife. If I tried to withdraw he would cut my throat before I could get back to the ladder. There was only one thing to do and the terror I was in made me do it quickly. I shouted with all the force of my lungs and I launched myself forward headfirst, arms flailing, hoping to get to grips with him before he could use the dagger, a forlorn hope, I knew it, he was poised to strike as I came. But this heavy fall of my body slipped the rope that was holding the nearer corner of the platform, it swung free and the platform tilted sharply. Spaventa, still in his crouch, dagger still in hand, was precipitated backward through the parting in the curtain and disappeared from view. I felt myself sliding after him and grabbed at a fold in the silk. It held and I was left dangling there, half enveloped in the curtain, a ridiculous sight, I have no doubt of it—though at that moment I was very far from considering the effect on the spectators.

Lupinus was there below me. His eyes were starting out of his head as he looked up: he had heard my bellowing, seen one man come flying out of the curtain, another left hanging there. A man was sent for the ladder I had left outside, and I descended, much shaken. Spaventa had landed on lilies but they had not sufficed to break his fall. He was on his back, looking up to the ceiling. His right foot was turned outward at an unnatural angle and his breath came noisily, as if something within were clogging his lungs. He had crawled to recover his knife; it was loosely clasped in his hand and seemed oddly like a crucifix that he was holding for his comfort.

I came to stand near him, not too near, and he transferred his gaze from the ceiling to my face. "The purse bearer," he said. "You bore me ill fortune. I should have killed you at Potenza, when it came into my mind to do it."

"Your days of killing are over," I said. Even now, in the way his eyes fastened on me and his grip tightened on the knife, there was something in him that daunted me and overbore my spirit, and I turned away from him without speaking more.

What followed is soon told. Others had gathered, as happens strangely quickly when there is accident or injury. I recounted the part I had played, though briefly: my suspicions of the shrouded platform, placed as it was to overlook the King's viewing place, my decision to investigate, my discovery of the assassin. Lupinus bore me out in much of this, and I was thankful now that I had spoken to him.

Since it touched on the safety of the King's person, word was sent to the Household Guard, and four came, with a captain in charge of them. The crossbow and a single bolt—all Spaventa had deemed necessary—were recovered from the folds of the silk where they had rested. Spaventa himself, white to the lips but completely silent, was lifted onto a litter, and we all, including Lupinus and the man who had seen me take the ladder and the three women who had been bringing in the flowers, were escorted first to the Precentor of the Chapel, then afterward, and with him also now part of the company, before the Magister Justiciar at the Vice Chancery, Robert of Cellaro.

Here the story was repeated, and once again I was supported in my account by the witnesses. Afterward I asked for a private audience, and this was accorded me. It was the Magister himself who heard me, and my words were taken down by his notary. I told of my earlier suspicions, the request that had come from the Curia Regis to our diwan to furnish the purse, the false story I had been told by Atenulf and Wilfred, my meeting with Spaventa at Potenza and the delivery of the money, his unguarded words which I had afterward construed into an intention to murder the King on this Sunday, the Day of Transfiguration.

I did not speak of Yusuf Ibn Mansur and our talks together concerning this mission of mine to Potenza. I did not utter his name at all. Neither did I speak of my discovery of the secret compartment and my reading of the documents kept there, with their strong suggestion that Conrad Hohenstaufen was the inspirer of this plot and perhaps also the paymaster. Even if it was true that my betrayal of Yusuf was not common knowledge, it was beyond all doubt that this corpulent and pale-faced man who was the King's Chief Justiciar, who listened so impassively to my words, knew the traitor's part I had played. He would have been there with those who tried Yusuf, if trial it could be called; it would have been he who delivered the judgment, appointed the punishment, saw it carried out. But there was an authority greater than his in the Kingdom of Sicily, one that made use of his voice and his eyes, one who would require to be told that all had gone well . . .

For the rest, I was as full and frank as I knew how to be, judging it the safer course. Spaventa would be put to the question and he would give names, mine among others. Attempting to conceal that I had carried the purse to him would have been far more dangerous than admitting it. I had acted in good faith, I laid emphasis on that. And it was I, after all, who had frustrated this malignant design.

I was kept under guard for a good while afterward, though why so long I do not know—perhaps they had found others to question. During the time I was held there King Roger, from his viewing place in the north transept, celebrated the Day of Christ's Transfiguration, and there was no trace on the wall opposite of anything that might offend his sight.

XXVIII

I NEVER SAW SPAVENTA AGAIN. He died in the hands of his questioners, but not before yielding names. Atenulf and Wilfred were arrested and racked in their turn, as also was the Lombard mosaic worker who had set the scaffolding in place. Gerbert succeeded in escaping to Swabia, where he was well received and later became Father Confessor to Prince Otto. These things I learned only later. I was still keeping to my rooms. I wanted no company, the feelings of weakness and illness were increasing on me.

Two days later the royal summons came, brought to me in person by Stephen Fitzherbert, Steward of the King's Household, which was already a sign that I was well viewed, as was also Fitzherbert's extreme affability toward me. He was a weather vane of a man, always turning in the breeze of the King's favor. Had the occasion been different he would no doubt have sneered at the poverty of my dwelling.

He waited below while I made ready. I had neglected to shave for a good many days now and had a short beard, which I decided to keep as not unbecoming—vanity persisted in me despite my wretchedness. Now it was only a question of choosing clothes that were not presumptuous in finery but sober and of good quality, not such a difficult choice but one that seemed heavy to me that day. The uncertainty of balance I had felt on learning the manner of Yusuf's death still visited me from time to time, as did the sensation of nausea I had experienced then. I was prey to sudden chills that made me shiver, even in that hot weather, and my eyes were giving me trouble. I had a sense of some obtrusion at the outer edges of my vision, and there was sometimes a strange distortion, with things stretching or contracting slightly, changing shape.

There was more to my reluctance than this. There were clothes in my chest that I could hardly bear to look at, let alone put on, those I had worn on my first visit to Favara, for example. And anything in which I had once taken pride bore in its folds the sound of Yusuf's voice and the look of his face when he complimented me on my appearance. Finally I chose a suit of dark brown velvet, unadorned with tassels or brocade, one I had possessed for a good while and was gone a little out of fashion, with pads on the shoulders and a waist that was gathered in.

Fitzherbert rode with me, talking all the while in his high voice, interspersing Sicilian phrases with his French—it was the practice now at court to use Sicilian in this way, for a colloquial effect. He was full of compliments for me. It seemed that my disabling of Spaventa had not been the fear-stricken blundering that I remembered, but intrepid and heroic and extraordinarily quick-witted and prompt. "To see the threat that no other saw, to make that leap of mind—it was brilliant, everybody says so," he gushed. "And then to confront him in that manner, single-handed, and wrestle with him and throw him down, such courage and readiness, everybody says so."

By "everybody" he meant those at court who had learned of it. But I was glad for his talking in this strain; it kept him from reference to Yusuf. I said little in reply, but he did not mind this, being highly content with the sound of his own voice. When we reached the palace I was delivered to the care of the Household Guard, who escorted me to an anteroom in the royal apartments, and here I waited some while. It was Giovanni dei Segni, the King's notary and close adviser, who came for me, and he too smiled upon me, and his smile was blurred, as if seen under water, and Yusuf's death was in it. I was led, with the guards still flanking me, through the portals of the audience chamber, and I saw the seated figure in the high chair on the dais at the far end of the long room, saw the gleam of the circlet round his head, the scarlet and gold of his mantle.

I stopped in the doorway and made a reverence that brought my forehead not far above the marble of the floor. And I heard the King's voice, loud, with some hoarseness in it: "Let him come forward alone."

He spoke in French but it was not the language of my fathers, it had the accents of the south. The guards fell back from me, but still for some moments I remained where I was, body inclined and eyes cast down.

"Come forward, Thurstan Beauchamp." The voice was softer now. "Come forward here to me."

I walked forward and rarely have I felt so alone as on that walk, as if I were in some desert place, under a vast and empty sky. I stood at the foot of the steps and still I did not look at him, but glanced beyond to the figures behind him and saw Gilbert of Bolsavo there, Master Constable Designate, whom I had last seen riding behind the King into the castle of Potenza. There were two with him, very splendid in the livery of his retainers, and one of these bore a sheathed sword laid flat in his gloved hands.

"Closer yet," the voice said.

It was not awe that kept my gaze from his face, though he would have taken it for such. I think it was a kind of fear, not of his person or his power, but of finding confirmed the misgivings I harbored in my heart. The plans that had been laid for my entrapment and my coercion into treachery, these he would not know—they were the devices of the spiders. But Yusuf's death, the manner of it and the haste, these things he must surely know, just as he must know the long and faithful service Yusuf had given him. With his full knowledge and consent this thing had been done. For a brief while, as I stood there below him, my soul was placed in peril by the Evil One and I was tempted to set all down to the mystery of the King's power, to restore him, serene in majesty, to his silver barge, gliding over the dark waters below which the creatures feasted and fought. Perhaps it was to save myself from this surrender of reason that I looked up to his face now, saw it for a moment only, sharp-eyed and fleshy below the coronet; a moment only, but there was time enough to see the marks that the anguish of fear and pride had made, time enough for me to know, finally and forever, that there had never been a silver barge to keep afloat, that this my King, to whom I had vowed my service, was a man with a face like other faces I had seen, the face of one who lived with us in the dark water, among the other creatures feasting and fighting there. And in that same moment, as

this knowledge came to me, my sight failed, the face of Roger of
Hauteville slipped and distended and lost its form and I lowered
my eyes to the glow of the ruby that hung on his breast.

"My beloved subject, up here to me," he said, and he raised a
hand and beckoned.

I mounted the steps until I was immediately below him. Here I
knelt—it was too close for standing. How often I had dreamed of
kneeling thus before him, to hear at last his praise for my devotion
and feel my soul absolved by this praise for all the things I had said
and done in his service.

"We thank you from a full heart," the voice said above me. "We
have been told of your courage and your quickness of mind. If all
his subjects were of your temper, the King would need have no fear
of foes." His voice had broken slightly on these last words, and
when he spoke again it was more quickly and warmly. "Thou hast
earned the King's gratitude, and he will not forget."

I had not raised my eyes again to his face after that slipping and
distortion. I was looking at his hands, which were broad in the palm
and had black hair on the knuckles. I saw them make a very quick
and sudden movement upward, saw them go behind his neck to the
silver chain that held the ruby. He leaned forward and placed the
pendant round my neck and I felt the touch of his hands as he fastened it. His face was close to my own and there was a sweetness to
his breath like that which comes from keeping sugared comfits in
the mouth.

"You will learn what it means, the King's gratitude," he said, in
tones more sonorous and measured now. "This that I place round
your neck is but a token."

I would have risen, but he stayed me with a gesture. "We hear
that you have long aspired to knighthood, to join the order that be-

longs to you by birth. By the power invested in me, I name you knight."

A moment later I felt the buffet of the *collée* on the side of my head, a light blow but it sent a pain through me. "Rise," he said, "Sir Thurstan Beauchamp, be brave and faithful in my service, that God may love thee."

A wave of heat came over me. I felt the blood flush in my face and I heard my voice replying with the words I had uttered so many times within myself in the days when I still thought to be knighted: "So shall I, with God's help."

Gilbert came forward and he was carrying the sword, still sheathed, and a belt. He came to a stop at the foot of the steps. I went down to him and he unsheathed the sword and tendered it to me, holding the hilt toward me. I took it and kissed the hilt and he returned the sword to its sheath, and the King left his chair and came down to me, descended to my level, and girded me with the sword. "God go with you, sir knight," he said. "I have bespoken a fief for you in Calabria with forest and ploughland." His face was not steady to my sight, the mouth and jaw contracted strangely and all that was in my mind was a fear of staggering and the anguish of a question: how had he known that knighthood had been my dearest wish? It was the same question that had beset me on hearing words almost the same from the mouth of Bertrand of Bonneval. I had buried my disappointment deep. I had spoken of it to no one, not for many years. Only she had known, Alicia. That night in the courtyard of the Hospitalers all had come forth from me in the warmth and sympathy—as it seemed—of her presence. In recounting my disappointment I had thought to be resuming my hopes . . .

This man, who had just blessed me and girded me with the sword, had learned of these hopes of mine. In gratitude he would have inquired. The purveyor of spectacles who had saved his life . . . They who had trapped me were the same who had answered his questions. It must be so; theirs was the only knowledge of it. He would not know of this entrapment. It was beneath his notice, who was concerned with threats of invasion, with the loss of his colonies in North Africa, the fall of his revenues from the sale of wheat, the continued refusal of the Pope to recognize his kingship. I was too low for his knowledge. But Yusuf's case was otherwise— Yusuf had been chosen. The perfect victim: high born, wealthy, a distinguished figure among the Moslems. The crime had been devised, the mode of punishment studied . . .

The certainty of this came to me like an access of sickness—I shivered with it. How and in what order I retired, I do not know. I remember retreating with bows, I remember being again flanked by guards. The return to my house is a page on which memory has left no marks. When I dismounted I could hardly walk in a straight line.

XXIX

I HAD STRENGTH enough left to tell Pietro to look after my horse, get up the stairs, put the ruby in my strongbox, and take off my outer clothes. The sword I let fall to the floor. My head was throbbing and when I lay down and looked up to the ceiling it seemed to tilt, as if I had drunk too much. Almost at once I fell into a state that was between sleep and waking. Shallow dreams came to me, too shallow for sleep, glimpsed in the air above my head or in the corners of the room, never seen for long and never distinctly, sometimes dissolving in mist, sometimes sliding away. Yusuf came and he was in shining white like Christ on the Day of Transfiguration and he was trying to explain something but when I interrupted him to ask his pardon his face was lost to me and I saw that his robe was dark with blood. Mohammed came, he too in white. He had no face but I knew him by the strangler's cord he held in his hands, gloved hands, he held it like an offering, like a sword. It was Alboino holding out a paper to me. I saw his sorrowing face as he spoke of the daily wrong, and I saw Bertrand's, pleasurable and full of care, as it had been when he cut out the hart's tongue.

How long I lay like this I do not know. Darkness gathered round me and the light of another day. Someone gave me to drink and he had the face and voice of Stefanos. Then the room was dark again and I woke in this darkness because of the smell of sweetness pervading the room, which I thought at first was caused by the lilies that lay on the floor, but it came from some sugary thing that is dissolved in the mouth and breathed out and I knew the king was breathing in this room though I could see nothing, he was beckoning me to rise, to mount toward him, the water was gathering here below, lapping round me, but I could not see the way to the steps, the water rose around me, I was struggling in it, others too, I saw their dim forms twisting in the water and I looked up and saw the silver of the barge far above me and rose to it but when my head broke the surface there was nothing there, only reflections of light that stretched and shrank and a fire burning in the distance. Then all was quiet and I was walking among fields that I knew and they were lying under a thick cover of snow, fresh and shining and unmarked, such as I remembered seeing in my boyhood in the north of England.

This snow was cool, I felt it on my forehead and chest. I opened my eyes a very little, to see sunlight in the room and Nesrin's face above me, and it was her real face, it did not slide away. She held a bowl and a cloth and just for a moment my eyes were able to dwell on her face without her knowing it, because she was looking down at my chest where she was about to lay the cloth. And this, her not knowing, gave a look of calm to her face, in its ministering purpose, that was new to me, making her seem, in my weakened state, still feverish as I was, a person at once closely familiar and entirely strange. It will be with me always, this presence of hers when I awoke, her care as she held the bowl, her mouth that could sometimes seem bitter softened with this care. Then she saw my look was on her and her expression changed, the eyes narrowed a little, something of a smile came to her face.

"If you open your eyes wide, you think I fly away? All the night you talked to ghosts, but I am not one."

But I closed my eyes instead, perhaps indeed not quite believing, wanting to keep this face of hers locked safe. "How did you come here?" I said.

"I come up the stairs, like any person."

"No, I mean . . ." What I meant I did not know. Her presence there was like a miracle to me.

"He tried to stop me, he below who keeps the door."

"Pietro."

"He said you are sick, you want to see no one. I tell him I know better what you want. I tell him stand aside."

This made a sort of laughter within me, or perhaps only a prospect of laughter, remembering the night we had first met and the jesting of the others and her serious face in the firelight. I was naked under the sheet, I realized now. "You took off my shirt," I said.

"I take off everything. You are burning hot, like a fire inside you. You are sweating all over, you are talking to spirits. I need to bathe you, to make the fever less. How can I do that if you have the shirt? You fight with me, you think I try to rob you."

She had found me ugly and disordered, among tumbled bedclothes, the sweat of sickness lying on me. "You will stay?" I said. "You will not go?" If she promised this I knew I could sleep.

"How strange man you are. You think Nesrin leaves you when you are sick?"

"The water feels good. It has a good smell also. It scents the room. What is in it?"

She was saying something in reply but I was asleep before I could catch the words. I lay in slumber all through the afternoon, without a dream that could wake me. When I opened my eyes the lamp was lit and she was sitting on cushions on the floor near the bed, and I thought she must have got these cushions from Caterina, as they had not been in the room before. Her head was lowered over her work—she was joining strands of wool together, over and under, with a hooked piece of wood, and the movements of her hands were very rapid and sure.

I felt weak but my head was clear and there was no impediment to my sight. I looked at Nesrin as she sat there intent on her work, her long hair tied back with a single ribbon to keep it from her eyes. She was wearing loose pantaloons of a kind Arab women sometimes wore, and she sat cross-legged. I would have liked to linger in this watching of her, her quiet presence gave me such heart, but I was afraid she might surprise me in it and think me one who spied, so I spoke a greeting to her and she glanced toward me and smiled, but in a way that seemed half startled, as if my words had interrupted some secret thought.

"So, you are awake," she said. "I go down to get some soup for you. I make it, I *made* it, while you were sleeping. It is broth of mutton with lentils."

"It will be very welcome." In fact I felt hungry for the first time in many days. I was to learn later, from a Caterina divided between resentment and admiration, that Nesrin had taken command of the kitchen during my illness and would brook no opposition to her plans for the feeding of me.

And very good the soup was, but my strength was depleted, I

could not manage my bowl and spoon without spilling, she came and sat by me and fed me as if I were a child and made a joke of it so that I felt no loss of dignity. Afterward we talked for a while, then I slept again, but more fitfully now, with some slighter spells of fever still returning. She was there when I opened my eyes—she kept a low lamp burning. I felt the touch of her hands and heard sometimes the murmur of her voice—she spoke in her own language to me as she bathed my brow. What was in the water to make it smell so good? Again I asked her. There was nothing, she said. It was fresh water from the well in the street.

Next day I felt much recovered and able to talk for longer. Nesrin had not known of my illness till she came to the house, but she had known of my absence from the diwan; Stefanos had told her of it during her Greek lesson. She had known of Yusuf's end—this too from Stefanos—and been afraid for my safety. There was an irony in this that I lacked the courage to explain to her. It had occurred to me only now, in these calmer hours of my recovery, that my falsehoods against Yusuf had been kept secret because this was the best way of ensuring silence on my part. Of course, silence could be ensured by killing me, and they would do this if they felt it necessary. But in Calabria I would be far enough away. If no other denounced me I would be unlikely to denounce myself, unlikely therefore to relate the circumstances of the betrayal, my part in Yusuf's murder. Why had it taken me so long to understand this very simple thing? My years at the diwan had taught me nothing. I had spent my spirit in shame, in fear of recognition, fear of being known. Now the appearance of justice would be preserved and the knowledge of my lies would remain with those who had coerced me, and so provide them with the means to coerce me again if ever they saw a need for it. These were among the first clear thoughts of my recovery and they were among the most desolate, because I knew that if by some chance I was ever in the king's mind again they would be his thoughts too.

As I say, I had not courage to speak of this with Nesrin; I was too afraid of her judgment. How could she not think ill of me when I thought so ill of myself? But we spoke of other things during this time that I was gaining strength again though still keeping to my bed. I asked her what I had intended to ask that night after the dancing when we had been alone together for the first time and I had wanted to keep her with me, about the Yazidis and the things they believed in. Her Greek was now so much improved that she was able to explain it to me without much faltering. There were many Yazidis, she said, among the people who lived far to the east, close to the lands of the Syrians and the Armenians and around the big lake they call Van. The people of Mount Ararat too? I asked her, being still much intrigued by the fact—or fable—that she had her origins in this place where the human race found firm ground again. Yes, she said, many of those who lived on the slopes of Ararat were Yazidis. But she herself did not believe in that story of the boat.

"Why is that?" I asked. I wanted to prolong the talk we were having, in my position of rest, with the pillows at my back, absorbed in watching the quick glances of her eyes, the small frowns that marred her brow when words would not come easily, the movements of her mouth as she spoke.

"Well," she said, "it is not possible, the time is not long enough to build a boat so big." When she found the Greek word she felt to be the right one she would emphasize it with a small air of triumph. "We must *remember*, it is only one family," she said.

"And who is the God of the Yazidis?" I asked.

"He who rules is *Malak Tavus*. This name has two parts. *Malak* is angel. *Tavus* is bird. He is the bird that spread the tail behind and very proud." Here, still sitting where she was at the edge of the bed, shifting her haunches from side to side, she danced for me, shoulders back and arms spread out, turning her head to look proudly behind her. "Very beautiful tail."

The dance itself had been greatly beautiful too. Also, whether by intention or not, very alluring, throwing her breasts into prominence. Returning her gaze to me she must have seen some look in my eyes, for she nodded a little and said, "Your health getting better, I *notice*, Thurstan Bey."

"You mean a peacock," I said, in some confusion.

"Yes, *tavus*."

"So the God of the Yazidis is a peacock."

She made a face of pity and patience. "Not god. *Malak Tavus* is the Peacock Angel, he is not peacock but has *form* of peacock. Is difficult to understand?"

"No," I said, "no."

"He has six angels to help him, they go here and there, they have many tasks. But he is not god, god is above him, we do not know the form of god—how can a person know the form of one who made the world and the sun and the stars?" She made a quick gesture as if flicking a fly away. "He made them just like that, for a game. He had joy to make them but after he does not care, he leaves everything to the Peacock Angel. He never judge, he never *punish* anybody. He forgave Shaitan and took him back to be chief of the angels. So there is no wrong. Well, there is wrong, but it is not to do with Shaitan, as you Christians believe, because he is not Shaitan, he is chief of the angels now. I do not know the word for this kind of wrong."

"You mean, there is no sin?"

"Yes, I mean that. There is wrong but there is no *sin*."

She was very clear about this difference, and convinced, as I could see from her face. It was hard for me to think of a god who did not judge, hard to imagine a religion without promise of reward and threat of punishment, though glimpsing the freedom there might be in such a view. But I said nothing of this at the time. She was confiding her beliefs, and I felt it brought us closer in understanding.

"If you do much wrong," she said, "you will be less in your next life."

She left soon afterward, saying she would return later. I remember sitting there, still propped up in bed, and looking round the room she had just left. For a while her voice and movements still seemed to stir in the air. Then it was as if the room darkened.

XXX

WHEN I NO LONGER kept to my bed she did not come any-
more. For three days, as my strength returned, I sought to
see my room in its own light and not somehow dimmed. The light
of day that entered by my window—the window I had valued so
much, which had made me want the room in the first place—fell
short of the glory that was desired. And the knowledge grew that
this lack would continue so long as I was alone there: the light that
was missing could return only with her, with the shrug of her shoulders, the toss of her head, the proud carriage of her body.

During these three days I considered my prospects and posses-
sions; the latter were soon counted, but the former took on luster as
I thought of sharing them with Nesrin. I had the title of knighthood
that had been bestowed upon me, though in circumstances very far
from those I would have wished. I was in royal vassalage and could
count on the king's goodwill so long as I was no danger to him. My

fief lay across the water in Calabria, distant enough from this island of Sicily that had brought me to ignominy and shame.

On the fourth day I went on foot to seek her. Where she lodged had been told me by Stefanos and was present in every detail to my mind. I was approaching the shop of the saddle maker, which was halfway along, when she came out into the street and turned toward me. I saw recognition come to her face, saw her smile, and I was swept with happiness at this chance meeting, a joy that came as revelation: I had wanted her in my room, to bring back the light, as if it could dwell only there. But here in the open, under the sky, she was clothed with it. And it came to me, as I walked toward her and hoped for other meetings life might give us, that I could be a bearer of light for her also.

Something of this should be said, I felt, as I drew near to her, something to mark the happy chance of this encounter, which had depended so much on the timing of our steps. But no words came to me; I could only gaze at her. She, on the other hand, had something immediately to impart to me, I saw it on her face—I was to learn that she always gave voice, in the first moments of meeting, to what was uppermost in her mind.

"I forgot to tell you," she said. "We Yazidis do not come from seed of Adam."

"Do you not?"

"No, God turned aside from Adam to make the Yazidis. He made us separate."

I looked at her for a moment in silence. The eagerness with which she had spoken was still on her face. She was dressed very lightly in the Arab style, and wore no undershift—her cotton bliau, slashed at the sides, allowed a glimpse of brown skin beneath. She had blackened her eyelids with kohl and wore small rings of copper in her ears.

"I well believe it," I said, and the fervor in my voice made her smile. "Why did you not come back?"

"I did not think you need me."

"Not need you?"

"When you are sick, yes. But when you are not sick you are the big lord of the diwan."

Under my guidance, without saying much more, we walked together to the Church of San Giovanni degli Eremiti and sat there on a marble bench, close to where, in another life as it seemed now, I had watched Gerbert and Atenulf talking closely together.

"I was not such a big lord," I said. "And I am not a lord of any kind now. All that is finished."

I told her then of my knighting, though not the true reasons for it, only that I had earned the gratitude of the king. In truth I could not bring myself to tell her of the tangled courses that had led me to confront Spaventa in the Royal Chapel, all the ugly tale of my weakness and folly, the traitor's part I had played, the ruined world I had wept for: Yusuf's, my father's, my own. All that lay behind me now, or so I wanted to believe, removed by sickness and delirium and corrupted vision, in another land, another life, there where the king had a changing face and hands that hesitated.

"I cannot stay here in Sicily," I said. "I cannot stay at the diwan, after what has happened. It would not be fitting in any case, now that I am made a knight. But the king rules also in Calabria, and he has made me a grant of land there that I would be lord of. We could live away from the court."

"We?"

"I want you to come with me. I do not want to go anywhere without you. Life without you is like my room when you have left it."

I would have said more but she stayed me, raising a hand with great gentleness and laying it for a moment against my cheek. She was silent for a time, looking before her. And this silence disconcerted me, when I was offering my life to her.

"I would go with you anywhere in the world," she said at last. "My heart says so. But I was already in Calabria."

"And so?" I stared at her, feeling my jaw slacken at this unexpected reply of hers.

"I like to go forward, not back. I know you are the man for me the first night I see you, so splendid you are. I know it when I see your eyes, when I hear your voice. I dance for you. You are not a stranger. I *recognize* you."

Wishing to reciprocate—or perhaps not wishing to be outdone—I said, "Yes, I felt the same when I saw you there in the firelight."

"No, it is not so, you did not see me. Of course, you look at me in a certain way, but many men do that. You do not see me, you make the wrong shape."

"What do you mean?"

She made a quick, impatient gesture in the air before her, using both hands to sketch the shape of a globe. "You make a shape of us, five persons, not one, we will dance for the King, we will get money, you will get good words and praises. I try to make you see me, I try to make jokes, I dance for you when they are trying to make the dress . . ." She gestured again, this time joining slender fingers and drawing them swiftly apart in a straight line.

"The Dance of the Measurements," I said, and the memory of it came vividly into my mind.

"Measurements? That is the name for it? I dance for you, and you begin to see me, yes? God gave me this body of a dancer. Dancing is my life. What is Nesrin in Calabria? Always the same place, every day the same. Do you call her after supper to dance for the Normans with their red necks?"

I was completely taken aback by this speech, and wounded by it. I was laying my life before her and she was rejecting it. Perhaps she had a fear of being treated ill . . .

"Do not be sad," she said, and again she laid a hand against my face. "I do not speak about your neck, it is beautiful."

"They will accept you," I said. "I will make them accept you. It will go ill with any who offer you offense."

"You do not understand. It is not them that does not accept. It is Nesrin that does not accept. You are doing the same again. You make a shape that is not true and you keep to that shape and do not see it is the wrong one. You tell us to bow and count before the dance, that is wrong shape, you know it is wrong, you know it while you tell us, but you keep to it, nothing can change you. Then the dance came to break the shape. Do you not see? If we do not break the bad shape, it will break us."

My hurt had faded as I listened. Looking at her face, which was turned a little away from me as she spoke, at the dark lashes over the lowered eyes, the molding at the corner of the mouth—features dear to me now, amounting to all I thought was beauty in woman—I knew she was right, though she did not know, perhaps never would, of that wrongest shape of all I had made and obstinately held to against all likelihood until it had broken my truth and fidelity and brought my world to ruin.

"I love the road," she said. "That is another wrong shape you make, here is poor wild girl from a far place, needing shelter and

look after and one same place. But that is not my need. I never know
one home place since I am a small child. I like to see new places, always moving. Also you, it is the same for you, you have no home
place. You are a fine singer, I never heard one like you. I watched
you when you sang. You were inside the song, and a song has no
home place. You sang for me and you looked at me and saw me, and
I knew I was in your heart, I knew it then. Why you think I go with
you afterward? Because you are a big lord in the diwan?"

"It was the most wonderful night of my life." I thought of enlarg-
ing on this, to tell her about the fire and the moon, but I saw from
her face that it was not the time. It would have been lost on her, she
was too intent on what she had to say.

"You play the viele?"

"Why, yes. Also the mandora. Well enough to accompany my
singing if need be."

"I can dance to the viele. And you can sing and make the words
and perhaps make the music that belongs to the words. Together
we are something not seen before—never seen such a dancer and
such a singer and two so beautiful people. We get money—they
throw more than we can gather in our hands. And we see new
places all the time."

Her eyes were shining. There was love for me in them and love
for the idea of traveling thus. She was so beautiful to me that I could
barely sustain the light of it. Whether she was right to see this future
for us I could not tell. I knew only that I wanted to be with her. My
title of knighthood was worthless—I knew it now at last. Her rejec-
tion had stripped away the last shred of value I placed on it. I knew
it for the reward of corruption, a gift from the ruined world I had
wept over. A memory came of that dark night at the castle of
Potenza and of the French knight who had so praised my singing at

a time when I had been too cast down to listen fully to his words. I had never thought of myself as one who might make song a means of living and a way of life. But I had remembered the knight's name. Perhaps this, finally, was the right shape.

"We could go to Paris," I said. "There would be a place for us there—we would find a welcome there, I am assured of it. You could dance and I could sing. Not in the street but at the royal court."

I did not look at her as I spoke. I was unfastening the clasp at my nape, which held the chain of the ruby—the same gesture the king had made.

"Paris," I heard her say, in the calm tone of one whose delight is very great. "That is a city I am very much wishing to see."

"I want you to have this." I leaned close to her as we sat there, and fastened the chain of the ruby round her neck and arranged the gem so that it lay between her breasts. "It is not to wear thus," I said. "It is for the dancing. I cannot tell if the chain be too long or too short to lie across your hips, your lovely hips. I want you to wear the ruby in your navel when you dance, and I will make a song about it and everyone in Paris will sing this song about the ruby that lies in the beautiful navel of Nesrin the dancer."

She clasped the stone for a moment, then looked down at it as it lay in her palm. "When I dance it will always be for you," she said. "Let us go and see if it fits me well." She smiled and her eyes looked into mine. "You will play the viele for me, and I will try if the red stone lies in the right place. We will have a dance of the *measurements*."

A Note About the Author

Barry Unsworth won the Booker Prize for his novel *Sacred Hunger*. He is also the author of *The Songs of the Kings, Losing Nelson, After Hannibal,* and the international bestseller *Morality Play*. He lives in Italy.

A Note About the Type

The text of this book is set in Monotype Bulmer. Designed by William Martin in 1792, this type was named after the printer who used it in his Shakspeare *[sic]* Press editions, and was thought of as England's answer to Bodoni (from Italy) and Didot (from France). As a text face, beautiful and practical Bulmer gives any page an elegant feel.